Praise for

Heidi Swain

'Sweet and lovely. I guarantee you will fall in love
with Heidi's wonderful world' **Milly Johnson**

'More Christmassy than a week in
Lapland – we loved it!' *Heat*

'Sparkling and romantic' *My Weekly*

'The queen of feel-good' *Woman & Home*

'The most delicious slice of festive fiction:
a true comfort read and the perfect treat to
alleviate all the stress!' **Veronica Henry**

'Sprinkled with Christmas sparkle' **Trisha Ashley**

'A story that captures your heart' **Chrissie Barlow**

'Grab a glass of mulled wine and enjoy this
sparkling, snow-filled romance' *Culturefly*

'Fans of Carole Matthews will enjoy this
heartfelt novel' **Katie Oliver**

Heidi Swain lives in Norfolk with her family and a mischievous black cat called Storm. She is passionate about gardening, the countryside and collects vintage paraphernalia. *Underneath the Christmas Tree* is her thirteenth novel. You can follow Heidi on Twitter @Heidi_Swain or visit her website: heidiswain.co.uk

Also by Heidi Swain

The Cherry Tree Café
Summer at Skylark Farm
Mince Pies and Mistletoe at the Christmas Market
Coming Home to Cuckoo Cottage
Sleigh Rides and Silver Bells at the Christmas Fair
Sunshine and Sweet Peas in Nightingale Square
Snowflakes and Cinnamon Swirls
at the Winter Wonderland
Poppy's Recipe for Life
The Christmas Wish List
The Secret Seaside Escape
The Winter Garden
A Taste of Home

Heidi Swain

Underneath the Christmas Tree

**SIMON &
SCHUSTER**

London · New York · Sydney · Toronto · New Delhi

First published in Great Britain by Simon & Schuster UK Ltd, 2021

Copyright © Heidi-Jo Swain, 2021

The right of Heidi-Jo Swain to be identified as author of this work has been
asserted in accordance with the Copyright, Designs and Patents Act, 1988.

1 3 5 7 9 10 8 6 4 2

Simon & Schuster UK Ltd
1st Floor
222 Gray's Inn Road
London WC1X 8HB

Simon & Schuster Australia, Sydney
Simon & Schuster India, New Delhi

www.simonandschuster.co.uk
www.simonandschuster.com.au
www.simonandschuster.co.in

A CIP catalogue record for this book is available from the British Library

Paperback ISBN: 978-1-4711-9584-6
eBook ISBN: 978-1-4711-9585-3
Audio ISBN: 978-1-3985-0060-0

Typeset in the UK by M Rules
Printed and bound in Great Britain by CPI Group (UK) Ltd, Croydon, CR0 4YY

MIX
Paper from
responsible sources
FSC® C020471

To Sue and Fiona
With love and thanks for everything you do
xxx

Chapter 1

By the time I'd poured my third glass of wine, the assortment of travel brochures and bundles of notes on the floor next to my laptop were more of an untidy heap than the regimented piles I'd previously organised them into. However, in spite of the mess, and the rapidly emptying bottle, I had finally made a decision about my future *and* succeeded in narrowing my favoured travel destination down to just two options. Feeling impressed, I downed another mouthful of Merlot to congratulate myself.

I sat cross-legged in my PJs on the sitting room floor and thought about the milestone I had just achieved. I had been putting it all off for far too long but I was finally going to see something of the world and then, the moment I landed back in the UK, I would set about launching my own business. All that was left to do now was instigate my plan to free up more funds and pick between the Japanese Tea Trail Tour and the Northern Lights extravaganza. Both looked incredible, but my savings would only allow for one epic adventure.

I leant back against the sofa and closed my eyes, exhausted as well as tipsy, but nonetheless feeling grateful for the six gruelling weeks I had just spent teaching art in a struggling high school. I had been devastated when I had been made redundant from my role of art therapist in another school the previous summer and had covered the last few weeks of someone's maternity leave in a different school to tide me over. It had been hell, but it was finally over and I understood now exactly why the universe had stepped in to shake things up a bit.

Had my former job not become the victim of yet more funding cuts, I would simply have carried on in my original role and not made the brave decision to set up my own art therapy business, which was what, deep down, I had wanted to do for years.

Had Mum been around to counsel me, I knew that was exactly what she would have said too. She would have told me it was fate and that when I came out the other side, I would be able to see the real reason behind why it had all happened. That had been the sort of woman she was. A bubbly, glass-half-full personality, full of hope and optimism.

She had sadly passed just a couple of weeks after I turned eleven, her heart having given up on life long before it should, so she hadn't been there to hold my hand through the turbulent time, but now I was through it and I could see the point, as well as my exciting new future. Setting up and working independently I would be able to support many more struggling youngsters than just those who had come my way in one school.

'Better late than never, Liza Wynter,' I told myself as I heaved my tired body on to the sofa and snuggled into the cosy nest of cushions I liked to cocoon myself in when I was feeling in need of a hug.

My mobile buzzed on the seat next to me and, without thinking, I reached for my ponytail and swept it over my shoulder. The familiar action offered some comfort, but not quite enough. I didn't need to look at the screen to know who was calling and I sank further into the cushions, nudging the phone away with my foot.

True to form, David, my late father's business partner, had rung every day of October. When Dad had died four years ago, David had kindly stepped up and taken over managing the Christmas tree plantation on the outskirts of Wynmouth on the Norfolk coast and his determination to coax me into showing an interest in it had never waned. As soon as autumn took hold and cards, lights and gifts appeared in the shops, he would instigate his far from subtle strategy to coax me back all over again.

'Just come and take a look at everything,' he would say. 'It's come on even further this year.'

I didn't doubt it, but I had no desire to see it. I couldn't stand the place.

'Let me just get this term out of the way,' I would bat back ad infinitum. 'And then we'll see.'

I hadn't been back since the day of Dad's funeral and

there was nothing in my new plan that would change that. I knew David's intentions were meant kindly and that if he'd understood the reason behind my reluctance to return, he wouldn't have pushed, but that was one of the many conversations with him I had never felt ready to have.

I held sixty per cent of the shares in Wynter's Trees but did nothing more than draw an annual bonus at the end of the tax year. David held the other forty per cent of shares and was legally obliged to keep me informed as to how the business fared throughout the year. I did take a cursory look through the books, so I knew Dad's dream venture was thriving, but that was as far as my involvement went. As far as it would ever go.

Even though my negative feelings for the plantation and the business were justified, I still felt guilty that David, and more recently his son, was left to deal with it all. Consequently, I only ever took half of what we had originally agreed I should draw and the rest was ploughed back into the plantation. That was going to have to change now though, I realised with a jolt.

In order to fund my new business, I was going to need every penny I was entitled to. I didn't relish the thought of telling David that I would be taking my full share and knew I certainly shouldn't attempt it after drinking a bottle of wine. Therefore, I ignored my ringing mobile and snuggled deeper into the cushions.

'Hello,' I croaked, what felt like mere moments later.

'Liza?'

'Um,' I winced, grappling with the phone.

'Liza, it's me, David.'

'David,' I repeated, my heart sinking in my chest.

My mouth felt dry and my head throbbed as I hoisted myself upright, scattering the cushions and sending the pain level soaring.

'So, you are still with us then?' he huffed, sounding unusually put out.

'Barely,' I whispered, as I gingerly inched my way to the kitchen sink.

I tucked the phone against my neck, which had a painful crook in it thanks to falling asleep on the sofa, and filled a glass with water. I was amazed to see it was light outside and realised I'd been out for the count all night.

'Well, I'm sorry if I've caught you at a bad time,' David continued. 'It is early, but as you no doubt know, I've been trying to get hold of you all month. In fact, had you not picked up today, I was going to make the journey to visit you this afternoon.'

That was a change to our usual back and forth. Ordinarily he just kept ringing until I eventually answered at a date so close to Christmas that it made travelling to Wynmouth for the festive season impossible.

'You were?' I swallowed.

'I was,' he said, more softly.

Listening to the change in his tone, I felt bad for screening his calls. Generous to a fault, kind, caring and hardworking, Dad couldn't have picked a better partner to help run the business. I had been so shocked when I lost Dad that I never really took onboard just how selflessly David had stepped into the breach. That said, I still wished he hadn't picked up the 'make Liza fall for Wynter's Trees' placard Dad had never stopped waving.

'I really need to talk to you, Liza.'

'I'm sorry I haven't picked up before,' I apologised. 'This term has been pretty awful.'

David knew I'd been made redundant and subsequently taken the maternity cover contract.

'But it's over now?'

'Yes,' I said. 'School broke up yesterday.'

'And you aren't going back?'

'God no,' I blurted out, without thinking.

'That bad, was it?' he chuckled.

'Um,' I conceded.

I had no desire to relive just how bad it had been. Had I been in two minds whether a return to full-time teaching was for me, the students at Elmwood High had hastily settled the argument.

'So,' David carried on. 'Have you applied for another post?'

It was tempting to lie to stave off his attempt to nag me into visiting, but I couldn't bring myself to do it.

'No,' I said, 'I haven't.' But then quickly added, 'but I'm very busy. I'm planning a trip and after that . . .'

I let the words trail off. I still wasn't ready to tell him about my business plans and the repercussions they would have for my Wynter's Trees annual reinvestment.

'After that?' he asked.

'It doesn't matter.'

'Good,' he pounced. 'Great, because there's something I need to talk to you about.'

I felt my defences crank up a notch in readiness to fend off whatever it was he was going to say.

'You know there's no point in asking me anything about running the place,' I quickly put in. 'It's a Christmas tree farm and I don't know a single thing about growing trees, do I? Whereas you're a world-leading expert now. Just carry on keeping me up to date via email, and we'll be fine.'

Of course, I knew that Wynter's was so much more than a 'Christmas tree farm'. It was an institution, a local treasure, a much-loved focal point of the county's festive calendar, but it wasn't a part of mine and it never would be.

Dad had moved me from my childhood home in the Scottish borders just a few months after we lost Mum. He was mad on Christmas, always had been, and when the opportunity to buy the plantation and site, which had never been properly utilised by its previous owner came up, he had jumped at the chance.

'It's the fresh start we need, Liza,' he had told me as he loaded up boxes and bags into the moving van. 'It's what your mum would have wanted us to do.'

But I didn't want a fresh start. I wanted to stay living in the house that was full of Mum, snuggle down in the bedroom where she used to read me bedtime stories, stay with my friends as we settled into the new routine of high school.

Dad might have been, but I wasn't ready to leave any part of my mum behind.

'You'll soon settle in,' he had said, sounding optimistic and almost cheerful.

I resented him for that and if I was being brutally honest with myself, I don't think I had ever stopped. In reclaiming his life, he had removed me from everything that I held dear. If I had found the words to explain that to David, then he would have understood why my feelings for Wynter's Trees were never going to change, rather than clinging to the hope that one day I'd have this magical epiphany and move back.

Striving to find the courage to speak up, along with the words, the memories flooded in. I bitterly remembered all too vividly how, as the plantation became popular and I resigned myself to it, the new school bully realised it gave her all the ammunition she needed to single me out.

The ridicule and name calling had been incessant and I had hated Wynter's all over again. At eighteen, I couldn't wait to head back north to university and, aside from the day of Dad's funeral, I hadn't been back to Wynmouth since.

'But you rarely respond to my emails,' David fairly pointed out. 'In fact, if it wasn't for the end of year books, I don't think you'd have a clue about how the place is doing at all.'

'I'm not that bad,' I said, trying to play it off, even though I knew he was right.

'In that case,' David shot back, 'you know what I'm ringing to discuss, don't you? You know exactly what it is I've been making multiple calls to talk to you about.'

I had assumed it was the usual, me going back to Wynter's for Christmas, but his tone suggested otherwise.

'Well,' I said, craftily switching the call to speaker so I could access my emails and carry on with the conversation. 'It could be any number of things,' I blagged, furiously scrolling. 'There's the health of the trees . . .'

'The trees are fine,' he cut in. 'It's been one of the best years so far, growth wise.'

'I was just about to say that . . .'

'This is about me, Liza.' He said, sounding frustrated. 'This is to do with Wynter's and me.'

'You?' I gasped, abandoning my inbox and taking him off speaker. 'You aren't ill or anything, are you, David?'

I knew my question gave away that I hadn't in fact read whatever it was he'd written about, but I didn't care. I just needed to know he was all right. I couldn't lose him too.

'No,' he said. 'I'm not ill.'

I felt my shoulders drop at least three inches.

'I'm retiring.'

'You're what?' I choked.

'I'm retiring,' he said again.

I pulled out a kitchen chair and flopped down on to it. That was the last thing I had been expecting him to say.

'That's the last thing I expected you to say,' I blurted out, the words echoing my thoughts.

David chuckled. He sounded far happier about the prospect than I did. What was going to happen to Wynter's? David *was* Wynter's now.

'And before you start to panic,' he smoothly carried on as if it was all decided already, 'I'm not leaving you in the lurch. I'm planning to sell my shares in the business to Edward.'

'To Edward,' I repeated.

Edward was David's son. He'd worked alongside his father since returning from his aunt's forest farm in New Zealand a couple of years ago. I'd never met him, but I knew he was as mad about Wynter's as David was. In fact, I got the impression that the whole family, which was spread across the globe, had sap rather than blood running through their veins. I supposed he would be the right person to take the reins.

'He's been working with me here for almost two years now and he knows the business inside out,' David forged ahead. 'He's more than ready to take it on. He's got some great ideas about how to keep Wynter's current and your dad's plans moving along. He's got far more vision than I've ever had. I've kept things ticking over, but Edward can see far into the future.'

I knew what he was saying made perfect sense, but it didn't stop me having a moment of panic. David couldn't leave. Dad and I might not have seen eye to eye about a lot of things, but David was my last link to him. I had lost so much of my parents; I couldn't lose him too.

'But you can't retire,' I blurted out. 'Wynter's Trees just wouldn't be the same without you, David.'

'I'm sixty-nine,' he gently reminded me. 'I should have gone years ago. I only stayed on . . .'

I didn't give him the chance to finish his sentence.

'Age is just a number,' I forthrightly told him. 'And what will you do with yourself? You'll be bored witless.'

He was always on the go. He'd hate a quiet retirement.

'No, I won't,' he said and I could tell he was smiling. 'I'm going to see my sister.'

'In New Zealand?'

'That's right,' he said, sounding well pleased. 'She's handing over her farm to my niece and nephew and the two of us are going travelling together. We should have done it years ago,' he absently added.

Well, that trumped my argument. Clearly David had no intention of settling for a quiet retirement.

'I see,' I said, forcing myself to not sound resentful. 'That sounds wonderful.'

'It will be,' he said happily. 'And I couldn't have picked a better time to go. Wynter's Trees is thriving, Liza. Your dad's potted Christmas tree idea was a masterstroke and the same families are coming back every year to rent their trees and there's going to be even more happening when Edward potentially steps up.'

'There is?'

'If you really read my emails,' David tutted. 'You'd know that.'

'Yes,' I agreed. 'I suppose I would.'

'So,' he carried on, 'I take it you will come back now, won't you?'

'Come back?'

'To meet Edward. I need your approval before I can sell him my shares.'

'There's no need for that. I trust you David, I don't need . . .'

'Yes,' said David. 'You do. We're not going to do anything until you've had a look at the place and got to know Edward, and not only because that's what the legal terms of the business dictate.'

'I could video call him,' I lamely suggested, desperate to put the inevitable off.

'Look,' David snapped, sounding cross, 'I can't book my flights or make any proper plans with my sister until this is sorted, Liza. Do you really want to be the person responsible for stopping me from going?'

I shook my head.

'Do you?'

'No,' I croaked. 'I was shaking my head, but I'm still happy to sign my approval online. Surely your solicitor can settle it that way, can't they?'

'This isn't about *settling*, Liza.' David insisted. 'I want you to meet Edward. I think it's important that you get to know him. Going forward, it's going to be just you and him and I'll feel better about leaving if I know the pair of you already know each other.'

I was beginning to feel desperate and there was a tight band of pain slowly wrapping its way around my chest.

'Given that you're not working at the moment,' David pointed out, 'the timing really couldn't be better, could it?'

'But I need to make my plans for this trip,' I feebly said.

'That's as maybe,' David astutely responded, 'but you have

unfinished business here, Liza. You know you do. And until you face up to it, your life is never going to work right. It won't matter where in the world you run to; the loose ends you still have to tie up here will always be at the back of your mind, waiting to trip you up.'

It was a low blow, but a perfectly placed one.

I had unplugged the landline and turned off my mobile after David's call, but I needn't have bothered because when I reconnected everything a few days later, there were no waiting texts or messages. There were no further emails either.

The silence was a surprise, but the quiet had given me the time and space to mull everything over and within that time, I had made another big decision. A huge one, actually. I wasn't going to tie up the loose ends David had flagged up; I was going to cut right through them.

If this Edward was as ambitious as his father suggested, then he would doubtless jump at the chance of buying my shares too. He could become the sole proprietor of Wynter's Trees. And, as a result, I'd be free of my father's unwanted legacy *and* I'd have even more money to dedicate to setting up and launching my art therapy business. It was the perfect plan.

'David, hi.' I said, once I'd plucked up the courage to call him back. 'It's Liza.'

'Liza,' he said, clearly surprised.

'This might come as a bit of a shock,' I quickly said, before I could change my mind, 'but I've been thinking about what you said and I've decided you're right. I do need to come back.'

'You have?' he asked. 'You do?'

He sounded flabbergasted, but given that he'd been trying to coax me into returning for the last four years, that was only to be expected.

'Yes,' I reiterated. 'I have and I do. I'm coming back to Wynmouth and I'm going to get to know Edward.'

'Well, that's wonderful!' He sounded absolutely over the moon, but I knew his good mood wouldn't last once I arrived and explained what I had in mind.

Had I been able to sort it all online I would have been tempted, but given the care David had lavished on the business and the way he'd tried to look out for me, even though I hadn't let him, I knew I owed it to him to give him a face-to-face explanation.

'This really is the best news,' David gushed on. 'I'm so pleased and I know Edward will be too.'

I hoped he was right about that. I hoped Edward would be so pleased he'd jump at the chance of investing further and taking Wynter's Trees on single-handed.

'That's great,' I said, staving off the pins and needles of guilt my ulterior motive induced. 'I'll be arriving next Thursday.'

'Marvellous.'

'And I was wondering,' I carried on, 'if you might be able to find me somewhere cheap and cheerful to stay in Wynmouth. I'm still saving for my travels, after all.'

'It would be easiest to stay in Wynter's Lodge, wouldn't it?' David suggested.

That was the name given to the wooden house built by my father on the plantation site driveway. A lump lodged in my throat as I thought of the pretty porch swing and wraparound veranda. It had been a beautiful house, but I'd never felt at home there.

'I suppose,' I frowned, as I imagined myself opening it up and dusting it down.

'No point spending money when you don't need to, is there?'

'I guess not,' I conceded, but even as I agreed, I knew I was going to be confronted by more than the ghosts of Christmases past when I crossed the threshold.

'That's settled then,' David happily sighed. 'We'll see you on the fourth. You'll be here in time for the fireworks.'

I knew there were going to be fireworks, just not the sort he was expecting.

Chapter 2

After my call to David, I spent the next few days dithering over my decision, but on Thursday, as planned, I loaded up my ancient car, which had been an eighteenth birthday present from Dad and which I couldn't bring myself to trade in even though it was becoming increasingly unreliable, and set off for Wynmouth, on the north Norfolk coast.

During the journey, and when I was tempted to turn back, I reminded myself that if I wanted to see my plans through properly then this visit really was the only option. However, rather than head straight to the lodge when I crossed the county border, I delayed the moment by taking a detour into the little coastal village. Ostensibly it was to see if anything had changed, but in reality, it was to buy a few more minutes in which to mentally prepare.

There were no new additions to Wynmouth as far as I could tell, but what had always been there looked, to my eyes at least, a little more cared for. The village sign, set in the green, had recently had a fresh lick of paint and the shops around the edge appeared smarter too. The pub, the Smuggler's Inn, was sporting a different exterior colour and the row of brick and flint former fisherman's cottages which led down to the beach were in good repair.

The sudden intrusion of another plethora of memories ensured I didn't linger, but instead wove my way back around the narrow lanes and out of the village, failing to spot the sea because the tide was too far out. As the road twisted and turned, I fell to wondering if Wynter's Trees was going to look as cared for as the village and I didn't have to wait many minutes to find out.

'Well, that's new,' I observed, as I turned off the road and on to the drive. 'Welcome to Wynter's,' I read aloud, as I opened the passenger side window and leant across the seats to take in the personalised board which told visitors they'd arrived.

The sign was well over eight-foot high and featured a very jolly Santa, sleigh and reindeer soaring over what looked like the acreage owned by Wynter's Trees.

The artist had done a good job and I wondered how much it had cost to have a bespoke sign designed and painted. I couldn't remember any email about it but I knew I could have done it for a fraction of the cost. Then I remembered that I didn't draw or paint for myself anymore so it wasn't worth thinking about.

I put the car in gear, released the stubborn handbrake and carried on along the drive, which was now enchantingly flanked on either side by rows of tall red and white striped candy canes. They lit the way in the gathering darkness and, like the sign, weren't the only new additions. There was also a five-bar gate blocking entry to the yard, but even if there hadn't been, I would have rolled to a stop at that point anyway.

'Wow,' I whispered, pulled up short by the sight of the lodge, which was on my left and set back, almost amongst the trees.

Tears pricked my eyes as I took it in and acknowledged that my memory had failed me. In my head it was much smaller and I'd forgotten how intricately carved and painted the bargeboards which gave the place its authentic gingerbread feel, even in the height of summer, were. It was a home fit for Santa himself and for a few years it had been mine. They might have been unhappier than I would have wished for, but there was no denying, the aesthetic was idyllic.

The lights in the lodge were all switched on, giving the rooms a warm glow, and there was smoke curling out of the chimney. David had gone above and beyond to welcome me back and my intensely emotional response to the sight of the lodge, which I had never formerly felt any affection for, was a surprise. However, it wasn't quite as much of a shock as the piercing noise of an alarm which began to screech when I tried to open the gate.

I covered my ears and took a hasty step back; my burgeoning tears banished as I looked about me, half expecting to see a police car racing up the drive.

'You were supposed to call!' yelled a man's voice from the veranda a few seconds later. 'You were supposed to let me know when you were here and I was going to let you in!'

The guy, draped in a bath towel which was far too small for his towering frame, pulled on a pair of work boots and ran over to where I was standing, open mouthed and wide eyed.

He was at least a foot taller than me and thickset, and there was a smattering of freckles covering his broad chest and shoulders. His hair was dark or at least, I assumed it was. It was hard to really tell because he'd clearly just jumped out of the shower and was sopping wet. When he turned around, I noticed that he'd got what looked like a pine tree tattooed down the length of his broad back, but it was difficult to make out the details in the harsh glare of my car lights and already agog, I felt it would be rude to stare.

'There,' he said, punching buttons on a keypad and thankfully silencing the noise. 'That's better.'

'Much,' I nodded in agreement, my ears ringing.

'You must be Liza Wynter,' he said, running one hand through his hair, while the other held on to the precariously positioned towel.

'Yes,' I nodded. I felt winded by the unexpected drama of my arrival and the proximity of his near nakedness. 'Yes, I am and I'm sorry about the noise. I hadn't realised the gate would be alarmed.'

'Never mind,' he dithered. 'No harm done.'

He had started to shiver, which was hardly surprising

given that he was sodden and it was the chilliest evening of autumn so far.

'And I'm guessing you're Edward?'

'Yes,' he nodded, running his hand through his hair again. 'Sorry, I should have said. I am Edward, although more or less everyone calls me Ned.'

'Ned,' I repeated.

He was certainly a good-looking potential proprietor. Not that how he looked mattered. But then again, Wynter's Trees needed someone physically fit at the helm and this guy fitted that description perfectly. I felt my face start to colour as I imagined him effortlessly hefting trees about.

'Dad did message you,' he said, biting his lip to stop his teeth chattering. 'He sent a text when we realised you were going to be late.'

'I must have been driving when it came through,' I said. 'Although I'm not really late because I never said what time I'd be arriving.'

Ned nodded. 'Dad also said he'd forgotten to tell you he wouldn't be around until the weekend now.'

'Oh,' I said, feeling disappointed. 'No, he hadn't mentioned that.'

That was annoying too. I had been hoping to get straight down to business, but I could hardly talk to Ned about my plan without his father present.

'Never mind,' said Ned, picking up on my disappointment. 'It'll give you time to get to know the place again without him breathing down your neck.'

He said it without sarcasm, and I noticed there was a hint of a smile playing about his lips. I guessed he knew how often and how hard his dad had tried to get me to come back. I didn't point out that getting to know the place again was the last thing I intended to do.

'Look,' I said instead, noticing he was in danger of becoming frozen to the spot, 'why don't we go inside? You're going to catch your death out here.'

'Good idea,' he said, looking down at me. 'It is a bit brisk, isn't it? And I've left the shower on. Can you manage to bring your stuff in?'

'Of course.' I said, wondering why exactly he was using the bathroom in the lodge.

The shock of seeing him half-naked meant it hadn't registered before and there was no chance to ask him because he eagerly, and not surprisingly, sprinted off. I pushed the gate further open, drove my car through, then closed it again and transferred my few bits of luggage from the boot to the veranda before taking a deep breath and lugging it inside.

Finding myself back in the lodge felt every bit as uncomfortable as I had expected it to and as I looked about the place, I felt satisfied that my mission to cut all ties with the business was the right one. I would endure this unwelcome onslaught of emotions, with my mind firmly focused on convincing Ned to buy me out and my eyes trained on next year's calendar, the travel brochures and my business plans back in my flat.

'New year, new start,' I whispered. 'New year, new me.'

Looking at the room in more detail, I realised it didn't look as if it had been abandoned and shut up at all and it didn't smell or feel like it either. It was warm and cosy, thanks to the roaring log burner, and there was the delicious scent of something hearty coming from the kitchen. If I hadn't known better, I would have said the place was being lived in but that couldn't be right, could it?

Heavy footfall on the stairs drew my attention and I gasped as Ned came back into view and a dog started barking somewhere.

'What on earth?' I frowned, further poleaxed by his choice of clothes. 'Why are you wearing that jumper?' I blurted out. 'It belonged to my dad.'

Ned looked fondly down at the chunky snowflake patterned navy knit which encased his broad chest and flat stomach.

'No,' he grinned, smoothing it down, 'this is definitely mine. I've got a whole collection of them and from what my dad has told me about yours, I don't think I could fit into his. They wouldn't be long enough, would they? Although,' he said, his eyes sparkling, 'I am every bit as much of a fan of the festive season as your father was.'

I felt my face flame as I realised he was right. He was much, much taller than Dad and there was no way he could have squeezed himself into any of his jumpers. The one Ned was wearing was oversized, even on him and looking at the pattern more closely, I could see it wasn't the same. It was very similar, but not identical.

'Sorry,' I swallowed, still lingering on the lodge threshold. 'I can see it's different now. The sight of it just took me by surprise.'

'No worries,' he shrugged. 'Can I take your coat?'

I took a further step into the room and gave Ned another tick on my mental checklist. His love for all things festive would be a great help when it came to asking him to buy my shares. Anyone as keen on Christmas as my father had been would be thrilled at the prospect of owning somewhere as seasonally spectacular as Wynter's Trees.

'Thanks,' I said, handing over my coat.

'I hope you don't mind that I've moved in,' Ned carried on, heading towards the utility room on the far side of the kitchen, which was where the barking seemed to be coming from.

'Moved in?'

'Yes,' he said. 'After the last break-in Dad and I decided I needed to be permanently on-site, but of course you know that already.'

'Did you?' I frowned again. 'Do I?'

'Yes,' he said, looking back over at me. 'Dad emailed you about the damage to the barn from the last break-in months ago and then about me opening up the house.'

'I must have missed the update,' I said, wondering which of the many emails I'd received and merely skimmed over held those particular nuggets of information.

'Dad has said that you tend to be a bit slack in the inbox department,' Ned admitted.

23

'Has he?'

Given that David had let me know, I could hardly take umbrage at the fact that Ned was living in the lodge and actually, he looked so at home I couldn't help thinking that was yet another plus point. Him already being so settled in the place would make his taking over feel like a logical next step rather than a great change and upheaval. Had I been fond of the lodge and had a hankering to live in it myself, his presence might have rankled, but as it was, this arrangement was just fine.

'Now,' he said, as he hung up my coat and then put his hand on the utility door handle as the barking reached a whole new level. 'How do you feel about dogs?'

'I love dogs,' I said, moving to stand nearer the sofa and quickly adding, 'as a rule.'

'Excellent,' he grinned. 'In that case, brace yourself, and don't worry, this fella's all bark and definitely no bite.'

I opened my mouth to ask what he was about to unleash but was practically bowled off my feet before I got the chance.

'This is Bandit,' said Ned, introducing me to the huge husky with the thickest coat and bluest eyes who had skittered across the wooden floor at breakneck speed and into my arms. 'Second line of defence in the keep Wynter's safe campaign. He's an absolute softie, but no one who turns up with criminal intent needs to know that.'

Once he'd said a very thorough hello, Bandit sat panting at my feet and looked up at me as if butter wouldn't melt. I wasn't sure if he was as innocent or as well behaved as he was trying to make out, but he was beautiful. I gave him another fuss, my fingers practically disappearing in his thick coat.

'He's a rescue hound,' Ned further explained. 'His original owners hadn't had him five minutes before they realised they weren't going to be able to cope with him.'

'And can you?' I asked, raising my eyebrows as I abandoned my post next to the sofa which had served as no defence from Bandit's enthusiastic welcome. Not that I really minded, because he was so lovely. 'He must need a lot of exercise.'

'Just about,' Ned laughed. 'And he does. I'm a keen runner, so he gets a good few miles under his belt with me most days.'

I supposed you didn't get a physique like his from felling trees alone and I could easily picture the pair of them pounding around the plantation.

'He's perfect for this place,' I pointed out, although I was sure Ned was already aware of that.

'I'm hoping for snow this year,' he told me. 'The photo opportunities with him will be too good to miss.'

'Yes,' I agreed. 'And he could be the perfect mascot for the website too.'

In my mind's eye, I could easily imagine the idyllic snowy scene on the homepage, enhanced by Bandit's blue eyes and elegant stature, but then I gave myself a shake and shrugged the image off. What the Wynter's Trees website looked like was nothing to do with me.

'Are you hungry?' Ned asked, making Bandit's ears prick up. 'Not you pooch,' he tutted, 'I was talking to Liza.'

'I am a bit,' I said.

'Good,' Ned nodded. 'I thought you might be, so I've made a steak and ale stew in the slow cooker. I hope that's all right? You're not vegetarian, are you?'

'Sounds great,' I said, and right on cue my stomach growled. 'And no, I'm not.'

'In that case, why don't you put your bags in your room and freshen up and I'll start plating up?'

I didn't turn the lights on in my old room. In fact, I barely opened the door. I just put my bags on the floor and nudged them inside with my foot. I'd deal with any emotional reaction to the sight of the room at bedtime and in private. I wasn't really expecting there to be one, but then I hadn't expected to well up at the sight of the lodge either, so it was probably best to err on the side of caution.

'I meant to say,' said Ned, handing me a plate filled with stew, soft and fluffy dumplings and glossy, green kale, 'I've taken the spare room opposite yours. I hope that's okay?'

'Of course.'

'I have been in the big double room,' he said, his eyes briefly meeting mine. 'But only to bleed the radiator and occasionally open the windows.'

'Thank you,' I quietly said.

That had been Dad's room and I knew it would still be just as he had left it. Not for the first time, I wished I'd had the courage to make decisions about what I wanted to do with his and Mum's things when I was at the very bottom of the pit of grief, rather than having to face it all now.

'So,' said Ned, when I didn't say anything further, 'Dad tells me you've been working with some challenging students for the last few weeks, what's that been like?'

He poured us both a glass of wine and I told him some of the more amusing anecdotes I'd accumulated, along with further details of what my real job as an art therapist entailed and how much I missed it.

Being stuck in a classroom for the last few weeks had hit hard after all the hours I'd formerly spent outside with the small groups of students I supported, encouraging them to use the natural world both as inspiration for their work and as a balm for their troubled souls. I didn't venture into details about my freshly formed business plans. It was my intention to only reveal those when Ned, David and I were all together.

From what his dad had already said, Ned struck me as an astute businessman and I was pretty certain that he would pick up on the fact that an enterprise such as the one I had in mind would require more than a teaching salary and savings to get it off the ground.

The conversation between us flowed easily, and I was grateful that Ned had gone to the trouble to make my first evening back as stress free as possible. As I looked across at him, I realised just how like David, in that respect, he was.

'So,' I said, turning my attention back to the focus of David's recent call, 'do you think it's going to take long to get the papers drawn up to sell and transfer your dad's share in the business to you?'

Ned helped himself to another ladle of stew, then looked at me. Now his hair was completely dry I could see it was touched by chestnut highlights.

'I'm not sure, to be honest,' he told me. 'All Dad's done so far is brief his solicitor about what might be happening. He didn't want to do more than that until we'd met and you'd decided if you were happy for him to sell to me or not.'

There was no doubt in my mind that Ned was going to win my seal of approval. In fact, he was already well on his way to receiving a gold star, hopefully along with my share in the business too.

'Why?' he asked. 'Are you in a rush to get away again? I was hoping to run you through the new ideas I have for the place. You never know, you might even fancy sticking around to help me get some of them up and running.'

It wasn't the time to explain that whatever he had in mind wasn't going to matter to me because I was planning to leave for good, so I just played along and tried not to feel too guilty about it.

'I'm not in too much of a rush,' I told him, choosing my words with care. 'But I'm going to travel soon, so I won't be staying here for long.'

'Dad did say you had plans to see a bit of the world,' Ned nodded. 'And he's told you he has too, hasn't he?'

'Yes,' I said. 'New Zealand.'

'And that's just for starters,' Ned laughed. 'I reckon

he and my aunt will be taking a full global tour if Dad
has his way.'

'That would be amazing.'

I'd never had David down as a global explorer before. I
had assumed his roots were too established in Norfolk to
take such a monumental trip.

'And where are you heading?' Ned asked me.

'Japan,' I told him, 'Or maybe Iceland.'

'Wow,' he whistled. 'Not both?'

I thought about that. 'Perhaps,' I eventually said. 'It's
going to depend on what Father Christmas puts in my
stocking this year.'

If my shares raised enough, and I was careful with my
budgeting, travelling to both sides of the world might turn
out be a possibility.

'In that case,' Ned smiled, emptying the last of the wine
into my glass, 'you'd better make sure you're on the nice
list, hadn't you?'

Chapter 3

Ned insisted on sorting the kitchen after our meal so I took myself off for an early night. Thankfully, my former bedroom didn't strike the same emotional response as my first glimpse of the lodge had, but I did experience a lump in the throat moment when I opened my wardrobe and found my old box of art supplies stacked inside.

Mum had been an accomplished painter and seeing the talent in me too, Dad had encouraged me to embrace my artistic gift and apply to art college after my A levels, but I didn't. I opted instead for teaching and a more structured and stable career path. I might have dreamt of being an artist, but Dad had followed his dreams, and his actions and choices had rather put me off following the whisperings in my heart. That was about to change now, however, with the creation of my own business which utilised my skills, but it had taken me years to work my way up to doing it.

It was barely light when I woke the next morning and I

felt weighed down in the bed, pinned to the mattress and unable to move. I hadn't felt like that since the weeks after I'd answered my flat door and found two police officers waiting to impart the horrific news about Dad and which had blown my world apart for the second time.

'Have I made a mistake in coming back here?' I cautiously whispered into the near darkness but then the weight shifted and I felt Bandit's warm breath close to my face. 'Oh, Bandit,' I said, feeling relieved. 'It's just you.'

I tried to shift him but he wouldn't budge and I buried my face and fingers into his soft, warm coat. It felt surprisingly soothing and I wondered if he was one of those dogs who could sense vulnerability in humans. If so, he was probably more keyed in to my true emotions than I was. I had arrived at Wynter's Trees with the intention of being all business, but I was already wondering if my mission was going to be as cut and dry as I originally hoped.

'Morning,' beamed Ned, who was in the kitchen, dressed and looking far too chipper given the early hour when Bandit and I padded downstairs. 'Coffee?'

'Coffee would be great, thanks,' I said, flopping down on the sofa in front of the already lit log burner.

'I see you've got company,' Ned nodded at Bandit, who was now sitting next to me with his head resting on my lap.

'He was on my bed when I woke up,' I said, stroking his head. 'Did you let him in?'

'Nope,' said Ned, handing me one of the lodge's Portmeirion holly patterned mugs. 'Huskies are the Houdinis of the dog world and this one can get in and out of anywhere. I daresay he thought you'd appreciate the company. He's an intuitive soul and my guess is he's picked up on how hard it must be for you, coming back here for the first time since . . .'

His words trailed off and I took a sip of the coffee, even though it was still a little too hot.

'Sorry,' he said. 'I didn't mean . . . that is, I'd told myself I wouldn't mention . . .'

'It's fine,' I briskly said, changing the subject. 'So, what's on the agenda for today?'

'Well,' he said, keenly grasping the alternative topic, 'Bandit and I are now going for a run. Would you care to join us?'

'I don't think so,' I said, smiling at the thought of my legs, trying to keep pace with his gigantic strides. 'But thanks for the offer. I'll stay here and shower instead.'

'Fair enough,' Ned grinned, and I wondered if he was thinking the same thing. 'We'll see you in a bit.'

The sun was up by the time I'd showered, dressed and breakfasted and with no sign of either Ned or Bandit I decided to have a look around outside. Admittedly, one Christmas tree looked much like another to me, but after being shut in classrooms for the last few weeks, I was craving fresh air and if I ventured far enough, I'd be able to see the patch of land Dad and a few other locals had invested in and turned into a sort of nature reserve. Earmarked for development, battling to save the site had turned Dad into even more of a local hero and I couldn't deny, I had been proud to see the plot saved and transformed.

The air was crisp and fresh and I was pleased I'd pulled on Dad's battered old wax coat, which still hung on its familiar hook next to the front door, because there was a definite coastal nip in the air. Sometimes I forgot just how close Wynter's Trees was to the sea and the impact that could have on the weather. The place seemed to have its own microclimate and that morning the barometer was set to bracing thanks to the breeze.

As I strode out among the rows of trees, I hoped I wasn't about to turn a corner and be bowled over by Bandit and Ned, but there was no sign or sound of either of them. As I looked around, it struck me that everything felt both familiar *and* different. David was right, the trees had grown well.

Many of the rows I had previously been able to look over the top of, now practically towered above me. Not a particularly difficult feat given I'm only five foot three, but the change made me very aware of how much had moved on in my absence. Those larger trees, I guessed, were the ones destined to be eventually cut for display for outdoor venues. It was just the ones in pots which were annually rented out and returned, but where were they?

I walked further into the plantation and then stopped, pulled up short by the sight ahead of me. Whereas before there had been a few dozen container grown trees, there were now what looked like hundreds, all neatly arranged in size order and regimented rows.

I wondered what Dad would have made of the spectacle. I knew he would have been proud, but would he have been surprised by just how impressively his vision had taken off? David always sent me lists numbering the rented-out trees, but that didn't have anything like the same impact as seeing them lined up for myself.

Container-grown trees had been the original inspiration behind Dad's environmental ethos. He always hated seeing the streets filled with dried out and dead trees throughout the first two weeks of January and had made it his mission to encourage families to rent trees on a yearly basis. I could remember him telling me that Norway spruce were the favourites because of their strong pine scent and that you could happily keep a tree growing in a pot for about twelve years before it needed planting out.

I was surprised I could remember. Even though I had never been interested in the business, I seemed to be able to recall a bit about it. I guessed if you heard something often enough it stuck, and Dad was always repeating the same spiel when waxing lyrical about the virtues of a rented tree to visitors, while our family friend, Sue, smilingly handed around freshly baked reindeer cookies and mugs of marshmallow-topped hot chocolate.

Dad made picking a Wynter's tree a memorable occasion and it was his in-depth knowledge and special extra seasonal touches which kept folk coming back, right from the first year of trading. I could see for myself now that David and Ned had more than competently carried those traditions

34

on. The number of trees awaiting collection were all the visual proof anyone would need to see that the venture was thriving.

I read a couple of the laminated labels attached to the trees which ensured the right family got the right one every year, but there were no surnames I recognised. I was amused however to read that lots of the trees had names of their own. Belle was a popular choice, as were Elsa and Kristoff. There was even a Clark 'Sparky' Griswold. I smiled as I wondered if that particularly impressive specimen was destined to survive the season.

In spite of the bright blue sky and accompanying sunshine it was still chilly as the wind whistled through the plantation. I began to shiver and, abandoning my plan to make it as far as the nature reserve boundary, walked briskly back to the yard, arriving in it as Ned and Bandit came out of the office. They must have finished their run just after I'd set out.

'Have you been for a walk?' asked Ned. 'I wondered where you'd got to.'

'Yes,' I said, 'I've been craving fresh air. Although I hadn't taken into account the brisk sea breeze. I could have done with some gloves. It's cold today, isn't it?'

'Yes,' he agreed. 'It is a bit sharp. But at least you found that old coat.'

'It was Dad's,' I said, pulling it tighter around me. 'I was pleased to find it still hanging in its usual place.'

'I haven't moved anything,' Ned told me. 'I wouldn't dream of changing or rearranging any of it.'

'I appreciate that,' I said, feeling choked by his thoughtfulness. 'I am going to get around to sorting everything out soon.'

'There's no rush,' he shrugged. 'It's yours to do what you want with as and when you feel like it. I'm just the lodge's caretaker.'

Knowing I was going to ask him to buy me out the moment I could get him and David together, there actually was now a need for me to feel like it quite soon.

'So,' Ned carried on, 'how did you find the trees?'

'Green,' I told him. 'And tall.'

Ned rocked back on his heels and laughed. My knowledge, in spite of Dad's efforts, didn't run much deeper than that.

'I was surprised to see so many in pots,' I added. 'That side of the business has really taken off, hasn't it?'

'Absolutely,' Ned agreed. 'Your dad was really on to something when he came up with that idea. He was well ahead of the game and even though there are other businesses offering a similar service now, none of them are a patch on Wynter's. Not that I'm biased or anything,' he chuckled.

I felt further reassured that his love for the place practically guaranteed that he was going to want to take it on, lock, stock and barrel.

'Well, the success it is today can't *all* be down to Dad's ideas.' I pointed out. 'You and your dad have cleverly capitalised on what he started. It's definitely a growth industry.'

Ned rolled his eyes at my pitiful pun.

'We have,' he smiled, 'and it is. And with that in mind, I want to tell you more about the huts.'

'The huts?'

'Yes,' he said. 'The beach huts, but first I think you'd better have a look at your tree.'

I followed him back over to the barn at the side of the yard which was where the office, stores and Santa's grotto were located.

'It's really starting to struggle,' Ned said, as he came to a stop in front of a tree which was in a huge pot outside the barn door. 'It's had far longer in a container than it should. I wanted Dad to ask you about planting it out last year, but he said to wait. He was certain you'd want to do it yourself. With some help of course. It is pretty big, after all.'

I swallowed hard as I looked at the tree I no longer recognised.

'You can see it's beginning to flag,' Ned carried on, unaware of the impact his words were having, 'in spite of the extra tender loving care I've been giving it and if it doesn't get moved on soon, I think we'll lose it.'

I couldn't say anything.

'Hey, are you all right?' Ned asked, frowning down at me when he finally realised, I hadn't responded to anything he'd said.

I pulled in a ragged breath, and slowly let it out again.

'Is this,' I swallowed, 'is this . . .'

'Your family tree,' Ned finished for me, his tone softer. 'Yes,' he said, 'this is yours, Liza.'

I couldn't believe it was the same tree that Dad had chosen to have in the lodge soon after we moved. It had been the focal point of our festive celebrations for years.

'I think I've found the perfect spot for it.' Ned said kindly.

I quickly reminded myself that I didn't care about the tree or anything else still here for that matter. I didn't care about a single thing that was connected to Wynter's Trees, and yet, the sight of that damn tree ailing in its too tight pot, had somehow succeeded in tearing my heart in two, just like my first glimpse of the lodge had.

'I'll have a think about it,' was all I could huskily say.

'All right,' Ned nodded.

The expression on his face told me that the look on mine gave away exactly how I was feeling. I turned away and, with an effort, recalibrated and shifted focus back to the real business in hand. I had to get a grip, and not get caught up in the sentiment I was floored to find I had attached to a few random things. I took a deep breath and lifted my chin as Bandit nudged his damp nose into my clenched fist and it was then that I spotted Dad's truck.

It hadn't registered when I'd set off for my walk, but there was no missing it now. The 1950 red Chevy pick-up had been a huge investment and it had been the perfect vehicle for ferrying trees about and getting the business noticed. I'd always hated being taken to school in it because it got me noticed too and earned me the hated nickname, 'Elf'.

'What's going on with the truck?' I frowned, walking over to where it was parked.

I hated it for another reason too. It had been off the road the night Dad had been hit by a drunk driver who was three times over the limit having gone completely over the top at his office Christmas party. Had he been cocooned in the tank-like Chevy, rather than the little courtesy car from the garage, he would have most likely walked away from the carnage.

'Why is it up on this platform?' I pointed, banishing further sickening thoughts of the night of the crash which I knew would send my mood plummeting.

There was so much more attached to the memory of that time than anyone else knew and I had no intention of revisiting it.

'Because we don't use it anymore,' said Ned. 'But as it's so iconic, we had it decommissioned and parked here on permanent display.'

So much for not changing anything I began to seethe, feeling nettled.

'But this truck encapsulates pretty much everything Wynter's stands for.' I snapped. 'It was Dad's pride and joy. He loved it.'

'Well,' said Ned, looking taken aback by my transformation from upset to annoyed, 'Dad did explain our reasons for doing it in . . .'

'An email,' I bit back. 'Of course, he did, but I can't quite remember the details now, so perhaps you could enlighten me.'

'Sure,' Ned shrugged. 'Basically, the decision to take it off the road came down to its environmental credentials. To tell you the truth,' he said fixing me with a challenging stare which took me by surprise, 'given your Dad's motivation to set the business up with a view to helping the planet, I'm surprised he ran it at all.'

'He ran it because it attracted more business than that thing could in a million years,' I huffed, pointing at the red Mitsubishi pick-up which I now realised had been drafted in to replace the Chevy.

'Perhaps,' Ned patiently said, 'but it's MPG is outstanding and even though I agree that it doesn't have the same appeal as this vintage treasure, we have to move forward with a view to what's best for the business. And the environment.'

'I thought you said you hadn't changed anything.' I sarcastically said.

'I haven't in the lodge,' he shot back. 'It's not my home, but out here is different. It's my job to keep things current, practical and cost-effective and besides, you've never objected to any of the other changes we've made.'

Given my track record for neglecting my inbox, I could hardly refute that.

'We aren't going to fall out over this, are we, Liza?' Ned asked, looking concerned.

'That depends,' I churlishly said, even though the last thing I wanted to do was make an enemy of the man I had pinned to solve all my problems. 'What's going to happen to the Chevy now? Is it just going to sit here and rot?'

'Of course not.' Ned tutted, sounding offended. 'It's regularly inspected and it's loved and polished too. Last

Christmas it proved perfect for photo opportunities. We put a tree in the back, added some lights, and folk loved it. Bandit even featured in a few of the shots. And the customers tagged Wynter's Trees every single time they shared a shot on social media. It might not be on the road anymore, but believe me, it's still drawing customers in and from even further afield than before.'

I supposed it would make a beautiful backdrop for a seasonal snap.

'Well, that's something I suppose,' I said, feeling appeased. I knew I should apologise, but couldn't bring myself to do it. 'I'm going to head back to the lodge,' I said instead. 'I need another coffee.'

Neither Ned nor Bandit followed me and I was grateful to be left alone. I spent the rest of the morning pottering about in the lodge. I could see that Ned had been true to his word and he hadn't changed or moved a thing.

I was just pulling Dad's old coat back on with a view to going out to apologise when I heard a vehicle revving on the drive and looked out to find the biggest lorry being slowly squeezed through the, by comparison, narrow gate. I rushed out the door to stop the driver before they got too far.

'You're in the wrong place!' I shouted up to the cab. 'The beach is that way,' I added when I noticed what was strapped to the trailer. 'You'll have to reverse back down the drive because there's no room for you to turn around here.'

'It's all right,' said Ned, coming out of the barn. 'He's not lost.'

It was then I remembered, he'd mentioned beach huts earlier.

'What's going on?' I frowned.

The driver jumped down and shook Ned's hand.

'Abbie's so excited about this, Ned,' he beamed, looking at me as he clapped my companion on the back. 'And the whole village is talking about it.'

'Talking about what?' I asked.

'Check your inbox,' Ned grinned.

'Where are they going then?' the driver asked Ned.

'Over there,' he pointed. 'The ground's all prepared so it should be quick to lift them off and get them set in position.'

'Ned,' I said, tugging at his sleeve to get his attention. 'Why exactly are you taking delivery of four beach huts?'

'They're for the new Wynter's shopping experience,' he said, pulling me out of the way and moving to guide the first hut into place. 'I know Dad's description was a bit vague, but the gist of it is, we're renting these to local crafters so they can sell direct to the public. Every single one has been booked and we're going to have extra food and drink in the barn to further compliment the venture too.'

'But the farm is only open for a few weeks every year, surely it won't be worth it.'

Ned shook his head. 'Not anymore,' he said. 'We're opening at certain times throughout the autumn too and properly from the middle of November now. People will be able to walk among the trees *and* do some Christmas shopping while they're here. The huts were supposed to be set up in Wynmouth but after a couple of problems, I suggested we do it here, where the site is more secure and there's already a festive vibe. Everyone jumped at the chance.'

'But Wynter's is about renting trees,' I reminded him, 'and visiting Santa, not selling Christmas tat.'

He looked shocked. 'The people coming here to sell are all small bespoke designers with fledgling businesses,' he said crossly. 'They operate along the same lines as we run this place. Quality first. You'll see soon enough. Had you read all the emails, you'd already know.'

I opened my mouth to object, but couldn't because he was right. It wasn't his fault that I hadn't engaged in any of what had been going on. I might own the bigger share in the business, but if I could pull my plan off soon none of it would be anything to do with me. I needed to keep Ned onside, not provoke and piss him off.

'Sorry,' I said.

'It's fine,' he said, running his hands through his hair, before he moved to the spot prepared for the second hut. 'Well,' he added, 'not really fine, but understandable. Being back here can't be easy for you.'

'It isn't,' I admitted.

'You're bound to feel a bit mixed up.'

'I do.' I swallowed.

'I get that.' He nodded.

'Are you always so nice?' I demanded, but found myself beginning to smile.

'Yes,' he grinned. 'Of course. I'm the ultimate good guy.'

Watching the way his eyes crinkled as he smiled and the tenderness behind his words, I could well believe that.

Chapter 4

I left Ned checking out the arrangement of his new venture and went back to the lodge. As I closed the door and glanced back at the row of huts, I couldn't help thinking how perfectly they sat in the yard.

There was more than enough room for them and they looked as though they'd been there for far longer than five minutes. Even though I didn't know exactly what they were going to be stocked with yet, in my experience bespoke designers meant quality, so they'd be a great draw. If Ned played his cards right then Wynter's Trees might well turn out to be one of the top go-to Christmas attractions in the area.

I hung Dad's coat back on its hook and picked up the framed photo of him and Mum from the bookcase next to the log burner. I wondered what Dad would make of the changes Ned was making. He would have most likely been upset to see the Chevy taken out of service, but he would have accepted it on the environmental grounds Ned had flagged up.

'Waste not, want not,' I could imagine him saying as he admired it on display.

He would have loved that the vehicle still had some purpose and would have been the first to have his photo taken standing next to it. And even though Mum knew nothing of Wynter's Trees, she would have adored the huts. I could remember her shopping with care and opting to buy from small producers because they offered something unique. She had been shopping local, I realised, long before it became a trendy buzzword.

'Good god!' said Ned, bursting through the door a little later and bringing with him a cold rush of air. 'It's absolutely pouring out there.'

He was soaking wet again, only clothed this time and Bandit, who was by his side, didn't look much drier. Ned shook his jacket out on the veranda and then gave the dog a rub with a towel which was kept next to the door for that purpose.

'I hadn't noticed,' I said, as Bandit skittered over to me, his claws scrabbling to grip the wooden floor, but I could see Ned was right.

'I hope it stops soon, otherwise tonight will be a wash out.' He tutted.

'Tonight?'

'It's bonfire night and there's a party happening on the beach.'

'Oh right,' I mused. 'I seem to remember your dad mentioning a firework party.'

Since finishing work, I'd rather lost track of the date which felt strange, given that my entire working life had been governed by the calendar.

'No fireworks,' Ned elaborated, 'because you never know where the waste will end up, but there's going to be a bonfire, sparklers and some fabulous food. Do you fancy it? You'd be most welcome. You might run into someone you know.'

That wasn't very likely because I'd never really socialised with anyone in the village. Wynter's Trees was located too far out to make it possible for my teenage self to get to the beach without parental assistance and given that the Chevy was Dad's favoured mode of transport, I preferred to stay at home, rather than draw the extra unwelcome attention. I hadn't passed my driving test until a few weeks before I left for university, by which time it was too late to form lasting local friendships.

'I don't think I will, but thanks for the offer,' I said. 'I'm still feeling washed out from the hectic term, so I'm going to have another early night.'

'Fair enough,' said Ned. 'As long as you're sure?'

'I am.'

'I was hoping to have the chance to tell you a bit more about my plans for the huts before I went,' he added, glancing over at the clock. 'But I've offered to help set up and if I don't get a move on, I'll be late. If you did come, I could tell you on the way.'

'There's no need,' I told him. 'It's fine.'

'But I don't want you thinking . . .'

'I don't think anything,' I cut in, waving his words away. 'Honestly.'

'Hang on,' he laughed. 'You don't know what I'm going to say yet.'

'Yes, I do.' I smiled back, because I found it impossible not to when he looked so amused. 'You were going to say you don't want me thinking that you're going to fill the huts with mass-produced plastic crap.'

He shook his head.

'Weren't you?'

'Yes,' he admitted. 'Well, something like that.'

'Well, I don't think that,' I insisted. 'Especially not since you set me straight so quickly. In fact, I'm looking forward to seeing the huts set up and stocked. And I'm looking forward to meeting these small business owners you're so keen to help out too.'

The words flowed out and rather took me by surprise. I put them down to my desire to see the business continuing to thrive and looking like an even more irresistible prospect.

'Well, that's great,' said Ned, scratching his head.

I got the impression that he had been expecting more of a battle than an easy ride.

'In that case, I'll get ready and go,' he carried on. 'And I'll shut Bandit in the utility room before I leave. That way you might get an undisturbed night. You're sure you don't want to come? Some of the people who will be selling from the huts are bound to be there.'

'No, it's okay,' I reiterated. 'I need some sleep, but thanks for asking.'

I didn't much like Bandit being banished and Ned hadn't been gone many minutes, leaving behind a lingering trace of luscious woody aftershave, before I unlocked the door and let the dog back out again. He gave me an accusatory cerulean 'I should think so too' stare, obviously aware that I had been the cause of his eviction from the hearth.

I apologised with a treat from the locked cupboard which contained his food and then settled down on the sofa and fired up my laptop. There they all were, David's multiple emails explaining what had been happening along with the details of the potential future changes.

I skimmed a few, but properly read the details of others and soon got the gist that Ned was keen to vastly extend the Wynter's Trees season and not with a view to just boosting profits.

Most recently there had been a Halloween party in the barn and a spooky trail around part of the plantation to help raise funds for the village hall which was in need of repairs, and there was another email explaining that more trees were going to be donated to local causes this year along with the reasons why. There was further future investment earmarked for the nature reserve too. A bird-hide named after Dad was apparently in the pipeline.

I went to bed, further reassured of Ned's commitment to the business and I happily snuggled down under the duvet and contentedly ran through the words I would say when I spoke to him and David about my plans the next day.

'My dear, Liza,' beamed David, rushing to greet me, when I went over to the office early the next morning. 'I'm so happy that you finally agreed to come home.'

'So am I,' I told him as he pulled me in for a hug, and in spite of the fact that I'd never really considered the place 'home'.

That said, in just a few minutes, I would finally be able to explain why I was so happy to be here and that was something to smile about.

'I knew you would be,' he said, releasing me and looking over to Ned. 'Didn't I say to you, that if we could just get her here, then everything would be fine?'

'You did,' Ned agreed, 'many, many times.'

Suddenly I found it wasn't so easy to return the look David was giving me. It was obvious that he was still harbouring the hope that I might move back for good.

'So,' he said, ushering me into a chair. 'How are you finding things? I know some of it has probably been a bit tough, but you're all right really, aren't you?'

The eagerness in his tone tugged at my heartstrings. David had tried so hard to look after me in the past and I'd blocked him at every turn. Going forward, I decided I would accept his kindness and his help. That is, assuming he would remain kind and helpful once I'd told him what I was planning to do.

'Yes,' I nodded. 'I'm fine, but you're right. Some things have been harder than others. For a start, it was a shock to see the truck out of action.'

I hated the thing with a passion and yet the sight of it permanently grounded had still taken some getting used to.

'But I wrote about that,' he said, his brows knitted together.

'And as you know,' Ned reminded him, with a mischievous grin, 'Liza doesn't always read her emails. Do you Miss Wynter?'

'No,' I blushed, staving off the desire to stick my tongue out at him. 'I don't. Although last night, I did work my way through a lot of what you'd written, David, and I've got a much better idea about things now.'

Ned looked impressed.

'And what do you think about the beach hut project?' David keenly asked.

'I really like it,' I told him. 'Ned knows I was a little sceptical at first, but now he's explained about the quality of the designers who will be stocking it, I think it's a wonderful idea. And I love the community focused projects too. You've got a great resource here, especially in terms of outside space and it's great that it's being used to its full potential.'

Ned looked even happier.

'Well, that is wonderful,' smiled David, 'but you just said, *you've* got a great resource here. Surely you mean *we*, don't you, my dear? This is still a co-owned business don't forget, even if you do prefer the role of silent partner.'

'Um,' I said, taking a deep breath and sitting up a little straighter. 'I'm pleased you picked up on that, David, because there's something I want to talk to you about in terms of my role in the business.'

Ned pushed back his chair and picked up the open file of papers on his desk.

'I'll leave you to it,' he said.

'No, don't go.' I insisted. 'This involves you too, Ned. In fact, it's more about you than your dad, but I didn't want to say anything until we were all together.'

He sat down again and he and David exchanged a questioning look. I tried to remember how I'd formed the words before I went to sleep, but now the moment had arrived, they'd all got jumbled in my head. I knew this was what I wanted, but now it came to asking for it, it wasn't as easy as I thought it would be.

'What is it?' asked Ned. 'You've got me worried now.'

I shook my head. 'No,' I said, 'don't be worried. It's nothing bad.'

'What is it then?' David demanded.

'Well,' I began, lacing my fingers together in my lap. 'I've been giving my future and my role here a lot of thought recently . . .'

A swift glance at the hope lighting up David's eyes left me in no doubt that he was willing me to say I was moving back permanently.

'And?' encouraged Ned.

'And,' I said, pulling in another breath, 'I've decided, like you, David,' I added to try and make it sound as if we were in it together, 'I'm going to sell my shares in the business.'

'You're going to what?' David gasped, all the colour draining from his face.

'Sell my shares,' I repeated.

He looked absolutely horrified.

'There are things I want to do with my life,' I elaborated, but for some reason holding back my plans to set up my own business, 'and I'll need capital in order to achieve them. The only way I can raise it is by selling my stake in the business.'

Neither man said a word.

'You did say that my life wouldn't work right until I'd sorted a few things out here, didn't you, David?'

Ned shot his father a look.

'And having thought it all through very carefully, I now know that severing my connection to this place is a sure-fire way for me to do that.'

Ned shook his head.

'You must know I've wanted to cut my ties to Wynter's for a long time, David,' I softly said.

'You always told me that you thought Liza would eventually come back,' Ned accusingly shot at his father. 'Just give her time, you said, and she'll come round.'

'That was never going to happen.' I clarified. 'Not in a million years. Why did you think I'd stayed away?'

'Jesus,' he muttered, thrusting his hands into his hair and making it stand up on end.

'And now you're retiring, David, this feels like the perfect time . . .'

'For who?' Ned interrupted. 'Who the hell are you planning to sell to? We don't want just anyone taking over. They're going to have the bigger share. What if they see things differently? What if they don't envisage the same future for the place as I do?'

He was beginning to sound desperate.

'That's not going to be an issue,' I tried to say reassuringly.

'But how can you be sure, Liza?'

'Because,' I said, 'I want to sell my shares to you.'

'To me?' he spluttered.

'Yes,' I said. 'I want you to take over the whole place, Ned.'

My words hung in the air and a silence I hadn't been expecting replaced the whoops of joy I had assumed would follow my announcement. I had thought the pair of them would be thrilled, but neither man looked excited at all.

'But Wynter's Trees needs a Wynter at the helm,' David said eventually.

'Wynter's Trees hasn't had that in a very long time,' I pointed out.

I turned my gaze to Ned. He looked paler than David.

'I can't buy you out, Liza,' he distractedly said. 'It's going to be a push for me to buy Dad's shares.'

I hadn't been so naïve that I assumed he would shake my hand and pass over the cash there and then, but I had thought that his excitement to take over would guarantee a promise that he would find a way to make it happen. A firm and immediate 'no' had never entered into the equation when I had played this moment out in my head.

'And before you suggest it,' Ned said, addressing his dad, 'I'm not buying Liza out instead of you. You've already put your trip off once for this place, I won't let it happen again.'

'What does that mean?' I frowned. 'When did you put it off, David?'

Ned opened his mouth to speak, but David cut him off. 'It doesn't matter,' he resolutely said, brooking no contradiction. 'Are you really sure you want to do this, Liza?'

'I am,' I said, lifting my chin.

'I can't believe it,' he sighed. 'This is the very last thing I was expecting you to suggest. I thought when you agreed to come back, that you might . . .'

'What?' I cut in. 'Somehow fall in love with the place when I drove through the gate? That would be a fairy tale, David, and I don't believe in fairy stories. Do you, Ned?'

He didn't look as though he knew what he believed anymore.

'Wouldn't you like to be sole proprietor?' I asked him.

'I don't know,' he said, his voice shaking a little. 'I've never thought about it. Given that Dad's always been so convinced that you'd come back, I thought you would too, and after this redundancy. Well, I thought this was it. Whenever I've thought about the long-term future, I always imagined the two of us working here together, side by side.'

For the briefest moment, I allowed myself to imagine what that future might look like. Working with Ned was a tempting prospect. The sight of him, kitted out in a chunky knit, certainly made my pulse race, but my heart beat fast when I thought about my life without Wynter's Trees in it and setting up my own business too.

'I'm sorry,' I told him, repeating what I'd already said, 'but that was never going to happen.'

'But your reaction to the lodge, and the tree, I thought . . .'

'None of that meant anything,' I firmly said.

The office fell quiet again.

'I suppose I could have a go at trying to raise the money,' Ned finally said, 'but it will need some serious thinking about first and even then, it will take a while. I'm not even sure if it's what I want.'

So much for my assumption that he would snatch my hand off. I was feeling every bit as poleaxed as the two men.

'I do appreciate that I've rather sprung this on you,' I acknowledged.

'Good,' said Ned.

'Might I suggest something?' David tentatively asked.

'That depends on what it is,' I told him, feeling ruffled that he had genuinely thought that one day I would move back, and worse, that he had let Ned believe it too.

'Well,' he said, 'as Ned's just mentioned, he's going to need time to think about all this and you've literally just arrived back, Liza.'

'So?' I frowned. 'What difference does that make?'

'So,' he said, 'you still haven't really given the place a chance.'

'To do what?'

'Grow on you, of course.'

Ned let out a bark of laughter.

'I know my own mind, David,' I firmly said, feeling exasperated, 'and I'm not going to change it. And I really need the money.'

'I appreciate that,' he said. 'And surely you can appreciate that Ned needs time.'

'What exactly are you asking me to do?' I sighed.

'Stay up until Christmas,' he suggested. 'It's not all that far away and as well as giving Ned time to think it will also help you determine whether or not you're doing the right thing. The longer you stay here . . .'

'I'm not going to change my mind,' I interrupted, the words this time coming through gritted teeth.

'You need to drop it, Dad,' said Ned, turning to his father. 'Liza's mind is made up.'

At least we agreed on something. Ned then looked at me.

'That said,' he carried on. 'I do need this time, Liza. It's going to get really busy here soon and this isn't a decision I can afford to rush into. I'm not going to decide overnight.'

'Of course,' I agreed, because it would have been ridiculous not to. 'I'll stay,' I said, staring hard at David, 'but only because I can get on with sorting out the lodge and things. One hint that you're trying to make me change my mind, David, and I'll be off.'

He held up his hands in surrender.

'I wouldn't dream of it,' he smiled, but I wasn't sure I believed him.

I was shellshocked by the reaction to my announcement. I hadn't been expecting David to be particularly thrilled, but I thought Ned would have been delighted. I could appreciate that it was a huge undertaking for him, but one I had reckoned he would be immediately willing to embrace.

I always knew it would take time to raise the money, but it had never entered my head that he might not want to. Still, he'd asked for time and I had that in spades. I would sort out the lodge while he mulled it all over, perhaps help out a bit around the plantation to keep David off my case too, and hopefully the end result would be worth the sacrifice of a few weeks.

Having finally shared my plans, I then drove to Wynmouth for a restorative walk along the beach. Within seconds of jumping down on to the sand, I was feeling pleased I'd had the foresight to add one of Mum's homemade knitted hat and scarf combos to Dad's wax coat, because it was freezing. The tide was on its way out which meant I could peer into the crystal-clear depths of the rockpools, but I didn't linger. The bracing wind whipped the sand up and about and my cheeks stung as I readjusted the scarf so only my eyes were uncovered.

It felt a far cry from the sunny summer days I could remember paddling in the sea and collecting shells, but as it was November, I supposed that was hardly a surprise. Feeling buffeted by more than the breeze, I left the beach and made a beeline for the shops.

'Can I have half a dozen eggs, please and six rashers of smoked bacon?' I asked in the butcher's. 'And four breakfast sausages.'

The sea air had given me an appetite and I rather fancied cooking a good old-fashioned fry up for dinner.

'Actually, make that five sausages,' I amended, thinking that as I was including Ned in the feast, a small meaty treat for Bandit wouldn't go amiss.

Next, I stocked up on mushrooms from the grocer's and a beautiful looking loaf from the baker's. Wriggling my toes to encourage the blood flow, I was just beginning to warm up when my temperature was sent soaring.

'Well, well, well,' said a voice behind me as I was about to leave. 'If it isn't little Miss Christmas. I'd recognise those homespun knits anywhere.'

My heart first sank in my chest and then began to pound. I took a deep breath and squared my shoulders, but it was no good. Neither action made me feel any braver. Or taller.

'It is you, isn't it, Elf?'

Reluctantly, I turned to face my nemesis.

'I knew I was right,' she said, clapping her hands together and looking me up and down in much the same way she used to at school.

Chelsea Chalmers was much taller than me and I felt myself shrinking to Lilliputian proportions in her unwanted presence.

In spite of all my efforts as a high school staff member to root out her kind and support any student who found themselves on the receiving end of negative singling out, I *still* couldn't put into practice the techniques I had taught others.

'Chelsea,' I croaked, before clearing my throat and trying again. 'Hi. Yes, you're right. It is me.'

I pulled off Mum's hat and ran a hand through my long dark hair, forcing myself to look at her.

'You look . . . different . . .' she faltered.

'Well, I should hope so,' I swallowed, 'we haven't seen each other in over ten years.'

'That's true,' she said, 'but as you can see, I haven't changed a bit.'

'No,' I said, looking at her overly made-up face, 'I can see that.'

Someone behind me sniggered and I quickly pushed my way out of the shop, my legs wobbling like a plate of jelly. David really had no hope that I would change my mind about moving back permanently when Chelsea Chalmers still lived in the vicinity. I had no desire to spend the rest of my life looking over my shoulder for her.

I packed my shopping in the chilly boot of my car and walked down to the pub to treat myself to lunch, determined that Chelsea wasn't going to run me out of the village.

'What can I get you?' asked the landlord.

After my unexpected encounter, I would have liked a double measure of something that would burn my throat and settle my nerves, but as I was driving, I thought better of it.

'I'll have a Coke please and a look at the lunch menu if you have one.'

'One Coke coming up,' he smiled, 'and the menu is over there,' he added, pointing to a board which was propped up next to a brightly burning fire.

'Right,' I said, reading the list. 'Wow, it all sounds delicious. What do you recommend?'

'If you're a seafood fan, then I'd go for the mussels,' he suggested. 'They're in season right now and they're cooked fresh with just a hint of chilli.'

'Perfect for this weather,' I said, looking out the window as the wind rattled the frame.

'Exactly,' he grinned. 'They'll soon warm you up.'

'I'll have those then, please,' I said. 'And some bread too.'

'Grab a seat and someone will bring it over.'

'Thanks.'

I chose the table closest to the fire and noticed that I wasn't going to be the first diner enjoying a steaming bowl of wine and chilli-enhanced mussels. They were clearly a popular choice, as was the pub. It was surprisingly busy for a blustery day in November.

'One bowl of mussels,' announced a woman wearing a Smugglers Inn apron, as she carefully placed them along with a rustic roll and a little ramekin of butter on the table.

I had warmed up enough to take off Dad's jacket and having now got over the shock of running into my old enemy, was very much looking forward to my meal.

'Wow,' I said. 'They look amazing.'

'Thank you,' she smiled. 'They're my mum's recipe. She runs a café on the beach and cooks her Caribbean fusion dishes for the pub. I'm Hope,' she added.

'Nice to meet you Hope,' I smiled up at her. 'I'm—'

'Liza,' she quickly said. 'You're Liza Wynter, aren't you?'

'Yes,' I said. 'Yes, I am.'

'Enjoy your mussels, Liza,' she said, before heading back to the bar.

I had no idea how she knew my name and tucked in, keenly mopping up the leftover liquor with the butter smothered bread. No sooner had I finished eating and drained my glass than Hope came back, bringing with her a slice of chocolate cake and a small jug of warm chocolate sauce.

'Dessert is on me,' she winked. 'And this isn't Mum's creation, it's mine.'

'Wow,' I said, hoping I'd got room for it. 'Thanks, but you didn't need to do that.'

'Consider it a thank you,' she said, smiling again.

'But I haven't done anything.' I frowned, feeling confused.

Hope sat down in the chair opposite mine. 'Oh yes, you have,' she said, sounding panto-ready. 'You've agreed to have the beach huts up at Wynter's Trees, haven't you?'

'Oh,' I said, feeling my face colour. I could hardly take the credit for that. 'I see. Well, the huts are there, but they're nothing to do with me.'

'I know Ned has been the driving force behind the

project,' she cut in, 'but nonetheless, everyone's very grateful to you both. It wouldn't be happening if you hadn't given the idea the go ahead.'

'Is it that big a deal?' I asked, pouring some of the sauce over the already moist cake.

'God, yes,' she said. 'Lots of people were relying on them for their festive income, but when the green, which was where they were originally supposed to go, became waterlogged after the last autumn storm, it was suddenly all off and everyone was devastated.'

'I see.'

'And then,' she carried on, 'having scrapped the hut idea, we tried to move into the village hall, but that was no good either because the roof is in need of repair and the insurers have deemed it unsafe for public use.'

'Oh dear,' I sympathised, guessing that was why the money raised from the Halloween event at Wynter's Trees was set aside for the hall.

'But it's sorted now,' Hope smiled. 'Not the hall yet, obviously, but the beach hut project, which everyone had their hearts set on in the first place. Wynter's has saved the day. It's safe and secure and already attracts hundreds of visitors. It's the best possible place for everyone to be.'

'It does sound like the ideal amalgamation,' I agreed.

'It is,' she said. 'You must be so proud of what your dad created. He really helped put Wynmouth on the map and I just know everyone who has signed up to sell in the huts feels the same way.'

I felt unexpectedly choked knowing Dad's legacy still meant so much.

'Do they?'

'Of course,' said Hope. 'Business start-ups, especially in the current economic climate, need all the help they can get. I should know, I've set up my own in the last couple of years and being able to put everyone who is in the same boat, in the same place, with the business your dad created as a backdrop is going to be just the boost we all need.'

She certainly sounded excited about it all and not for the first time, I acknowledged that Ned had struck on something wonderful that had the potential to benefit a lot of people.

'Well,' I said, 'like I mentioned before, it's really nothing to do with me. This is all Ned's hard work. I'm just a silent partner. It's been years since I've even visited.'

'But you're back now,' Hope winked. 'And rumour has it, for good. I just know that with the two of you working together, the place is going to go from strength to strength.'

I didn't have the heart to tell her otherwise, but neither did I want her assuming that I was back in Wynmouth forever. I would have to talk to Ned and ask him what we were going to tell people before everyone jumped to the wrong conclusion. The future of Wynter's Trees was in his hands now and the sooner folk knew that, the better.

Chapter 5

Still full from my delicious lunch and digesting Hope's mention of the rumour which suggested that I was back in Wynmouth to run Wynter's Trees with Ned, I didn't much fancy cooking the ingredients I'd picked up for my dinner, but they didn't go to waste.

I had planned a lazy Sunday lie in when I climbed the stairs to bed that night, but Ned was up and crashing about long before it was light and I found him in something of a tizz when I gave in, got up and went to begin a stint at the stove.

'Good morning,' I said, making an effort to sound cheerier than I felt.

'Hey,' he responded, barely looking up from the desk drawer he was rifling through.

'What are you looking for?' I asked, bending to fuss Bandit, who was looking forlorn.

I got the impression that he was feeling as frustrated about the early start as I was and I hoped Ned's apparent dip in joyful mood wasn't all down to my desire to sell up. If the crashing about was some sort of subliminal sign indicating how he really felt, then it was going to be a long, and headache inducing, few weeks.

'A marker pen,' he mumbled. 'Or a Sharpie. Anything thicker than a biro.'

'To throw about?'

'What?'

'It was a joke.' I smiled. 'A bad one apparently. I have a whole box full of markers in my room. What colour do you want?'

'Oh,' he said, abandoning the drawer, with a heavy sigh. 'Right. Black. Or navy. Anything dark. Thanks,' he added, his voice following me up the stairs as I headed back to retrieve what it was he wanted.

It turned out he was planning to write the names of everyone who'd hired a hut on separate pieces of paper so he could pin then them to the doors, letting them know where to go when they arrived.

'It's going to be busy today,' he told me, sounding slightly harassed at the prospect. 'Everyone's coming to start setting up and I want it all to go smoothly. Two people have their own huts and the other two are being shared,' he elaborated, scribbling a name in tiny letters in the corner of one of the sheets of paper. 'I thought this might be a nice touch.'

'Well, let's hope they've all got good eyesight,' I quipped.

'Why?'

'Because they're going to need magnifying glasses to read

that,' I said, eyeing the paper and miniscule lettering. 'When are you expecting everyone?'

'From ten onwards,' he said.

'Plenty of time yet then,' I yawned.

'But I need to exercise Bandit, check a couple of the trees, make sure the paperwork's all in order ...'

'Have a wash,' I further added. 'Eat breakfast.'

'Luxuries,' he sighed, screwing the paper up. 'I'll have time for neither food nor a shower this morning.'

'Look,' I said, grimacing as he added a tiny name to another sheet. 'Why don't you leave me a list of everyone's names and I'll write them up while you go for a run *and* I'll rustle up some breakfast too. That way you won't be so hangry when everyone arrives that you scare them all half to death.'

He pinned me with an intense stare. His dark grey eyes had a hint of green I noticed, and were as flecked as his freckled skin.

'Really?' he asked, sounding so surprised I was offended. 'You'd do that?'

'Of course,' I insisted, dragging my eyes away from his. 'Your dad's cajoled me into staying, so I might as well make myself useful when I can. That said, I do have an ulterior motive,' I admitted.

'Another one,' he muttered, holding out the pen. 'What is it this time?'

Our skin briefly touched as I took the pen and I felt my face flush. It was the briefest moment of skin-on-skin contact, but an unwelcome butterflies in the tummy feeling accompanied it. I hastily put it down to a combination of needing more sleep and feeling put out by Ned's peevish tone, rather than a potential spark of attraction.

'Go for your run,' I swallowed, nonetheless unsettled by my body's reaction, 'and I'll tell you when you get back.'

'All right,' he agreed, dashing off to change into his running gear. 'I won't be long.'

The high-cholesterol breakfast I cooked up was exactly what we needed. Cooking it was a distraction and stopped me further analysing the '*oh my god, we just touched*' moment and Ned, just as I'd predicted he would be, was far happier once his belly was full. He was thrilled with the name signs I'd drawn up and hastily laminated, just in case it rained, too.

'These look fantastic,' he said, shuffling through the pile.

I'd written everyone's names in the middle in cursive lettering and added a simple but pretty border of bright green holly leaves and shiny red berries to the corners. The pattern helped fill the space and looked appropriately festive. They hadn't taken long, but I'd enjoyed embellishing them.

'We're having a grand opening and late-night shopping event on Thursday.' Ned carried on, eyeing me speculatively. 'Word of mouth has been our main source of advertising so far, but do you think you could come up with a poster and flyer decorated like these, that we could distribute around the village?'

I couldn't remember any mention of the event in David's emails, but I knew there was no point grumbling about it. In fact, I was now resolved to not moan about anything for fear of giving either man the wrong idea. If I objected to anything, they'd assume it was because I cared and the last thing I wanted to do was fan the flames of any hope they were still holding on to.

'I don't see why not,' I therefore acquiesced, sneakily feeding Bandit the last pieces of the sausage I'd cooked for him. 'If you think they might pull a few more customers in.'

'I'm certain they will,' Ned nodded as a car horn sounded outside.

He swallowed down his last mouthful of breakfast and rushed over to the window.

'They're keen,' he said, at last sounding more excited than exasperated. 'It's Theo and Wren. Do you want to come out and meet them before the others arrive?'

'No,' I said, feeling a bubble of nerves mingle with the big breakfast in my belly, 'I'll be out in a bit, but before you go, I just want to ask you something.'

'Oh yes,' he said, 'I forgot you said there was something. What is it? If you're going to ask if I've made a decision about taking on the business yet . . .'

'No,' I said. 'Of course, it's not that. I promised I'd give you time and I'm sticking to that.'

Ned looked relieved. 'What is it then?' he asked, looking over to the window again.

'When I was in Wynmouth yesterday someone mentioned

they'd heard I was back and they were under the impression that I'm staying for good and going to run this place with you.'

'The good old village grapevine,' Ned tutted. 'Well, it hasn't come from me.'

'I wasn't suggesting it had,' I quickly said. 'But I don't want people getting the wrong idea about why I'm here. It probably doesn't matter in the grand scheme of things, but to me it feels deceitful, letting locals assume I'm back to help run the plantation.'

'Because you might be going again, you mean?'

'Because I will be going again,' I firmly corrected.

'So, you want to tell them you're selling up?'

'If that's all right, with you.'

Ned puffed out his cheeks and then let out a long breath. 'I'm sorry, Liza,' he said, 'but it's not. I'd rather we didn't tell anyone. Not yet anyway.'

'Oh.' I hadn't expected him to say no.

'The thing is,' he explained, 'if people get wind of it, I'll be inundated with advice and, no matter how well meant, I don't need it. I have to make this decision for myself, with no interference from anyone.'

Given the gargantuan nature of the situation, I could see the reasoning behind his remark.

'And then of course there's the flip side,' he added.

'The flip side?' I frowned.

'Yes,' he smiled. 'If folk know you're planning to sell, they're bound to go out of their way to convince you to stay.'

'Shit,' I said, biting my lip. 'I hadn't thought of that. Like you and your dad, you mean.'

'Not me,' he shrugged. 'You clearly know your own mind and I'm intrigued to hear more about this business idea you've got, but I can't account for what Dad and everyone else will say and do.'

It was a relief to know that he knew I meant business. No pun intended.

'All right,' I relented, because his argument made sense. 'We won't say anything.'

The car horn sounded again and Ned began to pull on his coat.

'I'll tell Dad not to say anything,' he told me. 'Not that I think he will, given how badly he wants you to change your mind, and we'll see how things stand in a couple of weeks.'

'All right.'

He looked as though he was about to say something else, but then changed his mind. He picked up the signs and made for the door with Bandit on his heels.

'I'll go and pin these up and then come back to help tidy up.'

I knew that wasn't what he'd originally been going to say.

'No, it's fine.' I insisted. 'You go and get on. I get the feeling it's going to be all hands on deck today.'

'Yes,' he said, as another early arrival lined up behind the first. 'I think you might be right.'

From my vantage point behind the sitting room curtains, I could see the yard was heaving before ten o'clock and counting the number of people rushing about, carrying boxes, bags and shelving units to and fro, I guessed everyone on Ned's list had arrived.

They were certainly eager and even though I was fascinated to find out what the many boxes and bags contained, I hung back, taking my time to load the dishwasher and plumping cushions on the pretence of being too busy to go out and introduce myself to the group of strangers.

That said, I had spotted one familiar face among the throng. Hope had arrived in a farm truck with a man who I guessed was her partner, given that they had kissed while unloading boxes, and they were now ferrying those into the barn, rather than one of the huts.

I was just toying with the idea of hiding out upstairs for a bit when Ned strode in, bringing with him a blast of freezing air which was fast becoming his trademark arrival.

'You all sorted?' he asked, his cheeks flushed with cold. 'Only I said I'd come and fetch you. We're just stopping for a quick break, so now's the perfect time to say hello.'

I would have much rather waited until everyone was back in their own huts and I could have faced them in smaller numbers, but lingering in the lodge for too long had put paid to that.

'All right,' I nervously said. 'I'll just grab a coat.'

'Layer up,' Ned advised. 'It's really cold.'

He wasn't wrong. The air that hit me was almost as chilled as that which had blasted me on the beach the day before, but at least I could blame the plummeting temperature for my rosy glow, rather than my nerves.

'Everyone,' Ned loudly said, drawing their attention. 'This is Liza Wynter.'

'Well, of course it is,' said a woman I knew very well. 'Hello, my darling.'

'Sue,' I swallowed. 'I had no idea you were going to be here.' I'd written her first name on one of the signs, but hadn't made the connection. 'How are you?'

'All the better for seeing you,' she said, jumping up and pulling me in for a hug. 'It's been too long.'

Sue and Mum had been the best of friends back in the village where we lived up north. She had moved to Wynmouth after her second marriage and was the person who had flagged up the plantation sale to Dad. Given that she had been so instrumental in the move, which had been such a disaster for me, I could have continued to cling to the grudge, but she was so warm, friendly and kind, I couldn't hold it against her any longer. Along with David, she had tried hard to support me after Dad's death but I hadn't let her in. Now, feeling comforted by the warmth of her embrace, I rather regretted that.

'It has,' I agreed, taking in her smiling face and plump rosy cheeks. 'Far too long.'

'It's wonderful to have you back,' she grinned.

She and Mum had run a sewing group back in the village, teaching anyone who was interested how to knit, sew, crochet and stitch. They were all skills they knew were fast being lost and were determined to pass on. Mum had carried on after Sue left, and I knew she had got something similar going in Wynmouth. Or at least she had.

'Is your group still going?' I asked. 'Sue's Sewing Circle, isn't it?'

'That's right,' she proudly said. 'And yes, it's still going strong. You should join us.'

'Not me,' I laughed. 'I'm still better with a paintbrush than a needle.'

'And on that note,' said another woman, stepping forward. 'I know who you are too.' I wracked my brain, trying to recall her face, but couldn't. She must have been just a couple of years younger than me. 'I'm Wren,' she said, 'and I can remember you from school, Liza.'

'Oh,' I said, feeling my heart sink. 'You can?'

She no doubt remembered my nickname and the ridiculing Chelsea endlessly subjected me to. I had been hoping to avoid further reminders of those dark days.

'Yes,' she said, 'I was in awe of your artwork. Your exam portfolio which was on display in the hall was phenomenal.'

'Oh,' I flushed, completely taken aback, 'thank you.'

'Are you a full-time artist now?'

'Oh no,' I smiled. 'I'm a school art therapist. Or I was until earlier in the year. I was made redundant at the end of the summer term.'

'Oh no, I'm sorry to hear that,' Wren sympathised.

'It's all right,' I told her. 'It's actually led me to better things.'

'Exactly,' said Sue, with a satisfied smile. 'Their loss is our gain. If you hadn't been made redundant, you wouldn't have come back and we're all thrilled you have. It was about time!'

I was desperate to correct her, but bit my lip and went

along with what I'd promised Ned as he quickly introduced me to everyone else. There were lots of names to remember, but my teaching experience helped fix them, as well as their wonderful sounding enterprises, in my head.

Hope and her mum, Sophie, along with Hope's partner, Joe, were setting up in the barn, rather than one of the huts. The two women were in charge of the Wynter's Trees catering, which got me off hot chocolate duty, while Joe was selling the wild bird seed he and his brother grew and harvested on their nearby family farm, along with other bird food products. It was a relatively new diversification venture, but proving to be a lucrative one.

'And I'm a silversmith and sea-glass jewellery maker,' Wren told me, as she darted about in much the same manner as the diminutive bird she was named after. 'I'm going to be selling my jewellery and sharing a hut with my other half, Theo.'

'I'm a potter,' Theo explained. 'Only part-time though. I'm a gardener too, but as there's not so much work around over the winter, I can focus on messing about with clay for a few more hours every day.'

'He does more than mess about with it,' tutted Hope on hearing his self-effacing tone. 'His pieces are functional and fabulous. Oh, and he's, my cousin,' she added with a wink.

'And as you might remember, I retired early,' Sue told me. 'But I got bored very quickly and decided to start selling my soft furnishings. I've got shelves full of vintage fabrics and I turn them into cushions, lampshades and bunting.'

'And we're Abbie and Noah,' said a young woman, who pushed herself forward in a wheelchair. 'But we're not a couple.'

I remembered the lorry driver who had delivered the huts had mentioned someone called Abbie.

'Definitely not a couple,' Noah quickly confirmed. 'I'm a wildlife photographer who makes wire sculptures and Abbie . . .'

'Fell off her horse eighteen months ago,' said Abbie, speaking for herself, 'and would have run mad, or I would if I could, until Sue introduced me to felting and I've just launched my first collection of wild birds.'

'Her tits are amazing,' said Noah, with a completely straight face. 'So realistic.'

Everyone burst out laughing and Noah rolled his eyes.

'You lot are so immature,' he tutted, striding off, but we could see he was smiling.

'I'm not going to be in this thing forever,' said Abbie, patting the arms of her chair, 'but my recovery is taking a little longer than expected so, in the meantime, I'm keeping busy hanging out with this lot and seeing if I can make a go of running a small business.'

'I think you're all amazing,' I told them, feeling in awe of both their determination and incredible skills. 'And I'm certain your products are going to prove popular with everyone who visits Wynter's. Ned was really on to something when he suggested siting the huts here, wasn't he?'

Everyone nodded in agreement and I only then realised

there was one woman who hadn't introduced herself. She was wrapped in a sort of patchwork cloak and stood slightly apart from everyone else.

'Hi,' I said, when our eyes met. 'I'm Liza.'

'I'm Lilith,' she said, then quietly added, 'I'm going to be selling greenery and making wreaths and swags on-site.'

'How lovely,' I said.

'I'm more interested in Yule, than Christmas,' she elaborated, her eyes sparkling and her cloak swishing as she became more animated. 'As you may have worked out.'

'Right,' said Ned, clapping his hands together, before I had an opportunity to answer her. 'Let's get this show on the road, shall we?'

I helped Abbie ferry a couple of boxes from Noah's car to the hut the pair had been assigned. It was the first one in the row and at the bottom of a slight incline that led to the others.

'Ned's thought of everything, hasn't he?' Abbie laughed as she easily negotiated her way inside the hut.

'It would appear so,' I agreed, putting down the boxes. 'Give me a shout if you need an extra pair of hands with anything else, won't you?'

'Well,' she smiled, 'as you've offered, I could do with a hand with the painting. Ned has said we're allowed to decorate but I can't reach the high bits.'

'In that case,' I smiled back, 'give me a brush and I'll make a start.'

*

By late afternoon, the light was fading fast and not even the warmth supplied by the delicious spice infused lunch that Sophie had kindly provided was enough to stave off the biting cold. Everyone had made a great start personalising their beach huts but there was still a way to go before they were officially opened the following Thursday.

Not everyone was going to be able to get back every day, so before they all left, Ned and I went around and made a list of who needed what and I offered to do anything I could to alleviate the stress and help make the launch the success I could see everyone wanted it to be.

Having promised Ned and David that I would stay until Christmas, I was pleased that as well as sorting through things in the lodge, there was going to be plenty for me to do and I'd already got my eye on a few offcuts of wood in the barn that I was planning to turn into signs. Now I knew everyone's business names and a bit about them, I could paint them accordingly and if I got on with the project straightaway, I would be able to hang them on their doors before the launch.

'Your mum and dad would be so proud of you,' said Sue, singling me out for another hug as everyone got ready to leave. 'I know it's taken you a long time to work your way back here, and I know the complicated reasons why better than anyone else, but you're here now, and that's all that matters.'

I squeezed her back and tried not to think of all the people I was going to disappoint when they found out the truth behind my return. Ned had been right earlier when he'd warned me that if everyone knew of my plans to sell, they'd spend the whole time trying to convince me to change them. If I shared my business idea, they might well tell me they loved it, but when it came down to it, I bet they'd love to keep a Wynter at Wynter's Trees more.

'Isn't it?' Sue smiled, pulling away a little so she could look at me.

'Yes,' I nodded, feeling my heart race. 'That's all that matters now.'

Chapter 6

During the next few days, I didn't have a spare second in which to start sorting the lodge or mull over the implications of Ned's request that we should keep my plans under wraps. There was no time to fret over the plethora of feelings and unexpected regrets Sue and her kind words had unleashed either. It was all hands on deck to get ready for the grand opening event and the days flew by in a frenetic whirl of activity.

There was always someone, besides Ned and David, on-site and more often than not they needed a hand. After prioritising the design, printing and distribution of the posters and flyers Ned had asked me to make, I then moved from one hut to the next, assisting in tasks which ranged from hanging shelves, to draping lights and even arranging displays. Given the beautiful products on offer, that was my favourite task.

I made painting the bespoke door signs a clandestine evening project and had set myself up in a corner of the sitting room, after making Ned promise not to peek. I would have been happy for him to just tell me he wouldn't look, but he'd insisted on making it a pinky promise. As he had wrapped his little finger around mine and looked deep into my eyes as he made his vow, I had felt another rush of internal fizzing, far stronger than the one which had coursed through me when I had handed over the pen on Sunday morning.

I could no longer deny, that the longer I spent in his company, the more I liked him. As in *liked him, liked him*, not just thought he was a good guy and the right man to buy my stake in Wynter's Trees. There was a definite spark there and an instant attraction and I was grateful to have painting the signs to focus on when we returned to the lodge at the end of every day, rather than lounging on the sofa and talking through his plans for the place.

It was hard enough internally acknowledging that, during my time helping set up the huts, I had felt a little of the magic my father had always insisted weaved its way about the place, so I certainly didn't need to throw developing feelings for Ned into the mix as well. Consequently, I strove to keep myself continually occupied and ignored the stirrings in my heart.

'So,' I said, from behind the makeshift screen I'd set up as I finished the plaque which was to adorn Abbie and Noah's beach hut door, 'is there much left to do tomorrow?'

I could cope better talking to Ned if he was at a distance, just far enough to make his freckles a blur was ideal.

However, when I looked over the top of the screen and saw him stretched out, surrounded by paperwork and with Bandit asleep on the rug close by, my libido longed to join him. I quickly bobbed back down again.

'The bird feeders and baths should be here between eight and nine in the morning,' he told me, 'so I'm going to get those set up early and then I'll make a start on the extra lights.'

It had always been Dad's dream to extend the nature reserve as far into the plantation as possible and Ned and I had decided to set up a couple of bird feeding stations, in and around the yard, which would hopefully help further achieve that vision. One was going to be right next to the lodge and the other, next to the barn. They were supposed to be squirrel proof and I hoped they lived up to their glowing online promises. We wanted to attract more fluffy, feathered finches and their kind, not more furry grey pillaging creatures.

'More lights?' I asked, quirking an eyebrow, even though Ned couldn't see it.

Mum had always maintained you could never have too many twinkly lights and given all the extra strands Ned had already hung up, he obviously subscribed to the same sparkly seasonal theory.

'I thought we should try and give Blackpool a run for its money this year,' he said, and I could tell from his tone that he was smiling.

'Or Buddy Hall, from *Deck the Halls*,' I said, stretching out my back and rolling my shoulders, before standing up.

'Don't be absurd, Liza.' he teased. 'There are nowhere near enough lights to be seen from space. Although,' he added, tapping his pen against his chin, 'you have just given me another idea.'

I shook my head as he scribbled something extra on his lengthy to-do list, but didn't ask what it was. My participation in the Wynter's Trees festive plans, and achieving the final few things on Dad's wish list, had already stretched my involvement as far as I was willing to let it go.

'Would you like a hot chocolate?' I asked, turning off the desk light and walking over to the kitchen.

'Oh yes, please,' Ned nodded. 'That's just what I fancy.'

'With or without marshmallows?'

He twisted round and shot me a look loaded with disbelief. 'Are you serious?' he gasped.

He looked utterly outraged.

'Oh, my mum would have loved you, Ned,' I laughed.

The words tripped easily off my tongue but the moment they were uttered, I felt a lump form in my throat. What with Sue being a member of the beach hut crew and Ned's fondness for festooning lights, Mum had been on my mind a lot during the last few days.

'Do you really think so?' he asked, as I busied myself pouring milk and cream into the pan and setting it to warm on the stove.

'Yes,' I huskily said. 'I do. And,' I added, blinking hard to banish a prickle of tears, 'Dad would think you're the perfect fit for this place too.'

As Dad had seamlessly settled into the routine of life at Wynter's Trees, I hadn't thought it possible for there to be another soul in the entire world who was as in love with Christmas as he was, but here Ned was. The embodiment of festive feeling and capable of making my heart race at breakneck speed.

'Wow,' he said, setting his list aside and wandering over to watch me prepare the copper hammered mugs which had always been my favourite. 'That's really something. And what about you?'

'Me?'

'Yes,' he said, sounding a little unsure. 'What do you think?'

I let my gaze flick quickly to his.

'Given that I hadn't know you for longer than five minutes before I was asking you to buy me out of the business, that should be obvious, shouldn't it?'

I could feel a blush beginning to bloom.

'Yes,' he said. 'I guess, but I get the feeling there's something else.'

'Something else?' I croaked as my mouth went dry.

'Um,' he nodded.

'No,' I said, 'nothing else. I think you're great.'

My cheeks glowed an even deeper shade of red.

'Well, that's all right then,' he softly said, 'because I think you're great too.'

I'd suddenly completely lost track of what I was supposed to be doing. The pan was dangerously close to boiling over, so I quickly turned it off and turned my attention to the cupboard where Dad had always kept his supply of chocolate.

'Liza,' Ned throatily said.

I was just about to turn around when his phone began to ring.

'You'd better get that,' I said, reaching up for a bar that was eighty per cent cocoa and breaking it in half.

'Damn,' he muttered, pulling the phone out of his pocket as I broke the generous chocolate chunk into smaller pieces and slid them into the pan. 'Hello.'

He was still talking when the chocolate had completely melted, turning the milk dark and velvety smooth. I placed his marshmallow-laden mug on the table next to him and quickly took myself off to bed. As I sipped my drink and slipped between the sheets, I couldn't help thinking I was going to have to find a way to nip my developing feelings for Ned firmly in the bud and fast.

By mid-afternoon on Thursday, excitement for the evening launch had reached fever pitch. The whole of Wynter's Trees was engulfed in a party atmosphere and I was surprised to find that I was well and truly caught up in it.

On more than one occasion I wished I could tell my dad that I finally had some idea about what he had meant when he talked about the enchantment of the place, but I was battling hard to temper my enthusiasm. I'd only been here a week and knew that when reality struck, along with the sense of post-Christmas isolation, it wouldn't take long for the novelty to wear off.

Wynter's Trees had proved surprisingly manageable, fun even, in this teeny tiny dose, but long-term it still wasn't the place for me. And, as I didn't want Ned or David interpreting my current enthusiasm and willingness to help out as anything more meaningful, I knew I was going to have to dial my reactions down a bit. I was still fully committed to my travel plans and setting up my own business. Nothing was going to sway me from those.

'Liza!' called Wren, beckoning me over. 'Did you make all these?'

She pointed along the row of huts at the signs which I had very much enjoyed designing and painting. In the end, I hadn't hung them on the doors because they were going to be pinned open, but had nailed them in place below the gable ends instead.

With the gables slightly overhanging they would be protected from the worst of the winter weather and with a small light, cleverly installed by David, fixed above each one they stood out well. And that was in spite of the extra lights which Ned had hung and which lit the yard to the point where it was almost brighter than a summer's day.

'I did,' I said. 'Do you like them?'

'They're wonderful,' said Abbie, wheeling herself out from her hut and looking up at hers and Noah's.

'You've clearly still got the artistic knack, Liza,' winked Sue. 'You know, you could start a small business of your own selling these.'

'That's a nice idea,' I told her, 'but my heart's still in my job.'

She looked at me and frowned and I realised I'd just hinted that my stay at Wynter's Trees wasn't a long-term proposition.

'Liza!' shouted Ned, thankfully saving me from having to think of something to say to cover my mistake. 'Can you give me a hand?'

'I'd better see what he wants,' I said, readily abandoning Sue and the others.

That had been a close call.

'What's up?' I asked Ned who sounded stressed.

'I can't get this blasted tree to sit straight,' he huffed, pointing an accusatory finger at the potted tree which was supposed to be artfully arranged in the back of the Chevy. 'There's something wrong with the bloody thing.'

I'd never seen him looking so stressed, not even on the day when I had told him and David of my intention to sell, and quickly climbed up into the back of the truck. The problem was immediately obvious.

'That's because you've left your hammer in here,' I tutted, wrenching it out from under the pot, which then sat perfectly straight.

'Damn,' he said. 'I've been looking all over for that.'

'Are you okay?' I asked.

I had earlier assumed that everyone was caught up in the party atmosphere, but Ned looked far from being in a celebratory mood.

'No,' he said, and I noticed his hands were shaking a little as I handed him back the hammer. 'Not really.'

'Come with me,' I commanded, jumping back out of the truck, before whistling for Bandit and guiding the pair of them into the office where David was sat behind the desk, a pile of papers one side and a checklist on the other.

I pushed Ned into a chair and Bandit rushed to his side. Ned buried his hands in the dog's deep, warm fur and let out a long breath.

'What's wrong?' David frowned.

'Not sure,' I shrugged. 'I just found him having a melt-down about a wonky tree.'

'I was not having a meltdown,' said Ned, looking up.

'I was talking about Bandit,' I joked, relieved so see a smile tugging at the corner of Ned's mouth a moment later.

'If you're still worried about the insurance,' David said to his son, 'don't be. I've been through everything with a fine-tooth comb and everything and everyone is covered.'

'What insurance?' I asked.

'In fact,' David continued. 'I was just checking it all again, to make extra sure and it's all fine, Ned.'

'Insurance for the plantation, do you mean?' I asked again.

'For the plantation, for the huts, for serving the food, for pretty much everything,' said Ned. 'And then there's Santa's DBS check which still hasn't come through.'

'Yes, it has,' said David, waving a sheet of paper. 'It's here. I printed it off a few minutes ago and Nick's now getting changed ready to welcome the children.'

Ned let out another long breath and sat back in the chair, his long legs stretched out in front of him. Bandit rested a foot on his thigh and looked adoringly up at his owner. Clearly, there was a whole lot going on behind the scenes that I knew nothing about and to be honest, I was rather grateful not to have been involved if the worry lines that were currently etched across Ned's brow were any indicator of how stressful running the place could really be.

Dad had never shown so much as a hint of it, but then he hadn't launched a venture which could impact the lives of anyone other than his and mine.

'Nick,' I said, only just realising what David had said. 'Seriously?'

My dad's name had been Nicholas and now we had a guy called Nick taking on the role of Santa. What were the odds? No one could accuse Wynter's Trees of being anything other than authentic.

'Yes,' smiled David. 'He's new this year and his wife's helping out too.'

Dad always regretted that he didn't have time to don the red outfit, boots and beard, but in order to have managed that he would have had to clone himself. Personally, I was thankful he'd hired someone else for the role. Chelsea would have had a field day if Dad had been Father Christmas too.

'So, Santa's here tonight?' I smiled, dismissing thoughts of Chelsea and remembering the lengthy queues of excited children.

'He is,' said David. 'In the usual spot in the corner of the barn. And he'll be here every time the huts are open too. Even though the school-aged children won't be here during the week, the little ones might be and Ned's arranged a visit from the local mother and toddler group and the playgroup, haven't you?'

'Yes,' said Ned, distractedly running his hands through his hair. 'I must have been mad. We're never going to keep on top of it all.'

Bandit threw me a concerned look.

'Of course, you will,' I stoically said. 'It's bound to be busy though and this first extended open season will be a steep learning curve, but I've no doubt you'll handle it and I'm here.' I added. 'I'll carry on helping where I can.'

'I suppose you're right,' Ned said, looking margin-ally calmer.

'Of course, I am,' I told him. 'And if it does prove to be a bit too much, you'll just have to draft in some extra help for a few weeks.'

There were already a couple of volunteers milling about wearing tinsel enhanced high-vis jackets to help with the parking so I knew Ned wasn't going to be short of extra help if he really did get stuck.

'I do have someone who helps on the farm when it gets busy,' Ned told me, 'and I suppose the huts will be the responsibility of the business owner's, won't they?'

'Exactly,' I said.

'I just want everything to be perfect.'

'Perfection is an illusion,' said David, paraphrasing

Charlie Mackesy. 'If you're expecting perfection, then you're going to be disappointed, son. Far better to enjoy the good bits and deal with the odd blip as it happens.'

There was a brisk knock on the door and then a belly appeared, held in by a shiny buckled belt. A rosy cheeked face came next, surrounded by a haze of white hair and a slightly unkempt beard.

'There's quite a crowd gathering,' beamed the guy who could only be Nick.

I couldn't rein in the smile which spread across my face. His voice was so deep I had no doubt that his laugh would be wonderful.

'Thanks, Nick,' said David. 'We're coming now.'

He tottered off to take up his station in the screened off corner of the barn which had always served as a grotto. It had its own tree and electric woodburning stove, and was softly lit, with festive music playing, to add to the magical ambience. The memory of it almost tempted me to go and pay a visit myself.

Ned and David stood up and I clipped Bandit's lead to his collar, just in case he got a bit too excited.

'Where did you find the cushion for Santa's belly?' I quietly asked David.

Father and son looked at each other and grinned.

'He brings his own padding,' David told me with a wink and together we left the office laughing.

Nick had been right. Since I'd dragged Ned into the office, lots of people had arrived and were standing in a noisy group, waiting for someone to step up and officially open proceedings. I was just beginning to panic that person would have to be me, when Ned jumped into the back of the Chevy and the crowd fell quiet. David stood beside me and I ran a hand over Bandit's fur to settle the flutter of nerves which had bubbled up in anticipation of what Ned was going to say.

'Good evening,' he said, smiling broadly and looking much happier than he had just a few minutes before, 'and welcome to the launch of the first ever Wynter's Trees festive shopping night.'

Everyone cheered and I could see the beach hut crew all eagerly waiting outside the huts to welcome the visitors and make some sales. Wren gave me a thumbs up and I waved back.

'As you know,' Ned continued, 'the beach huts were originally destined for Wynmouth but we think they look right at home here, and we hope you do too.'

This was met with more cheers and some enthusiastic clapping.

'By we of course,' Ned carried on, 'I mean David, my wonderful dad who has been running this place for the last four years and none other than Liza Wynter herself, who we are thrilled to have here with us tonight.'

More clapping followed and Ned looked at me and grinned. I wondered if he thought the crowd's enthusiastic response to my presence might have some impact on my decision to sell. Blushing as a few curious glances came my way, I knew it wouldn't.

'This is going to be my dad's last Christmas at the farm,' Ned then carried on, his voice catching as he looked fondly at his father, 'and I'm determined to make it a good one. Wynter's Trees is a truly magical place and even though we have made a few changes, I want you all to know that Nicholas Wynter's legacy and his love for Wynmouth and the surrounding countryside is still at the heart of everything we do.'

'Hear! Hear!' shouted David, making me jump.

As everyone clapped again, I felt Bandit lean heavily into my legs, as if he knew I needed some extra support.

'I'm delighted to have Liza's blessing for this exciting new venture,' said Ned, smiling down at me again, 'and I would dearly love to invite her up here to say a few words.'

He laughed as I returned his look with what must have been one of sheer terror.

'However,' he said, 'I don't think she would ever forgive me so, without further ado, I declare the evening, open!'

A breath I hadn't realised I had been holding, rushed out of my lungs and the crowd surged forward. Some people headed straight for the huts, while others made a beeline with their little ones to queue for an audience with Santa and the rest were seduced by the smell of the delicious food Hope and Sophie had cooked up. That pair were the pied pipers of the food world.

'I'm just going to take Bandit back to the lodge,' I said to David, before Ned reached us. 'He's a bit restless.'

'Good idea,' David agreed. 'Then you can have a proper look at everything.'

Bandit made no protest when I settled him in front of the log burner with a chew from his treat box and I took a moment to compose myself before venturing back outside.

The atmosphere was amazing. The scent of mulled cider and wine filled the air, mixing and mingling with the food. There were carollers singing, lights twinkling and overall, there was the sound of laughter. The queue for photos in front of the Chevy was almost as long as the line to visit Santa and the throngs of people going in and out of the huts carrying brown paper parcels and bags suggested that the tills were ringing too. It was all absolutely perfect and I hoped everyone would continue to come back in droves in the run-up to Christmas.

As I wrapped my gloved hands around a warming mug of cider, and looked about me, I knew that this clever idea was exactly what Wynter's Trees needed to move it forward and that the clever, handsome and kind man behind it, had fast found his way into my heart.

Chapter 7

In spite of the fact that the inaugural event carried on far longer than any of us expected it to, almost everyone was back early the next morning. The huts would be opening again at the weekend and then, other than Mondays, staying open every day right up until Christmas and, as a result, the beach hut team needed to take stock of what they had sold and try to calculate how much more they would need in order to meet future demand.

David had sensibly suggested that we all meet in the barn before getting down to work so we could compare notes and address any problems the previous evening might have flagged up. I was surprised to find I felt very much like a member of the team and a willing one at that, and in anticipation of the meeting, I was awake extra early.

I took the opportunity to enjoy a few peaceful minutes looking over the plantation boundary and into the edges of the reserve as the sun came up. It was a fresh start, but invigorating too and I felt wide awake and much refreshed by the time I joined the others.

'Everything ran like clockwork,' said Wren, echoing what some of the others had been saying as I walked in. 'Theo and I both made plenty of sales and the set-up in the hut worked really well.'

Theo would be joining us after he'd finished his few Friday gardening jobs and I already knew that he and Wren were planning to split their time between selling in the huts, producing more stock and in Theo's case, keeping his other business running. They were certainly going to be busy.

Sue and Lilith were happy too. There had been plenty of room in their huts as they had one each. They were both planning to work onsite whenever possible, setting up tiny work stations so the customers could watch them create, but sadly the same couldn't be said for Abbie.

'I ended up having to stay behind the desk,' she said, sounding a little glum, 'because I was worried I'd squash someone with this wretched thing.' The thump she gave her wheelchair was far from affectionate. 'I might be able to work in there, because felting doesn't take up much space, but I can't really move around.'

'We just need a re-jig,' Noah said consolingly. 'We'll shift things about a bit this morning and reorganise the space. After all, that's what last night was for, wasn't it, Ned? To iron out any wrinkles.'

'Exactly,' Ned said, quickly backing Noah up. 'And if you're not happy with the set up by the end of today, then maybe we could ask Hope and Sophie to move into your hut and you and Noah could have their space in the barn instead. There'd be more room for you to manoeuvre in there, Abbie.'

I wasn't sure that would work because the queue for food would clog up the doorways of everyone else's huts but before I could point that out, Sue kindly stepped in.

'Or you could take my hut, Abbie and I'll move in with Noah,' she kindly suggested. 'Liza and I could do a super speedy repaint and sign adjustment, couldn't we?'

'Absolutely,' I agreed. 'That would be no problem at all and I'm sure Lilith would offer to switch to the barn if she were here, too.'

'I really want us to stick together, Abs,' said Noah, 'but whatever works best for you will be fine, my lovely.'

Abbie looked much happier after that and when Nick and his wife, Edith, offered to take on the responsibility of keeping Santa's sack stocked up with small, ethically produced gifts, Ned did too.

'It will free you up a bit more,' Edith said, patting his arm. 'We'll keep everything ordered and topped up and give you the receipts for what we've put in at the end of each week. I'm guessing the budget is the same as last year? Nick said David had already told him what that was.'

'That would be a weight off my mind,' Ned said gratefully. 'Thank you and yes, we'll stick to the same budget.'

With the few issues satisfactorily addressed, Ned made everyone tea and I carried the tray round the huts, taking the opportunity to chat as I went.

'So, how are you really settling in?' asked Sue when it was just the two of us. 'It's not too difficult being back here, is it?'

I knew she was asking because she had always felt guilty that I hadn't settled in. Had she not told Dad the plantation was up for sale, we probably wouldn't have left my former and much-loved childhood home. Had that been the case though, I now had the sense to see, Wynmouth might not have had the benefit of the nature reserve or the plantation.

'No,' I therefore generously said, 'it's not too difficult. I thought it would be, especially as everything in the lodge is still as Dad kept it, but actually it's okay.'

Sue looked relieved.

'And how are you getting on with Ned?' she asked.

'Really well,' I told her. 'But then, who wouldn't? He's as mad on Christmas as Dad was.'

'He's mad on trees too,' Sue chuckled.

'That's true.'

I thought of the tattoo running down the length of his spine and hoped my pupils hadn't dilated in response.

'He loved working on his aunt's forest farm in New Zealand.' Sue carried on, unaware of my dreamy expression.

'I bet it was an amazing place.'

'It certainly looked it from the photos he showed me.'

'So, why did he come back?'

'To be with David of course,' she said, as if I should know. 'He's fiercely loyal to his family and the increased workload here was getting a bit much for one man.'

I felt my face flush. Family loyalty was something I had never felt.

'Which makes him the perfect person to take over, doesn't it?' I unguardedly said.

'Where are you off to then?' Sue frowned.

'Oh,' I swallowed, realising I'd almost spilled the beans. 'After Christmas, I'm going travelling for a while,'

Sue pressed a hand to her ample chest.

'That's all right then,' she laughed, looking relieved. 'You had me worried for a minute. I thought you were going to say you were leaving again for good.'

'You'd better take this tea,' I told her, nodding at the tray. 'Otherwise, it'll be cold.'

'Thanks, love,' she said, picking up one of the mugs.

'I'll leave you to get on,' I added, quickly rushing off.

My breath streamed ahead of me as I regathered my wits. That had been a close call. The sooner Ned gave me the nod to tell everyone the truth, the better.

'How's it all looking out there?' David asked when I ventured back over to the office, later in the day.

Both he and Ned were working at their desks. David had been engrossed in paperwork and Ned was frowning at his laptop screen. I was certain there hadn't been anywhere near that amount of admin when Dad ran the business.

'Good,' I said. 'Noah and Abbie have completely rearranged the space in their hut and they're going to see how they get on over the weekend.'

'Well, as long as they're both sure,' Ned muttered. 'Because there won't be time to make big changes after then.'

'Of course, there will,' I responded, surprised by his gruff response. 'If everyone pitches in, it'll take no time at all, but I'm sure it won't come to that. A few of us have just been in there, playing the role of customers and Abbie could move about much more freely. Besides, I doubt there'll be the same concentrated influx of people as we had last night, will there, David?'

'I wouldn't have thought so,' he thoughtfully agreed. 'It'll be more a steady flow of footfall now.'

'We hope,' Ned said gloomily.

Considering the success of the night before, he sounded remarkably morose.

'Right then,' I said, backing out for fear of saying the wrong thing and further darkening his mood, 'I'll leave you to it.'

Ned didn't say anything further and David gave me a sympathetic smile. I wasn't quite out of earshot before he spoke to his son.

'I don't know what's up with you, my boy,' he said, 'but you need to snap out of it. You're not usually so stressed. I know the huts are a big change and so is the plantation being open for longer, but it's what you wanted, isn't it?'

I heard Ned push his chair away from the desk and sigh.

'Yes,' he quietly said, 'you know it is and last night proved that having the huts here is going to work well.'

'So, what's the problem?'

Ned was quiet for a moment.

'I'm scared I'm not going to be able to raise the money to buy Liza out,' he eventually said, 'and if I don't, who the hell is she going to end up selling to?'

'So, you do want to take it all on, then?'

'Of course, I do.' Ned told him. 'How could I not? That said, I'd still prefer it if she didn't sell at all.'

'Well,' said David. 'You never know, she might change her mind.'

'No, she won't, Dad,' Ned firmly said. 'She's got her heart set on this big holiday and mystery business and if I can't get the funds fast enough, we could end up with a total stranger in charge. They'll have the bigger share, remember, and therefore the final say.'

'Liza might not be as attached to this place as you are, Ned,' David was quick to say, 'but I know her well enough to know she won't sell to just anyone.'

'I really hope you're right about that, Dad.'

'I know I am, and at the end of the day, if you have to buy her shares instead of mine . . .'

'No way,' Ned cut in. 'You deserve your retirement, Dad. I'm not going to do anything to jeopardise that.'

I knew I shouldn't have been eavesdropping, but I couldn't tear myself away. Sue had been right about Ned's sense of family loyalty.

'And I'm worried about flying solo,' he then huskily said. 'What if I take on this massive financial risk and then can't run this place on my own? Wynter's Trees would be ruined and I'd never forgive myself.'

He was clearly as concerned about doing right by my dad's legacy as he was about protecting his dad's retirement.

'That won't be an issue.' David insisted. 'You're more than capable Ned, but if you want me to, when I've finished trotting around the globe, I can still help out a bit. And you never know, you might decide to look for a partner yourself in the future.'

For some inexplicable reason, I felt myself bristle at the thought of someone else coming in.

'That's true,' said Ned, sounding a little less anxious.

'But rest assured,' David firmly added, 'you won't have any problem managing this place. And I just know there's still a chance that Liza might change her mind.'

Ned didn't say anything further and I slipped away. I now had more of an understanding about how he was really feeling about it all and knew that David was still hoping I'd change my mind. The best thing I could do now was find a way to boost Ned's confidence in himself so he wouldn't put so much faith in his dad's words. I knew without a shadow of a doubt that Ned was the right man to take over Wynter's Trees, I just needed to make him believe it.

'You should come,' said Theo, who had arrived at the plantation late in the day grubby, but also happy about how well the previous evening had gone. 'It's going to be a good night.'

'I'm sure you could do with a break,' added Wren, giving me a nudge. 'And I know Ned could, because he never stops working.'

The pair were trying to cajole me into going to the pub to listen to one of the locals tell tall tales over a drink or two and they wanted me to take Ned along, too.

'But it's the first full day of opening up here tomorrow,' I pointed out, 'and I'm sure Ned would prefer an early night.'

Theo shrugged, but Wren wasn't giving in so easily.

'A pint or two would help him relax,' she astutely pointed out. 'He's been wound-up all week and I can't remember the last time I saw him in the pub.'

'But what about Bandit?' I frowned. 'I'm not sure how long he can be left home alone.'

'He can come too,' said Wren. 'They've got a dogs welcome policy which I know for a fact extends to include beautiful Bandit.'

'Well, in that case,' I caved, 'I'll ask, but I'm not making any promises.'

To my surprise, Ned agreed to the impromptu excursion and later that evening he, Bandit and I, with me driving so Ned could have a drink, arrived at the packed pub. We were a little later than planned because my old jalopy had taken a bit of encouragement to turn over. She didn't much like standing idle and I had to promise I'd pay her a bit more attention before her engine reluctantly spluttered into life.

'Crikey,' I said, as we crossed the threshold and our ears were assaulted by a barrage of noise I hadn't been expecting, 'it's packed.'

'It's tall tales night,' shivered Ned, more the result of my car's intermittent heater than the outside temperature. 'It's always popular.'

'There's Wren,' I said, picking her out as she stood up and waved in our direction. 'She and Theo have got a table. Why don't you take Bandit and go and thaw out and I'll get us a drink?'

'All right,' he agreed, pulling his furry friend a little closer to his side.

Bandit wasn't fazed by the noise at all, but he was nose to nose with an enthusiastic Jack Russell terrier. Thankfully both tails were wagging in greeting.

'I take it they've met before?' I asked Ned, nodding at the dogs, before he moved off.

'Yes,' he said. 'The terrier is Skipper. He belongs to George who will be regaling us with all manner of myths and legends tonight.'

I was relieved to hear the dogs were happily acquainted. There was barely room to move, so a canine scrap would have caused mayhem.

'Thank goodness for that,' I said, bumping into Ned's side as someone squeezed by. 'Sorry,' I flushed, trying to move away but finding I couldn't. 'I think I'd better try and get to the bar. What do you fancy?'

Ned looked at me for a moment and his lips quirked. I felt my breath catch in my chest, as I wondered what he was going to say, but needn't have worried.

'Lager, please,' he smiled. 'Just a half though,' he hastily added. 'I want a clear head for tomorrow.'

'I hardly think one pint will knock you off your feet,' I pointed out, but he'd already moved too far away to hear.

In spite of what he'd said, I ordered him a pint for fear of not being able to get to the bar again and had just finished paying when I heard an unwelcome voice behind me.

'Elf,' said Chelsea, making my stomach twist. 'No hat and pointy shoes tonight? If you're running errands for Santa, you should have bells on, surely?'

There didn't seem to be quite the old sting in her words but she laughed loud enough to catch the attention of everyone close by. I was relieved that no one reacted to her joke, even though I knew they'd heard what she'd said.

'Forgive me for stating the obvious, Chelsea,' I said, buoyed up by her lack of support, 'but we're not at school anymore. Why don't you move on?' I suggested. 'Like everyone else has.'

There was a ripple of amusement for my retort and she looked thoroughly taken aback. Inside, I felt every bit as shocked by my response as she looked.

'I was only kidding,' she muttered. 'It was just a joke.'

'An old one,' I snapped, before picking up the tray of drinks, 'and not a good one,' I added as I weaved my way over to the table.

In spite of my shaking hands, I'd barely spilt a drop. I felt rather chuffed by my little victory but couldn't share what I'd done because that would lead to me having to explain the humiliation I'd suffered in school, and I had no desire to revisit either past hurts or the stupid nickname that came with them.

'I said a half,' Ned frowned, when I handed him the pint, but his brow cleared when I explained why I'd upped his order.

'I don't think we'll be getting served again,' I said, looking back towards the bar. 'So, I thought I'd make the most of the landlord's attention while I had it.'

'Don't worry about that,' Theo laughed, but nonetheless he gratefully accepted the pint I'd got for him along with another for Wren. 'I've got Hope on speed dial. She'll keep us topped up.'

I wasn't sure if he was joking or not, but when he whipped out his phone and his cousin appeared with four more drinks just as everyone was settling down to listen to the evening's entertainment, I guessed not.

George, it turned out, had a wonderful way with words and by the time Sam, the landlord, and his partner, Tess, were getting ready to call time, he had held us all in his thrall for well over two hours. There had been laughter, tears and genuine fear induced by the collection of stories he had told and even though I got the impression that a fair number of the locals had heard them before, he had such a talent, he still managed to keep them gripped.

I had been so enraptured that I hadn't noticed much of what was happening around me, but Wren's gentle nudge brought me back to earth with a bump.

'That was amazing,' I told her as everyone clapped and George took a bow. 'Although, I'm rather pleased I didn't know about the ghosts of the lost lovers when I was growing up.'

'Tragic that one,' nodded Theo, who looked a little tipsy.

'Totally,' I agreed.

Ned nudged my other side, handed me Bandit's lead and stood up.

'Are you going to be all right getting him home?' asked Wren, as we watched my companion try to negotiate the path back to the bar.

We both giggled as he failed to manage two steps in a straight line.

'Oh crikey,' I gasped, looking from him to the stacked up empty pint glasses on the table. 'How many of these are Ned's?'

'All of them,' said Wren. 'And he's not usually a more than a couple of pints man.'

There weren't that many empties, but if he wasn't used to more than two pints, then what was there was more than enough to make him feel every bit as tipsy as he looked.

'Well,' I said, biting my lip as I wondered how he'd fare with the stairs back at the lodge, 'you did say you thought it would do him good to relax, didn't you?'

The crisp winter air did nothing to sober Ned up and having sung a medley of Christmas classics, all out of tune, on the way home, I had a job to get the key code out of him when I pulled up at the gate. Eventually I parked the car, thanking her for getting us home, locked the gate, released Bandit and helped Ned out of his seat and on to the veranda.

'You'll have to let me go if you want me to open the door,' I told him. 'I can't keep you upright *and* let us in, Ned.'

He was leaning heavily against me and it was all I could do to stay on my feet and not crumble under his weight. Not that I would have minded finding myself under him, but it was a cold night and besides, I wasn't supposed to be entertaining illicit thoughts like those.

'I know,' he said, looking down at me and starting to laugh. 'But I think I might fall over if I let you go.'

Had he not been half-cut and if it was the end of a first date, that would have been a very romantic line, but as it was ...

'How can you be *this* drunk on six pints?' I demanded, starting to giggle myself.

'I had six?' he said, his eyes wide. 'I'm not a drinker, Liza. That's, what ...' He let go of me to add up on his fingers and I had to reach for him as he pitched backwards. 'That's three times more than I ever have.'

'Well,' I said, holding him steady by grasping the front of his shirt, 'at least you still have the wits to work that out.'

I could already tell he was going to feel rough in the morning, but I wasn't going to shoulder any of the blame. It was Theo's fault because he had told Hope to keep them coming. And Ned's of course, for drinking them.

'Right,' I said, 'let's get you inside and you can drink some water. It might not be a bad idea to take some painkillers up to bed with you too,' I added. 'For when you wake up.'

'That's an excellent idea,' he said, slurring slightly and smiling down at me. 'You're very organised.' He held my gaze for a second and I tried to ignore how the bewitching sight of his speckled eyes made my tummy flutter, even though they were slightly unfocused. 'Can I tell you a secret?'

'If you must,' I swallowed, before hastily looking away.

'You know before, when we were in the pub?'

'Yes . . .'

'And you asked me what I fancied?'

'Um,' I commented, feeling my temperature soar in spite of the cold.

'I wanted to say you, Liza,' he whispered as if he was confiding the biggest secret.

'Did you?' I gasped, thinking back to the moment.

I knew it was the beer talking, but he had looked at me a bit oddly when I'd asked the question and he hadn't had so much as a drop then. I wondered if he really meant it and, more importantly, if he had worked out that I fancied him too.

'I did,' he seriously said, making more of an effort to stand on his own two feet. 'Because I've fancied you from the very first moment that I set eyes on you, Liza Wynter. Even though I was freezing my nuts off because you'd set the alarm off and I had to come out in just a towel to turn it off. Do you remember?'

How could I not?

'Vaguely,' I smiled, 'and, I'm sorry about that . . .'

The rest of what I was going to say was cut off as he stepped forward and wrapped me tightly in his arms. Before I could resist, not that I wanted to, he softly brushed his lips against mine. He pulled away for less than a second and then kissed me again, deeply this time and with all the technique I had imagined he had at his disposal. By the time we broke apart, my temperature had climbed high enough to make a thermometer pop and my body was yearning to take the moment further.

'Sorry,' he said, closing his eyes, which were all pupil, but just as quickly opening them again. 'I shouldn't have done that.'

'Kissed me or closed your eyes?'

'Both,' he said, letting me go, running his hands through his hair and almost falling over as a result.

Just for the briefest moment, I felt hurt that he regretted it, but then common sense kicked in and I acknowledged that in view of everything we had going on, and in spite of the fact that I fancied the pants off him and now knew he felt the same way about me (assuming it wasn't all beer talk), a more intimate relationship was a complication we didn't need.

'Well, that's disappointing,' I smiled, making light of it while brushing the moment off at the same time, 'because I thought it was a decent way to end the day.'

'I don't know about that,' Ned drunkenly grinned, 'I always think a bacon sandwich is a fitting end to a trip to the pub.'

Chapter 8

As soon as we were back inside the lodge, Ned forgot all about his hankering for a bacon sandwich but it was immediately obvious when he emerged the next morning, cradling his head in his hands, that he wasn't going to forget the impact of six pints of lager in a hurry.

I wasn't going to forget them anytime soon either because I'd laid awake for much of the night thinking that if he could kiss like that drunk, then what was he capable of sober. I knew I wasn't supposed to be thinking anything like that, but in the long watches of the night, my brain seemed to have a mind of its own.

'Morning,' he huskily said, as he gingerly descended the stairs and slumped on a stool at the kitchen counter.

His voice was unusually deep and very sexy.

'Good morning,' I responded, ignoring the fluttering in my tummy. 'I thought you were getting up extra early this morning.'

'I planned to,' he winced, 'and I would have done, if it wasn't for you and your bloody pint glasses.'

'Don't blame me,' I said, wiping down the counter. 'I was only responsible for the first one. It was Theo who kept them coming and you didn't have to drink them, did you?'

'I suppose not,' he muttered.

Our fingers briefly touched as I passed him a mug of coffee and I snatched my hand away, almost upsetting the contents. Thankfully Ned didn't seem to notice. I looked at him, tousled and rugged, and thought the best thing I could do would be to put a bit of distance between us until I got over my night-time fantasy fest. I swilled my empty mug under the tap and put it in the dishwasher.

'Are you and Bandit going for a run?' I asked.

Bandit's ears pricked up, but Ned slowly shook his head.

'I can't,' he groaned, sliding off the stool again. 'Not when my head feels like this. I don't think I'm even going to be able to manage the pounding of the shower.'

'Have a bath then,' I suggested, swallowing hard as an image of his wet freckled skin and water running down the length of his tattooed back filled my head. 'I'll take Bandit for a walk,' I offered, desperate to get away. 'It won't be the same as a run, but at least he won't be going stir crazy by the end of the day.'

'Thanks,' Ned smiled weakly. 'That would be great and could you open the gate when you go out? That way everyone can let themselves in if I fall asleep again.'

I shot him a look.

'I'm kidding,' he said. 'I'll be raring to go once the painkillers have kicked in.'

'Good,' I sighed, 'because I won't be coming to wake you up in the bath.'

Ned grinned, looking more like his usual self.

'You've already seen me soaking wet and wrapped in a tiny towel,' he teased. 'I can't imagine there would be many more surprises.'

For the sake my sanity, I chose to ignore that.

After opening the gate, Bandit and I walked around the plantation. I could see that Ned and David had recently made a start moving some of the potted trees about, no doubt getting them in the most logical order for delivery and collection.

In just a couple of weeks the business would be beyond busy and in just over a month many of the trees would be indoors, decorated and adored then, after fourteen sparkling days, they would be back at Wynter's, patiently marking out the next fifty weeks.

Thinking of other people's trees and how they decorated them, pulled my thoughts back to the family one. Ned had been right to point it out and I felt bad that it was still languishing in its pot. I might still have had plenty of time to get things done, but the sooner the tree was sorted, the better.

'Come on, Bandit!' I called, striking off in a different direction to the one I had been thinking of going in.

For the most part, the plantation site was flat, but there was a slightly raised mound, close to the furthest boundary, which Dad said was the best spot for stargazing. When Bandit and I reached it, I could see there was nothing growing there and wondered if it would be possible to plant the tree either atop or next to it.

It felt like the ideal tribute to mark the spot where Dad and I used to lay out, wrapped in layers and with a Thermos apiece as the constellations shifted and shone. I swallowed away the lump in my throat and called Bandit to heel. I didn't often allow myself to think too deeply about any of the few things I had enjoyed about living at Wynter's and now, just as I was poised to part with the place for good, was hardly the time to start letting them back in.

My mobile vibrated in my pocket as Bandit and I walked along and I pulled it out, surprised to see a message from my former colleague, Caitlin. We had started our teaching careers at the same time in the school where I had eventually taken on a more nurturing role.

Caitlin taught English and her job hadn't fallen prey to the funding cuts like mine. With a position like the one I'd taken, I'd always known redundancy was a risk and after the death knell sounded, I wouldn't go as far as to say I felt bitter, but I hadn't kept in touch with her as regularly as I could have done.

> Hey Liza. Just a quick message to see how you're getting on. I called round to the flat last night but you weren't in.

I felt bad for not letting her know I had come to Wynter's Trees for a few weeks.

> I don't know if you're interested, but there's talk
> of an art-based support position opening up at
> the new academy. Have you heard about it? I
> don't know any details but can find out if you're
> keen. Let me know! School is hell btw, but then
> it always is in the run up to Christmas.

Just a few weeks ago, I would have jumped at the opportunity, but not now. Caitlin was right, the few weeks leading up to Christmas were hell and the thought of going back into a school to help a few students, when my own business could be geared up to assist potentially dozens, was not an appealing thought.

But none the more for that, I didn't have an endless amount of money at my disposal and if Ned couldn't raise the funds to buy me out, I was going to need to do something. David had been right when he said I wouldn't sell to just anyone and so, along with explaining to Caitlin where I was, I asked her to send on anything about the position that she could find out.

'Bandit!' I called, halting his sudden interest in a squirrel which had shot out of a tree. 'Come on.'

The yard was abuzz when we got back. I left Bandit with David in the office, then went to let Wren know that I'd managed to get Ned safely back from the pub in one piece.

Obviously, I gave her a doctored version of events, but she revelled in my description of his out of tune singing and subsequent thumping head.

'Well,' she said, adding more pairs of snowflake stud earrings to her display, 'he's none the worse for wear now. He was whistling when he came out of the lodge a few minutes ago.'

I was surprised, but relieved he'd negotiated his ablutions unaided.

'I'm pleased to hear it,' I said.

'I think your evening together, away from here, has sorted him out,' Wren nudged.

'You're making it sound like a date,' I blushed. 'It was hardly that.'

'Well, whatever,' she grinned. 'He's clearly back on track now.'

'Here you go, Wren,' said Sue, striding into the hut and thankfully putting a halt on the conversation. 'Bunting as promised. Morning, Liza.'

'Morning.'

'You all right, love?' Sue asked, scrutinising my complexion. 'You look a bit flushed.'

'I'm fine,' I said, louder than I intended. 'I'm just back from walking Bandit and it's brisk among the trees.'

'That explains it then,' she accepted, before turning back to Wren.

'And here are your earrings,' said Wren, handing Sue a little paper envelope, embellished with her logo, which was of course, a wren.

'Are you doing swaps?' I asked, recovering enough to pay attention.

'Sort of,' said Sue, opening the envelope and moving to look in the mirror Wren had set up as she pushed the star shaped silver studs into place. 'We thought it might be a nice touch to have a couple of things from other makers in our own huts.'

'Abbie has promised me a wren,' said Wren, 'but I already know I'm not going to be able to part with it.'

'But that won't stop you pointing folk in the right direction to find her collection once they've admired it, will it?' Sue pointed out.

'That's true,' said Wren, opening out the string of festive bunting Sue had stitched.

'This is lovely,' I said, holding up one end, while Wren climbed on to a chair, no doubt flouting every health and safety rule Ned had written up, to hang it. 'We could do with some in the barn.'

'I've just dropped a load off,' said Sue, tucking her grey curls behind her ears, the better to show the studs off. 'Ned's hanging it now.'

'I told you he was feeling better,' giggled Wren, as she stepped back down. 'He wouldn't be negotiating heights if he wasn't.'

'Has he been unwell?' Sue frowned, no doubt wondering why that would be the cause of amusement.

'Hungover more like,' I told her.

'He got blotto in the pub last night,' elaborated Wren. 'I have no idea how Liza managed to manhandle him home.'

117

'He was fine,' I said, looking back at the bunting and willing my cheeks not to flame again.

'That looks great, Sue,' said Wren, her gaze following mine.

'Yes,' said Sue. 'It does. I'm pleased with how well that mix of patterned fabrics works together. I'll tell you what's not looking so good though.'

'What?' Wren and I chorused.

'Santa's little corner in the barn,' said Sue, wrinkling her nose. 'I've just been and had a look at it and it's definitely more shabby, than chic. I didn't notice Thursday night because of the lighting, but in the cold light of day, it's looking a bit chipped and jaded.'

'More grotty, than grotto?' Wren suggested.

'Definitely,' Sue confirmed sadly.

I excused myself and went to have a look. Sue was right. Dad and I had painted the original backdrop together and by the looks of it, it hadn't been touched up or repainted since. The sight of it, so dated and worn, made my heart sink, but not for long.

There was nothing I could do about it during open hours, but as soon as the last customer left and the huts were closed, I set to with the brushes and paint from the storage area and speedily began to rectify the situation and bring the mural, back to life.

'What are you up to?' asked Ned, when he eventually materialised from the office, long after his dad had left.

'A bit of a touch up job,' I said, standing back to look at

all the extra bits I'd started to add. At this rate Santa and his visitors would think they really were in the snowy landscape of Lapland. 'Sue pointed out earlier that it needed a bit of attention. It looked all right in the evening, but not quite as pristine as it used to in the day.'

'Um,' Ned nodded, taking a closer look, 'I suppose it is a bit worse for wear now you've got the spotlights on it and I can see which bits you've been working on. I feel bad for not noticing before.'

'It doesn't matter,' I shrugged, trying to sound blasé. I didn't want him thinking my enthusiasm to bring the painting back to life meant that I was developing an attachment to the place. 'I've got all this time on my hands,' I therefore added, 'so I might as well do something with it.'

'Are you going to stop for supper?' he asked, pulling out his phone to check the time. 'Now I'm feeling better, I'm ravenous.'

'I ate earlier,' I said, 'but there are some leftovers. Sophie gave us some curried crab. If you fancy it, you'll just need to warm it through and there's plenty of bread to go with it.'

'Oh right,' Ned nodded. 'Fair enough. I'll see you later then.'

Repainting the grotto frieze was just the excuse I needed to avoid spending the evening curled up in front of the log burner with him and Bandit and I managed to keep going long after he'd turned in for the night. Lost in my thoughts I hadn't noticed the cold seeping in or how stiff my legs had got from kneeling on the floor. I felt like a pretzel by the time I locked up and hobbled back over to the lodge.

I was back out again early Sunday morning which effectively put paid to mine and Ned's paths crossing over breakfast and given the response I'd had from Caitlin to my message, that was probably just as well.

She had promised to find out what she could about the job and ended her reply with the words 'Ned sounds hot!' I didn't think I'd typed anything to imply that, but reading my message back, I realised I had put more emphasis on what he looked like than on his business credentials and thought a bit more time apart would be no bad thing.

The paint I'd added to the grotto had completely dried overnight, thanks to the efficient space heaters I'd left set on low and when Nick and Edith took up their stations ready to welcome the next line of visitors, they were both well pleased with what I'd done. The essence of what Dad and I had created was still very much in evidence but it had now been brought up to date.

'If the queue gets really long,' I said to Edith, 'you could get the children to try and count all these new snowflakes.'

'That's a great idea,' she beamed. 'And the number of baubles on the tree,' she added, looking closer. 'I'm sure there are more than before.'

'There are,' I laughed. 'Lots more!'

After I'd packed the brushes and paints away, I found the urge to carry on lingered. I hadn't been bitten by the creative bug in a very long time, and I looked about for other things I might be able to freshen up or give a festive twist to.

'Here you are,' said Ned, sounding exasperated when he found me rooting about in the stores. 'I've been looking all over for you.'

I knew he had been because I'd been one step ahead of him all morning, dodging out of sight whenever he was in the vicinity. The tactic had worked, until now.

'Well,' I said, stumbling as I stepped back over one of the little carts used to move the potted trees about the yard when it was too busy to use the truck. 'Here I am.'

Ned held me gently by the elbow while I regained my balance and I was so quick to pull myself free, that I nearly went over again.

'Was there something in particular you wanted me for?' I asked, eyeing the carts and wondering how I could make them look more Christmassy.

I was surprised Dad had left them unembellished. Practically everything else had some sort of festive themed adornment.

'No,' said Ned, pulling his hat further over his ears. 'Not really. I just wanted to check in. I didn't see you at all last night and this morning you were out of the lodge even before I was up. You are all right, aren't you?'

'Yes,' I said, 'of course. I just like to keep busy. I'm not very good at twiddling my thumbs,' I added to ensure there was no way he could misinterpret my rising activity rate.

'Well, the grotto looks great,' he said. 'I was beginning to think . . .'

'What?'

'Oh, it doesn't matter.'

'No,' I said, 'go on.'

He pulled his hat off, ruffled his already mussed-up hair and stared down at me. I forced myself to meet his gaze and wondered if my blue eyes looked as hypnotic to him as his flecked ones did to me. *He's already told you he fancies you*, an impish voice in my head reminded me.

'What were you beginning to think?' I asked again, sweeping my hair over my shoulder.

I already had a pretty good idea what it was, but wanted to hear him say it.

'I was thinking,' he said, finally breaking eye contact, 'that for someone who claims not to care, you've gone to an awful lot of trouble over that mural.'

Yep, that was it.

'Please don't get the wrong idea, Ned,' I beseeched him. 'Painting the grotto has absolutely nothing to do with me falling in love with Wynter's Trees.'

It's all about stopping me from falling in love with you.

'Right,' he swallowed. 'Fair enough.'

'I'm just used to being busy,' I carried on. 'Especially at this time of year. The run up to Christmas in school is manic, so I'm not used to doing nothing in November.'

'That makes sense,' he said, sounding disappointed. 'Do you miss it?'

'Yes,' I said, without hesitation. 'I do, although not the festive madness. I considered my role an important one and I like to think I'd made a difference, but cuts had to be made and student welfare didn't rank as highly as hitting targets and finding new ways to deliver the curriculum.'

'That doesn't make much sense to me,' said Ned.

'Me neither,' I shrugged. 'I'd far rather play a part in sending confident students who have been taught self-care and how to look after their mental health out into the world, than legions of kids who knew a bit about algebra that they'll never use. That's why I want to set up my own business. I'm going to combine art therapy with an emphasis on how nature and time spent outdoors can nurture and heal.'

I stopped to draw breath, conscious that it was the first time I'd said aloud what it was I was planning to do.

'That sounds amazing.' Ned thrilled me by saying. 'And you're right. Those are the skills that really count. They're the sort of things that should be on the curriculum, aren't they?'

'Well,' I grinned. 'I think so.'

'Your business is going to be amazing, Liza.' He praised, making me glow inside and out. 'I know it's going to be a huge success.'

The businesses success depended on whether he could raise the money to buy me out, but I didn't say as much.

'Anyway,' I said, turning the conversation full circle. 'in answer to your original question, I am all right, I'm just keeping myself busy.'

I wanted to add, *and not falling in love with Wynter's Trees*, but having now explained my business idea, I didn't think I needed to further hammer the point home.

'And out of mischief.' Ned grinned.

His words confirmed he'd taken what I'd emphasised and explained to heart and I was grateful for that.

'Oh, I don't know about that,' I laughed. 'I'm always up for a bit of mischief!'

Why did I say that?

'Oh right,' Ned laughed back, running a hand around the back of his head, 'well, that's good to know.'

'I'd better let you get on,' I said, feeling a total fool.

'Yeah,' he said, looking at his watch. 'Dad wants to look at some of the potted trees before it gets dark and I want to talk to everyone before they lock up. Theo especially. I missed him yesterday and he owes me a box of painkillers.'

I didn't want to think about painkillers because that reminded me why he had needed them, which in turn kick-started thoughts of that cosmic kiss ... that heart-stopping moment that I had been striving all weekend to ignore.

'Talking of trees,' I said, as he made to walk off, 'I think I've found somewhere to plant the family one.'

'Fantastic. Whereabouts?'

'Right at the furthest boundary overlooking the reserve,' I explained. 'There's a slight mound. You'll have to tell me if you think it's suitable or not.'

Ned shook his head.

'You know it.' I frowned. 'Is it no good?'

'Of course, I know it,' he laughed. 'It's the very place I was going to suggest.'

'Oh,' I said, taken aback.

'Great minds think alike,' he grinned and then he caught my eye and I felt like I was freefalling. 'It's a magical spot,' he carried on. 'The very best for watching the stars.'

I nodded, because I didn't trust myself to speak.

'Ned!' came David's voice from the plantation. 'Are we going to look at these trees?'

'Yes,' Ned shouted back, still looking at me. 'I'm on my way.'

Chapter 9

As I lay in bed that night my mind was awash with a million thoughts, many of which would never have existed had I not given in to David's pleading and made my way back to Wynter's Trees. Along with the turmoil I still felt every time I relived Ned's goodnight kiss, I was also perturbed to find there were also stirrings of what could only be described as softening feelings for my former home. It was all very disconcerting.

I tossed and turned, thumping the pillows into a hopefully more sleep-inducing shape and felt grateful that I'd had the sense to announce my desire to sell up so soon after my arrival. Had I delayed, my memories of stargazing, the presence of the family tree, my work on the mural and creative sign making, could have led me down a very different path, in spite of what I'd told Ned earlier. I squeezed my eyes shut and eventually drifted into an uneasy sleep and a night of unsettling dreams which all involved me, him and a reindeer skin rug.

Neither Ned nor Bandit were in the lodge when I went down to breakfast, feeling both groggy and guilty about the steamy dream. Ned's barely warm mug and damp towel and Bandit's empty food bowl, suggested they'd already had a run and headed over to the office. I was grateful for the peace and quiet and lingered over my breakfast, reliving certain moments from my sexy slumber, even though they really should have been banned before the watershed.

Finally ready to face the day, I switched Dad's coat for my better fitting and cleaner Barbour, which I had previously left behind. There was a 4x4 I didn't recognise parked in the yard, but I soon worked out it belonged to the person laughing in the barn.

'If you want them back, then you'll just have to come and get them, won't you?' crooned a seductive female voice.

The words were followed by a mischievous giggle. There was a brief silence and then Ned answered. To my ears, he sounded every bit as amused as his as yet unidentified companion.

'I'm hardly going to do that if you only keep letting me catch you when you're positioned under the mistletoe, am I?' he said.

I could tell me was smiling and my heart gave a slow and heavy thud in response.

'I don't see why not,' the woman purred. 'It didn't stop you last year, did it?'

'That was a one-off,' said Ned. 'And you took advantage. You knew I'd had too much to drink.'

My heart beat faster and I wondered if Ned only made a habit of kissing women when he'd had a skinful. If that was the case, then I'd really made too much of his inebriated embrace and determinedly pushed the now tainted memory of it away.

'If you say so,' came the woman's voice again and I rushed to rattle the barn door before walking in.

Bandit gave a gruff bark then, realising it was me, bounded over. I bent to fuss him, putting the moment of looking at the owner of the flirtatious voice briefly off. I might not have seen her yet, but I couldn't miss the huge ball of mistletoe which had been lashed to the office ceiling and which definitely hadn't been there the day before.

'Liza,' said Ned. 'I didn't realise you were about.'

'I've just come over from the lodge,' I told him, noticing his face was flushed.

'Come and meet Maya,' he said, stepping aside to reveal the woman standing next to him.

She was incredibly pretty and in her early twenties. Her dark blonde hair was swept into a high ponytail and her face, free of make-up, had a healthy outdoor glow. She was much taller than me and, as so often when faced with tall and attractive women, I felt immediately inadequate.

'Liza,' she beamed, tossing a bunch of keys at Ned before reaching for my hand and pumping it up and down. 'I'm so pleased to meet you at last!'

I was totally taken aback. Her welcome was both warm and genuine and not at all what I would have expected, given that I'd just interrupted her sultry seduction.

'I'm here to help with the trees,' she beamed, looking thrilled at the prospect. 'And I'm totally in love with this place. Always have been! Aren't the beach huts *amazing*?'

She let go of my hand and stared down at me.

'Um . . . yes,' I stammered. 'They are.'

'Sorry,' she laughed, when she realised I was feeling dazed. 'I tend to talk too much.'

'You certainly do,' said Ned, earning himself a playful thump on the arm.

'Are you here to work?' I asked. 'It's rather early.'

'Oh, I'm used to dark starts,' she told me, with a wave of her hand. 'My family own a farm up the road, so this is more mid-morning to me.'

'Right,' I nodded. 'I see.'

'We're going through the order book today,' said Ned, 'and looking over the biggest potted trees. Maya's become quite an expert in tree health over the last couple of years.'

'Ah, thanks Ned,' she said, giving him a gentler nudge. 'There's not much for me to do on the family farm at this time of year,' she then told me. 'So, I work here instead and I absolutely love it.'

'You've already said that,' teased Ned.

'Have I?' she frowned. 'Sorry, I'm a bit starstruck.'

'Starstruck?' Ned frowned.

'Yes,' she said, gazing at me. 'I've told you a million times how much this place meant to me was when I was growing up, Ned, and now I get to work alongside Liza Wynter herself.'

Ned rolled his eyes. 'That's me out of favour then,' he sighed.

'Please don't say that,' I told Maya, turning warm under her scrutiny. I was bound to be found wanting. 'There's really nothing special about me.'

Maya shook her head in disbelief. She wouldn't hear a word of it and I couldn't help but smile. In the few minutes since I'd met her, she'd made me feel far less inadequate than I had when I walked in. I appreciated that, even when her next words took me by surprise.

'You told me she was pretty, Ned,' she said in a very loud whisper, 'but you never mentioned that she was self-effacing, too.'

'Oh Maya,' Ned groaned, turning crimson, which made me feel even better. 'You're incorrigible. Go and do some bloody work.'

'But what about the . . .' she said, her eyes flicking to the ceiling and the big ball of mistletoe. 'I had to wrestle that into my truck this morning, don't I even get a peck on the cheek as reward?'

Maya was bold as well as incorrigible and she had the ability to make Ned's smile stretch far wider than I had ever seen it. As good as she had made me feel about myself, I realised I was a little jealous of her. She was beautiful, totally in love with Wynter's, an expert in the business and, judging by the look on her face, rather smitten with Ned. Looking at the pair of them standing side by side, I could see they would make the perfect couple.

'No, you don't,' tutted Ned, taking a step away from the mistletoe. 'Bugger off and make yourself useful in the yard for a bit while I get the books out.'

'There!' she grinned at me. 'Listen to the way he talks to your employees, Liza. I see a disciplinary in your future, if you're not careful, Edward.'

Ned shook his head.

'I can help with the trees too, if you like,' I piped up, even though I had no desire to head out into the chilly plantation. 'Many hands and all that.'

'No, it's all right,' said Ned, opening the filing cabinet. 'We've got a system in place and the job won't take long once we get going. I'm sure you've got other things to do to keep you occupied.'

I should have been grateful that Ned had someone so competent to work alongside him, especially as after Christmas he was potentially going to be in sole charge, but I would have much preferred it if his colleague was someone less attractive. I had absolutely no right to think it, but that was how I felt.

In spite of my twinge of unjustified jealousy, Maya's constant and cheery presence, combined with the overheard conversation about Ned kissing her when he was drunk, did have one positive benefit. It very effectively put the lid on me mooning over memories of our kiss and the explicit reindeer rug fantasies.

Her timely arrival turned my thoughts back to my travel

and business plans, but there was an unsettling feeling in the back of my mind, that neither felt quite as all-consuming as they had before. I still had every intention of pushing ahead with both, but while I was at Wynter's Trees, and with Ned still to make a formal offer for my shares, they felt further out of reach than they had before.

'You all right, my love?' Sue asked towards the end of the week, when I was doing the tea round in the huts. 'You've been looking a bit glum the last few days.'

There had been a consistently steady flow of shoppers to the beach huts and it was obvious that Ned's offer to set them up at Wynter's Trees had been the right one. Many of the people I spoke to had travelled further than before and with the added benefit of Hope and Sophie serving food and drink, they were staying longer and consequently spending more too.

With this in mind, I knew I should have been on cloud nine, but I felt as though I'd come up against a brick wall. My creative mojo had taken flight again, I couldn't bring myself to start sorting out the lodge and Maya's laughter seemed to follow me everywhere. I should have been grateful that she had an uncanny knack of stepping between Ned and me, and maintaining the distance between us that I had been aiming to achieve, but even that was beginning to bring me down.

'I'm just feeling a bit flat,' I told Sue, with a shrug.

I wished I could have explained what was really going on in my world and talked it all out with her, but Ned had told me he still wasn't ready. Consequently, I was beginning to feel weighed down by the battle of conflicting feelings which were building within me and which I had to keep to myself.

Sue eyed me over the top of the cushion she was sewing. 'Why's that then?' she asked. 'I thought you were finally feeling excited to be here. You positively threw yourself into repainting the grotto, so I assumed you were settled and enjoying getting stuck in.'

'I was,' I said, my voice thick in my throat, because it wasn't the whole truth. 'I am.'

'I know you weren't happy when you were growing up here,' she said, 'but you've seemed quite content these last couple of weeks.'

It felt so devious, stringing everyone along. My apparent contentment had grown from me feeling safe in the knowledge that I would soon be leaving for good, and that was deceptive enough in itself, but now, on top of that, lots of other things felt like they were getting muddled too. I would have to talk to Ned again and insist we set the record straight.

'Or you did,' Sue carried on, when I didn't say anything, 'until a certain someone came back to work.'

I followed her gaze into the yard where Maya was striding out, her long slender legs carrying her along and her glossy ponytail jauntily swinging.

'It's not Maya,' I hastily said.

'Hmm,' Sue sniffed.

'I'm thrilled she's here,' I insisted. 'She's a great help to Ned.'

I watched as she disappeared into the barn. I knew Ned was working in the office and wondered if she was about to succeed in cornering him under the mistletoe.

'He's going to need all the help he can get now David's retiring,' I inadvertently said.

'He's got you, hasn't he?' Sue frowned.

'Well, yes,' I swallowed. 'But you know what I mean. Maya's proper help, isn't she?'

I backed out of the door before she could answer.

'I better go and give Bandit his lunch,' I said. 'I promised Ned I would as he's so busy.'

I eagerly accepted Wren's invitation to go to the pub on Saturday night and as she had already arranged to meet Abbie, I didn't feel obliged to ask Ned. A girl's night out, was just what I needed, even if it was only for a quiet drink in the local.

'If you want to have a drink,' Wren kindly offered, when I arrived, 'you can leave your car in the village and I'll drive you home. I'm sticking to Coke tonight.'

'Whereas I look as though I need of shot a rum with mine, do I?' I laughed.

'No,' said Wren.

'Yes,' said Abbie and we all laughed.

'Thanks for the offer,' I said to Wren, 'but I'm not fussed.'

Given what had happened to Dad, I never touched a drop of alcohol before getting behind the wheel.

'So,' I said, 'where are Theo and Noah tonight? You mentioned they had plans, Abbie.'

'They're at a stag do in Norwich,' she told me, rolling her eyes. 'Noah's brother is getting married and he insisted Noah went to the party. He's taken his partner, Michael, with him, but as neither were keen, they roped Theo in on the assumption that he would have more experience.'

I didn't know about his partner, but from what I knew of Noah I could guess that a stag night in the city wasn't his cup of tea.

'Which he hasn't,' Wren laughed. 'But he's tagged along to lend some moral support.'

'It's really not Noah's sort of thing, is it?' I asked.

'Really, really not,' said Abbie. 'He and Michael have been dreading it for weeks.'

'Bless them,' I sympathised. 'It's not a good feeling getting cajoled into doing something you'd rather not, is it?'

I was thinking of David talking me into coming back to Wynmouth, but obviously couldn't say as much.

'I used to get roped into doing all sorts of crazy things at school,' I said instead. 'The sponsored Go Ape Treetop Challenge was the worst.'

'Oh god,' Wren shuddered. 'I'm rubbish with heights.'

'So am I!' I told her. 'That's why it was the worst.'

They couldn't help but giggle as I told them about how much fun the students had had at my terrified expense.

'My legs were trembling for weeks,' I finished up, which was no exaggeration.

'You should set something like that up at Wynter's,' Abbie mused.

'Not possible,' I told her, feeling relieved even though it wouldn't have impacted on me. 'Wrong sort of trees and anyway, Ned's got enough on his plate without worrying about the health and safety aspect of a venture like that.'

'That's true,' Abbie agreed.

'But at least he's got you to share the load now David's retiring, Liza.' Wren pointed out.

'Oh,' I said. 'He doesn't need me. He's more than capable of managing on his own.'

'And he's gorgeous to boot,' Wren giggled.

I had no idea what that had to do with his business skills.

'Wren!' said Abbie, shaking her head. 'You're practically a married woman.'

'With twenty twenty vision,' she laughed. 'I might be head over heels for Theo, but that doesn't mean I haven't got eyes in my head. Ned's a hunk and a half.'

'He is a dreamboat,' smiled Abbie, staring off into the middle distance. 'And us three aren't the only ones who think so, are we?'

I didn't think it was worth pointing out that I hadn't offered an opinion.

'Are you talking about Maya?' I asked.

'Who else?' smiled Abbie.

'I'm not so sure,' frowned Wren. 'You know what she's like. She flirts with everyone!'

'They would make the perfect couple though, wouldn't

they?' I sighed. 'I bet tree sales go through the roof when Maya's front of house.'

'No way,' said Abbie. 'Not this year anyway. Folk round here are more excited about seeing a Wynter front and centre than Maya's pretty face. You might not be aware of it, Liza, but your return to Wynter's Trees has caused quite a stir.'

I hadn't heard that myself, but it made me feel even worse about keeping my secret. Not only was I going to upset the beach hut crew, I was going to let down the entire population of Wynmouth too.

'Well, I don't know about that,' I said, 'but you can't tell me that having someone around who looks as good as Maya isn't good for business.'

'No,' conceded Wren. 'Perhaps not.'

'And she's such a lovely person too,' Abbie added. 'She stepped straight in after I'd had my accident, offering to help with my horse. She exercises him and has him stabled on her family farm. I probably wouldn't have been able to keep him had she not been around.'

'She's the whole package all right,' I said, as a lightbulb moment landed.

Ever since I'd overheard Ned telling David that he was scared he wouldn't be up to the task of running Wynter's Trees on his own, I'd been looking for ways to boost Ned's confidence. Momentarily blinded by my misplaced jealousy of Maya, I hadn't been able to see the solution which was literally towering over me.

'And I don't know about you two,' I said, 'but I think

we should help Maya get Ned under the mistletoe before Christmas.'

My new friends didn't look so sure.

'Come on,' I encouraged. 'They're made for each other. All they need is a bit of coaxing.'

'I think it'll take more than that,' said Wren.

'On Ned's side anyway,' added Abbie.

'Rubbish,' I loudly said, banging my glass on the table. 'Ned and Little Miss Perfect, are a match made in heaven!'

'Pipe down,' said Wren, tugging at my sleeve as out of the corner of my eye, I spotted Maya striding across the bar and out the door.

'Bugger,' I said as Abbie and Wren shook their heads. 'Do you think she heard me?'

'Call her Little Miss Perfect?' frowned Abbie. 'Er, yeah, I think she might have done.'

'But I wasn't being mean,' I hastily pointed out.

'We know that,' said Wren, 'but I daresay she didn't catch the whole conversation, did she?'

'Damn,' I sighed.

We were still in the pub when Sam called time and Tess began clearing the tables. I had put off driving back to the lodge in case Maya had already told Ned her version of what she thought she'd heard. The fact that he was still up and looking grumpy when I slipped through the door warned me that that was exactly what had happened.

'I've had Maya on the phone,' he gruffly said before I'd even got my coat off.

'Look, Ned,' I said. 'I can explain ...'

'She seemed to think that you, Wren and Abbie were talking about her in the pub,' he interrupted. 'You weren't bitching about her, were you?'

'No,' I hotly said. 'Of course not.'

'That's what I told her ...'

'Although,' I cut in.

'Although what?'

'Although, I did say something that she might have taken the wrong way.'

'Oh?'

'I called her Little Miss Perfect,' I said, feeling a total fool. 'But not in a mean way,' I quickly added. 'Just because she is.'

Ned looked at me and quirked an eyebrow. 'You think Maya's perfect?'

'Well, duh. Don't you?'

'Perfect for Wynter's Trees, you mean?'

'Yes,' I said. 'She's total employee of the month material.'

'Well, yes,' he said. 'I suppose she is.'

I let out a long breath. I was off the hook.

'But she heard my name mentioned too,' said Ned, immediately catching me again.

'I just said that the pair of you work well together,' I told him.

There was no way I was going to explain my matchmaking mission. Given that Ned had, albeit drunkenly, told me he fancied me, I didn't think he'd appreciate my efforts to fix him up with someone else.

'You didn't happen to mention that you were hoping to sell up as well, did you?'

'No,' I said. 'Of course not. I promised I wouldn't and I haven't told anyone.'

Ned ran his hands through his hair and I noticed how tired he looked. Even though he had broached the subject, I knew it wasn't the moment to tell him how difficult I was finding it to not say anything and how guilty I was feeling about misleading everyone.

'I'll explain to Maya,' I said. 'I should have gone after her when she left the pub.'

'It would be good to clear the air.' Ned sighed. 'I want to make your last few weeks connected to Wynter's Trees good ones, so the last thing we need are misunderstandings among the team.'

I appreciated that he could acknowledge that this Christmas was to be my last, but his insistence that we keep my plans quiet was going to be the cause of the biggest misunderstanding of all.

'I know it must be hard for you,' he then kindly said, 'being back here properly for the first time since you lost your dad, but I want to give you a Christmas he would be proud of, Liza.'

'That means a lot,' I whispered, emotion suddenly outweighing annoyance, as I turned towards the stairs and away from that look in his eye. 'Dad would appreciate that,' I swallowed, 'and so do I.'

Chapter 10

As I went through my cleanse, tone and moisturise routine that night, I played over the conversation I'd just had with Ned. I was deeply touched that he wanted to make my final December connected to Wynter's Trees so special, but my appreciation was marked by an unexpected hint of sadness.

I hardly dared to entertain the idea, but was I feeling upset because he wasn't fighting for me? I should have been delighted that he wasn't thinking I'd be seduced by the sight of the place bedecked in its seasonal finery, like I guessed David still was, but I felt as far from thrilled as it was possible to get. It was irrational and infuriating. Aside from not letting me tell everyone my plans, Ned was behaving exactly how I had initially wanted him to, but for some reason his kind and considerate conduct didn't satisfy me.

Perhaps I should have another chat with him and David and see if I could persuade him to let me talk about my intentions to Sue at least? The future I was attempting to create didn't feel real all the while I was cocooned inside the lodge and spinning out these surreal few weeks helping in the huts. Maybe putting the cat among the pigeons would be the wake-up call I needed to bring my emotions to heel, and launching my 'get Ned and Maya together' plan of action might help too.

Unfortunately, my freshly formed plan didn't get off to the best of starts. Maya's truck was nowhere to be seen the next morning and neither was she. I initially panicked that she hadn't turned up because of what I'd said in the pub, but then David reminded me it was Sunday and she wouldn't be in. I wanted to ring her mobile but he said he couldn't let me have the number, which was fair enough. Thwarted in my quest, I headed back to the lodge and, noticing the date on the calendar, grabbed an apron, determined to make the most of the day, in spite of the less than satisfactory start.

'What's going on?' Ned frowned, when he came back for lunch and surveyed the chaos in the kitchen. 'It smells like Christmas in here.'

His expression was transformed as the heady fruit and alcohol enhanced scent filled his nostrils.

'Good,' I said, blowing my fringe out of my face. 'It's supposed to.'

Even my desire to embrace stir-up Sunday hadn't been straightforward, because I'd forgotten the kitchen cupboards wouldn't be stocked in the same way Dad used to keep them. However, rather than give up, I'd speedily swapped the apron for my car keys and dashed to the nearest supermarket for supplies. My little banger appreciated the extra run and since arriving back, I'd been going great guns, hence the fabulous festive scent. The whole lodge smelt reminiscent of Christmases past, so I knew I'd got something right.

'What exactly are you doing?' Ned asked, picking up Mum's ancient recipe book which was open on the counter and covered in a light dusting of flour.

'Playing my part in making my last Christmas here memorable,' I told him, my voice cracking as I added. 'I want to make my dad proud, too.'

Ned put the book down again and I knew he was watching me. I kept my eyes firmly fixed on the huge bowl of rum soaked fruit I was mixing. My arm was beginning to throb, but I didn't stop. I didn't want to do anything that might betray the mystifying feelings I was doing my utmost to control.

'It's stir-up Sunday,' I elaborated. 'Mum always used to make our cake and pudding today and after she died, Dad carried on, so in line with the tradition, I thought I would too.'

The words came out in a rush.

'What size are you making?' asked Ned.

I was pleased he hadn't said something sympathetic.

'This isn't for just one pudding,' I told him. 'I thought they would make nice parting gifts. I'm going to give everyone in the huts one, along with your dad, Nick and Edith and Maya, of course.'

I risked a glance and the smile Ned gave me made my

heart flutter in response. Clearly, it was going to take a while for it to toe the same line as my head was trying to.

'That's a really lovely idea,' he beamed.

'I'm pleased you think so,' I puffed. 'And as you're so impressed, and my arms are about to drop off, you can go and wash your hands, then come back to help. You'll be able to make your wish while you're helping me out.'

'My wish?'

'Yes,' I said, checking Mum's recipe again. 'It's another tradition. You make a wish when you stir the pudding. Mum, Dad and I always used to do it.'

'Does that mean we get a wish for each pudding?'

'No,' I laughed, realising there were going to be close to a dozen, 'don't be so greedy. We'll both wish on the one I'm making for the lodge.'

'All right,' he agreed, looking deep into my eyes, 'if there's really any magic in it, one should be enough, shouldn't it?'

'I'd say so,' I nodded, longing to know what he was going to wish for.

Making good on my commitment to help Ned make my last Christmas at Wynter's Trees a memorable one and my dad proud, I was up extra early on Monday morning, ready to apologise to Maya the moment she arrived. I also wanted to throw myself into another creative idea which had landed the evening before and would require both artistic and practical skill and distract me from my more unsettling thoughts.

'Now what are you up to?' Ned asked, when he found

me taping sheets of paper together on the floor in front of the log burner.

Bandit, keen to get involved, was getting in the way, but I didn't have the heart to push him aside and consequently the paper was becoming rather crumpled.

'It's a surprise,' I said as Bandit took an exploratory bite of the sheet he was laying on. 'Hey,' I tutted. 'That's not helping, hound.'

'Come on,' said Ned, patting his leg. 'Let's go for a run and leave Liza to her crafting session.'

I soon finished drawing up the outline of what I had in mind and was rifling through the barn stores when I heard someone behind me. It was still rather dark and thanks to the inadequate overhead light, I was struggling to see what was there.

'Do you know if there are any sheets of MDF or bits of ply kicking about anywhere?' I called over my shoulder, assuming it was Ned. 'I don't want to go and buy new, if there's some leftover.'

'I wouldn't know,' said Maya's voice. 'My forte is trees that are still growing.'

'Maya,' I said, jumping down from the stepladder. 'Just the person I wanted to see.'

'I am?' she asked, sounding surprised.

'Yes,' I said, brushing dust off my jeans. 'Of course, you are. I owe you an apology.'

'That's funny,' she smiled. 'That's exactly what I was going to say to you.'

'You were?'

I knew what I was sorry about, but she had nothing to apologise for.

'Yes,' she said. 'I shouldn't have called Ned after I heard you talking in the pub. I'm sorry I did that.'

'No,' I said, shaking my head. 'I'm sorry, Maya. I'm sorry I said something that made you feel bad, but I promise you, we weren't being mean. Far from it in fact. I was actually telling the others that I think you're perfect. Little Miss Perfect might have sounded like an insult, but it wasn't meant that way.'

'You really think I'm perfect?' Maya asked, her beautiful eyes widening and her cheeks flushing prettily.

There was absolutely no false modesty attached to her question and I realised that what you saw was very definitely not what you got where Maya was concerned. She might have looked catwalk-ready, but she didn't have the confidence to strut down it.

'Well, yeah,' I said, as if it should have been obvious. 'Have you seen you, Maya?'

Her cheeks burned brighter but she didn't say anything.

'You've got brains and beauty,' I told her. 'Not forgetting six-foot long legs that I'd kill for and you're lovely too. Now I think about it,' I added, 'I should hate you really.'

She laughed at that, but then looked sad.

'If I'm as perfect as you seem to think I am,' she quietly said, 'then how come I'm not inundated with admirers? I haven't had a date in forever.'

My guess was that the guys who wanted to ask her out were probably a bit intimidated by her looks, but if they found the courage to have a conversation with her, then they'd soon realise what a pussycat she was. Not that I was going to tell her that, because my plan was to get her and Ned together!

'Oh, I shouldn't worry,' I told her. 'I think that situation's going to change soon.'

'Chance would be a fine thing,' she sighed. 'I think that was why I went and told Ned that I'd heard you talking about me. I thought he might feel sorry for me and pay me a bit more attention.'

'Well,' I said, 'if it makes you feel any better, he was quick to jump to your defence.'

'He was?'

'I hadn't even got in the door before he was demanding to know what I'd been saying.'

Maya brightened considerably after that and told me she'd got a few missed calls from him, and Abbie, registered on her phone when she'd turned it back on.

'There,' I said, 'I daresay he wanted to make sure you were okay.'

'And Abbie probably did too,' she pointed out. 'But there were more calls from Ned.'

I tried not to feel jealous and instead focused on the fact that stage one of my matchmaking mission was finally launched.

'Did you say you were looking for wood offcuts?' Maya asked. 'I'll give you a hand if you like.'

I was happy to return to my new project and once she'd helped me dig out some sheets of ply, I explained what I hoped to achieve, even though I had no idea how to do some of it.

'I can help you there,' she said, quickly gathering the wood and sketches together. 'Leave it with me and I'll bring them back before you know it.'

True to her word she arrived back a short while later.

'Are these what you had in mind?' she asked, when she beckoned me over to show me, out of sight of the office.

'Oh yes,' I said, clapping my hands together. 'They're perfect. Thank you so much.'

'It was no bother,' she said. 'My dad had the equipment to cut them and they've turned out really well.'

'They'll look even better when they're painted up. Do you fancy giving me a hand?'

'Oh no,' she laughed, shaking her head so hard her ponytail bounced. 'I'll help you fix them in place, but if you want them to look half decent, don't even think about passing me a paintbrush.'

When we knew Ned had gone back to the lodge and David had gone home, Maya helped me carry everything back to the barn where I hid it all away, ready for the next day. Ned had already told me he was going to be off-site and I thought I could easily set something up which would keep my clandestine crafting out of sight.

'Will you get them all finished tomorrow?' Maya asked.

'No,' I told her, 'but I'll be able to make a good start.

Hopefully they'll be done and fixed in place by the end of the week.'

'I can't wait to see them.'

'Me neither,' I said, wondering if Bandit might be able to give the idea the launch it deserved.

'So,' Maya said, following me out of the barn. 'We are okay, aren't we, Liza?'

'Yes,' I said, locking the door behind me. 'Of course, we are. It was just a silly misunderstanding and entirely my fault. Although I'm pleased it happened.'

'You are?'

'Yes,' I told her, 'because if nothing else it's proved how much Ned thinks of you, hasn't it?'

'Has it?'

'Believe me,' I said seriously, 'he wouldn't have reacted the way he did if you didn't mean something to him, Maya.'

'Well,' she dreamily said, 'we are friends.'

I looked at her, rosy cheeked and so pretty and knew there was potential for them to be much more than that. They worked so seamlessly together. How could Ned not find that combination of brains and beauty irresistible?

'I think there's rather more than friendship between you,' I said, fleetingly wishing I was on the receiving end of those words, rather than dishing them out.

Maya looked thoughtful.

'Sometimes I do too,' she nodded, 'but we only ever seem to get so far before he backs off. The closest we've ever been was the result of a tipsy Christmas kiss last year.'

'I daresay he's mindful of your professional relationship,' I pointed out. 'You're his employee and he's your boss, so he's probably reluctant to cross the line. I know he values the work you do here and wouldn't want to lose you if you did start something up and it went wrong.'

Maya mulled that over for a moment or two, before linking her arm through mine.

'In that case,' she grinned, 'I'll have to find a way to convince him that nothing will go wrong, won't I?'

I nodded but couldn't bring myself to agree. In my head, I was all for getting Ned and Maya together, but my heart still felt nowhere near as keen.

Chapter 11

Having set the matchmaking wheels in motion, I made sure I stayed out of the way as much as possible during the next few days. Emboldened by my encouragement, I knew Maya wouldn't waste a moment in finding ways to convince Ned that starting a romance with her wouldn't jeopardise their professional relationship. And, even though I knew that, should she succeed, it would further my cause, I had no inclination to witness either her endeavours or their outcome.

'Knock, knock.'

'Hey Noah,' I said, looking up to find him peeping around the temporary screen I had set up in the storage area at the back of the barn.

I had been trying to keep my new project under wraps, but with limited success. Everyone had been popping in and out, and sneaking a look, aside from Ned. Once he'd got wind that I was making something which would further enhance Wynter's seasonal feel he told me he would rather wait and see the finished result.

'How's it going?' Noah asked.

'This is the last one,' I told him, stretching out my back. 'What do you think?'

'Inspired,' he said, clapping his hands together.

'Now all I have to do is fix them to the carts and we'll be in business.'

The ply sheets had been, thanks to Maya's dad, cut into the shape of sleighs which I had further transformed by painting bright red and decorating to look like the real thing. I had also added, in flowing white script, the words, *Wynter's Trees Transport* along the sides. I had enough to bolt on to the sides of each cart, hopefully giving them the appearance of real miniature sleighs and I further hoped I might be able to encourage Bandit to pull one for long enough to get some video footage and a photo or two to send to the local press.

'You're so clever, Liza,' Noah gushed.

'Thanks,' I self-consciously said, struggling to accept the compliment. 'To be honest, I'm surprised Dad hadn't come up with something like this years ago.'

'From what I can remember,' said Noah, cocking his head. 'He was more practical than creative. The decorative flourishes are definitely more your forte, my love.'

Dad had said something similar the day he drove over to see me for what turned out to be the last time. I hastily pushed aside the memory and forcefully blinked away the tears which always arrived whenever it managed to squeeze its way in.

'Thanks, Noah.' I said again before changing the subject. 'Have you and Michael finally recovered from your stag night experience?'

Noah rolled his eyes and shook his head.

'Just about,' he said, with a shudder. 'I don't know what my brother was thinking, insisting that we tagged along, although actually, some good has come out of it.'

'Oh?'

'We've talked practically every day since,' he confided, sounding pleased. 'We'd drifted apart a bit after I came out, but we're closer now than we have been in a long time. And he really likes Michael, which has made Mum happy too.'

'That's fantastic.'

'It is,' he agreed. 'It's nice to feel that he needs me again. Only this morning, I was calming his nerves.'

'Pre-wedding jitters?'

'Mmm,' Noah nodded. 'I told him to follow his heart. Not that he's *really* having doubts, but that's always the best course of action, isn't it?'

I hoped that was a rhetorical question because I tended to follow my head and good old-fashioned common sense, rather than my heart. I had adopted the strategy the day I left school. Hearts, I had realised by then, were vulnerable organs. Mum's had let her down, and mine had been irreparably damaged by her death, it was then further crushed by Dad's decision to move us and then stamped all over by Chelsea. I was better off ignoring it.

Of course, it had taken a further blow after Dad's crash

and since arriving back I'd had no choice but to acknowledge the reaction it had whenever Ned was in the vicinity, but thanks to my head coming up with the plan to get him and Maya together which would enable me to soon be on my way, it was back under control again.

'I mean,' Noah carried on, 'the heart wants what the heart wants, and following your head is all well and good but it can be a bit soulless, don't you think?' He didn't wait for me to answer. 'When it comes to matters of love, it's the heart that counts. Now,' he said, with a nod to the sleighs, 'do you want me to give you a hand to bolt these on?'

Everyone had left by the time Noah and I had finished and with Ned away on business elsewhere again, I decided to line the carts up outside so they looked poised for action. There would be no way he could miss them when he came over to the office the following morning and I hoped he'd like them as much as I did. Using ply had ensured the additional weight was minimal and I had attached them high enough to ensure there was decent ground clearance.

'What's the matter with you?' I frowned at Bandit who growled when I let him out of the office.

I hadn't had him sit with me while I had been painting because the fumes had been a bit on the strong side and then I'd ended up leaving him a little longer so he didn't get under mine and Noah's feet while we finished up. I hadn't realised he was going be so put out.

'It's been for your own good,' I told him, but he shot round the side of me and straight out into the yard.

Perhaps he'd read my mind about being the Wynter's Trees poster pooch and was making himself scarce before I had a chance to hook him up to a sleigh.

'Bandit!' I shouted after him as he bypassed the lodge and headed straight for the plantation. 'It'll be great publicity!' But he didn't stop. 'Oh, for pity's sake.'

I was in no mood to go chasing after him in the dark. Not when a hot bath and lazy supper beckoned. I was looking forward to an evening alone where I wouldn't have to spend all of my time trying not to look at Ned.

'Come back you crazy dog!' I bellowed, but to no avail.

Grabbing a torch and locking the barn door, I turned up the collar of my coat, swore a bit and tramped off after him. I hadn't made it far when I realised he'd stopped running and switched his efforts to barking madly. I quickly followed the sound. He'd got surprisingly far, and I was out of breath when I finally reached him.

'What on earth are you playing at?' I scolded, but Bandit was not alone.

Cowering behind the tree he was guarding was someone that I first assumed was a man, but it turned out, when I shone my torch in his face, was a tall teenager.

'Jesus,' he winced, screwing his eyes up against the glare.

'Who the hell are you?' I scowled.

'No one,' he flinched as Bandit took a step closer, further buoyed up by my presence. 'I'm no one. Call this bloody dog off, will you?'

'Not until you tell me what you're doing here.'

'I'm not doing anything!'

'You most certainly are,' I retaliated. 'You're trespassing on private property.'

Bandit let out another bark and lunged forward.

'Bandit,' I said sharply. 'Here.'

To my astonishment, he stopped barking and sat down. With no lead to hand, I was relieved he was willing to do as he was told. I wondered if the same could be said for the sulky looking lad I had no idea what to do with.

'I know I shouldn't be here,' he said, sounding mulish, 'but I'm not doing any harm.'

'I'll be the one to decide that. Come out from behind that tree and bring anything you've got, or taken, with you.'

He did as I asked, in spite of Bandit's low growl and I shone my torch around the tree. I couldn't see anything that shouldn't be there.

'I haven't pinched anything, if that's what you're think-ing,' he quietly said. 'I've just come here to walk.'

'Walk?'

I didn't believe that for a second. I wondered if this was the culprit who had been responsible for the increased secu-rity around the farm.

'Yeah,' he sniffed, burying his hands which were glove-less, into his jacket pockets. 'Walk.'

'But you must have walked miles just to get here,' I pointed out, as another thought occurred. 'Unless you're not alone?'

If he'd got a lift, and they'd parked a vehicle out of sight then the trees could be harbouring an accomplice, or even two, that I hadn't seen. I quickly shone the torch around, but then realised that Bandit would still be in guard dog mode if there were more people hanging about.

'I am alone,' the lad said, 'and it's not all that far cross-country from the village.'

'Which village?' I frowned.

'Wynmouth,' he sniffed again. 'I walked from Wynmouth.'

'But why?' I gaped. 'That is far. Really far. It's literally miles away.'

It was quite an undertaking, even more so when you weren't properly dressed for the weather which, taking in the fabric of his jacket, he wasn't.

'Like I said,' he shrugged. 'I just fancied a walk.'

'You'll have to do better than that if you don't want me to call the police,' I said, reaching for my mobile, even though I knew there was no signal among the trees.

'You're not going to call the police from here, are you?' he tutted.

Not liking the change in the lad's tone, Bandit stood up again, but didn't bark. Thankfully his change in posture, was enough to weaken the impostor's regained attitude.

'I often come here,' he relented, his shoulders sagging, 'and to the reserve, but no one usually sees me.'

'What do you come here for?'

I couldn't interrogate him for walking around the reserve because that was open to everyone, whereas Wynter's Trees wasn't. Not generally after dark anyway.

'Like I keep telling you, just to walk,' he explained. 'It's so peaceful here. No one to moan at me or nag me. I can just walk up and down a bit. The trees smell nice. I used to come here with my nan when I was little.'

Suddenly he looked more like a small boy, and a vulnerable one, than a bolshy teen already the size of a man.

'Come on,' I said, moving off, 'let's go back to the lodge. It's freezing out here.'

The lad didn't move and I turned to look at him.

'Don't even think about running off,' I told him, my eyes on Bandit. 'He'd hunt you down in a heartbeat and he's got an extremely high prey drive.'

'What does that mean?'

'It means it's in his instinct to take a chunk out of you if he catches you.'

Once inside, I added a log to the burner, leaving the door open to further spread the warmth and got out two mugs, while the lad rubbed his hands in front of the flames, closely watched by my canine companion. So much for my evening of relaxation. I had no idea what I was going to do with him, but my years of teaching told me there was something troubling him. Why else would he be tramping over the countryside in winter to walk around some rows of Christmas trees?

'Tea, coffee, or a hot chocolate?' I asked him.

'Nothing,' he shrugged. 'I really should be getting back.'

'Well, I'm having a drink,' I told him. 'Because I'm freezing and it will warm me up.'

'Coffee then,' he said. 'Black, no sugar.'

'I'm having hot chocolate,' I said. 'It's just as easy to make two as one.'

'That then,' he said. 'Thanks.'

I handed him a mug of marshmallow-topped hot chocolate and a spoon and sat on the sofa while he sat cross-legged in front of the fire with Bandit for company.

'He's all right really, isn't he?' the lad said, giving him a tentative stroke.

'He's wonderful,' I said.

Bandit edged closer and rested his head in the boy's lap and my remaining concerns completely subsided. There couldn't be much bad about him if Bandit had befriended him already.

'What's your name?' I asked.

'Liam,' he said, taking a sip from his mug before spooning out the melting mallows. 'Crikey. This isn't like any hot chocolate I've ever had before.'

'Good, isn't it?'

'Amazing,' he said, before looking up and replacing his smile with a frown. 'Are you going to report me to the police?'

'No,' I said. 'I wouldn't have invited you into my house and made you a drink if I was going to do that, would I?'

'Dunno,' he shrugged. 'You did mention them before and, in my experience, adults often send out mixed messages. I don't know where I stand with them half the time.'

There was a whole heap of heartache attached to those

two sentences, and even though my heart went out to him, I wasn't about to delve deeper. The last thing I needed was to get attached to a local waif and stray, even if my instinct was screaming at me to help him.

'Well,' I said, 'you scared me half to death out there Liam and I had to say something to make sure I was getting the truth out of you, didn't I?'

'Did you believe what I said about me just wanting to walk then?'

'Yes,' I said, looking straight at him. 'I did. My dad used to love walking through the trees, at all times of day and night and whatever the weather so I don't consider you as crazy as some people might.'

He gave a huff, which might or might not have been amusement.

'I remember your dad,' he then said with a smile.

'Most people around here do,' I sighed.

'You don't like walking around the place then?' he asked. 'You are Liza Wynter, aren't you?'

'Yes,' I said. 'I am and I haven't had much chance to until now. I've been away for a while.'

'You should try it,' he quietly said, staring into the depths of his mug. 'The sunsets over the reserve are stunning and there's a spot on a mound in the plantation that's amazing for watching the stars.'

I curled my legs up under me.

'You really do know the place well, don't you?'

'I do,' he nodded, turning red, 'but I've never messed

about with anything. I used to come up the drive, but then the bloke who's usually here had that gate and cameras put up so I had to sneak in another way.'

'If you'd asked him,' I said, 'he probably would have been happy for you look around, you know.'

'Doubt it,' he muttered.

'How old are you, Liam?'

'Fifteen,' he told me. 'And I can't wait to leave school and get a job. Not that there's much doing around here, especially if you come from a family like mine.'

I itched to ask what sort of family that was, but didn't.

'In that case,' I said, making the suggestion, which took me completely by surprise, 'how do you fancy working here for a bit?'

I knew Ned probably wouldn't appreciate me taking on another member of staff but Liam clearly loved Wynter's Trees and I could just tell the lad needed a helping hand. From the little he'd said, I could deduce that he had no faith in any of the adults in his life and needed something to focus on if he was going to stay out of trouble.

'There are four Saturdays between now and Christmas,' I calculated, 'and it's going to be busy here, what with shifting the trees and having more shoppers on-site. I can't say exactly what you'll be doing, but we could do with an extra pair of hands, if you fancy it.'

'You're kidding.'

I shook my head.

'I was going to put a sign up in the barn this week,' I

fibbed, so he didn't think I was making him a pity offer. 'But if you take it on, I won't need to. I might even be able to give you a few extra hours in the holidays.'

Liam's expression was transformed.

'How does five pound an hour sound?'

'That's more than the minimum wage for a sixteen year old!'

'I know,' I said, 'and that's because I'll be expecting you to work extra hard. And once you've proved your worth, I might even throw in the occasional Liza Wynter hot chocolate special with your lunch.'

I thought that might be the clincher, but Liam wasn't so sure.

'I'll have to check at home,' he said, sounding suddenly less excited.

'That's all right,' I said. 'I'll talk to your parents if you like.'

'No,' he said, draining his mug. 'Best leave that to me.'

It was starting to drizzle so I drove him back to Wynmouth. He wouldn't let me take him all the way to his house, so I dropped him off on the green.

'And don't worry about transport,' I told him. 'I can pick you up and drop you back if your mum and dad can't run you.'

'Why are you doing this?' he asked, as he unbuckled his seatbelt.

He sounded heartbreakingly suspicious.

'Because Wynter's Trees needs some extra help,' I said.

'You obviously love the place as much as my dad did and that's good enough for me.'

'I'm really sorry about what happened to him,' he kindly said. 'I lost my nan this year. It's tough, isn't it?'

'So tough,' I swallowed.

'I'll ring the office tomorrow,' he said, as he climbed out.

'And I'll see you Saturday,' I called after him.

'But we don't need more help,' Ned objected. 'I don't want more help. What you should have done, Liza, is report the little sod to the police.'

The argument had carried on, right from the moment I'd told Ned what had happened late the evening before and it had completely taken the shine off my cart conversion unveiling the next day. With hindsight, what I should have done was shown him my handiwork before blurting out that I'd recruited a lad who I'd found wandering around the plantation after hours, but it was done now.

'These are amazing,' Ned said, momentarily distracted from our disagreement as he cocked his head and pulled one of the sleighs backwards and forwards.

'I made sure there was decent clearance,' I said, highlighting all the effort I'd gone to, to think of the practicalities as well as the aesthetics. 'And I thought we could maybe take some promo shots with Bandit somehow harnessed up to the front.'

'That's a brilliant idea,' Ned nodded. 'He'll love that.'

'I wonder if he's strong enough to pull a tree,' I pondered, biting my lip.

That would make an even prettier tableau.

'And you know, the little kids love sitting in these,' Ned carried on, the shadow of a smile eradicating his frown. 'They'll be clamouring more than ever for their parents to pull them about the place now.'

I had assumed the carts were used solely for transporting trees, but if children loved them too then that was fine by me. A plump, rosy cheeked two-year-old wearing a padded snowsuit being pulled about in a miniature red sleigh with the family business name emblazoned down the side by a willing husky would make the perfect feel-good festive story.

'In that case,' I wheedled, tracking back to our original conversation, 'maybe our new assistant can make sure everyone lines up and takes it in turns.'

Ned's frown made a sudden reappearance and I regretted bringing Liam up again.

'And he could take over the beach hut tea round,' I hastily added. 'And keep Santa's sack full of toys while Mrs Claus talks to the children before they go in. And he's a tall lad too who loves the trees more than anything. I'm sure a bit of extra muscle and exuberance wouldn't go amiss when you and Maya are busy.'

Ned looked at me and shook his head.

'Maybe,' he said, 'but . . .'

I never found out what he was going to say next because a car screeched up the drive and into one of the parking spaces. The driver then gave three sharp blasts on the horn which had everyone peering out of the huts.

'Oh, you have got to be kidding me,' said Ned, his head dropping.

'What?'

'What's the name of the lad you offered this mythical position to, Liza?'

'Liam,' I shrugged, squinting to see who was behind the car wheel.

'Would that be Liam Chalmers, by any chance?' Ned tutted as he looked towards the new arrivals.

'Hey lady,' shouted Chelsea, through the open car window. 'I want a word with you.'

Chapter 12

It turned out my instincts, honed over years of working with troubled teens, were right. Liam really did have a whole heap of baggage. The biggest bit was Chelsea-not-so-charming-Chalmers. The mere sight of her made me momentarily regret that I'd been hospitable to Liam and spontaneously offered him some work.

'Chelsea,' I said, forcing myself not to turn back into the schoolgirl she had been so adept at intimidating, as she leapt out of her car and slammed the door shut. 'Welcome to Wynter's Trees.'

'You have got to be frigging kidding me!' she growled, shooting me a withering look.

'Hey,' said Liam, who I hadn't noticed was in the passenger seat and was now climbing out. 'I think you should just . . .'

Chelsea spun round.

'Don't you dare tell me to calm down,' she fired at him, sounding livid. 'Not again. So,' she said, whipping back around as she strode through the gate, 'what have you got to say for yourself? What the hell were you playing at inviting my lad in to your home for a hot chocolate and then into your car? I thought you were a teacher. Surely you know that sort of behaviour isn't allowed?'

I took a moment to try and make sense of what was happening and thanked my lucky stars the place wasn't particularly busy. I had wondered last night if I was doing the right thing, but what else could I have done? Sent the lad back over the wet fields, freezing cold and inadequately dressed when he wouldn't let me call his family? And then another thought landed, why had Chelsea just called him, 'my lad'?

'Liam,' said Ned, thankfully not taking the opportunity to add further weight to his argument that I shouldn't have offered Liam a job, 'why don't you let me show you around properly? Liza's been telling me your interview went really well and that you've got the right attitude to help us out here in the run up to Christmas.'

Chelsea looked dumbfounded and I could have kissed Ned, not that that was allowed. He hastily led Liam towards the plantation, leaving Chelsea and I facing each other. I opened my mouth to say something, but her shoulders slumped and I couldn't be sure, but I thought her eyes were full of tears as she dropped her gaze to the ground. I had been going to suggest we talk in the office, but changed my mind.

'Shall we go into the lodge?' I said instead, keen not to draw further attention from anyone in earshot. 'I was just about to make myself a coffee.'

*

Chelsea, although recovered, looked rather out of place in the lodge and when she recoiled from Bandit's friendly advances, I ushered him into the utility room. Liam had readily made friends with my four-legged chum, but I didn't think Chelsea was going to and didn't want to aggravate her again.

'Do you take milk and sugar?' I asked.

'Just milk,' she said. 'I'm sweet enough.'

Even though the remark was classic Chelsea, I could tell there was something more complicated behind the motivation for her visit than raking me over the coals for offering Liam a job and giving him a lift to Wynmouth.

'There you go,' I said, handing her a mug before sitting at the opposite end of the sofa.

She inhaled the strong aroma before placing it down on the side table.

'There really was nothing untoward about last night,' I began, keen to keep Liam out of further trouble, when she didn't say anything. 'I genuinely thought Ned might need some extra help what with the beach huts being here now and . . .'

Chelsea held up a hand, thankfully to stop me, rather than slap me.

'I know that's bullshit,' she calmly said, 'so don't even say it.'

I tried to swallow away the lump in my throat. Was I going to survive this situation with my reputation intact?

'Not the untoward bit,' she amended, soothing some

of my fears, 'but the stuff about offering him a job. There was no job, was there? You caught him here, didn't you? Prowling about the place?'

I didn't know what to say for the best.

'I know he comes here,' she carried on, her tone softening. 'The last time I tackled him about it, he promised me he's never pinched or damaged anything.'

'He wasn't technically doing anything wrong when I found him last night,' I quickly said. 'He was just walking. He told me likes to walk here and that he used to come and visit with his nan.'

Chelsea nodded and laced her fingers together. Her eyes looked bright again.

'Yeah,' she said, her voice thick in her throat. 'They always came together, every December. They never missed a year.'

'You didn't come with them?'

Chelsea tutted. 'I think we both know the answer to that one, don't we, Liza?'

I almost choked on my drink. She only ever called me Elf.

'Yes,' I said, recovering. 'I suppose we do.'

'We lost Mum at the beginning of the year,' she continued.

'I'm so sorry,' I said. 'I know how hard that is.'

She turned to face me and I could see my own sadness reflected right back at me.

'I know you do,' she said, a sob catching, 'and that's been playing on my mind so much recently. I know I didn't show it when you first arrived back, because ... well ... because I'm stupid sometimes, but I am sorry, you know. Now I know what you were going through when you moved here, I hate myself all the more for what I put you through too.'

I never thought I'd see the day when Chelsea Chalmers would apologise to me and as much as I treasured it, I hated the reason behind why she was doing it. I wouldn't wish losing a mum on anyone, whatever their age.

'I appreciate that you've thought that through,' I told her, 'but I don't want you hating yourself for it, Chelsea. Grief is hard enough to cope with and if you throw guilt into the equation too, it's nigh on unbearable.'

I knew that better than anyone given the circumstances surrounding how I'd lost Dad.

'It hurts so much,' she whispered, 'and it's even harder for Liam.'

'From what he told me, I guessed they were close.'

'Oh Liza,' she murmured. 'You don't know the half of it.'

'What do you mean?'

She turned away and picked up her mug. Her hands were shaking as she wrapped her fingers around it before taking a long sip.

'Sorry,' I said. 'I didn't mean to pry.'

'No,' she said, putting the mug down again. 'You're all right. It's just that I didn't come here expecting to say all this today and especially not to you.'

'A heart to heart wasn't what I thought you had in mind when you leapt out of your car, I must admit,' I told her, with a small smile.

I thought she might laugh at that, but instead she took

a deep breath and turned to me again. Her expression was serious, her pencilled brows knitted together and her mouth a thin line. She pressed a cerise painted nail to her temple.

'It's harder for Liam,' she quietly said, 'because he thought my mum was his mum too.'

I took a moment to let that settle.

'I'm not sure I understand.'

'Forget it,' she said, shaking it off.

I wasn't sure I could.

'Now,' she carried on, 'about this job.'

'I know it's weird,' I told her, ignoring her pointed change of direction, 'but you can talk to me, Chelsea. I'm not going to gossip to anyone about you behind your back, you know.'

I had never thought I'd be able to forgive her for what she'd put me through, but she'd lost her mum too and I realised now that she'd had to deal with more than that alone. If I could help her, and Liam, then I would.

'God,' she said, with a flash of her former anger. 'You really are bloody perfect, aren't you?'

'Far from it,' I said, imagining myself standing next to the wonder that was Maya, 'but I am a good listener.'

She wilted again and a few seconds later the words began to flow.

'I had Liam when I was fourteen years old,' she told me. 'Me, him and Mum moved to Wynmouth a year later. Mum raised him as her own and I retook a year at school which is why I'm older than you are.'

I hadn't realised she was.

'I had to repeat year ten and I made a point of picking on you from my very first day because I didn't want anyone to mess with me. You, with your festive obsessed father, were the easiest target and that was why I singled you out.'

I looked at her and blinked, taking a moment to let it all sink in. That certainly explained her earlier actions, which had resembled those of a tigress protecting her cub.

'So, you used me as a smokescreen.' I stated rather than asked. 'By getting our classmates to laugh at me and scrutinise my life, they didn't bother to delve too deeply into yours?'

'Yes,' she said, lowering her eyes. 'That's the gist of it.'

Thinking back, I remembered that my first year at school, before she had arrived, hadn't been all that bad. On a personal level, I'd been in bits, but the academic side of things had been okay. However, Wynter's Trees had been fully operational by the time Chelsea arrived and that was when my school life had taken a nosedive. The few friends I'd made who thought Wynter's Trees was cool, soon changed their minds when Chelsea rocked up.

'Liam only found out the truth after Mum died,' Chelsea said with a shudder. 'For some stupid reason, I got it into my head that telling him would help but it didn't and we've been struggling to make the switch from sibs to mum and son ever since.'

'Bloody hell, Chelsea,' I said, automatically reaching out and squeezing her hand.

She resisted for a moment, but then grasped mine back.

'No one else knows,' she said, before releasing my hand and rifling through her pockets for a tissue. 'We haven't told anyone yet and I think that's why Liam comes here. It's intense, just the two of us at home now and he needs a bit of peace and space.'

'What's going on?'

Our heads snapped up and there was Liam, her son, framed in the doorway.

'Come in, Liam,' I said, beckoning him over.

'Is everything all right?' asked Ned, following Liam inside.

'Yes,' I said, looking at my old adversary. 'Fine. Chelsea and I have just had a catch up and now we're working out the best way to get Liam to and from work, aren't we?'

Liam looked relieved.

'Yes,' she sniffed. 'I'm going to bring him in, in the mornings, and . . .'

'One of us will take him home,' I finished.

'That would be great,' she said, 'because I'll be at work by then.'

'That wouldn't be an issue, would it?' I asked Ned.

'Not at all,' he said. 'And Liam's just told me he's off school all day today because of an inset day.'

'That's right,' said Chelsea. 'Random timing, but that's the headteacher for you.'

'In that case, I was wondering,' said Ned, 'if I could borrow him for a bit? Maya isn't in today and I could do with an extra pair of hands to help with a delivery I have to make in Norwich?'

He explained there were a few trees intended for destinations called Nightingale Square and Prosperous Place which were located in the city centre and as the trees were on the large side, they would take a bit of manoeuvring.

'What do you think, Liam?' Chelsea asked him.

He was practically bouncing up and down at the prospect of starting so soon and Ned threw him one of his waxed jackets to wear over his clothes.

'See you later then,' Liam beamed, as he followed Ned back out again.

'I'll drop him home later,' Ned called over his shoulder before the door closed.

'Crikey,' said Chelsea. 'I can't remember the last time he looked so happy.'

She looked pretty pleased too and with the guys back to work, we talked a little longer and I reassured her that her secret was safe with me. I did, however, warn her that Liam had told me he'd lost his nan, rather than his mum this year.

'Thanks for the heads up,' she said. 'I know it's all going to come out sooner rather than later, but I appreciate that you won't be talking about it. That really means a lot, especially given everything I put you through in the past.'

I looked around the decorated yard, and at the few customers still milling about, as we walked back to her car.

'I can see why I was such an easy target,' I smiled. 'Christmas every day is hardly the norm, is it?'

I was surprised to find that knowing her motives for

singling me out, had somehow made what she'd done a little more bearable. Not a lot, but a bit. Suddenly, it didn't all feel quite so personal.

'No,' she agreed, 'it's not, but that's not the only reason why I picked on you. I was jealous of you too.'

'Jealous?'

'Um,' she said, looking back at the lodge. 'Your life looked pretty perfect from where I was standing. Yes, you'd lost your mum, but you had a dad who loved you and the perfect Christmas every year. I would have loved that.'

I thought back to how surprised Maya had been when I said I considered her perfect and realised that my reaction to hearing Chelsea's words about my own life was similar to Maya's. Disbelieving. Sometimes it was hardest to see the things that were right in front of you for what they were.

'Anyway,' Chelsea said, 'we're not kids anymore, are we? We've moved on, right?'

'Absolutely,' I agreed.

Before long she'd find out exactly how far I was planning to go.

After the success of the trip to Norwich, Liam was a good ten minutes early the next day and raring to go, which was just as well as the gate was barely open before customers started flooding in. Everyone in the vicinity seemed to have Christmas on their minds and as the sky was clear and the sun was shining, it was the perfect weather for shopping outdoors.

With so many families arriving and popping their kids in the carts, I made the most of the opportunity to take some photos of the Wynter's Trees sleighs in action, asking permission from parents first of course, and with Bandit thankfully on his best behaviour, he was more than happy to pose and be petted.

'How's your first day working onsite going?' I asked Liam, who seemed to be everywhere.

'It's brilliant,' he beamed, his cheeks glowing. 'But I can't stop. Ned needs me to help move some trees. I'll see you later.'

He bounded off, resplendent in a Wynter's Trees fleece that Ned had sent him home with the evening before. I don't think I'd ever seen anyone other than Dad wear one with such pride.

'He's going to be worth his weight in gold,' Maya told me, as she walked over and filled the space Liam had left. 'He's literally not stopped all morning.'

'A bit like you then,' I said, taking in her complexion, which was every bit as flushed as Liam's, as she flicked through a file full of papers.

She gave me a wink and headed back to the office and I took a moment to look about me. Everything at Wynter's Trees was running like a well-oiled machine and I felt like a bit of a spare part as I watched it all happening. I knew that should have made me happy. Safe in the knowledge that my future absence wouldn't impact on the place at all, I should have felt satisfied that leaving for good wasn't going to be the cause of any problems for anyone, but just for that moment, I unsettlingly didn't.

After taking a brisk and bracing walk around the reserve, where I startled a handsome Chinese water deer and spotted plenty of pink-footed geese, I slipped back to the lodge, taking Bandit for company. I flicked through the notes I'd been making about my new business, along with the travel brochures, but the lure of the spectacular northern lights didn't inspire me that morning any more than the serenity in the reserve had settled my thoughts.

'Are you busy?' Maya asked, popping her head in just after I'd finished lunch and was loading the dishwasher.

'No,' I said, 'far from it. What's up?'

'Lilith's got a family emergency and is going to have to close up because everyone's too busy in their own huts to help out in hers.'

'I can do it,' I said, readily abandoning the dishes. 'I'll grab a coat.'

I felt it would be good to be doing something, rather than wandering aimlessly about. I had been thinking I'd head to the reserve again, with Dad's binoculars this time, but chatting to customers and keeping busy would probably be better for my unexpected dip in mood. I hadn't had all that much to do with Lilith, but I was certain I could sell at least a few of the stunning wreaths and glorious green garlands she made on her behalf.

'Actually,' said Maya, biting her lip, 'she's asked if I could man her hut, because I've got some experience in making wreaths and she's got a couple of orders that need finishing off. I wondered if you could possibly take my place helping Ned and Liam?'

'Oh,' I said, 'yes, of course. I'm happy to do anything and that sounds like a sensible switch.'

'You're sure?'

'Yes,' I said. 'You go over there now and I'll go and find Ned.'

'He's in the plantation.'

'Right.'

'And you'll need to wrap up,' she advised, 'because it's freezing and you'll need gloves too. We're shifting a lot of trees.'

'Already? It's only November.'

'I know,' she said, backing out again. 'Ned doesn't really like letting cut trees go so early because they'll be past their best by Christmas, but we can't turn business away, can we?'

'I suppose not,' I said, as she disappeared again.

I got suitably togged up and made my way through the busy yard. I could hear a chainsaw at work in the distance and it triggered a plethora of memories. Dad had always insisted on decorating the lodge early, but the tree didn't come inside until the second weekend of December, even though it was well hydrated and in a pot.

It had so much care lavished on it, it must have felt thoroughly spoilt and I hoped the trees I could see Liam feeding through the netting machine received the same level of attention now they were poised to fulfil their festive destiny.

'This netting is completely biodegradable and therefore environmentally friendly,' I listened to him explain to the family who were waiting for their tree. 'Which is of course completely in line with Mr Wynter's original vision for the plantation.'

He looked at me and grinned, before loading the tree back into the sleigh it had been pulled out of the plantation on and checking the receipt the eldest child held up and which confirmed that David, manning the till in the barn, had been paid.

'Merry Christmas,' Liam said, also remembering to hand over the Wynter's Tree care sheet. 'See you next year.'

'You sound like a total pro,' I told him as the family returned his kind words and wandered off. 'I had no idea the netting was eco-friendly.'

'Yep,' he said, patting the machine. 'Ned told me all about it this morning when he trained me on how to use it. Do you know where Maya's got to? She was helping shift the trees and ferrying the left carts back from the car park.'

'She's working in one of the huts now,' I explained. 'So, I'm taking on her jobs.'

'You'd better go and find Ned then,' he said, 'there's probably loads more trees that need moving by now.'

'Yes, sir,' I grinned with a mock salute, before marching off.

More often than not, the people buying the trees liked to pull them out of the plantation themselves, but that wasn't always the case and sure enough there were a couple of people waiting for assistance after I'd followed my ears and found Ned.

'Where's Maya?' he frowned, once he'd turned off the chainsaw.

I told him the same thing I'd explained to Liam and then got to work. Each of the trees had a specific coloured ribbon, based on their variety and size, which the customers gave to David so he knew how much to charge them. The system was a good one and worked well. It didn't take me long to get into my stride and the hours flew by with the tills everywhere ringing all afternoon.

I was making my way back from the car park at the end of the day with a sleigh in each hand and feeling tired and grubby when Liam called me over.

'Are you still working, Liam?' I frowned.

He'd been at it for hours but looked as keen as when he'd started.

'Yes,' he said. 'Ned said I can legally do up to eight hours on a Saturday if I want to.'

I was pleased Ned had checked the legalities involved in hiring a teenager, because that was something I hadn't taken into account at all.

'That's all right then,' I said, breathing hard, 'so what's up? Do you need a comfort break?'

'No,' he said. 'I'm good, but someone has left this in one of the sleighs,' he went on to explain, pulling a wallet, full of notes and cards out of his fleece pocket. 'I didn't see who it was so I haven't been able to track them down.'

I had just taken it from him, noticing that it was an old and slightly battered but still very beautiful Chanel wallet, when a woman came out of the barn and rushed in my direction.

'Oh, you've found it,' she beamed, clasping her hands together.

A much younger man followed her out, weighed down with shopping bags and with a frown etched deep across his forehead.

'It's here, Jamie,' the woman called over her shoulder, sounding relieved. 'I must have left it in this little cart we used to ferry our bags about.'

'For pity's sake,' said the man, identified as Jamie. 'I think you'd better let me take care of it, Mum.'

I handed it to her and she willingly passed it to her son.

'I didn't find it,' I said, keen to give Liam all the credit. 'My young assistant here spotted it and handed it in.'

'Well,' smiled the woman, turning her attention to Liam. 'That was most kind of you, young man.'

Liam nodded, but didn't look particularly impressed by her praise.

'What is it?' she asked him.

'Yes, Liam,' I nudged. 'What's wrong. You did the right thing looking after it until I came along, didn't you?'

'I know that,' he said, looking at Jamie and then down at his boots.

'I know what it is,' Jamie smiled. 'You're thinking your colleague shouldn't have just handed it over, aren't you?'

Liam's eyes snapped up again, but he didn't say anything.

'Of course,' gasped the woman. 'I could be anyone, couldn't I?'

'Well,' said Liam, turning as red as a beetroot. 'It's not very likely that two wallets could go missing in one day, but I think I would have asked you to somehow identify yourself before I handed it over.'

I felt my own cheeks flush.

'You're right, Liam.' I grimaced. 'I should have done that.'

The poor lad looked as though he wanted the ground to open up and swallow him, but he was completely right. This woman looked elegant and sophisticated but it didn't automatically follow that she was the owner of the Chanel wallet.

'Let's start again,' said Jamie, handing Liam the wallet.

'Good idea,' agreed the woman. 'Open it up and pull out a card. You'll see my name on any one of those. It's Catherine Connelly.'

Liam looked reluctant, but acquiesced, pulling out a black Coutts card. He read the name then handed it to me.

'Yes,' I confirmed, 'Catherine Connelly.'

'Sorry,' said Liam, handing me the wallet again.

'Don't you apologise,' said Catherine Connelly. 'You did the right thing.'

'You did, Liam,' I added. 'I should be the one apologising.'

I handed the wallet back and Catherine Connelly immediately opened it and pulled out a crisp twenty-pound note which she thrust into Liam's hand.

'Consider that a finder's fee,' she smiled at him. 'Thank

you for keeping my wallet safe. My husband gave it to me many Christmases ago and I would have been devastated to lose it.'

Personally, I would have been pretty upset about the lost cash too.

'Which is why I'm going to carry it,' said Jamie, tucking it into a pocket on the inside of his jacket.

'We've had a wonderful day,' said Catherine Connelly as she and her son drifted away. 'This place is charming. Utterly charming.'

Liam looked from his hand to me and back again.

'Thank you!' he called after them and they turned and waved.

'Well done, Liam,' I grinned. I still felt a bit of a fool, but praise where praise was due. 'What an absolutely fabulous way to end your day.'

Chapter 13

During the next few days, life at Wynter's Trees settled into a routine which I found rather comforting. Having spent practically my entire life in an educational environment in one capacity or another – first as a student and then as staff – my days and months were bound by the academic calendar and without the rigidity of it, I had felt a little adrift. At least that was in part what I put the unsettled feelings down to.

However, even with the new routine, I still had plenty of time for introspection and couldn't help mulling over what Chelsea had confided in me along with how her traumatic teenage years had impacted on mine.

I considered how if she and her family hadn't moved to Wynmouth then my life might have taken an entirely different course. Without Chelsea's persistent taunting, once the business was further established and I had come to terms with Mum's loss and accepted Dad's decision to move us, I might well have fallen in love with Wynter's Trees.

Without Chelsea's influence, the few friends I'd made

might have carried on admiring my unusual homelife, rather than turning it into the butt of their jokes. And that, in turn, might have meant I would have been happy to join Dad in the business and he would never have made that catastrophic final trip to visit me.

As pleased as I was that I was able to help her son, I was in danger of blaming Chelsea for Dad's crash and that was not a good place for my head to be. I knew I had to pull back from the self-destructive brink and when I woke on the first of December, I resolved to do my utmost to set Chelsea's revelations, along with the impact they may or may not have had on my life, aside.

'Good morning,' said Ned, when I joined him downstairs and found him cooking bacon and brewing coffee. 'Can I tempt you to a coffee and a bite of breakfast?'

'A coffee would be great,' I said, lingering longer than perhaps I usually would to fuss Bandit. 'Thanks.'

'I've grilled enough bacon for us both,' Ned told me.

'It's a bit early for me,' I responded.

'That's as maybe,' he smiled, looking a little sheepish, 'but I've got a packed day planned and you'll need some sustenance to keep you going.'

'Oh,' I said, stifling a yawn.

I supposed keeping busy could only help strengthen my resolve to keep my darker thoughts in check.

'What's on the work itinerary for today then?' I asked.

Ned sliced a roll, filled it with bacon, set in on a plate and held it out.

'Well,' he said, 'what I have in mind doesn't have any-thing to do with work.'

'I see,' I said, accepting the plate. 'What does it have to do with then?'

He focused on shaking the sauce bottle before adding a large dollop of ketchup to his own roll. I shuddered at the sight.

'What?' he smiled. 'It's perfectly healthy. This is locally made and so full of tomatoes, it practically counts as one of my five a day.'

'I'll take your word for it,' I tutted.

Ketchup was all right on chips, but in my opinion, abso-lutely nothing, other than a little butter, was required to embellish a decent bacon roll.

'You were saying,' I reminded Ned, just as he took the biggest bite and covered his fingers in ketchup.

'Well,' he chewed, tearing off a sheet of kitchen towel. 'There's no getting away from the date, is there? And I for one, wouldn't want to.'

I felt my face flush and put my roll back on the plate.

'The date?'

'The first of December,' he clarified.

He reached down the side of the counter and pulled out two large envelopes. He kept one for himself and handed the other to me.

'What's this?' I asked.

'Open it.'

I carefully slit open the top and pulled out an advent

calendar. It was a proper old fashioned one, covered in glitter and featuring Santa, jolly and rotund, flying through the star-studded night sky in his sleigh pulled by eight trusty reindeer. They were soaring over a village of snow-enhanced cottages and towards a very full moon.

'It's lovely,' I said, feeling rather choked.

'And I got one for me too,' Ned beamed, opening his and turning it for me to see.

His featured a snowy woodland scene and a variety of wild creatures and birds, including rabbits, foxes, badgers, robins and owls. It was very Matthew Rice.

'They're both lovely,' I told him, feeling relieved that he had flagged the date because it was the start of advent calendar season rather than anything else.

'I wasn't sure which one you'd like,' he frowned.

I wondered if he'd got one for Maya too. The pair were spending more hours together than ever, but whether the extra time in the office and out in the plantation was professional or private, I couldn't be sure. I was just gearing up to gently enquire but didn't get the chance.

'And of course,' Ned tentatively said, 'December the first isn't just about advent calendars, is it?'

I stared at mine, willing him to stop.

'It was also your dad's birthday, wasn't it?' he carried on, 'and the start of the festive season, as far as he was concerned.'

'Yes,' I said, clearing my throat. 'Yes, it was.'

'And with that in mind,' Ned continued, having gained

confidence from my succinct confirmation, 'I thought we could make a start decorating the lodge today and I have something else planned too.'

'If it's all the same,' I said, pushing my untouched plate away and sliding off the stool. 'I'd rather not.'

'But it's all sorted.' He beamed looking every bit as excited as Dad did when his birthday dawned. 'I thought we could hang the paper decorations and pin up the lights. I know it's too early for greenery and the tree, but we could do the rest. My dad said that's what you always used to do.'

'Ned . . .'

'Dad's shown me photos of how the lodge used to look, so we can replicate what you had before or create something completely new. It's entirely up to you.'

Considering it was 'entirely up to me' he should have stopped pushing when I said I didn't want to do it.

'We're supposed to be making this Christmas a good one, remember?' he added.

As unwilling as I was to accept it, he did have a point. I had previously said that I'd make this Christmas memorable and as it was the last December the first I was going to be spending at Wynter's Trees, I supposed I should make the effort to make it count.

'All right,' I said, taking back the plate. 'We'll do it. Though I'll eat this first and then we'll get the boxes out of the loft.'

'You don't have to worry about that,' he said, looking like

the cat who'd got the cream as he pinned our calendars side by side on the kitchen pinboard. 'I got the boxes out last night. They're in the utility room.'

The wave of nostalgia and plethora of memories which hit me as we unpacked the boxes was almost overwhelming. I hadn't spent a Christmas at Wynter's Trees in a very long time, and the boxes hadn't been touched since someone, David I guessed, and perhaps Sue, had packed them away after Dad's funeral.

I hadn't stayed long enough to do anything that day. I hadn't even come back to the lodge after the service. I had arrived at the church just a few minutes before the hearse and left swiftly after the formalities at the graveside. However, even though some of the memories associated with the decorations Ned and I carefully unpacked were painful, unwrapping the treasures felt like meeting old and long forgotten friends too.

'Did you make this?' he grinned, holding up a rather battered angel.

Fashioned from a loo roll tube, pipe cleaners, glitter, and paper doilies, my reception class effort looked a little rough around the edges, but at well over two decades old, that was hardly surprising.

'I did,' I proudly said.

'Wow,' said Ned, reverently setting her, or him, I couldn't remember, to one side. 'Your artistic talents shone through from an early age, didn't they?'

'Ever so,' I laughed. 'Anyway,' I added, 'you're not

supposed to be looking through those boxes. They're all for the tree. These are the ones we want.'

We pushed the tree decoration cartons aside and dived into the others. There was plenty to choose from and Ned reminded me that the lights for the veranda along with the deer family figures I had talked Dad into buying in lieu of real, live reindeer, were all stored in the barn.

'Can we sort those on Monday when we're closed?' I asked. 'If visitors see things being set up, it sort of takes away some of the magic, doesn't it?'

'Spoken like a true Wynter,' Ned laughed.

I didn't comment, but threw a pine cone, which had somehow made its way into one of the boxes, at him instead.

'Ow,' he winced, as it bounced off his head.

'Sorry,' I grinned, failing to stifle a giggle.

'Yeah,' he said, rubbing the spot where it had made contact, 'you sound it.'

He threw the cone back and I caught it, noting the mischievous look in his eye. I imagined a game of back and forth, a playful tussle, lingering eye contact, a breathless sigh and then . . .

'I've no idea how this got in here,' I briskly said, setting the cone to one side. 'Dad always insisted that anything borrowed from nature, should be returned to nature.'

Then I remembered, David and Sue wouldn't have necessarily known that. I daresay they had hastily packed everything away and returned it all to the loft. It must have been a dreadful and depressing task. I couldn't have faced it and felt guilty that I'd left it to them.

'There's some more here,' commented Ned. 'But don't worry, we can take them to the plantation later. I've got an outdoor activity planned for this afternoon.'

'In that case,' I said, checking the time as well as my darkening thoughts, 'we'd better get a move on.'

Within a couple of hours, the lodge was transformed. I had taken onboard what Ned had said about creating something new and rather than try and replicate what Dad favoured, I'd put my own stylish spin on things.

There were certainly enough decorations to create a whole new design. If fact, looking at what was left, there was enough to have at least a five-year rotation. I'd settled on a green and white aesthetic and with the warmth of the wood which the lodge was built from and the clear lights, it made for a striking combination.

'That's the last of them,' said Ned, as he climbed down from the ladder.

He'd been up and down more times than I cared to count since we'd started pinning up the garlands, but the effect was worth his exertions.

'Perfect,' I said, standing back and taking the space in.

The strands of lights were all warm white and the elaborate white garlands featured snowflakes, stars and intricate patterns. It was the kind of pared back colouring I knew Mum would have favoured over Dad's kitsch and gaudy combinations.

'It's certainly different,' said Ned.

'The green will come in when we've got the tree and the holly, ivy and . . .'

'Mistletoe,' Ned smiled, quirking an eyebrow.

'Yes,' I said, 'there might be room for that too.' Then added, 'we'll have to get Maya on the case.'

I had been dropping her into the conversation all morning, but Ned hadn't confessed how much he liked her. That said, the mention of mistletoe had sparked more of a reaction.

'Yes,' he smiled, shaking his head, 'she's the queen of that.'

Now her name had received a more positive response, I wished it hadn't, especially given what it was associated with.

'Although we'll have to be careful because the berries are poisonous,' I swiftly said. 'We'll have to keep it out of Bandit's reach.'

'That's a good point,' frowned Ned.

'Perhaps I'll order some artificial stuff online,' I suggested. 'I suppose we could fake it, couldn't we? It's not as if the stuff in here needs to be authentic because we won't be putting it to its ancient Greek purpose.'

'Ancient Greek purpose?' Ned queried.

'Yes,' I said, 'it was used during Saturnalia and later in wedding ceremonies because of its associations with fertility. It's been used for reconciliation purposes too.'

'Well,' grinned Ned. 'You never know . . .'

'It must be time for a drink,' I interrupted. 'Do you fancy a hot chocolate?'

With a mug of velvet smooth chocolate each, we toasted the lodge and Dad's birthday. I thought about what he would have made of my choice of decorations. Privately, I knew he would have considered them too refined, but outwardly he would have been delighted I'd put them up. He would have been ecstatic to see me finally embracing Christmas at Wynter's Trees.

'Are you all right?' Ned asked, as an unchecked tear rolled down my cheek.

'Yes,' I said, quickly wiping it away. 'Thanks for this, Ned. It was kind of you to take today off and make it special.'

'It isn't finished yet,' he reminded me. 'You know how much I want to make your time here memorable so there's something else too. And I do appreciate how much courage it has taken for you to finally come back.'

'It has taken a lot,' I agreed. 'But I'm pleased I've done it.'

'You are?'

'Yes,' I said, looking around again, 'I am. I know I could have asked you to buy my shares in a letter, email or even on Zoom, but your dad was right. It has been important for me to come back. It's been good getting to know you, Ned. There's no doubt in my mind that you're the right person to take over.' I added, wanting to reiterate that even though I'd helped decorate the lodge this year I wouldn't be around to do it again.

Ned didn't look as pleased to hear my vote of confidence as I hoped he would.

'He's asked me not to say anything,' he quietly said, his

words explaining his expression, 'but Dad's still shocked by your decision.'

I'd guessed as much. I wondered if he was still feeling that way too.

'I know,' I nodded. 'But I need to move on . . .'

I was about to ask if he'd had any success trying to raise the funds to buy my shares but was interrupted by a knock on the door.

'I'm sorry to bother you, Ned,' said Maya, as Ned beckoned her inside. Her eyes widened as she took in the decorations. 'But there's a chap on the phone asking for you. I can't make head nor tail of what he's talking about. Something about schools and for . . .'

'Tell him I'll be right there,' said Ned, cutting her off and thrusting his mug into my hands. 'I'll be back in a sec, Liza. Don't shift any of those boxes without me.'

Ned was actually gone for ages, but I didn't mind because I needed a little time to myself. Although enjoyable, certain moments throughout the morning had been intense. I had loved decorating the lodge, but the emotion of unpacking the decorations and the significance of the date, blended with the potentially playful moments with Ned and his admittance of David's continued shock regarding my decision to sell, had made for a heady mix.

'Right,' Ned puffed, sounding out of breath as he rushed back in just as I finished tidying away the boxes. 'Hey, I said to leave those.'

'I've only dragged them into the utility room,' I pointed out. 'As you'd said you'd got more lined up for today, I didn't want to waste time.'

'That's fair enough,' he said. 'Come on then. Grab your wellies.'

'What now?' I asked. 'I was just about to make some lunch.'

Ned looked at the clock and shrugged off his coat.

'I hadn't realised it was so late,' he tutted, then spotting the waffle maker added, 'but I suppose I could go for a bite of something.'

'You're very food driven,' I laughed. 'I'm surprised you're in such good shape.'

He ran a hand over his stomach which, courtesy of the day I arrived, I knew was perfectly smooth and toned.

'Well, I'm a busy guy,' he mischievously grinned. 'And I know lots of ways to burn off calories.'

'I bet you do,' I smiled back, unable to stave off both a laugh and the flames of desire I'd been trying to tamp down.

With our appetites eventually sated – it had taken a few attempts to get the hang of making waffles – and wrapped in multiple layers, Ned and I made our way, with Bandit on our heels, across the yard. The beach huts weren't particularly busy, but everyone was occupied so our progress towards the plantation wasn't interrupted.

'I hope you don't mind that I've gone ahead and made a start,' Ned said as I gasped at the sight of the Wynter's family tree nestled in the back of the truck, 'but it felt like today would be the perfect opportunity.'

'Of course,' I nodded. 'The timing couldn't be better.'

Having just about managed to keep my emotions in check while we decorated the lodge, I wondered if planting out the tree would be my undoing.

'It was far too big to put in one of the carts.' Ned smiled, with a nod at the tree before correcting himself. 'Sorry, I mean, sleighs.'

I climbed into the passenger seat and Bandit scrambled to push his way between my feet in the footwell. It only took a couple of minutes to reach the site I had picked out and which Ned had already had his eye on and, as the plantation had been roped off to stop anyone entering without David accompanying them, we were undisturbed.

'I can see you've prepped the site,' I said, nodding at the large hole which was already dug. 'Or was that Bandit's part in all this?'

Ned rolled his eyes and Bandit licked my chin before we climbed out of the cab.

There was a robin hopping in and out of the hole, no doubt looking for a tasty snack. It cocked its head as I walked to the reserve boundary and tipped out the bag of cones, I'd gathered from the decoration boxes.

'I knew it would take a while to dig out,' Ned told me as I pushed the empty bag into my coat pocket. 'So, I thought I'd get it ready. All we have to do now is the planting.'

He made it sound simple, but it wasn't the easiest of tasks. Fortunately, he had taken the time to wrap the lower branches so we didn't get too scratched as we manoeuvred it down the ramp and over to the planting hole.

'Crikey,' I puffed, as we pushed and pulled and Ned began cutting through the pot, while the robin scolded us for disturbing its foraging. 'I hope I haven't given you a hernia for Christmas.'

'Me too,' Ned laughed. 'I'd like to find something far less painful in my stocking from you than that.'

My face flushed because my mind had instantly conjured an image which involved completely different hosiery and such thoughts were far from appropriate given the signifi-cance of the occasion.

'I hate wasting the pot,' Ned grimaced as he struggled to free the root ball, 'but there's no other way of getting this brute out.'

'That's my fault,' I said, feeling bad. 'I shouldn't have forgotten about it.'

With another huge tug and with Bandit barking excitedly and skipping around us, the tree was liberated and Ned and I fell backwards on to the ground.

'Stupid dog,' said Ned, as Bandit jumped on him and began licking his face.

He pushed him off, scrambled to his feet and offering me a hand, pulled me up too.

'Right,' I said, brushing myself down, 'let's get planting.'

We took our time, making sure we checked the depth, then back filled the hole, before soaking the ground and adding a thick layer of organic mulch. I wouldn't have minded taking all week, if it meant the tree would survive.

'It will be all right, won't it?' I asked. 'It won't be too much of a shock because we've done this in winter instead of spring?'

'To be honest,' said Ned. 'I'm not going to make any promises, but the time of year isn't that big a deal. The site isn't frozen or waterlogged and I'm going to keep a close eye on it, so it's got the best possible chance of settling in.'

'I appreciate that,' I told him. 'And it certainly couldn't have stayed in the pot any longer. At least now, it's got a shot.'

I took a few steps back and felt my breath catch in my throat. Just as I'd imagined, it was the perfect position. With the landscape of the reserve opening up beyond it and the wide Norfolk sky overhead, it was a spot fit for a very special tree, which was exactly what it was.

The agitated robin was calmer now and already flitting about the branches. What was it that Mum had always said? *Robins appear when loved ones are near.* I wondered if she and Dad were looking down and watching me and Ned.

'Are you all right?' he asked for the second time that day as he came to stand beside me and put a comforting arm around my shoulders.

'Yes,' I whispered. 'I'm okay.'

I stroked Bandit's soft head and he flopped down by my feet, clearly exhausted from the excitement and exertion he had put into helping.

'Good,' said Ned, giving me a squeeze before gathering

the tools together and brushing them off, 'because we're not done yet.'

The light was beginning to fade as he pulled a thick rug and insulated bag out of the back of the truck.

'I hope you're not too cold,' he frowned, 'because I haven't got anything to drink that will warm us up.'

'What have you got then?' I asked, pulling the waterproof backed rug out from under his arm and spreading it out on the ground.

'Champagne,' he announced with a flourish as he pulled out two melamine flutes.

'Champagne!' I laughed.

'Of course,' he said, sitting down to reveal the bottle of fizz.

'That's extravagant, isn't it?'

'A little,' he said, as I sat beside him. 'But then this is a special occasion, isn't it? This tree deserves a toast, as does your dad's birthday.'

We'd already wished Dad a happy birthday with the hot chocolate but I was happy to go again. Ned popped the cork and pocketed it, before filling both flutes almost to the top.

'Cheers,' he said, tapping his drink against mine. 'And welcome home. For however long you're going to be here.'

'Cheers,' I said, my eyes resting on the tree. 'And don't you drink too much of this, not after what happened last time.'

Ned didn't respond and when I looked at him, I saw his cheeks were as rosy as mine had been earlier.

'I don't want to have to listen to you singing again,' I hastily added. 'That would completely ruin what's been a wonderful day.'

Chapter 14

I didn't know whether it was the surfeit of champagne, a reaction to the day's events, the date or a combination of all three, but by the time the bottle was empty, I was feeling tipsy, tired and even more emotional than I had been earlier. Ned and I lay side by side on the rug with Bandit draped over us, a most welcome insulating layer, and watched as the sky slipped from dusky to dark and the stars began to shine.

It wasn't the first time I'd laid in that spot, but with Ned it felt completely different. Or perhaps that was the fizz befuddling my brain. My head swam with thoughts of Dad and I wished, for what must have been the millionth time, that the outcome of his last visit to see me had been different.

'I suppose we should be getting back,' Ned eventually said.

'Mmm,' I agreed. 'You're probably right.'

I had no idea how long we'd been laying there and sat up slowly, making sure I kept still until the world stopped spinning. Between us we packed the things back into the truck and then took one last look at the tree.

'Don't worry,' Ned reassured me. 'I'll keep an eye on it.'

'I know you will,' I huskily said.

The sight of it, silhouetted against the star-filled night sky, caused another burst of emotion to bloom.

'I just wish Dad was here to see it,' I whispered, my breath streaming out and away in the chill crisp air.

Ned didn't say anything.

'I'll never forgive myself for what happened to him, you know,' I carried on, my usually guarded thoughts weakened by the impact of the champagne. 'If I could just turn back the clock ...'

My throat felt tight as I bit back the avalanche of words backing up in my brain. I wasn't drunk enough to forget that if I said them, I'd never be able to take them back. However, that didn't stop a strangled sob escaping my lips.

'Hey,' said Ned, wrapping his arms around me and pulling me close. 'You can't blame yourself, Liza.' I shook my head, his kindness further weakening my defences. 'None of what happened that night was your fault. It was just ...'

'It was,' I loudly said, the last guard crumbling as I put my hands on his chest and pushed him away. 'It's my fault he's dead.'

I stumbled back, catching sight of Ned's shocked expression.

'He wasn't supposed to be with me,' I sobbed, as a river of tears coursed down my cheeks, stinging as they mingled with the frosty air. 'He just turned up.'

'At your flat?'

'Yes,' I snapped. 'At mine.'

'I didn't know that,' said Ned.

'No one does,' I cut in. 'I've never told anyone because I knew they'd blame me . . .'

I cut the words off, turned away and blindly ran. I sprinted away from the tree, away from Bandit and away from Ned. Had it been possible, I would have run to the furthest edges of the world.

The track was rough and uneven, completely unsuitable for stumbling along in the dark and totally non-negotiable after drinking half a bottle of champagne. I'd barely covered any ground before my foot caught and I fell, jarring my ankle, tearing my jeans and grazing my cheek as I swiped something before landing heavily on the cold, hard earth.

'Liza!' shouted Ned, as Bandit flung himself down by my side. He whined in distress. As did I.

Then Ned was there, checking my bruised and battered body for breaks, before scooping me up and carrying me back to the lodge. I was grateful that everyone had long since left and no one was there to witness my stupidity.

Ned set me gently down on the sofa, pulled off his coat and caught his breath. I turned my face away, too mortified to face him. I heard him moving about in the kitchen and when I put my trembling hand up to my cheek it came away crimson with blood. The sight of it made me feel nauseous as well as stupid.

'I'm going to call Dad and get him to take us to the hospital,' said Ned. 'I can't drive because I've had a drink.'

I turned to look at him. The action made me feel dizzy but that was probably the result of the champagne rather than the impact of the fall.

'No,' I said. 'There's no need.'

Ned didn't look convinced.

'I didn't hit my head.' I told him. 'This is just a graze. A scratch from something I caught on the way down.'

'I want to be certain,' he firmly said.

'Please, Ned,' I begged. 'Don't. I was an idiot to run off like that, but it's my pride that's more wounded than anything else. This is just a scrape and a twisted ankle. Nothing more. I don't need to go to hospital and waste everyone's time.'

He shook his head.

'I honestly didn't hit my head,' I said again. 'I didn't lose consciousness, did I? I can easily clean these scratches myself and wrap a bag of frozen peas around my ankle.'

'No,' he resignedly said. 'You can't. But I can.'

While he fetched the first aid kit from the utility room, I wriggled out of my jeans and covered my legs with the throw from the sofa. It would have been pointless to clean my scraped knees and then pull the soiled fabric over them. I was able to put a little weight on my ankle, but not much.

'This might sting a bit,' said Ned, as he tenderly dabbed at the graze on my cheek.

I rested my head back and closed my eyes.

'You know,' he softly said, 'you might feel better if you finished saying what it was you started out there.'

His voice sounded close and when I opened my eyes his face was just inches from mine.

'I don't think so.' I swallowed, closing my eyes again.

He was quiet, but only for a moment.

'It's something you've carried with you for years, isn't it?'

I didn't answer.

'I bet it's nowhere as terrible as you think it is.'

'You're wrong,' I whispered.

'Why don't you let me be the judge of that?' he pushed.

'All right,' I gruffly said, pushing his hand away and hoisting myself into a more upright position. 'How about,' I said, looking straight at him, 'it's my fault that my dad died?'

My eyes filled with tears and I stared up at the ceiling, trying to force them back.

'You weren't the drunk driver . . .'

'No,' I cut in, 'but I was the daughter who argued with him, before he stormed off. Had I forced him to stay he wouldn't have been on the road, would he?'

Ned didn't say anything.

'So,' I said, 'now you know. Now you know, I'm responsible for what happened. I'm responsible for all of it.'

'No,' said Ned. 'You're not.'

'He wasn't even supposed to be at mine that weekend,' I carried on, ignoring what he'd said. 'I'd mentioned I was having a tough time at work when we talked on the phone and he just turned up.'

'To make sure you were okay?'

'To see if he could convince me to come home,' I blurted out. 'Again.'

'Here, to Wynter's you mean?'

'Yes,' I nodded. 'He never got it into his head, that I didn't think of this place as home and when I said as much, for the umpteenth time, we argued and he left.'

'I didn't know he'd seen you that night,' Ned frowned. 'What with the crash happening so close to Wynmouth . . .'

'I should never have let him leave,' I cut in. 'I was so angry. I'd told him that Wynter's Trees was *his* cure all, not mine. The last words we'd had were cross ones.'

Ned leant forward and dabbed my cheek again.

'Does my dad know about this?'

'No,' I said. 'I've never told anyone.'

'You should have told him,' Ned softly said. 'There's no way he would have kept asking you to come back if he knew what was really keeping you away.'

'How could I have told him this?' I whispered. 'He would have hated me.'

'He wouldn't,' said Ned, reaching for my hand. 'He would have helped you.'

I snatched mine away.

'I don't deserve help,' I bit back. 'I deserve to feel the guilt that's pressed down on me every hour since it happened.'

'No,' Ned firmly said. 'You don't.'

'I let him leave,' I reminded him. 'I let Dad leave after an argument and now I'll never get the chance to make my peace with him.'

'But that still doesn't make you responsible for what happened.'

'Doesn't it?' I scowled.

'No,' said Ned. 'God no. Your dad could have been on that stretch of road at that time for any number of reasons.'

'But had I not let him leave, he wouldn't have been.'

Ned bit his lip.

'You see,' I choked. 'It is my fault.'

'Did you ask him to go?' Ned asked, changing tack. 'Did you kick him out of your flat and slam the door behind him?'

'No,' I gasped, shocked at the suggestion. 'Of course not. I begged him to stay.'

'So, your dad left of his own free will and against yours? You didn't let him go, as you put it. He left, didn't he?'

'Well, yes,' I said, 'but . . .'

'Liza, look at me. You can't keep blaming yourself for the decision your father made to leave that night. Other people's choices are *exactly* that. Their choices. Not yours or mine or anyone else's. We're only responsible for our own actions and our own decisions.'

I thought about what he had said as he turned his attention to the cut on my knee. Dad *had* left of his own free will. I had begged him to stay, I had wanted to clear the air about Wynter's Trees once and for all, but he'd refused to listen. He refused to let me explain that while the place was his sanctuary, it wasn't mine and that I'd get through the difficult time at work and carry on.

Heidi Swain

'You need to let this go,' Ned seriously said, as he gently blew on the graze, 'otherwise you'll never have a happy life. It absolutely isn't your fault that your dad died and it's not your fault that Wynter's isn't the right fit for you either. From what Dad's recently told me, this place was thrust upon you during a very difficult time. It's no wonder you never fell in love with it.'

But I might have done. Eventually. Had Chelsea not poisoned it. Too late now. I closed my eyes and my mind flicked over, through and around my muddled thoughts. Was it time to let it all go? Not just my attachment to Wynter's Trees, but my guilt too. Ned had said my life wouldn't be happy all the time I hung on to it and that thought terrified me. I was planning a brand-new life, a new business and an exciting adventure, but what would be the point of any it, if I was never going to be happy? If I wasn't free?

Ned *was* right. It *was* time to let it all go. Even my desire for him.

'Liza?'

My eyes fluttered open again.

'Are you sure you didn't hit your head?' he asked, his eyes raking across my face before looking deep into my eyes.

'One hundred per cent,' I said, moistening my lips.

His gaze flicked to my mouth.

'You aren't feeling dizzy?' he throatily asked. 'Your vision isn't blurred, is it?'

'No,' I said, lifting my head and pressing my lips to his.

It was a soft kiss. Sweet and tender and it felt perfect. He began to kiss me back but I gently drew away.

'My vision is completely fine,' I told him. 'Thank you, Ned. I can see everything clearly now.'

Chapter 15

Without a word, Ned kindly fetched my PJs and helped me up to bed. I slept all the sweeter for that conclusive, soft lipped kiss and I would have laid late too, had he not woken me before he took Bandit for his run early the next morning.

I think he was still worried I might have been concussed and the look he gave me and the tender words he uttered, suggested that he might also have been thinking that the kiss I had bestowed upon him meant something.

It had meant something, but a different thing for me than him. For me it marked the end of my romantic feelings for him. Yes, I still fancied the pants off him and yes, he was a truly great guy, but if I was going to properly move my life forward, then hanging on to my feelings for him, the man I had already set up with another woman and who was in charge of the place I was going to great efforts to free myself from, would have been entirely counterproductive.

What I needed was a completely clean break and I hoped that if I didn't mention the kiss, or unguardedly throw him a lustful look, then Ned would soon work out that my post-tumble actions were purely the result of the emotional outpouring and the reaction of going backside over boobs. Therefore, launching straight into the spirit of the thing, before he and Bandit headed off, I sped the process along.

'I'm pretty certain I didn't hit my head in that tumble,' I said, rubbing my slightly swollen cheek, 'but I can't remember much about what happened after it.'

Ned, framed in the bedroom doorway, looked concerned.

'Well,' he began, 'you told me something . . .'

'Oh,' I said, glancing down at the duvet, 'I remember that.'

'Good,' he said, burying his hands in his hoodie pocket. 'I'm pleased about that, because I was hoping that talking it through might have helped. I really hope it's helped you come to terms with a few things, Liza.'

Baring my soul and explaining the guilt I'd been carrying for the last four years had been every bit as cathartic as he had suggested it would be. That had been a total, but very pleasant, and potentially life-changing, surprise.

'It did,' I told him. 'It has.'

'Good.'

'But after that,' I said, looking back at him and purposefully sounding vague.

'You can't remember anything?'

'No,' I shrugged. 'Nothing. I didn't do anything embarrassing, did I?'

'Of course not.'

Was it my imagination, or did he sound disappointed?

'But I am sorry about how yesterday turned out,' he carried on. 'I had hoped it would be a great day. I wanted it to be really special.'

'It was,' I firmly said, determined to let him know that his efforts had been worth it. The day had marked a very real turning point and I would be forever grateful for that. 'Aside from my stupid cross-country antics, it was absolutely perfect. A most fitting tribute to my dad and to everything Wynter's Trees represents.'

It really had been a wonderful mix of family tradition, seasonal activity and nostalgia and even though the way it ended had been draining, the epiphany more than justified the injured ankle and subsequent outpouring.

'That's all right then,' Ned smiled, his brow clearing. 'That's what I had been aiming for. Do you think you can manage to get downstairs on your own?'

'Yes,' I said, 'I don't think I'll have a problem.'

He unhooked my dressing gown from the back of the door and laid it on the bed.

'I'll get on then,' he said. 'I need to pop to Wynmouth later. Do you want anything picking up while I'm there?'

'I don't think so,' I said, 'but a lift would be great. I'm pretty certain I'm not going to be able to drive today and there's something I would like to do.'

Later that day, Ned dropped me at the church gate, having made sure I could hobble unaided. The sprain thankfully wasn't anywhere near as bad as it might have been and I slowly made my way to roughly where I remembered Dad had been buried. It all looked rather different because of the additional graves and I felt ashamed that I hadn't visited sooner. I felt another emotion when I spotted Dad's plot too. It hit me right in the stomach and took my breath away.

'My goodness,' I gasped, as I looked at the many festive trinkets and decorations which fittingly embellished his final resting place.

I knew some churchyards didn't allow for any kind of adornment because it made it difficult for the person responsible for cutting the grass, but that clearly wasn't the case in the churchyard in Wynmouth.

Unable to sit on the ground, I carefully lowered myself on to the bench closest. I noticed it had a brass plaque dedicated to Dad screwed on the back. I ran my fingers over the engraving. It had been made from a tree which had fallen in the reserve during a winter storm a couple of years ago and commissioned by the local community as a thank you for saving the land. The memory of Dad amongst the local community was bound up with so much more than just the twelve days of Christmas I realised. He might have been long gone, but his unique and lasting legacies were not forgotten.

Mum had instilled in me her love of nature and the changing seasons and I wondered if that was some of the reason behind why Dad had fought so hard to save the reserve site. I had accused him many, many times of leaving Mum behind when he moved us south, but this bench brought home to me that I was wrong. Just like he was now, Mum too was gone, but she hadn't been forgotten.

'So ...' I said, my breath catching as the chill breeze whipped around me.

On the journey into the village, I had thought about what I was going to say but now the words wouldn't come. It was freezing cold and I knew Ned would soon be waiting so, rather than say the words out loud, I ran through them in my head.

I apologised for not coming sooner, shared the weight and depth of the guilt I had carried and explained what I was going to do next with my life. I told Dad how I had struck upon a business idea of my own, one that combined my love of nature and art with my desire to help struggling students, and how I was going to fund it.

'Ned,' I said, finally finding my voice, 'is the perfect person to carry on running Wynter's Trees. He's a chip off David's block and even more full of ideas than you were, Dad.'

I carefully stood up again, taking care not to put too much weight on my injured ankle.

'Oh,' I added, 'and I'm going to see the northern lights.' My mind had suddenly settled on that as the trip I was going to take. 'I know you always wanted to go, Dad, so I'll go for both of us. I know we'll have a great time.'

I spotted Ned pull up at the gate and waved.

'I really am sorry I haven't been before,' I said, a lump forming in my throat. 'And I'll always be sorry that Wynter's

Trees wasn't for me, but I know I'm doing the right thing in handing it on to someone who loves it as much as you did. I hope you can be happy about that, Dad. I love you.'

I felt utterly exhausted, but as I hobbled back to the truck, I knew I had been purged of my guilt. It had been a long time coming and if it hadn't been for Ned, I'd still be dragging the weight of it around with me, like Marley and his chain in *A Christmas Carol*.

'All right?' asked Ned, solicitously hopping out to open the passenger door.

'You know,' I said, feeling light of heart as I leant on his arm so I could climb in. 'I really am.'

He looked surprised. I daresay he had been braced for tears. I know I had, but they hadn't come.

'Well, that's great,' he said, sounding relieved. 'Really great.'

'It is,' I told him, with a smile. 'I feel ready for anything now.'

I was raring to go the next morning and ready to face another busy weekend at Wynter's Trees. I was still pretty immobile, but I didn't let that dampen my spirits. Thanks to my heart to heart with Ned and my long overdue visit to Dad's grave, I felt transformed and determined to make the most of the rest of my time in Wynmouth.

'Good morning,' I beamed at David and Ned who were in the office even earlier than usual. 'It's freezing out there, but it's going to be a glorious day.'

The pair looked at each other and exchanged smiles.

'Someone's in a good mood,' laughed David. 'Even though she looks like she's gone a few rounds with Joe Bugner.'

'Joe who?' I frowned, wincing as the action made my bruised and cut cheek throb.

'He was a boxer in the seventies,' explained Ned.

'Oh right.'

'I reckon it's the max strength painkillers,' said Ned.

'No, it isn't,' I grinned. 'I'm happy.'

Spotting the signs, I could see David was about to launch into his familiar, 'I told you coming back here was a good idea' speech but Maya's voice floated through from the barn and he turned his attention to Ned instead.

'Can't you go?' Ned pleaded with him.

'No, because she called for you,' David pointed out, 'I'm pretty certain I would be a huge disappointment.'

With a sigh, Ned reluctantly pushed back his chair and ambled off.

'What's going on?' I whispered to David. 'I thought Ned would be jumping at the chance to meet Maya out there under the mistletoe.'

I guessed that was why she wanted him. There were bunches of the stuff appearing everywhere now. With Lilith on site, Maya had access to a constant, fresh supply and was always to be seen refreshing and replenishing.

'Between you and me,' David conspiratorially replied, 'I don't think Ned's all that keen on privately meeting Maya anywhere.'

I felt my good mood plummet. I had assumed their paths were now seamlessly aligned.

'Oh,' I said, resisting the urge to sneak a look to find out how Maya was faring for myself, 'I got the impression that they were fast becoming a couple.'

'I don't think so,' David further confided. 'But I do know is it's a long time since anyone asked me for a Christmas kiss.'

I'd forgotten that David was a widow. His wife had died a few years before he became a partner in the business, so his circumstances, in some respects, sadly echoed Dad's. I wondered if that had, in part, drawn the two men together. I also wondered how Ned had coped with losing his mum. Like me, he'd also experienced the aching pain of familial grief. It was a sad thing to have in common.

'Me too,' I sighed, as Ned sidled back in, looking sheepish. 'You might want to wipe that lipstick off your face before you greet the customers, Ned,' I suggested, feeling more put out than I should considering I'd gone to the effort of kissing him goodbye myself.

'Morning team,' beamed Maya, as she breezed in with Liam hot on her heels. 'Are we all ready for another busy day serving up Christmas spirit?'

'I am,' said Liam, who looked ready for anything and entirely smitten. 'I can't wait.'

I couldn't tell if it was the prospect of Christmas, being employed at Wynter's Trees or having the opportunity to work with Maya, that had got him so fired up.

'Can I take Bandit for a walk before I start?' he asked Ned.

'I wouldn't mind a few minutes among the trees before it gets busy.'

'Be my guest,' said Ned.

'Where does he get his energy from?' David laughed as boy and hound jogged off.

'Liam or Bandit?' asked Ned.

'Both,' said David.

'It's the exuberance of youth,' I told him. 'I used to have to cope with it every day at school. Sometimes there were getting on for thirty Liams in every class.'

'Ah youth,' David wistfully smiled. 'I remember it well.'

Ned rolled his eyes.

'I've got something for you, Liza,' said Maya, returning her siren shade lipstick to her bag and rifling through it for something else.

She pulled out a tube and held it out for me to take.

'What is it?' I asked, accepting it.

'Arnica,' she said. 'It's good for bruises. That one on your face is a real shiner now.'

Ned and I had told everyone I'd fallen over while planting the family tree. We'd kept the champagne, failed athletics and subsequent revelations to ourselves. My gaze momentarily flicked to his face but his expression thankfully gave nothing away.

'That's really kind,' I said to Maya. 'Thank you.'

'You're welcome,' she said, smiling brightly, before putting her bag in the staff locker and bouncing out again.

We all watched her go. She had just as much pep as Liam

did. With her glossy ponytail and her sparkly smile, she was an absolute vision and she had kindest personality too.

'You're a lucky guy, Ned,' I said, just to hammer home how blessed he was and in spite of what David had confided. 'A very lucky guy indeed.'

The weather on Sunday was every bit as grim as it had been beautiful the day before. The car park was half empty practically all day, but the lack of customers gave me the opportunity to have a proper catch up with everyone in the beach huts.

'Do you want to borrow my chair?' asked Abbie with a cheeky grin as I cautiously negotiated my way around the wet yard and into her and Noah's hut.

'That's very kind of you,' I told her, 'but I can just about manage. Thanks.'

Wren stuck her head out of her hut and then joined us, while Noah went to buy some lunch from Hope who had been cooking up a storm in the barn all morning and was destined to have lots left over if we didn't have a rush of visitors soon.

'So,' said Abbie, when Noah was out of earshot, 'how are you getting on with Maya? I saw the pair of you chatting earlier and it looked like you've been friends forever.'

'It feels like it, too,' I told her. 'We properly hit it off as soon as I'd explained that what she'd overheard in the pub was nothing like she thought it was. She's so thoughtful and hardworking. She's perfect for Wynter's.'

She was perfect for Ned too, but I didn't add that.

'And what about Chelsea?' asked Wren, with a nod to Liam, who was busy tidying the yard in spite of the rain. 'Have you really settled your differences with her?'

The pair now knew some of what Chelsea had put me through at school, but I hadn't breathed a word to anyone about any of what she had confided in me the day after I'd offered Liam a job.

'We've certainly cleared the air,' I said, with a happy sigh, 'And boy, do I feel better for it. If there's one thing I've realised since coming back here it's that if you can't see the whole picture, then things aren't always what they seem on the surface.' I thought for a moment and then added, 'and I've also worked out there's nothing healthy about holding on to past hurts either.'

'That sounds like a very healthy attitude,' said Sue, who had come in behind me and thanks to the drumming rain I hadn't heard.

'Ow,' I winced, as I flinched and jarred my ankle as a result.

'Oh, I'm sorry, my love,' she said, looking upset. 'I didn't mean to make you jump. Is that ankle still giving you gip?'

'Don't worry,' I said, 'Not really. As long as I don't make any sudden moves, it's fine. I've been careful in the yard though. It's so wet today, I've been worried about slipping.'

We all looked out at the driving rain.

'This will soon pass,' Sue sagely said. 'I wouldn't let a few hours of wet weather hamper you settling back down, my love.'

'I suppose not,' I tensely said, while privately cursing Ned because he still maintained he wasn't ready for me to publicly share my plans.

I looked up to find three pair of eyes staring at me and was just wondering if I could somehow drop a hint, when Noah came sprinting back across the yard.

'I've got stew and dumplings for everyone,' he said, putting down two brown bags, before shaking out his jacket and covering us all in freezing raindrops.

He passed around the reusable bowls and we all sighed with pleasure as we peeled off the lids and breathed in the delicious smell of herby dumplings and slow cooked stew.

'Hope wants the bowls back,' he told us, handing out eco forks.

'Thanks Noah,' we chorused, digging in.

I was especially grateful. Not only for my lunch, but also for the timely interruption. As I savoured the first succulent mouthful I vowed to make talking to David and Ned again the next thing on my to-do list. It was about time I had an update on Ned's progress and reiterated to David that I still hadn't fallen for Wynter's Trees.

Chapter 16

'Are you all right?' Ned asked over breakfast the next morning. 'You look a bit pale. Your ankle isn't still hurting, is it?'

Having decided to talk to him and David again I had opted for an early night to ensure I would be rested, refreshed and ready for the conversation. I didn't know how David was going to react when I restated my position or if Ned had even tried to raise the money to buy me out, but I wanted to be ready for whatever their responses were to what I had to say. Unfortunately, however, my plan to catch eight hours had failed and I'd spent much of the night tossing, turning and watching the clock. My pasty pallor was no doubt the result.

'No, it's fine.' I said, dredging up a smile as I helped myself to coffee. 'Not one hundred per cent obviously, but it's much better than it was.'

'That's good,' said Ned. 'You must be healthy for it to have recovered so quickly.'

'Healthy, but not especially fit,' I admitted.

'You should start running with me and Bandit,' Ned suggested.

'My legs are half the length of yours,' I pointed out, 'and I can't risk my recovery. I'll stick to walking.'

Ned didn't look convinced, but there was no way I was going to go puffing and pounding my way around the plantation.

'You never know,' he said, 'you might enjoy it.'

'Is this your way of saying I need to lose a few pounds ahead of the festive feasting?'

'Absolutely not,' he choked, sounding mortified. 'I was thinking more of myself. I wouldn't mind a bit of company out there every now and again, that's all.'

'In that case,' I swiftly said, 'ask Maya. I bet she could keep pace with you. She's a far better match for you than I am.'

Ned didn't comment and I waited to let the words settle. He'd see the sense in them in the end.

'Are you going to be busy this morning?' I asked, once a minute had passed.

'I'm going to be busy every morning between now and the twenty-fourth,' he beamed, his embarrassment forgotten.

He looked ecstatic at the prospect and was clearly keen to embrace another hectic Christmas.

'Of course,' I said. 'The collection service starts this week, doesn't it?'

'It does,' he gushed, 'and thanks to the upgraded online booking system we have a good idea of who will be coming for their trees, rather than having them delivered, and when, so there shouldn't be too many surprises. The trees are all good to go. They're looking fit, healthy and ready to fulfil their festive destinies.'

I wasn't at all surprised to hear it and admired how he'd got the whole season so competently in hand. I knew it was all part of his job, but it was an impressive feat nonetheless.

'You've certainly got everything efficiently organised,' I said admiringly.

'It has to be,' he told me. 'With the business going from strength to strength every year, and more trees being rented out, we need to have proficient systems in place. Can you imagine the upset if we gave the wrong tree to the wrong family?'

'I don't suppose that would go down particularly well when everyone's so invested in their own tree, would it?'

'No,' he shuddered. 'It wouldn't. It's the sort of fiasco that keeps me awake at night.'

My thoughts returned to my own disturbed night.

'Well,' I said, 'if there's anything I can help with, just ask and if there's any chance you and your dad have a spare minute today, then I'd really like to talk to you both. With it being Monday and the place being closed, I thought it might be the best opportunity to get the pair of you in the office at the same time.'

'Is it about the business?' he frowned.

'I'd rather wait until the three of us are together, if that's okay?'

'All right,' he agreed. 'And don't forget we're decorating the veranda today,' he reminded me, his smile back in place. 'It's a little late, but you did say you didn't want to spoil the magic by doing it in front of the visitors and this is the first chance we've had.'

'Oh yes,' I said, as I carefully slipped off the stool I was perched on. 'I did say something like that, didn't I?'

'You did,' he grinned. 'So much for being immune to the enchantment of Wynter's Trees, hey?'

'I'm not enchanted,' I told him. 'I'm simply encouraging you to stick to Dad's traditions.'

'Yeah, right,' he laughed.

I hoped he hadn't fallen in the same trap as his dad and was thinking I'd had a change of heart now I'd decorated the lodge and planted out the tree.

'You'd best come over at nine,' he said, as I headed for the stairs. 'Getting the three of us together will be a super start to the week.'

If my gut reaction was right, he'd most likely be feeling the exact opposite by half past.

No one was at the huts that morning but I had seen Maya's car arriving as early as usual. I made sure I gave her plenty of time to bestow upon Ned her daily greeting and only went over when I caught sight of her walking out of the barn.

Ned had been less than willing to answer her seductive call the day before, but I bet when the moment came, he had risen to the occasion and given it his all. Not that it was anything to do with me. My head was focused on our imminent conversation and I had no intention of scrutinising his face for further traces of lipstick.

'Good morning, my dear,' smiled David. 'Ned tells me you want to talk.'

He looked delighted at the prospect.

'Yes,' I said. 'I do. And as I know you're both busy, I'm not going to keep you long.'

I was surprised to feel my stomach roll in reaction to what I was about to say. It wasn't as if I was uttering the words for the first time. I had made my intentions clear weeks ago, but the look on David's face and his chipper tone gave the impression that he hadn't heard them, let alone taken them onboard. It finally dawned on me that agreeing to do things his and Ned's way had been a mistake. By staying on at Wynter's Trees, I had given them hope. False hope as it turned out.

'Sorry,' said Ned, as he rushed in with Bandit close behind. 'I lost track of time.'

I half hoped, half hated the idea that that was because Maya had got him in a spin.

'You're not late,' I nodded to the clock. 'I'm a few minutes early.'

'I was getting the veranda boxes out of storage,' he elaborated, as he hung a 'do not disturb' sign on the door before closing it. 'I found the stag easily enough on account of the massive antlers, but the doe and fawn twins were harder to track down.'

'Not a sentence you'd generally hear in everyday conversation,' David chuckled, 'but a fairly run of the mill one for Wynter's.'

I nodded in agreement.

'Did you find them?' he then asked Ned.

'Find who?'

'The doe and fawn twins.'

'Oh yes,' Ned said. 'They were tucked behind the snowman Liam insisted on inflating before he left on Saturday. Apparently, that was one of his favourite things to look at when he used to visit when he was little.'

David laughed again and I began to think we'd never get down to business if they kept talking about woodland creatures and seven-foot snowmen.

'So,' I said, pulling their attention back to me, 'as I've already said, I know you're both busy, so I won't keep you.'

Ned lifted his office chair around to the front of his desk and I pulled out the one next to David's. They both looked expectant and I felt my nerves hitch up another notch.

'Right,' I said, clearing my throat. 'I know it's not quite Christmas yet, but I wanted to have a quick chat following on from what was discussed during our last meeting.'

'It's been a busy time, that's for sure,' said Ned, 'so it would be good to have an update on how things stand.'

I was rather hoping *he* was going to be the one to update *me* because my stance hadn't changed in the slightest. All I wanted to know was, had he raised the money and could I tell everyone what my plans were?

'We've really enjoyed seeing you throwing yourself into everything,' David carried merrily on. 'Quite literally,' he added, with a nod to my ankle.

I knew he'd got completely the wrong end of the stick. I'd thrown myself into everything to pass the time, not because I was trying to learn the ropes.

'Right,' I said, biting my lip as my palms began to sweat.

'Go on,' said Ned.

His tone was suddenly the polar opposite of David's. It was resigned now, bordering on hard, and I realised he'd sussed why I'd called the meeting, even though his dad hadn't.

'Well,' I said, rubbing my hands down my jeans and forcing myself to look at him, 'what I wanted to ask, is whether you've had any opportunity to raise the money to buy me out yet? And I also wanted,' I carried on, before I chickened out, 'to say to you that we need to share the news about my new business. It feels deceitful having kept everyone in the dark for so long. We've let them come to the wrong conclusion about why I'm here.'

There, I'd said it. I'd said it all and the sky hadn't caved in and no one had keeled over. So far so good.

'I see,' Ned brusquely said.

Or not.

'You mean,' David stammered, looking crestfallen, 'that you still want to go ahead and sell? You still want to leave Wynter's Trees?'

'Of course, she does,' Ned rumbled.

'Yes, David,' I answered, trying to stay strong, even

though the look in his eyes was squeezing my heart. 'I do. I told you right from the start that I wouldn't change my mind, didn't I?'

'She did,' said Ned, running his hands through his hair. 'You were sitting in that chair when she said it, Dad. Are you going to leave before Christmas?' he then abruptly asked me.

'No,' I said, 'I'll still stay, if that's all right? I haven't made a start on sorting anything out in the lodge yet.'

I knew that was because I'd been preoccupied with my crafting, painting and generally helping out, so I supposed it wasn't entirely David's fault that he'd misread the signs.

'I've got loads to do and thanks to you, Ned, I can face doing it now.' I looked at the top of his bent head. 'I want to say thank you for helping me get my head straight. You've made such a difference.'

His head bobbed up and down, but he didn't say anything.

'Goodness me,' David sighed, just before the silence began to feel awkward. 'I really thought you'd change your mind, Liza.'

'I realise that now,' I softly said. 'I'm sorry, David.'

I knew I didn't have anything to say sorry for. I'd been straight with them both practically from the day I moved back and, as Ned himself had previously pointed out, I couldn't be responsible for other people's actions and decisions. But none the more for that, the apology had still slipped out.

Ned cleared his throat and sat back up again.

'To answer your first question,' he said, sounding all

business, 'I'm no further forward with the funding issue yet. And not because I was so deluded that I thought you'd change your mind, but because there's a lot going on here and it's a tricky time to sort anything other than trees.'

'I appreciate that,' I began.

'And with regard to your request,' he continued, a steelier edge creeping into his tone, 'I'd still rather wait to tell everyone.'

I was about to ask why, when Maya opened the door and stuck her head round the frame.

'I'm sorry to interrupt . . .' she said.

'Then don't!' Ned shouted, making us all jump. 'Can't you see the bloody sign?'

Red-faced and bright-eyed she backed out and quietly closed the door again.

'No,' I said, adamant that I wouldn't back down about telling everyone. 'I can't agree to that Ned, and there's no need to take your annoyance out on Maya.'

His flash of temper told me he was every bit as upset as David, even if he hadn't been as *deluded* as he had insinuated his father had been. I heard David get up and pour himself a cup of water from the cooler behind his desk.

'Are you all right, Dad?'

'Yes, yes,' he said, turning back around. He did look a bit peaky. 'I feel a bit of a fool, to be honest. I should have realised you wouldn't change your mind, Liza, but I never really believed it would come to this. I suppose I've just blocked it all out, until now.'

'I'm sorry,' I said again, 'but I did say . . .'

Ned put up a hand.

'We know,' he curtly said.

He stood up, and without another word, strode out. He didn't quite slam the door behind him, but it was a close-run thing.

'Oh dear,' David sighed.

'That didn't go how I hoped it would,' I swallowed, blinking hard as I stood up and returned the chair to its space under the desk.

'It's my fault,' said David. 'I should have taken your wishes onboard when you first expressed them.'

'Yes,' I nodded, as I gently laid a hand on his shoulder, 'you should, but I can understand why you didn't.'

I left him, finally absorbing the information I'd given him weeks ago and went to find Ned. I hoped he'd apologised to Maya in the interim, but when I caught up with him and saw how he was throwing boxes about on the veranda, I knew he hadn't.

'So, you're still not happy that I'm going to tell everyone then?'

'No,' he snapped. 'I'm not, but I know you'll go ahead anyway.'

'That's hardly fair, Ned.'

He stopped what he was doing and let out a long breath.

'I know,' he said, raising his arms and letting them fall again. 'I know it's not fair. I know that you were only restating what you'd already said and I know that you've never done anything deceitful to make either Dad or me think that you'd change your mind *and* I know that you want to move on, but there was still a part of me . . .'

'Still a part of you what?'

'That was deluded,' he shrugged, his bottom lip trembling a little.

I didn't know what to say. It was a shock to see him so upset.

'I'll sort this later,' he said, nudging the boxes into a row with his foot.

'Ned . . .'

'I need to apologise to Maya.'

I watched him stride away and found myself wishing I'd never come back.

Chapter 17

After our meeting and following few words, Ned made it painfully obvious that he didn't want to be in my company and barely looked in my direction for the next couple of days. He had made a stunning job of decorating the veranda, but whenever I walked into a room, he walked out of it, so there was no chance to either tell him how much I liked it or thank him for doing it.

The atmosphere inside the lodge was frostier than outside and given the confused looks Bandit was giving us, I could tell it was taking a toll on our four-legged friend. I was just starting to seriously consider leaving, when Maya came to find me.

'Are you busy?' she asked, when I answered the lodge door.

Before she used to just walk in, but after Ned had bitten her head off, she had taken to knocking and waiting.

'Not really,' I told her. 'Come in.'

'Thanks.'

'I was actually hoping I would get the chance to talk to

you alone,' I said, taking the opportunity as it was just the two of us.

'Oh?' she frowned.

'I wanted to say sorry for what happened on Monday. It was my fault that Ned snapped at you,' I explained.

Maya shook her head and slipped off her mud encrusted boots, before accepting a coffee and a seat on the sofa.

'In that case,' she said, looking far happier than I currently felt to be on the receiving end of his persistent bad mood, 'I should be thanking you.'

'Thanking me?'

'Yes,' she said. 'He's been a changed man since that meeting. I don't know what you said to him, Liza,' she laughed, 'but he's totally transformed, especially where I'm concerned.'

'Is he?' I swallowed.

Around me, he was all brooding and Heathcliff, but given the dreamy expression on Maya's face, I fathomed he was the ultimate Hallmark hero in her company.

'He is,' she grinned. 'He took me to the pub to apologise and he's been so sweet and attentive ever since. I was beginning to think he was a lost cause, but since Monday he's completely changed.'

The smile lighting up her pretty face suggested that he'd done considerably more than apologise. Had I realised that simply upsetting him would have thrown him into Maya's waiting arms, then I would have done it far sooner.

'He'll be dragging *you* under the mistletoe in no time,' I

said, the words sticking in my throat, 'rather than the other way around.'

Her playful wink told me all I needed to know.

I should have been happy that he'd finally realised that Maya was the girl for him, but now I'd got them across the finishing line, the victory felt rather hollow. At least, if I left early, I wouldn't have to endure watching their relationship blossom. I might have convinced myself Ned wasn't the man for me, but now it turned out, I didn't want him to be the man for anyone else either.

'Now all we have to do,' Maya thoughtfully said, drumming her fingers against the side of her mug, 'is find a match for you. Wouldn't it be wonderful if we could all spend Christmas together? Me and Ned,' she dreamily added, just to make sure I knew what she was getting at, 'and you and Mr Still to be Revealed.'

Personally, I couldn't think of anything worse.

'But before we do that,' she said, biting her lip, 'I don't suppose you can tell me what that meeting on Monday was about, can you?'

Her request gave me the perfect opportunity to spread the word that I was selling my shares in the business. I knew Maya wasn't the gossiping type, but armed with such gargantuan news she wouldn't be able to resist telling someone and, depending on who's ear her words poured into, then that would be enough.

'Sorry,' she said, shaking her head when I didn't immediately answer. 'Forget I asked. It's none of my business.'

'No,' I said, 'it's fine. I can completely understand that you'd want to know. Given Ned's reaction to you walking in, you're probably thinking it was something pretty important.'

'Yes,' she said. 'I am.'

'Well, it was.' I told her, gearing up to share, 'but don't worry. It was nothing to do with your job or Liam's, if that's what's playing on your mind.'

I don't know why, but I couldn't bring myself to say anything further. It was the ideal time and should have been, given the set-up and how much I wanted it to happen, the easiest thing in the world to explain, but I just couldn't do it.

'Thank goodness for that,' said Maya, wilting with relief. 'Now Ned and I are finally getting somewhere, I'd hate it if I couldn't work with him.'

'You've no worries there,' I told her. 'With David about to retire, you're needed more than ever.'

'Phew,' she grinned, wiping imaginary sweat from her smooth brow.

'And thanks for the thought,' I quickly added, 'but you needn't worry about finding someone for me to spend Christmas with either. I'm very happily single right now.'

'How about a winter warmer?' she giggled. 'A festive fling?'

'No thanks,' I breezily said. 'I'm good.'

'Sure?' she wheedled.

She sounded disappointed and I hoped she hadn't already got someone in mind.

'One hundred and ten per cent.'

'Oh well,' she shrugged, 'in that case, I'd better get back to work.'

She handed me her mug and stood up.

'Oh, but before I go, I have a favour to ask,' she said, sitting back down again. 'I can't believe I almost forgot.'

'What is it?'

'Well,' she said, 'I really wanted to go with Ned to Wynbridge tomorrow.'

'To Wynbridge?'

'Yes,' she said. 'You know, that place in the Fens. It's their Christmas tree auction this weekend and we supply a lot of the trees. Ned usually goes on his own to deliver them, but a couple of weeks ago he said that this year we could make the trip together.'

'Well, that's all right then, isn't it?' I shrugged. 'If he's already suggested it . . .'

'It was all right,' she cut in, 'but now he's changed his mind. He says he needs someone here he can rely on and who knows the rental system.'

'I'm sure David's au fait with it all, isn't he?'

'He is,' she agreed, 'but ideally there should be more than one person working on site. There'll be the cut trees to sell as well as some potted ones to book out and I was wondering if you might be able to help out. If you worked with David for the day, then Ned couldn't have any objection to me going with him.'

I was cross with Ned. I'd made it more than clear that if

he and David needed help, then they only had to ask. I had been planning to leave, but I wouldn't even consider it now. I wasn't going to let Ned's mood drive me away. I would stick it out, whatever the cost.

'Don't you worry,' I told Maya, thinking that a day away from Wynter's Trees could only serve to push her and Ned closer together. 'I'll sort it. I'm more than happy to help out.'

'Really?' she squeaked. 'You're sure you don't mind?'

'Of course not,' I insisted. 'Ned only had to ask.'

'Really?'

'Really. You'll get your trip out. Even if it is going to be a bit of a busman's holiday.'

'Oh, thank you, thank you, thank you!' she beamed.

'In fact,' I said, standing up, 'I'll go and sort it out right now.'

Maya was keen for me to tell Ned what we'd decided and we left the lodge together. She peeled off into the barn, having bestowed more heartfelt thanks, and I, following the sound of the chainsaw, carried on to the plantation. My ankle barely protested, which was a relief because if I was going to ensure Maya got her day away with Ned, then I was going to be standing on it all of the next day.

'Hello Liza,' said David, as I approached the line of trees that he and Ned were working their way through.

Every day Ned was felling a few, in a variety of sizes, to cater for those visitors who wanted a cut tree without the walk through the plantation or who simply didn't have time to browse. The felled selection was displayed in the yard and once a tree was chosen, it was then netted, paid for and driven away.

In spite of Dad's efforts to educate me, I hadn't given it much thought before, but since returning I had and I vastly preferred the fate of those trees growing in pots. Playing a part in the seasonal celebrations with the same family, potentially for years, was very special indeed. It turned out Dad did have a point and an important one. Not only did his vision make sense for the environment, it created a much-loved tradition too.

'Hi, David,' I called back. 'I need to talk to Ned. Has he nearly finished? I don't want to disturb him, if he's on a roll.'

Given his recent mood, I wouldn't dare.

'He's got a few more to do, but his arms could probably do with a break,' David told me. 'He's felled a quite a lot this morning, ready to take to Wynbridge tomorrow.'

'Yes,' I nodded. 'I know all about that now. Maya's just been telling me.'

'We aren't the only supplier for the auction,' said David, his voice lowering as Ned turned off the chainsaw and peace was restored, 'but a lot come from us.'

'What's up?' called Ned, first lifting the chainsaw visor, then one ear defender and then the other.

I couldn't help thinking he looked rather good in all the gear. The Kevlar reinforced trousers, jacket and gloves bulked out his already sizeable frame, and the steel toe-capped boots made him look even taller. Rugged, rough and ready was the description that sprang to mind before I had the chance to fend it off.

'What is it?' he asked, wiping the sweat from his brow with the back of his hand.

'I want to ask you something.' I said, fending the fantasy image off.

He opened his mouth to say something, most likely, '*You'll have to wait*,' but David stepped in.

'Your timing couldn't be better, Liza,' he smiled. 'I was just about to take the truck back to the yard and start off-loading these trees, wasn't I, Ned?'

Ned glowered at his father, who jumped into the cab with an agility that in no way matched his advancing years, and set off.

'What is it?' Ned fired at me again.

'Your trip to Wynbridge tomorrow,' I shot back, coming straight to the point.

'What about it?'

'Maya was under the impression that she was going with you,' I told him, 'but now she thinks you've changed your mind and you're going to leave her behind.'

'I have,' he shrugged. 'I am.'

'But she'd really like to go and I think it would be good for her to see how that side of the business works.'

Ned shook his head.

'Given what's in the offing, don't you think it's important that she has as much knowledge and experience as possible?'

'And I suppose you told her what's in the offing,' he snapped.

'No,' I said, lifting my chin. 'I didn't actually.'

He looked as surprised as I had been when I let the opportunity to tell her pass.

'Why not?' he frowned.

'It doesn't matter,' I said.

Truth be told, I didn't know why.

'Let's just focus on tomorrow,' I carried on. 'Surely, it would be useful for another member of staff to have some first-hand experience of how the run to Wynbridge works, wouldn't it?'

I didn't add that Maya was looking forward to spending the day with him off-site. Surely, he couldn't be so dense that he hadn't worked that out for himself.

'Yes,' he said, 'it would be great, but taking her would leave us too short staffed here.'

'But I think . . .'

'For fuck's sake, Liza,' he bit back, roughly pulling the helmet off and dumping it on the ground along with the chainsaw. 'What *you* think is irrelevant. How Wynter's Trees works and who knows what about it, is no concern of yours now, is it?'

Tears stung my eyes as his words hit their mark, but I refused to let them fall.

'Perhaps not,' I snapped back, 'but you know full well that I've offered to assist wherever and whenever I can. I don't understand why you're carrying on as if I won't help.'

'Because I can't allow myself to start relying on you!' he yelled.

'Not just for one day?' I shouted back.

'Not for a single hour.'

'But that's absurd.'

'It is what it is,' he shrugged.

'I don't understand ...'

'I know you don't,' he cut in. 'But I'm not going to spell it out for you.'

He snatched the helmet back up and shoved it on his head, snapping both ear defenders and the visor into place, before firing the chainsaw up again.

'Maya stays here tomorrow!' he shouted over the din. 'End of.'

I threw up my hands and walked away.

I don't know what happened between me walking out of the plantation and six o'clock the following morning, but I awoke to the sound of the truck and trailer rattling down the drive, Bandit's distant bark and the tinkle of Maya's melodious laugh as she locked the gate. There was a note on the kitchen counter when I went downstairs.

Dad said I had to take Maya.
He's coming in early. We'll be back by 8pm.

I screwed it up and threw it in the bin, refusing to let its succinctness further rattle me, before pummelling my skin under the shower and heading out into the crisp, frosty air.

The morning got off to a slow start, which gave me the chance to catch up with everyone in the beach huts. I found Sue replenishing her stock of festive bunting.

'I'm selling it as fast as I can sew it,' she happily told me. 'Not that I'm complaining. But what's up with you? You've got a face like a smacked . . .'

'Nothing,' I brightly said. 'I'm all right.'

She eyed me beadily. 'What time did the dynamic duo set off?' she asked, with a nod to the drive.

I wondered if it was a coincidence that she'd leapt straight from asking if anything was wrong with me to Ned and Maya's big day out. I *hoped* it was a coincidence.

'Six,' I told her. 'I heard them leaving at six.'

'He's another one with a puss on this week,' she observed. 'That wouldn't be anything to do with you, would it?'

Since I'd passed up the opportunity to tell Maya what was afoot, I hadn't felt further inclined to tell anyone. However, I hadn't dissected my change of heart in too minute detail. The only obvious reason I could think of, which was quite something considering we weren't really talking, was that I was keeping quiet for Ned's benefit. There couldn't be any other explanation.

'Hey, hey,' came an excited voice behind me. 'Check me out.'

'Abbie!' I gasped, watching her nimbly negotiate the path on crutches.

'Oh, good grief,' winced Sue. 'Please be careful,'

I knew David had gritted the paths, but I didn't think the conditions were the best for Abbie to try out her relearned walking skills, even though it was a thrill to see her out of her wheelchair for the first time.

'That's exactly what I said,' said Noah, bustling up behind her. 'But she wouldn't be told.'

With a frown knitting his brows and his hair all over the place, he looked totally stressed. Not at all his usual carefree and charismatic self.

'Don't worry,' Abbie puffed, as she stepped into Sue's hut. 'I'm done.'

'Here,' said Sue, shoving her chair under Abbie's bottom. 'Park yourself in this.'

Abbie sank gratefully into the seat, her face a picture.

'Twelve steps,' she beamed. 'Progress.'

'On thinly covered ice,' tutted Noah. 'I call it a death wish.'

'Hey Usain,' shouted Theo, from the yard. 'I couldn't keep up with you.'

Abbie rolled her eyes, but still looked every bit as happy.

'Next stop, the ten metres in a hundred minutes,' she quipped. 'What have you got there?' she then asked Theo who was carrying a large cardboard box.

'More jugs,' he told her. 'The Christmas ones, with the hand-painted holly and berries.'

'Oh good,' said Abbie. 'I saw you'd sold out again and I wanted one for my mum and another for my sister.'

'Great,' laughed Theo. 'Two sales before I've even opened.'

'Is Wren with you?' I asked, looking over his shoulder.

'Er, no,' he said. 'Not today. She was feeling a bit off colour, so she thought she'd leave running the hut to me today.'

'Again?' frowned Sue. 'That's the second time she's felt off in a week.'

'I know,' said Theo, with a shrug, 'something obviously hasn't agreed with her.'

The morning had started off quietly enough, but during the afternoon, the car park began to fill and I was surprised by the number of visitors.

'Is it usually like this on a Thursday?' I asked David, who was helping me until I got the hang of netting the trees.

I was quite a dab hand already, but nowhere near as fast as Liam. He clearly had the knack and could already feed the trees through far faster than I ever would.

'From now until Christmas it is,' David puffed, as we slid a huge tree through the machine, then balanced it back in the sleigh that the couple buying it had called into action.

'Thanks,' grinned the man, while the woman next to him wrestled extremely excited toddler twins back into their buggy. 'We can manage from here.'

The woman, his partner I guessed, didn't look at all inclined to agree and I smiled.

'Our grandchildren,' she explained. 'We look after them while my daughter works.'

The snowsuit-padded pair were clutching Wynter's Trees stockings, so I knew they'd already paid a visit to Santa and were now in raptures over the tree, although, given their age, I wasn't sure they appreciated its significance.

'How lovely,' I said, but I bet it wasn't. Not all of the time anyway. 'Merry Christmas,' I added as they walked away. 'It isn't too early to say that, is it?' I asked David.

'It's never too early here,' he beamed. 'Now here's a couple who have come to collect their potted tree. Come on,' he nudged, 'put the barrier around the netting machine and I'll show you how the system works. Cass! Tony!' he called. 'How wonderful to see you.'

As I watched him greet them, I realised that this was exactly what Wynter's Trees was all about – the personal touch. Adult customers were remembered, their growing offspring admired and their beloved trees cosseted and kept safe.

It was all part of the special service Dad had strived to provide and I felt an unusual swell of pride in my chest as I realised that he might not have had the opportunity to enjoy it for long, but he had achieved exactly what he had set out to all those years ago. It turned out that following his heart had worked out pretty well, for him at least.

David and I were still in the office when Ned and Maya arrived back, tidying up after a brisk afternoon's trading. Chelsea had kindly dropped off and driven back out to pick up Liam after his first ever after-school stint. He'd proved to be as indispensable as ever and had been brimming with more than his usual level of excitement because of some secret presents he'd come up with for everyone.

Ned and Maya were animatedly chatting when they walked in, but their voices quickly trailed off. I calculated they'd just about made it as far as the suspended ball of mistletoe before silence reigned; however, their goodbye must have been brief, because Ned appeared in the office doorway ruddy-cheeked and windswept almost before I had worked the equation out.

'You're back!' said David, even though I knew he had heard them come in when I did. 'How did it go? Where's Maya?'

'She's gone home,' said Ned, looking happier than he had been all week. 'She's pretty tired, having driven all the way back. The whole day was wonderful though. They took the lot. It's going to be a bumper auction for Wynbridge this weekend and the chap from the council was thrilled with the tree for the market square.'

As well as donating a tree for the green in Wynmouth, I knew that another had been given to Wynbridge and a third to a winter garden in Norwich. It was good to know that Dad's philanthropic spirit lived on.

'And what about the Wynthorpe Hall trees?' David asked. 'You dropped those off too, didn't you?'

'Yes,' said Ned, picking up the day's bundle of receipts, before glancing at the computer screen his father was updating. 'All good there too. I reckon Angus's festive spirit could have given Nicholas Wynter's a run for its money.'

No matter how keen this Angus was on Christmas, I'd have still put my money on Dad winning the race.

'And what about here?' Ned asked, throwing a look in my direction. 'No hiccups?'

'Everything ran like clockwork,' I told him. 'Like I said before, it's a great system you've got set up.'

Ned inclined his head, but carried on flicking through the receipts and when I remembered the terse note he'd left, I wished I hadn't praised his failproof planning.

'I got Liza working on the netting machine,' David enthusiastically said. 'She's quite the expert now.'

'A skill that will no doubt come in handy when she has absolutely no connection to Wynter's Trees in the future,' Ned muttered under his breath.

'Ned,' David warningly said.

I felt my face turn red.

'Sorry,' said Ned, but he didn't sound particularly contrite.

'We thought it might be handy for me to know, in case Liam needed a hand at the weekend, didn't we?' I smiled for David's benefit, rather than Ned's. 'I think I'll head back to the lodge now. Night, David. Thanks for today, I really enjoyed it.'

It came as a surprise, but I really had. The day had flown by and it had been both fun and informative.

'You were a great help,' David kindly said.

'Before you go,' said Ned. 'I want to tell you both something I heard about this place from the owner of Wynthorpe Hall.'

'That's Catherine Connelly, isn't it?' David asked.

Why did that name ring a bell?

'Yes,' said Ned, 'that's her. She said she and her son had visited a few days ago and she'd lost her wallet.'

'A Chanel one,' I said, suddenly remembering.

'That's right,' said Ned. 'She was relieved to get it back and most impressed with Liam. She said the lad was a credit to the place.'

'He's a credit to himself,' I said, feeling proud on Liam's behalf. 'I bet you're pleased I offered him a job now, aren't you?'

I slipped out before he had time to reply.

Chapter 18

When I went down to breakfast the next morning, safe in the knowledge that Ned and Bandit were out on their run, there was a gift-wrapped present with a label addressed to me, sitting on the coffee table.

I tore into the paper and discovered, to my delight, a leather-bound journal, complete with pockets, envelopes and plain and lined pages. It was absolutely exquisite and already a work of art in itself. As I flicked through it, a business card fell out. I picked it up and read it. The journal was from a stationer's in Wynbridge.

He hadn't signed his name, but this was clearly a peace offering from Ned. A very beautiful acceptance of my decision to leave Wynter's Trees and a wonderful tome in which to jot down my business ideas and perhaps even record the details of my adventure to see the northern lights.

I ran my hands over the cover, imagining myself filling it in and feeling relieved that Ned had finally calmed down. I hadn't thought he was all that changed when he'd arrived back from Wynbridge the evening before, but the gift suggested otherwise and I set about cooking breakfast feeling lighter of heart than I had all week.

'What's all this?' panted Ned, when he and Bandit burst in, having taken much longer than they usually would, and spotted the laden table.

'Breakfast,' I said, as Bandit skittered over to his water bowl. 'I thought I'd make enough for both of us and I wanted to say thank you for the journal too.'

I picked it up and stroked the cover. It was so tactile; I couldn't not caress it.

'I haven't got time for breakfast here,' Ned gruffly said, as I caught sight of Maya bending and stretching on the veranda, in close-fitting running gear. 'Maya and I have just had a run and now we're going to get showered and have breakfast in the office.'

'Oh,' I swallowed. 'Right.'

'It's a working breakfast,' he added. 'We've got the deliveries to run through. From today it's going to get crazy busy. With just a couple of weeks until Christmas, we're heading into prime tree buying season.'

It was a working breakfast and a bout of busyness that obviously didn't include me. But then, why should it? I put the journal down again.

'And that's from Maya,' he said, nodding at the gift. 'Not me. She picked it up in Wynbridge yesterday after we'd had lunch.'

It sounded like they'd had the perfect date. Lunch and

shopping in a pretty market town, combined with a bit of business. It was exactly what Maya had hoped for, and exactly what I'd gone out of my way to enable, I quickly reminded myself.

'Yay,' said Maya as she bounced in sporting a healthy glow and not at all out of breath as I would have been. 'You found it. Do you like it?'

'No,' I told her, picking it up again. 'I don't like it, I love it. It's beautiful Maya. Thank you so much. It was very thoughtful of you.'

'I thought it might come in handy for making notes about running Wynter's, while you're getting into the swing of things,' she explained. 'And Ned mentioned you were planning a holiday, so I thought you might want to record the details of that too. What with you being such a talented artist, I know you'll make it beautiful.'

'It already is,' I acknowledged, 'but I'll definitely add to it.'

I wasn't sure how I felt about her and Ned discussing me. He obviously thought it was acceptable to mention my plans for a couple of weeks away but, and I guessed this from Maya's buoyant mood and comment about Wynter's, he clearly hadn't shared my big life plan. I didn't know whether I should have felt grateful about that or not.

'I should have saved it for Christmas really,' Maya laughed, 'but I've never been any good at keeping secrets. Just don't go anywhere too wonderful on this getaway of yours,' she jokingly added, 'because you might not want to come back.'

'Right,' said Ned, 'we'd better get on. Maya, you take the bathroom upstairs and I'll use the shower down here.'

'Not upstairs with me?' she giggled as she skipped over to the stairs.

'Not today,' said Ned, striding off without a backwards glance.

Just as Ned predicted, the footfall at Wynter's Trees reached record breaking numbers that weekend. It seemed as if the world and his wife were determined to buy their tree, or have it delivered, and decorate it between the eleventh and twelfth of December.

The damp weather on Saturday didn't impact on customer numbers at all, and everyone was rushed off their feet. Ned hadn't assigned me anything specific when he doled out the jobs, but as soon as he set off, first with Maya and later Liam, to deliver trees, David set me properly to work.

Once the car park had finally emptied and the beach huts were closed that evening, David gathered everyone together in the barn to ask how their day had gone.

'I don't mind admitting now,' piped up Noah, 'that I had a bit of a wobble in the early days. My wire sculptures are quite expensive and I didn't think I was going to shift any, but after today, I've changed my mind.'

'Today's been better?' asked Ned.

'Much better,' Noah smiled. 'I've sold two. Both to returning visitors who had browsed before but came back today to buy.'

'That's great,' said Wren who, I noticed, was still looking peaky.

Theo rubbed her back and I wondered how long it would be before she was tucked up in bed with a hot water bottle. Not long, if the yawn she stifled was any indicator.

'And I'm out of festive bunting again,' said Sue. 'I'll have to make some more tonight, ready for tomorrow. I was hoping to eke it out and do it on Monday when we're closed, but it's been so busy today that it's all gone.'

'And I saw lots of your wreaths and garlands heading towards the car park, Lilith,' I pointed out.

She was such a quiet character; it was easy to forget that she was there half the time.

'Yes,' she said, 'I'm in the same boat as Sue now. I'll be making more wreaths tonight ready for tomorrow.'

Everyone nodded and Theo gave her a thumbs up.

'And one customer bought my entire collection of long-tailed tits,' said Abbie, making everyone gasp. 'She told me she's got some branches set up in her conservatory and is in the process of filling them up with birds created using different crafts. She loves felt and said mine have so much character she couldn't resist. Initially she only wanted one, but then . . .'

'I pointed out they live in flocks of up to twenty,' Noah cut in, 'and . . .'

'She took the lot!' Abbie finished up. 'She's promised to send me a photo and said I can use it on my Instagram account. Her indoor branch idea has given me some inspiration for photographing the rest of my collection too.'

'Assuming you have any left!' chuckled David and we all laughed.

Theo then told us how busy he'd been and Wren had sold more of her silver studs in one day than at any other event she'd ever attended.

'Thankfully I've still got lots in stock,' she said with a smile.

I was pleased about that because I rather fancied a pair myself. I particularly liked the ones with a snowflake stamped in the middle and there were Christmas tree ones too, which I thought might make a nice gift for Maya. Given the beautiful journal she'd gifted me, she was definitely on my present list.

After the brief meeting, everyone headed home and as Maya was driving into Wynmouth to meet some friends in the pub, she offered to take Liam.

'And what about the tree for the lodge?' David said to Ned, as everyone left. 'Are you going to take it tonight?'

Ned shook his head. 'No,' he said. 'It can keep until Monday.'

'But I thought . . .'

'Like I said,' Ned cut in, sounding harassed. 'I'll do it Monday, Dad. It's going to be busy tomorrow, so we'll sort it when we're closed. Assuming that's all right with you, Liza?'

'Yes,' I said, 'that's fine with me.'

I hadn't realised he'd got another tree lined up for the lodge and didn't ask about it, for fear of aggravating him further. I said goodnight to David and left Ned to lock up.

There was a pile of post on the mat. I picked it up and

heaped it on the kitchen counter before making a drink and heading upstairs for a long, hot bath. I'd already eaten, courtesy of Sophie and Hope, and wanted to make myself scarce before Ned got in. I had thought that he was finally getting over his annoyance with me, but apparently not.

Sunday dawned dry but dull and that worked in our favour because it meant the lights looked good from early on. I made sure I was up with the lark and raring to go. I was determined to get Ned to assign me a job that went beyond making endless cups of tea and coffee but if he refused, then I planned go back to David for further direction and hang the consequences. Fortunately, it didn't come to that.

'Oh,' I said, only just noticing, 'this post is for me.'

The large envelope in the pile I'd picked up the evening before had my name on it.

'Is it?' frowned Ned.

'Yes,' I said, holding it up for him to see. 'Look.'

I had no idea why I'd be getting post at the lodge. I hadn't sent off for anything or had anything redirected.

'Would you mind looking at it later?' Ned asked, as I began to open it. 'I want to run through a couple of things with you about today. We've no Liam and as it's potentially going to be the busiest day of the season, we're going to need you to help out a bit. If that's all right?'

It was on the top of my tongue to remind him that I'd already, on more than one occasion, said I was willing, but bit the words back.

'Of course,' I said, abandoning the envelope and giving him my full attention.

I listened intently as he ran through everything, especially the bit about who was coming to collect their potted trees as well as where he and Maya were going to be heading. I couldn't help noticing that he looked tired. There were dark circles under his eyes and the frown lines looked established enough to be a permanent forehead feature, even though I knew they weren't.

Given the miles he'd clocked up since the potted delivery service began, combined with those he'd added to the tally while delivering to places like Wynbridge, I supposed it was hardly surprising that he looked all in. At least I hoped that was the reason behind the bags. I'd hate to think that my request that he should buy me out had contributed to them.

'Because I wouldn't usually need her,' I heard him saying. 'You are listening, aren't you, Liza?'

'Yes,' I nodded, realising my focus had been side-tracked for a few seconds.

'Right well, as I was saying,' he continued. 'I wouldn't usually take Maya, but a few of the trees are quite big now and it's a struggle to manoeuvre them on my own.'

'Your dad and I will be fine,' I told him.

'And Joe,' he said, narrowing his eyes.

Clearly, I'd missed something in the few seconds I'd drifted off.

'And Joe,' I repeated, remembering who he was talking

257

about just in time. 'Your friend who sells his bird seed and is Hope's other half.'

'Yes,' Ned said, his brow clearing and his shoulders relaxing. 'He can do the really heavy lifting and stuff.'

Ordinarily, I would have felt aggrieved about a comment like that, however, being a little on the short side did put me at a disadvantage when it came to manhandling Christmas trees. It was nothing to do with brute force. I could lug them about well enough, but I did sometimes have a job seeing over the top and getting my arms around them, to feed them through the netting machine. Anything over six foot was definitely a challenge, so Joe's longer reach would be much appreciated.

'It's going to be especially busy early on,' Ned told me, 'because everyone will want to get their tree home and ready to decorate before they have their Sunday dinner, so make sure you have a big breakfast. You'll soon burn off the calories.'

'Duly noted,' I said, reaching for what Mum had always called the porridge pan. 'Shall I make enough for two?'

'Better make it three,' said Ned, with a nod to the window. 'Here's Maya. She'll have already had one breakfast at home, but she won't turn down another.'

He made her sound like a Hobbit, eager for her second breakfast, but as we watched her willowy figure climb out of her 4x4, I realised she was definitely more of a Rivendell elf. Her long, slim legs easily reached the ground whereas I would have had to jump out of the cab.

'I don't know where she puts it all,' Ned wistfully said, still watching her.

'Me neither,' I said, reaching for the honey.

I suddenly found I needed sweetening back up.

By late-morning I was beginning to feel muscles in places I didn't even know existed. Joe had done his share of lugging the trees about, but so had I. The little carts I'd converted into sleighs were holding their own in the yard, but they were no help when it came to lifting the trees into car boots and trailers and up on to roof racks.

'If they keep turning up in these numbers,' puffed Joe, looking thrilled, 'you'll be sold out in no time!'

David, who kept popping in and out of the office to see how many cut trees were left, was in complete agreement.

'I've never known it to be this busy,' he told us. 'It's quite extraordinary. I don't know what's going on!'

As I looked about, I could understand exactly why it was so hectic. Ned had cleverly created a one-stop Christmas shop and everyone was loving it. There were bespoke and unusual gifts championing the buy local ethos, there was food and drink to match every taste and appetite and the opportunity to walk it off with a stroll through the trees. Santa was installed in his grotto, music was playing, lights were twinkling and to top it all off, there were stunning trees to take home too.

But it turned out, that wasn't the only thing which had caused the sudden spike in visitor numbers.

'Have you seen this?' called Sue, who rushed over, waving a newspaper above her head. 'Look at the centre spread.'

She handed David the paper and jogged back to her hut while he opened it in the middle.

'Well, I never!' he gasped. 'Would you look at that?'

'I don't believe it,' I said, stepping up to take a better look. 'I sent those in ages ago, but never heard anything so assumed they weren't going to be used.'

'Head to Wynter's Trees for the full-on festive experience,' David read out. 'Enjoy Christmas shopping at the seaside and get to know the people behind the presents.'

As well as using the photos of Bandit pulling a sleigh that I'd submitted, and the beach huts, there was another of Ned looking god-like in a chunky knit and wellies. The journalist responsible for the feature had also made a secret shopper visit and based their glowing copy on that. There was a potted history of the place and a small image of Dad from the archives and a mention of the reserve.

'Look,' said Joe, thrusting his phone in mine and David's faces. 'The paper's Twitter account has got Wynter's trending and there are dozens of comments on the website. No wonder it's so busy!'

'You've done this, Liza,' said David, sounding choked. 'You've turned the place into an online sensation!'

'I just thought it would be good publicity,' I said, feeling shocked. 'I thought we'd get a couple of column inches at the most.'

'We've got a whole lot more than that!'

I looked about me, the idyllic sight causing a lump to form in my throat and just for a moment, I panicked. Had I made the right decision in telling Ned and David I no longer wanted to have a connection to Wynter's Trees? The place might not have been for me in the past, but from what I saw now, it looked pretty perfect.

Then two things happened in quick succession which knocked the thought clean out of my head. Firstly, I remembered that Wynter's was only like this for a few weeks every year and that it was in no way capable of satisfying the need I still felt to nurture struggling students, and secondly, Theo came rushing across the yard looking stricken. He grabbed me by the sleeve and pulled me away from David and Joe who were still looking at the paper.

'Whatever's wrong?' I asked.

The look on his face scared me so much it made me forget where I was for a moment.

'It's Wren,' he choked. 'I need to get her to the hospital.'

'What's happened?' I gasped, looking over to the huts. 'I thought she'd just picked up a bug.'

I'd noticed the day before that she still looked pale, but sometimes these things took time to get over.

'No,' said Theo, shaking his head. 'It's not a bug, she's pregnant.'

'Oh, my goodness,' I gulped.

That should have been cause for celebration, but the stricken look still fixed on his face left me in no doubt that it wasn't.

'She was pregnant before,' he said in a voice so quiet, I had to lean in to hear him. 'We got to about this far along and we lost it.'

'But that doesn't mean . . .' I began.

'She's had some blood loss during the last few days,' he swallowed, 'and the doctor said if it didn't stop, I was to take her in.'

'Of course,' I said, choking back a tear when I realised what he was telling me. 'Just go. I'll come and lock your hut. Where is Wren now?'

'With Sue.'

By the time we had pushed through the crowds to the hut, the troops had rallied and everything was organised. Wren and Theo's hut was closed and Noah was manning Sue's because she was going to drive the pair to the hospital. She'd already got Wren tucked in the back of her car under a blanket.

'Did you know?' Abbie asked me as we watched Theo join her on the back seat and Sue drive them away.

'No,' I said. 'I had no idea. Did you?'

'No,' she sobbed, before taking a deep breath.

'Liza!' I heard Joe call.

He was waving his arms to get my attention and I waved back.

'I'll just see what he wants and come back over.'

'No, it's all right,' Abbie stoically said. 'We can manage. You stick to helping with the trees. We're all organised here. Noah's taken a few bits from Wren and Theo's hut

262

and put them in Sue's, so they'll all still make some sales this afternoon. Not that it matters . . .' she added, her words trailing off.

I reached for her hand, but Joe called again.

'I'm sorry, Abbie,' I said. 'I'd really better see what he wants.'

'This chap has come to collect his family tree,' Joe informed me once I'd made my way back across the yard and was in earshot.

There was no time to assimilate any of what had just happened and I turned my attention to the man standing with Joe. He didn't look much better than I felt.

'I'm a bit nervous about it actually,' said the guy, who was on his own. 'It's a sort of rite of passage. I'm relatively new to the family and have been trusted with the task of picking up the tree. Apparently, it's been in the family for years and my prospective father-in-law has asked me to collect it.'

His nerves were obviously jangling and I forced myself to focus. There was nothing I could do for Wren right now, but I could get on with the task Ned had entrusted me with.

'No pressure then,' I said, conjuring a smile.

He shuffled from one foot to the other, looking mildly terrified and I got the impression that his potential father-in-law wasn't a man to be trifled with. Perhaps there really was a hand in marriage at stake.

'Right,' I briskly said, 'let's get you sorted.' Then I added, 'have you got any identification with you?'

I was stalling for time, trying to pick David out in the

crowd. I was happy to rent the tree out but as it was my first time doing it independently, and so particularly important, I wanted him nearby to oversee the procedure.

'I have,' said the man, wrinkling his nose, 'but it's got my name on. I haven't got anything with the family name on. Is it important?'

'No,' I told him, but I wasn't really sure whether it was or not. 'Don't worry. We can manage without it. Where's David?' I asked Joe who was standing next to me, talking to another family.

'Sorting something in the grotto, I think. Do you want me to fetch him?'

'No,' I said, seeing there was already quite a queue forming. 'It's fine. I can manage.'

I'd watched plenty of potted trees being rented out over the last few days and was clear on how the logging out system operated so I knew I could do it. I just needed to get on with it.

'So,' I said to the man who was looking more edgy by the minute as Joe rushed off to help a young couple select one of the cut trees. 'What was the name?'

'Stott,' he told me. 'The name is Stott and it's the Stott family tree that I'm here to collect.' He reeled the words off as if they were part of a script he'd been told to memorise. 'It's much-loved apparently and an important part of Christmas.' He sounded slightly bewildered by the family's attachment to the tree, but having walked through the potted part of the plantation, I could understand why it meant so much to them. 'I'd better not cock this up, had I?' he swallowed.

I led him over to the potted trees awaiting collection. As I began sorting through them, my head filled again with thoughts of what might be happening to Wren. Theo had looked positively terrified, so I couldn't even begin to imagine how she was feeling. I'd had no idea she was pregnant or that she'd previously miscarried, but then as a newcomer, or new returner to Wynmouth, that was no surprise. It wasn't the sort of information you shared with people you'd only just met, was it?

I could feel the lump beginning to form in my throat again and for two pins would have handed my nervous customer over to Joe. However, it was far too busy for me to bail, especially after I'd been so adamant about pitching in and helping out.

'Here it is!' announced the Stott family representative, making me jump, as he grasped a label and looked triumphant. 'I've found it.'

With his chest puffed out, he looked quite transformed. He was in full hunter gatherer mode.

'Oh, well spotted,' I said, blinking away my tears as I quickly checked the label. 'Let's sort the rental fee and then you can be on your way.'

He looked mightily relieved as he drove off.

'Another satisfied customer,' said David, as he came out of the barn, followed my gaze and watched the car turn out of sight. 'Are you all right, Liza, you look a bit pale?'

'I'm fine,' I rallied, knowing there was no time to get into what had happened to Wren. The best thing I could do was carry on and explain at the end of the day. 'Who's next?'

I kept checking my phone, having quickly given my number to Theo, but there was no word. I kept telling myself that no news was good news and carried on, netting trees as if my life depended on it. The busyness did help keep my mind occupied to a certain extent, but as three o'clock dawned, disaster struck and my head was filled with another crisis.

'It's Scott,' said the man I'd just shown one of the few remaining potted trees to. It was a fine specimen; tall, wide and in a vast pot. 'Not Stott,' he carried on. 'We're the Scotts and we're here to collect Doris.'

'This isn't her,' said the woman with him as she stepped forward. 'Unless she's grown about three foot in the last year and look, this label says Stott family.'

'We're the Scotts,' the man repeated, looking increasingly harassed.

'The Scott family,' the woman said again.

They had two kids with them. The eldest, a boy aged about fifteen, looked up from his phone and sniggered, no doubt enjoying the fact that someone else was on the receiving end of his mum's bad mood, and the younger, a girl, looked as if she was about to cry. The woman put her arm around the girl and gave her a squeeze, which soon set the tears flowing.

I couldn't believe this was happening. There was still no

word from Theo and when I looked up and spotted Ned's truck pull into the car park, I felt very much disposed to join in with the girl's wailing.

'Shit,' I muttered under my breath, feeling like the biggest fool.

'Kim,' said Ned, when he reached us, 'Andrew. Good to see you both. Hey Jasper, hello Daisy. I'm guessing you're here to collect Doris. She's grown loads this year.'

'Not three foot though,' muttered Jasper, with a grin.

I knew, given how tired Ned looked, that he was making a huge effort to warmly greet these annual customers he clearly knew so well and I also knew that he was going to go ballistic when he found out what I'd done. Hopefully not in front of them though. Not that I didn't deserve a public dressing down.

'Where is Doris?' he frowned, his eyes scanning the few trees still awaiting collection.

'With the *Stott* family, apparently,' said Kim, with a hard stare in my direction.

Ned's gaze swung to me. 'Oh,' he said. 'I see.'

I opened my mouth to explain, but David called me from the barn.

'Phone call, Liza!' he shouted.

'You'd better take it,' said Ned, through gritted teeth.

I didn't need telling twice and sprinted off.

'It's a chap asking for the young woman who's working here today,' said David, handing me the phone. 'As Maya's been out, that can only be you, can't it?'

267

'Theo?' I tentatively spoke into the handset, even though I knew it wasn't.

'No,' said a posh voice. 'Mr Stott actually.'

'Oh Mr Stott,' I blustered. 'I'm so sorry. My mistake with your tree has literally just come to light. I do apologise. It wasn't the fault of the man who came to pick it up at all,' I hastily added, hoping I hadn't cost him his betrothal. 'It was entirely mine. I muddled your tree . . .'

'With the Scott family tree,' he cut in. 'Yes, I can see that from the label. Had I been there I would have seen straightaway that this wasn't ours. Still, no harm done. Can you switch them tomorrow? You'll need to deliver and collect.'

'Of course,' I said, relieved that he was willing to be so understanding. At least that might help my cause when I went back to talk to Ned and placate the Scotts. Mr Stott's prospective son-in-law must have either been a bit of a wuss or the guy's bark was worse than his bite. 'I'll rectify the situation first thing tomorrow.'

'Excellent,' he said and hung up.

'What's going on?' David asked, looking concerned when I ended the call.

'Nothing to worry about,' I told him. 'A slight hiccup but it will soon be rectified.'

I rushed back out knowing I sounded more confident than I felt, but then again, I could calm a class argument with just one look, which was quite something for someone of my diminutive stature. Then I spotted Ned's face, which resembled a thundercloud, and wondered if my faith in my mediating skills was misplaced.

'Right,' I said, before anyone else had a chance to chip in. 'That was Mr Stott on the phone. He's acknowledged the mix-up and I've told him I'll switch the trees tomorrow and personally deliver them. Both of them.'

Ned looked taken aback.

'I'll drop this tree at the Stott residence, then load up Doris,' I said, smiling at the girl who was still blubbing but only because her mother seemed hellbent on encouraging her, 'and then deliver her straight to you.'

'But we wanted to decorate her today,' the girl snivelled.

The boy rolled his eyes. Bored with the drama, which obviously wasn't going to end spectacularly, he shoved his earbuds in and zoned out. At least that was one less Scott to worry about. I turned my attention back to the father.

'These things happen, sugarplum,' he was telling his daughter. 'I'm sure this lady didn't mean to give Doris to someone else.'

'She certainly didn't,' I quickly confirmed.

'This would never have happened when Mr Wynter were here,' said the wife, looking disparagingly at me.

I didn't think that was the moment to announce I was his daughter.

'You can have Doris at absolutely no cost this year,' I said, 'to compensate for my mistake.'

Ned was looking daggers at me.

'That sounds like a very generous gesture,' beamed Maya,

who I hadn't until that moment noticed. 'And how about a little something from Santa to say sorry, too?'

She handed the boy and girl a stocking apiece. The girl's tears dried instantly and the lad blushed bright red. He was too old for a stocking but Maya's lovely smile certainly seemed to strike a chord. I could have kissed her.

'We'll see you tomorrow then,' I said waving them off, having first made sure we had their correct address and postcode. I was going to need it and the Stotts' to make the switch, along with Ned's truck. I only hoped he hadn't got another full day of deliveries lined up.

Chapter 19

By then, a cloying drizzly rain had started to fall, the light was fading and Wynter's Trees was deserted. No one from the huts had come to give me an update on Wren and so I assumed they still hadn't heard anything.

I waved Joe off then followed Ned, David and Maya into the office knowing I had some explaining to do. I only hoped that when I told Ned that Wren had been taken ill and I had been distracted and worried about her, he would be a little more understanding about the mix-up I'd accidentally made.

'Bloody hell,' he said, running his hands through his hair before I had a chance to say a word. 'This is a right royal balls up, isn't it?'

I had seen Joe talking to him before he left and guessed he'd mentioned how busy we'd been, but Ned was clearly unwilling to accept the influx of extra customers which, I remembered, I had also been partly responsible for, as contributing to my mistake.

'If you would only let me explain, Ned . . .' I tried.

'I know none of this actually matters to you, Liza,' he cut in. 'Especially not anymore, but we take pride in our reputation here at Wynter's Trees and we would like to get through the season with it still intact.'

'Of course it matters to me,' I snapped.

'Why wouldn't it?' frowned Maya.

No one answered her.

'I'll cover the lost rental costs for the trees out of my own pocket,' I inadequately insisted. 'And whatever you think is right for the delivery.'

'Damn right you will,' grumbled Ned.

'Edward!' David warningly said.

'And how exactly are you going to make this miraculous swap?' Ned stormed on. 'You can't take the truck, because I need it. There are still trees to go out tomorrow. There simply isn't the time for me to go chasing all over the county clearing up the mess you've made today.'

Even though I had hoped I was wrong, I'd had the feeling that might be the case, right from the moment I'd rashly offered to make the swap.

'Oh,' was all I could muster.

I took in Ned's glowering expression and began to wonder if he was using my mistake over the trees to have another dig about my decision to sell up. It wasn't as if I'd fed either the Stotts' or the Scotts' trees through the shredder, and even though there were transport issues to resolve, the depth of his temper and his out of character reaction did feel a little over the top.

'Edward,' David said again. 'You're being too harsh. It was a mistake which could have happened to anyone.'

'A mistake!' Ned laughed, but it was obvious that he didn't find any humour in the situation. 'Dad, if I had a pound for every time you told me that mistakes like this could ruin the Wynter's Trees reputation and that we had to check, check and check again before we let a tree go, then I'd be retiring with you.'

'Of course, you wouldn't,' Maya mildly said. 'You're as melded to this place as Liza's dad was, Ned, and that's why you're getting your boxers in such a knot. You have to admit, Liza's already done as much as she can to sort it out.'

'But the trees are still in the wrong place and with the wrong families,' he said, this time through gritted teeth. 'And we have no way of moving them.'

'Well,' Maya continued, sounding completely unruffled, 'we're shut tomorrow and I know there's stuff to be getting on with, but I can easily borrow a truck from the farm and take Liza to switch the trees. It shouldn't take too long.'

David and I looked from her to Ned. If he accepted her offer, then she would have effectively saved me from a further tongue-lashing and two families' Christmases from being ruined.

'They're big trees,' Ned pointed out, thrusting his hands into his jacket pockets.

'And we're big girls,' she shrugged, kissing his cheek. 'Well, I am. Liza's more of a pixie, but she's plenty strong enough. Aren't you?' she said, winking at me.

'Absolutely,' I said, giving her a grateful smile.

'You should have asked for identification,' Ned further grumbled.

'I did,' I said, 'but the guy collecting the Stott tree wasn't a Stott so it made no difference because his last name wasn't the same.'

'The trees are only supposed to be released to family members or someone they've named on the release form,' he persisted.

'Well, no one told me that, did they?' I pointed out.

'And anyway,' said David, looking briefly at me. 'I signed the release form. I took care of them all today and I've just had another look at it and there was a note saying another family member was coming to collect the tree. I missed it earlier.'

I didn't mention that, strictly speaking, the guy wasn't yet a family member.

'Yes,' said Maya, looking thoughtful. 'Now you mention it, David, I think I took that call sometime last week.'

'Why didn't you mention that before, Dad?' Ned tutted.

'Because you didn't give me a chance,' David fairly pointed out.

Ned let out a long breath. He looked exhausted and we still had days to go before the end of the delivery service. I had been going to mention that I had been distracted about Wren too, but then decided not to. There was no point going over it all again and, as I still hadn't had word from Theo, I decided it was best left until I knew what had gone on.

*

True to her word, Maya arrived early the next morning in a huge truck and with a picnic basket tucked into the footwell.

'I thought we'd make the most of the trip,' she giggled as I scrabbled to climb into the cab after we'd manhandled the Stotts' tree and secured it in the back. 'Do you want a hand?' she asked, thankfully with no derision.

'No,' I said, as I finally got a foothold and heaved myself up, 'but thanks.'

I hadn't slept particularly well and there was still no word from Theo or Sue. I really hoped everything was all right. Maya hadn't mentioned anything about it either and I didn't have the heart to fill her in on what had occurred the day before. I knew I could have messaged Sue to ask, but couldn't bring myself to, for fear that she'd only have sad news to impart.

'Right,' Maya happily said. 'Let's go!'

The Stott residence was the perfect match for Mr Stott's voice – upper class and imposing – and the switch was soon smoothly made. He hadn't allowed the Scott tree to cross the Edwardian threshold, so Maya expertly manoeuvred Doris on to the sack wheels and between us we wheeled her back down the drive and then up the ramp and safely into the truck.

'Thank goodness you had a vehicle with a ramp,' I puffed. 'We never would have lifted either of these.'

'That's what I thought,' said Maya, grimacing as between us we dragged and loaded the Stotts' much taller tree on to the wheels. 'I'm going to need your eyes to guide me with this one, Liza,' she added. 'It's a lot heavier than Doris and too dense to see through.'

I had no idea how Ned managed to do this. No wonder he was happy for customers to collect and return their trees, if they had a vehicle big enough. On the website I'd seen that he marketed that aspect as being all part of the Wynter's *tree gathering experience*, but having tried it for myself, I realised it was actually more about saving his strength.

The cut trees for the Wynbridge auction must have felt as light as feathers after all the filled pots he'd been hauling about. Not only was there the weight of the tree but you had to take the damp earth it was growing in and the pot itself into consideration too.

'Here we are then,' I said to Mr Stott, conscious that he was watching our every move as we made our way up the path again.

'He's going in the bay window as usual,' he said, walking around the tree and inspecting every branch and needle. 'Put on a lot of growth,' he thoughtfully said. 'Might be the last year he makes it indoors. Next stop, the garden.'

I was pleased the family had plans to plant this one out. It was really too heavy to shift far and I could imagine the prospective son-in-law's mortification when he was informed of the mistake because Doris was nowhere near as big as this brute. It must have caused quite a stir when he arrived back with her, and not a good one.

'Would you like us to position him?' Maya asked and I shot her a look.

'No, no,' said Mr Stott. 'I'll get the chaps who help my wife in the garden to do that and I think I'll give Wynter's a ring and see about keeping hold of the tree this year. It might be better to plant him out sooner rather than later.'

I was relieved about both the positioning and the fact that no one would have to try and return the tree to Wynter's.

'I know you probably don't need this,' I said, having rushed to the truck and back again, 'but I forgot to pop one in Doris's pot yesterday.' I held out a care sheet for him to take.

'Doris?' he frowned.

'That's the name of the other tree.'

'Oh, right,' he smiled, taking the sheet. 'I think we have already got one of these kicking about, but we know what we're doing.'

'I'll leave it anyway,' I said, erring on the side of caution, 'if that's all right with you.'

'Don't want to get in more trouble with the boss, eh?' He astutely said, his bushy grey eyebrows twitching.

'Quite,' I agreed. 'And there's this one too.'

I handed him a second sheet which had planting out guidelines on.

'Thanks,' he said. 'Right. I think that's everything, isn't it? We now have the right tree and that fool of a boy will be able to sleep tonight.'

'It really wasn't his fault about the mix-up,' I quickly said. 'I should have double checked the label.'

'Yes, well,' he said, looking at the tree again. 'No harm

done and it's kept him on his toes. I daresay we'll have an engagement announcement over Christmas, if his courage doesn't fail him.'

After the phone call yesterday, I had thought the guy might have been a bit of a wimp, but having now met Mr Stott in person, I retracted that unfair assumption. He was the bravest of the brave to be taking on this man as a father-in-law.

I heard Maya clattering the sack wheels up the ramp behind me and beat a hasty retreat back up the drive.

'We'll leave you to your day then,' I said to Mr Stott, 'and again, I'm so sorry about the mix-up. Thank you for being so understanding.'

'That's all right,' he said. 'Ask David if there's anything to pay for keeping the tree, would you? I want to settle the account ahead of picking out another next year.'

I would look forward to telling Ned he'd said that. If Mr Stott was willing to choose another tree then the Wynter's reputation wasn't in the total tatters he imagined.

'Of course,' I said. 'Someone will be in touch. Goodbye.'

'See you next year,' Mr Stott called after me. 'It will be fun to start again with a tiddler.'

Just for a moment, I rather wished I was going to be around to see that.

'That'll be interesting,' said Maya, voicing my thoughts as I scrambled back into my seat and fired off a quick email asking David to update the Stott account and issue a final bill. 'I bet Mr Stott's idea of a tiddler won't be a teeny two-foot effort, will it?'

'Definitely not,' I laughed, feeling better now that the first part of the plan was sorted and had gone smoothly.

'You'll have to let me know what they go for.'

Maya indicated and pulled on to the road, side-eyeing me as she did so.

'Why, where are you going to be?' she frowned.

I felt my face flush. 'I mean, if I forget what he's just said,' I hastily said. 'Or I'm off-site when he visits.'

'I don't think you'll forget about this in a hurry,' Maya laughed.

'No,' I said. 'I don't suppose I will.'

I keyed the Scott postcode into the satnav and settled back into my seat.

'Are you missing your job, Liza?' Maya asked, once she'd driven a mile or two.

I wondered if my slip of the tongue had got her thinking about my change in circumstances.

'Yes,' I truthfully said. At least I could be honest about that. 'Although, at this time of year it's hectic. Imagine, if you can, trying to manage a whole load of teens, who pretend they're too cool to care about Christmas, from getting too excited about it.'

Maya gave a shudder. 'I don't know how you do it,' she said. 'I've got two younger brothers and a sister at home and negotiating my way through and between them is hard enough. The thought of a class of twenty.' She dithered again.

That no doubt accounted for her ability to stay calm in a

crisis. Growing up in a large family she would have seen and waded through her fair share of battles and rows.

'Nearer a class of thirty more like,' I corrected her. 'In mainstream school that is.'

Maya whistled under her breath.

'Would you consider going back to it?' she interestedly asked, as the Australian accented chap narrating directions on her satnav told her to take the next left.

'Not teaching in a mainstream school,' I quickly said, shrinking from the thought of the weeks I'd misguidedly just covered. 'But I would like to carry on in some way,' I told her. It was the most revealing thing I could say without giving away too much. 'I enjoy the nurturing role a lot more than regular teaching. Looking out for the kids who find school tricky and don't necessarily see Christmas as a good thing.'

'Are there kids who don't see Christmas as a good thing?' she laughed.

'Unfortunately, yes.' I swallowed. 'There are plenty of students who dread all the holidays. Not everyone is blessed with home being their safe and happy place, Maya.'

I could feel her eyes on me for a moment.

'God,' she said, her smile fading. 'That's a terrible thought.'

'For some it's a reality,' I said, sadly.

'So, do you use art in your counselling and therapy?'

'Yes,' I said, 'and we get outdoors a lot too. In my experience, the students are more willing to open up and share things in a relaxed and open environment. Outdoors we can potter and gather, with no eye contact, and then use what we find to make something or inspire a painting or a collage. You get the idea.'

'I do,' she smiled again. 'It sounds great. Fresh air is free and you can't beat time spent in nature when it comes to lifting your spirits and clearing your head.'

'Exactly,' I agreed.

'But that could be a real issue for you if you want to carry on with it.' She said, her eyebrows almost meeting as she frowned in concentration. 'I don't think there's anywhere near Wynter's Trees where you'll find a job like that.'

Unfortunately, she'd hit the nail on the head.

'And besides,' she carried on, 'won't you have your hands too full at the plantation to take on another job?'

We were heading into tricky territory again.

'But then, maybe that's what . . .' she said thoughtfully, then hesitated.

'Maybe that's what, Maya?' I prompted, when she didn't carry on.

She threw me another look.

'Well,' she said, 'I heard Ned talking to David about those outdoor schools.'

'What outdoor schools?' I frowned.

'I don't know really,' she shrugged, a blush blooming. 'Ignore me. I didn't hear the whole thing and besides, I shouldn't have been listening. Now, I don't know this area very well so I'd better concentrate.'

'Of course,' I said, looking at the satnav. 'I don't think it's too complicated from here though.'

Although intrigued about what she'd overheard, I let the subject drop. It was imperative that the trees were switched without incident and therefore, I turned my attention to the view and let Maya focus on the road and the Aussie accented directions.

It took over an hour to drive between the Stotts and the Scotts and I could well understand why Ned had been so hacked off. Had Maya not generously stepped in, he would have had to sort out my muddle and on top of all the other deliveries he had to make, it would have made for a very long day.

Both the Scott offspring were at school, so I didn't have the pleasure of seeing their reaction to being reunited with Doris who, according to her paperwork, had been with the family since Jasper was ten. I knew he would have pretended he wasn't fussed, but I bet he would have been fizzing inside and Daisy would have probably cried. She had come across as a lover of the waterworks.

'Here she is!' shouted Andrew who rushed from the house as Maya expertly reversed between two parked cars and up on to the drive.

'One Doris as promised,' I smiled, jumping out of the cab as Maya hopped into the back of the trailer and loaded the tree on to the wheels as competently as she had just completed the narrow reversing manoeuvre.

I was beginning to think there was nothing she couldn't do.

'Doris,' Andrew sighed as we wheeled the tree down the ramp. 'I'm afraid my wife couldn't be here to welcome her, but she's told me exactly where she wants her.'

'I bet she has,' Maya whispered and I had to stifle a giggle.

I wasn't at all upset that I wouldn't be seeing his wife, Kim, again and helped Maya guide the tree, which was nowhere near as large as the Stotts', and relatively easy to carry, into the house.

'You know,' said Andrew, once we'd put Doris in place as per Kim's most particular instructions, 'I'm not sure that's right.'

'Me neither,' said Maya, winking at me and playing devil's advocate. 'Surely she'd look better the other side of the fire.'

The fire in question was an electric wood burning stove, so Doris wouldn't come to any harm if she were pulled a little closer to the faux flames.

'I think you're right,' said Andrew scratching his head. 'She usually fits there a treat but the bit extra she's grown this year makes her look a bit cramped, don't you think?'

'I do,' I agreed, because it had been a bit of a squeeze to get her in.

'If we lift her up, could you,' he said, nodding to me, 'shift the tray across?'

I loved that Doris had her own bespoke tray to sit in and which collected any loose earth or water which would otherwise have ruined the carpet.

'Absolutely,' I said, suiting the action to the words.

'There,' said Maya, as they put her down again, 'much better and I'm sure your wife will agree.'

'That's definitely a better spot,' Andrew said, biting his lip, 'but I'm not sure if Kim . . .'

'Right,' I briskly said, handing him a copy of the same care sheet I'd given Mr Stott, 'we'd better get on. We've lots to do back at Wynter's Trees.'

'Of course,' said Andrew, who was looking a little doubtful about not following his wife's instructions to the letter. 'Can I offer you a drink before you go? I'd just boiled the kettle when you arrived.'

'Thank you, but no,' I said, following Maya out. 'We really must be going. Merry Christmas!'

'Merry Christmas!' he called after us.

As Maya carefully inched the truck back between the cars, we could see him through the window, striding about, looking at Doris from one angle and then another.

'I feel a bit bad now,' giggled Maya, as we drove off. 'She's going to give him hell for deviating from the plan.'

She didn't sound particularly sorry and I couldn't help but laugh along with her.

'She will, won't she?' I smiled.

I was about to comment further, but my phone started to ring. I scrabbled in my pocket for it, hoping it wasn't Mr Scott begging us to go back and return Doris to her original spot, but then felt guilty as I realised that for a few minutes, I'd forgotten all about Wren. I hoped, if this was the call I'd been waiting for, I was about to hear good news, rather than bad.

'Please let her be all right,' I whispered, fumbling to answer the call. 'Hello?'

'Hi, it's me.'

It was Ned and for the first time ever, I felt my heart sink at the sound of his voice.

'I thought I'd just give you a quick call to find out how you're getting on?'

It was a rubbish signal and I had a job to hear him.

'Good,' I shouted. 'We're all done.'

I felt relieved the switch had gone so smoothly, but Maya shook her head and rolled her eyes when I looked at her.

'What?' I mouthed.

'Never mind,' she muttered.

'And both families were happy?' Ned asked.

'Both families were thrilled,' I told him, but then they were getting their trees for free this year so, had I been in their shoes, I'd have been happy too. 'I've emailed and asked David to get in touch with Mr Stott about keeping their tree,' I added. 'They want to plant it out in their garden now it's had so many years in a pot.'

'Mmm,' Ned said ponderously. 'I suppose they might have got another year out of it, but that would have been pushing it. I'll make a note about sending a final bill.'

'There's no need,' I said, feeling rankled, but trying not to get too annoyed because he might not have heard what I said about sorting that because of the dodgy signal. 'I've already emailed your dad about it,' I repeated.

'Are you heading back now then?' he asked, ignoring what I'd just said.

'Yes,' I said. 'We've literally just left the Scotts.'

Maya tutted and I looked at her and shrugged.

'Well, don't rush,' said Ned. 'Given the time, you might as well stop and have some lunch on the way back.'

'All right,' I said, feeling crestfallen.

I got the distinct impression he didn't want me back at the plantation too soon, even if it was shut and I couldn't cause further mayhem. I supposed I should have felt pleased that we'd established a bit of distance as it would help make leaving again easier, but the truth was, his continued abruptness smarted a bit.

'How are you getting on?' I then asked him.

'Good,' he said. 'I'll see you later,' and with that he hung up.

I told myself it was the less than satisfactory signal that had kept the call brief and stuffed the phone in my pocket.

'What's with the face?' I asked Maya, who was still pouting.

'You should have said the traffic was heavy or something,' she admonished. 'Or that there was a hold up. We could have had a bit more time playing hooky and found somewhere to stop and eat lunch then.'

'It's all right,' I told her with a sigh. 'Ned suggested we should stop and eat anyway.'

Maya swerved a little as she looked at me, causing the car behind to toot.

'What?' I said, my eyes fixed on the road.

'Well, that's a first,' she gasped. 'He's always rush, rush, rush at this time of year.'

'I thought as much,' I sighed again.

'I wonder what he's up to?' she frowned.

'Nothing,' I said. 'He's up to nothing. He's just happy I'm going to be off-site for a bit longer and won't be able to bugger anything else up.'

'Oh, I'm sure that's not it,' she began, but the look I threw her silenced her.

As it wasn't too chilly, and we were already wrapped in multiple layers, we found a wooded picnic site and tucked into the delicious soup from the pot Maya said her mum always had on the stove in winter. There were sausage rolls from the Wynmouth butcher too, apples, also from Maya's kitchen and cookies which Hope had made. It was all delicious and we ate in companionable silence until our bellies were full.

'So,' I stole myself to ask once I'd thanked her for the tasty repast, 'how are things going with you and Ned?'

Maya wrinkled her nose and chewed her final mouthful of cookie wearing a thoughtful expression.

'Slowly,' she said, once she'd swallowed. 'Very slowly.'

She didn't sound very impressed with the glacial pace.

'Well, that's something,' I responded. 'Given what you told me before, it's far better than the not-moving-at-all that you've been stuck with in the past.'

'Mmm,' she said. 'I suppose, but I can't help thinking there's something nagging away that's stopping him from focusing on us.'

'What do you mean?'

'He's distracted,' she frowned. 'All the time.'

'Well, that's hardly surprising given the time of year, is it?' I pointed out. 'Maybe you need to wait for the end of the season for things to speed up. Come the spring there'll be less to do on the plantation and you can make the most of the beach.'

Sometimes I forgot that Wynter's Trees was located so close to the coast. I'd barely visited the village since I'd been back and I'd only seen the sea once. But then, given it was the middle of December, it was hardly the cosiest place to hang out.

'I don't know,' said Maya, fixing me with an intent stare.

I shifted in my seat, rather unsettled by her scrutiny. Given that Ned had my request to buy me out of the business preying on his mind, it was hardly surprising that he was distracted, but I wasn't about to explain that.

'Between you and me,' Maya added, biting her lip, 'I'm not sure his preoccupation is anything to do with work at all.'

I, of course, knew that it was *everything* to do with work and wondered how Ned would react if I suggested to him that he should talk to Maya about it. Given that I'd only fleetingly suggested the pair should start running together and as if by magic, Maya had instantly appeared in her figure enhancing running gear, he might consider it a wonderful proposal and embrace it with open arms.

'It's like his head is entirely somewhere else,' Maya carried on, 'and that's not like him at all, especially at this time of year.'

'But you have to remember how different this year has been,' I reminded her.

'What with you being back, you mean?'

'Well,' I said, 'there is that, but I was thinking more about the changes to Wynter's Trees that he's instigated. Setting up the beach huts and having the site open longer, as well as the barn, has taken a lot of organising. The place has been transformed and even though it has all gone smoothly enough, it's still a lot of responsibility for one person to carry.'

As my words flowed, I realised I'd hit the nail on the head. Ned really did have a lot on his plate this Christmas.

'You know what,' Maya said, brightening considerably. 'You're right. It's no wonder he's been a bit off, is it?'

My words had succeeded in lifting her mood again, but they'd made mine sink into my boots. My announcement to sell felt horribly mistimed. Poor Ned.

'No,' I said, 'it isn't, is it? And I've hardly helped, have I?'

'Of course, you have,' Maya insisted as she began tidying away the lunch things. 'The grotto painting and the cart conversions have been an absolute hit.'

'But the twisted ankle and the cock up with the trees,' I countered. 'They've hardly been my finest moments, have they?'

'Hiccups in the grand scheme of things,' Maya said, shrugging away my mistakes as easily as she swept the crumbs we'd made off the table.

She might have been able to forget about my recent blunders but they, alongside my big decision, became stuck fast in my head as we drove the rest of the journey back. I had previously told Ned that I would make an effort to make my last Christmas connected to Wynter's Trees a good one, and it was about time I did exactly that.

Chapter 20

It was well into the afternoon by the time we arrived at Wynter's Trees. The return journey had been hampered by heavy traffic and Maya and I had laughed conspiratorially that we had talked it up. We didn't chat all the way back however, because she'd locked the truck radio to Heart Xmas, (which she said would annoy the heck out of her brothers), and we'd sung along, as hilariously out of tune as each other, to every festive track. I had forgotten my worries for a while, although Wren was never far from my thoughts, and it felt like a much needed and appreciated respite.

My time with Maya had been a real tonic. We'd laughed so much my belly ached and my brain was in much better shape than it had been the day before. Maya was the human embodiment of what was meant by 'don't judge a book by its cover'. She was tall, slim and breathtakingly beautiful, but she was also generous, intelligent, completely modest and a rubbish singer. She was also the perfect match for Ned, in all things, and as much as that still pained me, I knew I had to reconcile myself to it.

'You coming in?' I asked her, when we reached the gate which was locked because the plantation was closed on a Monday.

There didn't look to be anyone working in the huts, but there was a light on in the barn and the doors were open.

'I'm going to make some hot chocolate,' I temptingly added.

'As appealing as that is, I'd better not,' she said. 'Dad will be wanting the truck back.'

'Of course,' I said, gathering my things together. 'You really got me out of a pickle today, Maya. Thank you so much for stepping in and helping out and please, thank your dad for the loan of the truck too.'

'It's no bother,' she lightly said. 'It's actually been really fun.'

'It has,' I agreed, although I was well aware that it would have been better all round had I not made the mix-up in the first place, 'and we've covered some miles. Make a note of them, won't you?' I added. 'Because I want to reimburse you for the fuel.'

Maya wouldn't hear of it and made a neat three point turn on the drive so I didn't have to open the gate. I watched until she was out of sight and then climbed over, landed carefully on my healthy ankle and headed for the lodge.

My breath caught as I opened the door. The main lights were all switched off, but the whole of downstairs was bathed in the warm glow of twinkling fairy lights. I stepped further in and closed the door noticing that the new lights were all artfully wrapped around a potted Christmas tree which was sitting in place of where the television had been, a little distance away from the log burner.

The significance of the position of the tree wasn't lost on me. It was where the family tree had always been displayed, although this of course, wasn't the original family tree. Ned and I had planted that a couple of weeks ago. Ned . . .

Positioning this new tree and covering it in lights must have been the reason behind his insistence that Maya and I didn't rush back. If he was responsible for the pretty sight, then I realised he *had* wanted to keep me away from Wynter's Trees for as long as possible, but not for the reason I had originally thought. He must have been planning to surprise me, and if that was the case, he must have forgiven me for my mistake. But what exactly had prompted this dramatic turnaround and change of heart, I wondered, assuming I'd read the situation right?

My mobile bleeped as a text message landed and I quickly dumped my bag and pulled my phone out of my pocket.

> Wren is doing really well. Sorry it's taken a while to let you know. It's been a bit touch and go but she's much better and, she's still pregnant! It's early days and she's got to be careful but we'll be back at the huts soon. Thank you for all your help yesterday. Theo x

I must have read the message a dozen times to make sure I'd understood it properly. Wren was okay and, most importantly, she was still pregnant.

Maya's kindness, coupled with the discovery of the beautiful tree had been enough to form a lump in my throat and a prickle of tears behind my eyes, but this much anticipated and reassuring message from Theo completely burst through my already weakening defences and my body was wracked with sobs.

They weren't refined tears either, but the noisy, messy kind and I gave in to them completely. I felt so relieved for Wren, and so wrung out after undoing the mess I'd made over the trees, that a few tears would have been justified, but I knew the emotional outpouring I finally succumbed to was about so much more than any of those things.

The river of tears which soaked my face and neck fell not just for my new friends and a couple of trees, but for the whole of Wynter's, along with everything it had come to represent. Ned, David, Maya, Chelsea, Liam and everyone else danced through my head on a sort of merry go round and I sobbed as I watched them all go by.

With Ned's help, since I'd arrived back in Wynmouth, I had finally unpacked the multiple boxes of mental baggage I'd been carrying, but I hadn't once allowed the dam to properly burst. Now my tears were washing everything away and I wholeheartedly allowed myself to be swept along with them. I sunk down next to the fire and finally gave myself permission to cry my heart out.

'Liza! It's me. Are you here?'

I was upstairs when Ned and Bandit eventually came in. I'd finished off my transformative cry out in the shower and was feeling a whole lot better. Granted, my eyes looked a bit red and swollen, but that was only to be expected given the gallons of tears which had poured out of them. I didn't think I'd ever have another one to shed.

'Yes,' I called back, somewhat huskily but feeling light in my heart. 'I'll be down in a minute.'

Wren was pregnant, my tree muddle had been rectified and I was on my way to tying up the loose ends which would free me from Wynter's Trees and set me off on my merry way. All was right with the world.

Aside from the fact that I still needed to convince my heart that my feelings for Ned weren't going to amount to anything. Okay, so not *everything* was right with the world, but the keel definitely felt more even than it had before.

'Hey,' Ned softly said, when I padded down the stairs in my animal print pyjamas and dressing gown.

'Hey,' I said back.

We stood staring at each other for a few seconds. I was reluctant to come all the way down the stairs. It was nice to look him straight in the eyes for once. Actually, it was a bit too nice. I hastily skipped down the final two steps.

'Come and sit down for a minute, will you?' he asked. 'I need to talk to you.'

The look on his face and the change in his tone told me I was forgiven and I realised I needed to keep busy around him. I knew that, having already looked deep into his eyes, a sit-down talk would be too much for my already rapidly thumping heart.

'Aren't you hungry?' I asked, nodding towards the kitchen. 'We can talk while I make us something to eat, if you like.'

Not that I had much of an appetite. I was still full from Maya's picnic. I thought about the fun the pair of us had enjoyed throughout the day. It felt imperative that I should keep Maya at the forefront of my mind if I was going to take my heart in hand.

'No,' said Ned. 'Food can wait.'

'Food can wait,' I gasped. 'Crikey, this must be serious.'

He plonked himself on the sofa and I reluctantly joined him at the other end. Bandit quickly, and thankfully, filled the space between us, but Ned clicked his fingers and the dog obediently jumped back down and settled at our feet. I would have much preferred it if he'd let the pooch stay put.

'So,' I said, as I leant down to stroke Bandit's head, 'what's more important than your supper, Ned?'

He let out a long breath.

'I know about Wren,' he huskily said.

I sat back up again and looked at him.

'Theo called earlier and told me what happened yesterday.'

I nodded.

'He told me it was chaotic when they left for the hospital and that they had to switch things around in the huts.'

'I was going to tell you,' I said, 'but the timing wasn't

right. The beach hut team were brilliant. They had everything in hand even before Theo came to find me.'

'They're a great bunch.'

'The best,' I agreed. 'I'm pleased you know now and I'm so pleased Wren is okay. Is that what you wanted to talk about?' I asked, making to stand up.

'No,' said Ned, putting a hand up to stop me. 'It isn't.'

I sat back again.

'I've had a look through the receipts from yesterday,' he carried on. 'It must have been bedlam, netting and selling that number of trees in that amount of time.'

'It was busy,' I conceded. 'But we managed. Just about. Aside from my stupid muddle over the Stott and Scott trees of course.'

Why had I brought that back up?

'Never mind that now,' said Ned, fixing me with his beautiful eyes. 'What I'm trying to say, pretty incoherently I know, is thank you, Liza.'

'Thank you?' I frowned. 'What for?'

All I'd done was make more work for all of us.

'For this,' he said reaching down the side of the sofa. 'Two whole pages dedicated to Wynter's Trees and all down to you.'

He opened the paper and spread it across his lap.

'Oh,' I said. I'd forgotten all about the newspaper article. 'It was nothing.' I shrugged. 'Pot luck, really.'

'No,' said Ned, 'it really was something. You made the effort to get in touch with the paper, Liza and that in turn has already helped to make this year the most profitable the plantation has ever had.'

At least something positive had come out of the day before.

'Well, in that case,' I said, 'I'm pleased. Shall we get some supper now . . .'

'No,' said Ned. 'Hang on. I haven't finished.'

I looked away from his face and down at my hands.

'I want to say sorry as well as thank you.'

'Sorry?' I asked, my gaze snapping up again.

'Yes,' he softly said. 'I should never have taken my temper out on you. Given how busy the place was, how short of staff we were for the visitor numbers and all the extra worry about Wren, it was no wonder there was a hiccup in proceedings.'

'But even so,' I put in, 'I should have checked that label more carefully.'

Ned shook his head. 'If I tell you something, will you promise not to go mad?' he asked.

'That will depend on what it is.'

He bit his bottom lip. It was an incredibly sexy look.

'What is it?' I demanded, willing him to talk again and stop turning me on.

He took a deep breath. 'When I realised which of the trees had been switched,' he told me, 'I was as angry at myself as I was with you.'

'Why?'

'Because I'd been meaning to change the labels to make the names more obvious and I was going to mention to Dad that they were both due to be collected yesterday too, but I forgot.'

Without thinking, I grabbed a cushion and whacked him with it. Bandit jumped up, keen to join in the fun.

'Are you telling me,' I said, hitting Ned again, 'that it was as much your mistake as mine?'

'I wouldn't go that far,' he said, putting his hands over his head when I threatened to inflict another feather filled blow. 'All right,' he conceded as I lined up my aim. 'It was about even.'

I dumped the cushion back on the sofa, much to Bandit's disappointment.

'Bloody hell,' I muttered. 'And to think I spent a sleepless night worrying about it.'

Ned had the grace to look a bit sheepish as he pushed his hair away from his face.

'Sorry,' he grinned.

'You don't look it,' I tutted. 'But at least it's all sorted now. Thanks mostly to Maya.'

Ned nodded.

'We had a real laugh today,' I told him, remembering our out of tune rendition of Mariah's most famous festive tune. 'She's a wonderful woman. You could certainly do a lot worse than her, you know?'

'She's certainly good for business,' he said, properly running a hand through his mussed-up hair and making it look even worse.

'That wasn't what I meant . . .'

'So,' he said, swiftly changing the subject. 'What do you think of this tree?'

Knowing he wouldn't be pushed, I let him get away with the switch of topic, but I was determined to track back to it at some point.

After a Nigel Slater supper of honey and mustard covered sausages and a mug of mulled cider apiece, we set about decorating the tree using the boxes I'd stacked in the utility room on Dad's birthday.

'I've been looking forward to this moment,' said Ned, liberating my primary school angel from the box. 'This is definitely going on the top.'

'Well,' I said, 'you'd better put it up there, because I certainly can't reach.'

'Oh no,' said Ned, pulling me to my feet and then picking me up in one swift and smooth movement. 'You have to do the honours.'

My breath caught in my throat and my heart started to canter as his arms tightened around me.

'Go on then,' he said, when I didn't move. 'Or do you need to be a bit higher?'

I quickly reached up and plonked the angel on the highest branch.

'That'll do,' I said, trying to wriggle free.

'It's a bit wonky,' Ned laughed, as he set me on my feet. 'Let's have another go.'

'No,' I said, backing off as he reached for me again and

Bandit barked and skittered around our feet. He was having a whale of a time. 'You do it,' I insisted. 'You can reach easily enough.'

With the angel finally positioned, we set to adding everything else. Lots of the baubles had belonged to my grandparents and there were a variety of handcrafted and sewn decorations too, all of which I knew Mum had made.

Dressing the tree took much longer than it used to, but that was because I wanted to examine everything. I wanted to savour every treasure and lock the sight of them, proudly displayed on the new tree, away in my memory for safe-keeping. I found the process far harder than I had expected to and it was a struggle for my head to acknowledge that this was the last time I'd ever decorate the lodge for the festive season.

Next year, I forced myself to think, it would be Maya and Ned standing together and doing this. Although they wouldn't be using the same decorations. I had already made up my mind to pack them up and take them with me when I left after Christmas.

'So, what do you think?' Ned asked, looking about him.

It must have been hours after we'd started but he hadn't rushed me once. In fact, I got the impression that he'd enjoyed listening to me explain the origins and anecdotes attached to each and every decoration.

'Do you think it's finished?' he queried.

I took a step back and drank the vision in. It was perfect, utterly perfect. Exactly how Mum and Dad would have wanted our family tree to look. I felt a fresh supply of tears rush to my eyes. So much for my earlier assumption that I was all cried out.

'I take it you like it?' said Ned, picking up one of my hands and giving it a squeeze.

'Yes,' I sniffed, wiping my eyes on my sleeve. 'I love it. It's beautiful. It looks very much like the tree Dad and I used to have.'

Ned nodded and pulled me into his side. I wrapped my arms around his waist and he kissed the top of my head. In spite of the difference in our heights, it felt so right snuggling into him. Surprisingly, we felt like the perfect fit.

'There's something I have to tell you about this tree, Liza,' Ned said.

'What is it?' I asked, looking up at him.

He led me back to the sofa and we sat down, closer this time. Our knees were almost touching and as soon as we were settled, he picked up my hand again.

'Your dad always had an eye on the future,' he began. 'You've said that yourself, haven't you?'

'I have,' I agreed. 'Many times. We've all of us said it, I think.'

Ned smiled. 'Well, this tree is proof of that,' he told me.

'What do you mean?'

'Your dad potted this tree up years ago, specifically for the lodge.'

'He did?' I choked.

'He did,' Ned confirmed. 'And there's another smaller

one too, barely bigger than a few branches right now, which will keep the tradition going for years to come.'

'I had no idea,' I smiled, through a haze of yet more tears.

'I can show you it, if you like?'

'Yes, please,' I sniffed. 'I'd love that.'

'I thought you might,' he said, leaning over and gently brushing my tears away. 'And you can take it with you of course, but I can't tell you how much I wish you were going to be here to watch it grow.'

I couldn't find the words either, but in that moment, I found myself wishing for exactly the same thing too. The thought of decorating Christmas trees that Dad had potted up for years to come, here in the lodge and with Ned by my side, felt like a bewildering, but very appealing prospect.

As one we leant towards each other and for the third time since I'd arrived back at Wynter's Trees we kissed. This time there was no alcohol involved and no bump on the head and it felt all the sweeter for that. Or it did until I remembered my dear friend, Maya. The sight of her beautiful face, and the thought of her generous spirit filled my head and my heart and I pulled away. Ned looked every bit as guilty as I felt as I muttered a hasty good night and rushed upstairs to my room.

Chapter 21

Given the furtive looks we exchanged over breakfast the next morning, I knew Ned and I were both feeling guilty about how our wonderful evening spent decorating the tree had ended. I had lain awake long into the night admonishing myself for leaning in and reciprocating and the tired expression Ned wore was all the evidence I needed to know that he had too.

Between us we managed to make vague small talk, but the silences between the stilted words dragged on and when my phone went off, I pounced on it, grateful for the distraction.

'Wow, that's great,' I smiled, as I read the most recent text which had landed.

There was another too, which had arrived a little earlier and I hadn't noticed before, but I would read that later.

'Good news?' asked Ned, looking up from his porridge.

'Yes,' I said. 'Fantastic, actually. It's a message from Wren.

She's going home this morning and has asked if I can drop a couple of things from the hut round to her cottage.'

'That sounds very positive.'

'It does,' I agreed. 'Obviously, Theo doesn't want to leave her alone.'

'Of course.'

'And she has a commission she was working on and which she can finish at home. I think she needs the distraction, but can you spare me? It's going to be busy today, isn't it?'

'Easily,' Ned eagerly confirmed.

I daresay he wanted to keep me away from Maya as well as the trees, but he needn't have worried. Given how guilty I was feeling, I was hardly going to throw myself across her path. In fact, I was grateful for the opportunity to stay off-site.

'What I mean is,' he amended, turning slightly pink, 'is that I think it's more important that you help Wren, than hang about here all day.'

'I agree,' I said, sliding off the stool and trying not to feel slighted by his turn of phrase. 'I'll go and get ready. Could you write down Wren and Theo's address for me?'

'Of course,' he said, reaching for the shopping list pad and pen.

Wren and Theo lived in one of the tiny former fisherman's cottages which were built along a narrow one-way lane alongside the pub and on the walk down to the beach. As the weather was so bright, I parked my car, which had been more than a little reluctant to start, in the village with a view to walking to the house. From what I could remember, there was no parking nearby anyway.

I planned to pick up a couple of things from the shop on the way, but first I read the other message which was waiting on my phone and was from my former colleague, Caitlin. As I scanned what she'd typed, I let out a long breath which could have been the result of annoyance, but was in truth, relief.

So caught up in the madness of Christmas at school, Caitlin had forgotten all about her promise to find out the details of the job she had previously mentioned and the post had now been filled. Rather than disappointment I was pleased that I wouldn't feel obliged to apply, although I would now have to give further thought to what I was going to do if Ned couldn't raise the money to buy me out. I had thought the post, should I secure it, might prove useful while looking for an alternative solution, but that wasn't going to be an option now.

I messaged Caitlin as I walked to the shop. I told her not to worry and pointed out that had I been that interested in the role, I would have reminded her or searched for it myself. She sent a reply almost instantly.

> Phew! That's all right then. I thought you were going to be fed up. Let me know when you're back – assuming you're still at the seaside – and we'll go for a drink. After this term, I'm going to need it!

The shop bell jangled as I put away my phone and opened the door. My arrival was met with a warm smile which seemed to be readily available everywhere in Wynmouth. I couldn't help thinking it was far more appealing than the anonymity and blank expressions associated with where I previously lived. After selecting some chocolates and flowers for Wren and a few other essentials, I carried on to the cottage.

'Hey,' said Theo, a smile also lighting up his face, when he answered the door. 'Come in, come in.'

He explained they hadn't been back long, but Wren was already tucked up in an armchair next to the fire and, even though she still looked a little pale, she was smiling too.

'Hey you,' I said, bending to kiss her cheek, which was warmed by the fire blazing in the hearth, 'I'm so pleased to see you.'

'I'm pleased to see you too,' she said. 'Thank you so much for coming. I hope they can manage without you at Wynter's this morning,' she added, with a frown. 'I know it's going to be busy today.'

'When I tell you about my mix-up,' I told her with a grimace, 'you'll realise why Ned was actually pleased to see the back of me.'

It felt good to have an amusing anecdote to share and which would hopefully take her mind off things. Although I still would have been happier not to have made the gaffe in the first place.

'Oh, I don't believe he was for a second,' Theo mischievously grinned, taking the bunch of flowers and bag containing the chocolates, milk and biscuits which I had picked up in the shop. 'From what I've heard . . .'

'Never mind what you've heard,' Wren cut in. 'Thank you for the flowers, Liza,' she said to me, her tone utterly changed. 'They're beautiful.'

'And the milk and biscuits are much appreciated too,' said Theo, who was still grinning from ear to ear. 'I'll go and put the kettle on before I put my foot in it, shall I?'

'Good idea,' said Wren, rolling her eyes.

I was intrigued, but he disappeared before I had the opportunity to prise an explanation out of him. While he was clattering about in the kitchen, I gave Wren the things she'd asked me to collect from the hut and she explained what had happened at the hospital and how she'd now got to take it easy for a few days.

When Theo came back in with the tea tray and a pretty enamel jug containing the flowers, I told them all about the Stott/Scott fiasco.

'Crikey,' said Theo, whistling under his breath as he poured the tea. 'Perhaps Ned was glad to see the back of you, after all. I bet he was like a bear with a sore head. He must have been fizzing.'

'He was,' I agreed. 'I've never seen him look so angry. I honestly thought he was going to banish me from Wynter's Trees forever.'

'Wynter's reputation means the world to him,' Wren put in, 'but I don't think he'd go that far. He's enjoying having you around too much to do that.'

'Is he?' I frowned, my gaze flicking from her to Theo. Now they both looked mischievous. 'What's going on?'

Neither said another word, but they exchanged a meaningful look. It was the sort of exchange that couples who know each other very well share, the kind that demonstrates how well they can read each other's minds.

'Nothing,' they chorused, then clammed up again.

My heart skittered at the thought that Ned had talked about me to his friends, but then the guilt descended. Theo and Wren's scant admissions implied that he'd confided something positive, but given he was now dating Maya, he really shouldn't have been saying anything like that about me at all, should he? But then, perhaps I was reading too much into it.

Given that he would have talked to them prior to the Stott/Scott fiasco, at a time when it looked like I might have proved useful around the place in the run up to Christmas, then I supposed he would have been more inclined to say nice things. I bet if he talked to them now, post tree trouble and after kiss number three, it would have been a completely different story!

'Liza?'

'Sorry,' I said, tuning back in to Theo's voice. 'What did you say?'

'I said, are you in a rush to get back?' he repeated, offering me a mug of tea.

'No,' I said, taking it. 'Not at all. In fact, I'm free for the rest of the day.'

'In that case,' he said, 'would you mind sitting with Wren while I make a quick trip to the studio?'

'Of course I wouldn't mind,' I said, smiling at Wren.

'I'll be fine on my own,' she said to Theo, in spite of my offer. 'I don't want to hold Liza up.'

'You're not,' I quickly said. 'I've absolutely nothing planned.'

'And I'll feel better if you're with a friend,' Theo said, bending to kiss her cheek. 'Just for this morning.'

'To tell you the truth,' I told her, 'I could do with a chat about something other than Christmas trees.'

Theo gave me a grateful smile. He might come across as laidback and light of heart, but I'd seen the look of fear on his face the day Wren went into hospital. He'd been every bit as scared as she was and I was more than willing to do whatever I could to make sure that expression didn't appear, on either of their faces, again.

'Oh, go on, then,' Wren said to him. 'I know you're itching to empty the kiln.'

'I won't be long,' Theo grinned, as he reached for his coat which hung on a hook next to the door.

The door opened straight on to the tiny front garden and I could see that even though the place was Lilliputian it was very organised. There were clever storage solutions everywhere and absolutely no clutter. I wondered if they would have to move to somewhere bigger when the baby arrived, but in view of the recent scare, didn't ask.

'Take as long as you need,' I called after Theo. 'Where even is your studio?' I asked Wren once he'd gone.

Her face lit up as she told me all about it. It was part of a former stable block at Home Farm, which belonged to Joe's family. She and Theo shared the largest space there and Hope ran her business from another converted stable next door. With Theo being Hope's cousin, it sounded very much like a family affair and Wren clearly loved it.

'It sounds perfect,' I told her.

'It is,' she said, and then her expression clouded.

'What is it?' I asked. 'Are you not feeling well?'

'No,' she said, 'I'm all right, thank goodness, although between you and me, I am worried about the beach hut.'

'It's fine,' I reassuringly said. 'I locked it after I'd been inside this morning. Everything's safe.'

'I know that,' she said, looking tearful, 'but it shouldn't be locked up, should it?'

She had a point.

'No,' I said, biting my lip, 'I suppose not.'

'Theo and I have been preparing for these few weeks for months. We've put in endless hours to make sure we would have enough stock to make the most of the expected customer numbers and now, just as the absolute peak time for sales has hit, this has happened and we're missing out.'

I didn't know what to say.

'That makes me sound awful, doesn't it?' she choked, turning red. 'I don't mean it too. And of course, I'd rather be here and healthy, than at the huts and not pregnant.'

'Wren, stop,' I softly said. 'You don't sound awful at all. I can completely understand why you're so upset. This time, in the run up to Christmas, must provide a big boost to your annual income.'

'Yes,' she said. 'It does. We make more now than at any other time of the year and without it . . .' she shook her head. 'Well, to be frank, I'm not sure I'll be able to keep going full-time and with a baby on the way, I'd rather not have to look for something part-time to help make ends meet.'

'I can see that wouldn't be ideal,' I said, chewing my lip.

'And Theo is insisting he's not going to leave me until I'm completely better, not that there really is anything physically wrong with me now, but it's a blow, this loss of income at such a potentially lucrative time.' She let out a shuddering breath. 'He wouldn't have gone to the studio this morning if you weren't here, you know,' she said sadly. 'I really don't know how we're going to manage.'

All the time she'd been talking I'd been channelling Winnie the Pooh and trying to think, think, think. The last thing she needed was more stress. She was supposed to be relaxing, and certainly not worrying about the demands of her and Theo's finances.

'I do,' I said, as a lightbulb moment landed. 'I know how you can manage.'

'You do?'

'Yes,' I triumphantly said, 'I do. I'm going to open and run the hut for you.'

She looked at me and blinked. 'But . . .'

'It's still got plenty of stock,' I carried on, 'and I'm sure Theo can leave you long enough to drop off more if he thinks I'll need it, and then I can sell it for you. Abbie or Sue can run me through the payment system as I know you all use the same one, and you can tell me anything about the products I need to know. I'll open first thing tomorrow and then you won't have to miss out on a single sale.'

I felt well chuffed to have struck upon an idea that would really help.

'But what about Wynter's?' Wren asked. 'I know you said Ned was angry about what happened, but now it's all sorted, surely he'll be expecting you to help shift the trees.'

'No, he won't,' I said, shaking my head. 'The delivery service ends tomorrow and then there'll be him, David and Maya in the yard, which is the usual team. They won't need me at all. And of course, Liam's on the payroll now too.'

If Wren and Theo agreed, this idea would not only save their festive sales, but also keep me out of Maya's way. I'd been trying to come up with a way to avoid her that wouldn't look too obvious and this was the perfect solution.

'Well,' said Wren, once she'd mulled it over, 'as long as you're sure. That really would be amazing and a huge weight off my mind.'

'One hundred per cent sure,' I told her. 'Maya helped me out of a tight spot with those trees yesterday,' I added, feeling my face colour, 'and now I can help you. It's the perfect pay it forward gesture.'

I tried not to dwell on thoughts of how I'd then stomped all over Maya's very generous act of kindness by kissing Ned, but then I remembered, he'd kissed me too. I hadn't leapt across the sofa and thrown myself at him, we'd very definitely met in the middle, drawn together by some unseen but irresistible force. Not that that excused what had happened, but it was a two-way street.

'All right,' beamed Wren. 'Theo should be at the studio in a few minutes. I'll give him a ring and see what he says. He might be able to remember how much stock is still in the hut and if he thinks we need more, he can bring it away with him this morning.'

'That's a great idea,' I agreed.

Theo was as keen on the plan as we both were and came back with a couple of boxes which I promised to set out in readiness to open up the next day.

'If you could do tomorrow, Thursday and Friday,' he said as we loaded the cartons into my car, 'then I should be back on Saturday.'

'Let's play it by ear,' I told him. 'There's no rush, is there? I can do easily do the weekend if you need me to.'

'But what about the party?' he said. 'Surely Ned will want you to help with setting up for that?'

'What party?' I frowned.

'Oh,' said Theo. 'I assumed you knew. Ned and David are having a thank you party in the barn on Saturday night for everyone who has helped at Wynter's Trees this year. Ned told me it's on track to be a bumper year and he wants to celebrate the success. All the beach hut crew have been invited. It's going to be quite a night.'

'Oh,' I said, arranging the boxes, to hide my embarrassment. 'I had no idea.'

'Ned must have forgotten to mention it,' Theo said consolingly. 'He's been so busy.'

'Yes,' I said, 'that's probably it. Either that,' I joked, 'or I'm not invited.'

Theo looked embarrassed then too.

'Right,' I said, slamming the boot shut and trapping my discomfiture inside along with the boxes, 'I think I'll take a quick walk along the beach. I'll keep you posted about how I'm getting on.'

'Thanks, Liza,' said Theo, giving me a warm hug. 'Wren and I really appreciate what you're doing for us.'

'It's my pleasure,' I told him, even more grateful that I now had a good reason to stay out of the office and away from Ned as well as his other half.

It was blustery on the beach and, aside from the occasional dog walker, deserted. I pulled my hat down and my collar up and set off along the sand. The wind rushed this way and that and as it pushed and pulled me to and fro, my emotions got dragged along with it. As well as walking through the plantation, Dad had often come to the beach when he needed to think things through and clear his head, but my thoughts felt even more muddled when I left than they had when I arrived.

'What's all this then?' Ned asked, when he found me still in Wren and Theo's hut after everyone else had closed up and gone home. 'Is Wren really all right?'

315

'She's fine,' I told him as I carried on, carefully setting out the stock, so I didn't have to look at him, 'but she's not ready to come back yet and Theo would rather be with her for a few days, so I've said I'll open the hut in that time on their behalf.'

'Oh right,' he said. 'I see.'

'Otherwise, they'll lose a huge chunk of their annual income,' I explained. 'From what Wren said they make a fair bit in the run to Christmas. That is all right, isn't it? They didn't ask me to do it, I put myself forward. I mean, you don't want me, do you?'

'Absolutely not,' he hastily said. 'I don't want you.'

I wasn't sure if they were intended to or not, but his words really stung.

'That's all right then,' I swallowed.

I knew we had to keep things between us straightforward from then on, but he didn't have to be quite so blunt about it.

'I just hope they know what they're letting themselves in for,' he then teasingly said, which made me feel a little better, as his mouth quirked into a smile.

'Ha, ha,' I said, rolling my eyes. 'Even I can tell the difference between pottery and silver jewellery.'

'That's all right then,' he laughed. 'Right, I'm going back to the lodge. Don't be too late, will you? You're going to be run off your feet tomorrow.'

'Has it been busy today?'

'Ever so,' he nodded. 'Thankfully, I've only got one delivery run to make tomorrow and then I can help out here after that. We're going to be all in by Christmas Eve.'

'You'd better save some energy for Saturday night,' I said, then wished I hadn't brought it up.

'Saturday night?'

'There's going to be a party, isn't there?'

'Yes,' he said. 'Crikey, I'd forgotten all about that. It's this weekend, isn't it?'

He sounded genuinely surprised that the date had crept up on him which in turn made me feel slightly better that he hadn't mentioned it.

'Apparently,' I said, brushing my hands down my jeans. 'Let me know if you need a hand with anything, won't you?'

'Thanks for the offer,' he said, 'but I'm sure it's all in hand. I put Maya in charge and you know how efficient she is. I'm sure she's got it all organised.'

'In that case,' I unguardedly said, 'it'll be mistletoe central here, come Saturday night.'

I had no idea why I thought it was a good idea to mention mistletoe. Mentioning mistletoe led to thoughts of kissing and that was the last place I wanted either of our minds to end up.

'I hope not,' said Ned, backing out of the hut. 'I've already had my fill of Christmas kisses this year.'

Chapter 22

Having offered to step into the breach for Wren and Theo, I didn't have endless hours to make a detailed dissection of what Ned might have meant about having had his fill of Christmases kisses, however I did manage to find a few seconds in which to obsess.

I knew he could have been referring to having had enough intimate moments with either Maya or me, and in spite of my guilt over betraying my friend, and the fact that I would soon be leaving for good, there was still a part of me jumping up and down and shouting, 'pick me, pick me!' whenever Ned glanced in my direction. I didn't like that version of myself in the slightest, but for some reason, I couldn't shake her off.

Wednesday was the first day I was in charge of running Wren and Theo's hut and, as it wasn't too busy, I had the opportunity to settle into the routine of serving and selling without any stress inducing queues or impatient customers. There was a steady trickle of people arriving and leaving, rather than the rush I had been dreading and, aside from running low on bubble wrap, the day went without a hitch.

I checked, checked and checked again whenever I keyed a payment into the card reader and I made use of the quieter moments to tidy, rearrange and write down exactly what had been sold. My desire to keep track of everything in such minute detail might have been a little over the top, but once bitten and all that and I did feel better for doing it.

Thursday however, turned out to be a totally different day and my nerves were set jangling from the off.

'Hey, Liza,' said Maya, the second I opened the beach hut door. 'How's it going?'

Our paths hadn't crossed at all the day before, but I had known my luck was bound to run out at some point. The sight of her fresh-faced and ready to spend another day working beside her beau made me feel more like a traitor than ever. Which, of course, was no less than I deserved.

'Good,' I told her, and doing my utmost to sound as if there was absolutely nothing the matter at all. 'Really good. Yesterday was great. I'm just hoping now that I've got the stamina to get through today *and* tonight.'

Wynter's was hosting another late-night opening event, much the same as the night the huts were launched, and everyone was bracing themselves for a brisk few hours of trading.

'I'm sure you'll be fine,' Maya kindly said, making me feel even worse. 'Although you do look a bit flushed. You're not coming down with a cold or something, are you?'

'No, no,' I said, waving her caring concern away. 'I'm fine.'

'That's all right then.'

'How's it all going over there?' I asked, with a nod to the barn.

I didn't particularly want to prolong the conversation, but my paranoia had me thinking that she might get a bit suspicious if the chat was all one way.

'Great.' She grinned. 'Did you see Ned's happy dance yesterday?'

'Is that what that was?' I couldn't help but smile. 'I did wonder.'

I had surreptitiously watched as he arrived back late in the afternoon, then leapt out of the truck and treated everyone to an unguarded and very public kitchen disco moment. It wasn't the kind of abandoned demonstration I would have had him down for displaying, but then I still didn't know him all that well, did I?

'He was so relieved to have finally finished delivering the trees,' Maya explained. 'And that all of the customers were happy, of course.'

That, I had discovered, was the most important thing here at Wynter's Trees. Customer satisfaction came above all else, with Dad's original eco-business credentials coming a very close second.

'He certainly looked happy,' I smiled. 'It must be a weight off his mind.'

'It is,' she agreed, 'but I know there's still something both-ering him.'

Was it perhaps the disloyal kisses, or concerns about

raising the money to buy me out, that was weighing heavy on his mind? Or even a combination of both?

'Maya ...' I began, but she cut me off.

'Anyway,' she briskly said, 'I mustn't stand here gossiping. I only really came over to give you this.'

She stepped aside to reveal a large roll of bubble wrap.

'I popped round to see Wren last night and Theo asked me to give you it.'

'That's great,' I said, nudging away the other words I had been about to say. 'Just what I need. How did you find Wren?'

'She was really good,' Maya told me. 'She's hoping to be back here next week.'

As Maya didn't mention what had been the cause of Wren's recent stay in hospital, I didn't either. However, I did wonder if our mutual friend's proposed return date to the hut matched Theo's. I couldn't imagine he would be willing for her to come back so soon.

'Theo said he had thought there was enough wrap here to cover all the stock,' Maya added, looking about. 'But luckily he had this at the studio.'

'I think I probably overdid the packaging on his pots yesterday,' I admitted, lifting the roll of wrap over the desk so it wasn't in the way.

'Better to be safe than sorry,' Maya laughed.

'My thoughts exactly,' I agreed.

Mending a broken pot wouldn't have been anywhere near as simple as swapping two trees had turned out to be.

'Right,' she said, 'I'll see you later. It's not going to be quite so busy on the tree front now because pretty much everyone has got their decs up, but there's still plenty to do.'

I didn't have time to admire Maya's work ethic and commitment to Wynter's Trees or feel worse about my bad friend credentials, because the car park was fast filling up as customers arrived in their droves. With schools breaking up the next day, I guessed lots of parents were making the most of the last opportunity to shop without their children.

As the morning slipped by, I realised I had listened to practically every customer telling me a tale about why they loved Wynter's Trees so much, as well as how they had been coming to the plantation for years. Everyone loved the inclusion of the huts and Sophie and Hope's menu was proving to be a popular draw too.

'Ned delivered our tree yesterday,' one woman told me, as she held up and admired a pair of Wren's sea-glass earrings. 'We've had the same one for six years and it's too big to fit in the car now. It was Mr Wynter who set us up with it originally. He greeted us like old friends, right from our very first visit.'

'That's really lovely,' I said, remembering the pride Dad had always taken in knowing the names of all his customers. A trait I'd now seen and appreciated in Ned.

It broke my heart a little though when I worked out that Dad had only given this woman's family their tree for a couple of years.

'That personal service and attention to detail is one of the things I love about this place,' she carried on. 'And it just keeps getting better and better. The kids still love visiting Santa and my other half is a huge fan of the truck. He had his photo taken next to it the night you first opened.'

'It's certainly proving to be a popular feature,' I agreed.

There hadn't been a day go by when we were open that I hadn't seen someone being snapped next to it and I felt pleased that Ned had found such a clever use for it after it had served its time on the road. I'd also noticed that if beautiful Bandit was in the vicinity, he was encouraged to pose too.

'And now we can shop here and have something to eat, it's totally worth the journey to get here.' The woman gushed. 'I hope you'll be doing it again next year?'

'I don't see why we wouldn't be,' I told her.

I couldn't imagine a single reason why Ned wouldn't want to carry on with the venture, but as it wasn't going to be anything to do with me, I didn't want to sound presumptuous.

'I'll take these,' she said, passing me the smooth green glass earrings. 'You know, I'd come and shop here throughout the year if the huts were open,' she carried on. 'Easter would be a great time to visit. You could have an egg hunt through the plantation!'

'That's an excellent idea,' I told her. 'I'll mention it to Ned.'

Once she'd gone and I had a moment to think about it, I realised there were far more opportunities to open up the place than were currently being used. Easter could potentially be as busy as Christmas with the right marketing and stargazing events would be great too. I knew Ned had been on the ball about Halloween and probably had all this in his head already, but it might be worth mentioning just in case.

I could already imagine the advertising headline – *Wynter's – not just for Christmas* – displayed on the website homepage and perhaps even in the press again. The plantation might be of interest to the local Brownies and Cubs groups too, assuming they were still running.

I sat and took a minute to assimilate just how much my opinion about the place, and what it should be used for, had changed over the last few weeks. I had initially been rather reluctant to embrace the beach huts the week I arrived, but Ned had been right about both opening the place up for longer and what Dad would have made of it all.

In an unexpected twist of fate, I found myself beginning to wonder if there was anything I'd missed about Wynter's Trees that could suit me and what I wanted. Was there some opportunity here that could somehow work in my favour too?

Once the minute was up, I set the thoughts aside. It was far too late to be daydreaming about anything like that. I'd told Ned and David I wanted to sell my stake twice now, and I'd set Maya and Ned on the path towards a happy ever after. The Wynter's Trees ship had, at last, well and truly sailed and that, I purposefully reminded myself, was exactly what I had wanted it to do.

*

As the afternoon rushed by and the customers kept coming, I had begun to worry that I wouldn't have enough stock to see me through the evening. Theo had messaged earlier to let me know he would drop more things in the next day, but I was keen to make the most of every opportunity to sell on his and Wren's behalf and had quickly devised a plan.

'Special delivery!' shouted Liam, when he and Chelsea arrived at the hut weighed down with boxes.

'Well, well, well,' I laughed, when I spotted Chelsea. 'Who's the elf now?'

She was sportingly wearing a striped green and red elf hat, complete with bells, and her face was lit by a minxy smile.

'I thought it was too good an opportunity to miss,' she laughed. 'And I know now more than ever that I should have had more sympathy for you, Liza,' she added, carefully putting down her stack of boxes. 'It's hard work being Santa's little helper.'

Liam rolled his eyes.

'Right?' I giggled. 'Seriously though, thank you for ferrying these. I really appreciate it and I'm sure Theo was grateful too.'

I had known Liam and Chelsea were going to be coming to Wynter's Trees for the evening because Liam had offered to help in the grotto, and as they didn't live too far from Wren and Theo, I had capitalised on the opportunity to ask them to collect more stock.

'He was,' said Liam, looking pointedly at Chelsea. 'But not for long.'

'What do you mean?' I asked, ripping into one of the boxes and starting to unpack it before the hut filled with customers again. 'What happened?'

'She happened,' Liam tutted.

Chelsea pulled another hat out of her bag, plonked it on my head and quickly set about artfully filling the shelves with the mugs and jugs I was unpacking.

'Who's she?' she frowned. 'The cat's mother?'

'No,' Liam laughed. 'Mine, apparently.'

'What did you do?' I asked, narrowing my eyes at my old adversary.

'I just told him a few home truths,' she said with a shrug as she jutted out her chin. 'I told him he can't keep cosseting Wren. There's nothing wrong with her now, but if he doesn't stop fussing, he'll make her paranoid when what he should be doing is helping her to ease back into things and letting her get on.'

'I see,' I said.

I was glad I hadn't been around to witness how that had been received. Chelsea obviously knew about the baby but had no qualms when it came to making her feelings and opinions known, even though the subject was a delicate one.

'I wasn't being harsh,' she said, shooting Liam a look.

I guessed he'd said different.

'He just needed telling.'

'You were right,' I was surprised to hear Liam say as he stepped aside to let a customer in, 'but you could have put it better.'

'Subtlety was never Chelsea's strong point,' I said in a mock whisper.

She gave me a look.

'Anyway, it worked.' she sniffed. 'Theo will be popping in tomorrow and then he'll be here all day Saturday and Sunday and Wren will be in for a while from Monday.'

'Crikey,' I gasped. 'Your words really did hit home, didn't they?'

Chelsea looked well pleased. I had been more than prepared to carry on selling, but I knew she was right about it all. It wouldn't do Wren any good to be fretting at home and it wasn't as if manning the huts meant she had to be on her feet all day. Everyone would keep an eye on her and I could still help out if it got really busy.

'Right,' said Liam, 'I better get to the grotto. The queue is out the door already!'

'Now you have an elf of your own,' I nudged, as Chelsea watched him go.

'He's a changed lad,' she wistfully said. 'Coming here has given him a real focus. Thank you for taking him under your wing, Liza.'

'I'm just pleased it's worked out,' I told her. 'And you are most welcome, but I haven't really done anything. He's just got on with things himself. He's very intuitive and has picked things up so quickly.'

'He's always been independent,' she said. 'I used to think he was naughty when he was little, but I can see now that's not what it was. He was just strong-willed.'

'I wonder where he gets that from?'

Chelsea gave the question a very dramatic eye-roll.

'And he's never been a fan of school,' she further said, 'but knowing he's got his job here on a weekend has kept him on track. His form teacher rang to tell me he's been turning in homework and there's been no disruption in class.'

'That's fantastic,' I said, feeling proud on both her and Liam's behalf. 'School is very much a one size fits all and if you don't fit . . .'

'You're fucked.'

'I wouldn't have put it quite like that,' I laughed, 'but yeah, you're right. That's why I loved my job using art as therapy so much. It gave the students who didn't fit an alternative for a little while every day.'

'I bet you were good at it too.'

'Thanks, Chelsea.'

I wondered if there might be the possibility of a job for Liam at Wynter's Trees beyond Christmas, maybe even full-time when he left school. Perhaps I could plant the idea in Ned's head before I left.

'Are you going to stay for the evening?' I asked. 'Or do you need to go? I can run Liam home later if that would help.'

'I had planned to go,' she said, turning to face me and in the process, making the bells on her hat jingle, 'but I think I'm going to stay. I can give you a hand if you like?'

The evening got busier and busier and I was grateful for Chelsea's help. David had bustled in at some point with refreshments in the form of mugs of hot chocolate and a couple of thick slices of spiced and fruity stollen.

He looked completely taken aback as he watched the two of us working so companionably together. I had to laugh at his dumbfounded expression. Had I been able to see into the future even just a few weeks ago, I knew I would have been wearing the same look of shock myself.

The carol singers were in fine voice and with a few snowflakes fluttering prettily down, the scene beyond the hut door couldn't have been more perfect. It wasn't that many days ago that I had reminded myself not to fall in love with Wynter's Trees because it wasn't like this for many weeks of the year, but with those potential ideas on how to extend the plantation opening times now bubbling away in my head, I realised that scenes like this had the possibility to become the norm, rather than the exception.

'Penny for them,' said Chelsea, making me jump.

We were leaning either side of the hut doorway as the visitors finally began to head back to their cars.

'Oh,' I said, pushing myself upright then rubbing my hands together and blowing on the ends of my fingers which weren't covered by my gloves. 'I was just wondering if I might have made a mistake about something, that's all.'

I hadn't expected to be so forthright and felt my temperature spike as a result.

'Not another muddle over some trees, is it?' Chelsea teased.

Clearly news of my mistake had reached Liam's ears.

'No,' I laughed. 'Nothing like that.'

'Want to talk about it?'

'Thanks,' I said. 'I really appreciate the offer, but I think I need to figure this one out for myself.'

'Well,' she said, leaning over and rubbing my arm, 'let me know if you change your mind.'

'I will,' I told her.

'Hey,' called Liam, as he jogged over from the grotto. 'You're here. I haven't even messaged you yet.'

Rather than just opting for a hat, he was dressed in a complete elf outfit, including shoes with bells on, and looked nowhere near as self-conscious as I would have. In fact, he didn't seem bothered at all. He really was one in a million.

'I haven't been home,' Chelsea told him, holding back the comment that I knew must have been brewing. 'Liza begged me to stay and give her a hand.'

Liam looked at me and raised his eyebrows.

'I couldn't have managed without her actually,' I grinned.

Chelsea pulled off her hat and ruffled her hair.

'And I've had a great time,' she said. 'I'd love to work somewhere like this. Although, somewhere with a bit of heat might be a bit more comfortable. I've got used to the temperature in the care home now. Shifts in there are stifling.'

Now we'd stopped moving, I could feel the chill reaching further than the ends of my fingers.

'You should give that some serious thought,' I told her. 'You're a great saleswoman.'

'I'll lend you this if you like,' said Liam, pointing at his costume. 'It's kept me warm tonight.'

'And drawn some comments, I would imagine,' Chelsea chuckled.

Liam shifted from one foot to the other and stared at the ground.

'What?' she frowned.

'Nothing,' he shrugged. 'Let's get home, shall we?'

Perhaps I'd been wrong to assume he hadn't minded wearing it.

'Nothing, my foot,' said Chelsea, eyeing him beadily. 'I know that look. What happened, Liam Chalmers?'

Liam looked at me and then to his mum.

'Bradley and Kyle turned up,' he eventually said.

'What, here?' Chelsea frowned.

Liam nodded, his shoulders slumped and all his former perkiness deserted him.

'What did they want with Wynter's Trees?' Chelsea demanded.

'Who are they, Liam?' I asked.

His tone inferred they weren't friends.

'Lads from school who I used to hang about with,' he sniffed.

'Troublemakers,' Chelsea added. 'Did they see you in that get-up?'

'Yep,' said Liam, 'but I don't care about that.'

'What do you care about?' I asked, wanting to get to the bottom of whatever was bothering him. 'What happened, Liam?'

'They went to Ned,' he said, and for a moment I thought

he was going to break down, but then he carried on. 'They went and told him that I was one of their gang and that if it wasn't nailed down, I'd pinch it and sell it.'

'Oh, Liam,' I gasped.

'And what did Ned say to that?' asked Chelsea, looking across the yard to see if she could spot him. 'Because if he's thinking . . .'

'He's not,' said Liam, cutting her off. 'He told them . . . well, let's just say he told them to leave.'

'I should think so too,' I was quick to say. 'We know you're not like that, Liam. We know we can trust you with everything.'

He looked happier when I said that, but only a little.

'We really appreciate that, Liza,' said Chelsea. 'Don't we, Liam?'

He nodded and gave me a small smile.

'Right,' she carried on. 'Come on, Liam the lanky elf. Let's get you home. It's the last day of school tomorrow and at this rate, you'll be too tired to go in.'

'I don't see why I have to,' he said, sounding more like himself. 'We never do any work in the last week.'

He had a point.

'Tough,' Chelsea firmly said, winking at me, 'you're going in.'

'You won't be there much longer,' I consoled him. 'And you don't want to give those lads any ammunition or ruin this great new track record your mum's been telling me about, do you?'

'Suppose not,' he said, 'but I've no idea what I'm going to do when I leave next year.'

'There's plenty of time to work that out,' I told him.

Chelsea turned to look at me. 'You know where I am if you fancy a chat,' she smiled. 'You weren't by any chance thinking about that forest thingy when you zoned out earlier, were you?'

'Hey!' Liam cut in.

'What?' she gasped, flinching at the sudden escalation in volume. 'What are you shouting like that for?'

He shot her a very stern and thin-lipped look. 'That doesn't matter now,' he gruffly said, his gaze momentarily flicking to me. 'Ned said it's not important.'

'What's not important?' I asked.

'Nothing,' he said. 'She's just got the wrong end of the stick about something, that's all.'

'She,' said Chelsea. 'Again!'

'Come on,' said Liam.

'But I thought . . .' Chelsea began, but he cut her off again.

'Just come on,' he said, striding away. 'I thought you wanted to go.'

'Boys,' she said, throwing up her hands. 'They're still a mystery to me.'

'Mmm,' I said, watching Liam march off. 'Me too.'

Chapter 23

With it being the last shopping day before the start of the school Christmas holidays, it was another busy day at Wynter's Trees and the visit to the grotto from the Wynmouth mother and toddler group made it even more memorable. I could hear the squeals of delight – and the occasional tears – from my spot in Wren and Theo's hut and when the group lined up in front of the truck to have their photographs taken, with Santa and Mrs Claus at either end, they did look very sweet, almost angelic.

'Don't they look adorable?' sighed Abbie, taking in the group which ranged from tiny babies in their mum's arms to around three and struggling to free themselves from their father's hand.

Noah looked at me and rolled his eyes.

'Tears before bedtime and at least one tantrum on the minibus home,' he sourly said. 'Possibly even some vomit, looking at how that one on the end is wolfing down those cookies.'

Abbie gave him a thump and, given her position in her wheelchair, very nearly made his eyes water.

'I love babies,' she dreamily said to me. 'I want at least three.'

'I guessed as much from the look on your face,' I told her.

'What about you?' Noah asked me, his eyebrows raised. 'How's your baby timer, Liza? Is it ticking like an internal timebomb yet?'

'Noah,' scolded Abbie, looking outraged. 'That's a very personal question.'

Noah shrugged. 'Sorry,' he said. 'I didn't realise it was such a touchy subject.'

'You're fine,' I laughed. 'It's not. Not for me anyway. I haven't heard my timer at all, but then I work with what those babies turn into. The decision whether or not to have kids is a huge one. I mean, you just said you love babies, Abbie, but they're only those bundles for a few weeks and then you're responsible for a little person.'

'That's true,' said Noah, who clearly had no paternal instincts and looked with disfavour at the line up as a ruckus broke out among the snowsuit brigade. The battle for the last cookie was on. 'Give it a couple of years and you've got *that* on your hands.'

He covered his ears and marched back into his and Abbie's hut as the wails reached a crescendo that only Bandit would be able to properly hear.

'He has a point,' I laughed, then spotted the look on Abbie's face. 'But each to their own.'

There were slightly more snow flurries as the morning passed, but nothing significant. From the winter months I could remember living near Wynmouth, heavy snowfall so close to the Norfolk coast had been a rarity but the falling flakes added to the atmosphere and made Wynter's Trees look even prettier. With the tree deliveries finally finished, Ned had spent some time putting up even more decorations and if the snow kept falling then the party on Saturday night was going to have the perfect seasonal backdrop.

'My goodness,' gasped Theo, immediately noticing all the gaps on the shelves when he popped in later that day. 'I knew you'd sold a lot from looking at the online banking, but seeing it like this is quite something.'

'I know,' I grinned. 'It's amazing, isn't it? And nothing to do with me. It's your products that have drawn the customers in. You and Wren are an incredibly talented duo. I hope you've got more stock.'

'Um,' he said. 'Wren's got more than I have, but we should be all right. If push comes to shove, I might see if some of my larger pieces will sell.'

I couldn't help thinking he should have made them available from November, but it wasn't my place to say anything. I got the feeling that he hadn't been all that confident when the hut opened, but fingers crossed the popularity of his and Wren's clever crafts had given him enough of a boost to realise that there was real value in what he produced at the wheel.

The recent boost to their bank balance had hopefully

helped him with that too. I was so pleased I had been able to play a part in making sure they hadn't missed out on this most lucrative, as well as most wonderful, time of the year.

'I think that would be a fantastic idea,' I encouraged him. 'Nothing ventured and all that. How's Wren feeling today?'

'She's great,' he said, his face breaking into a smile. 'Although a little nauseous, first thing but even that has made her happy.'

'Really?'

Theo looked wistful. 'She said she doesn't mind feeling a bit yuk in the mornings because it's all part of the pregnancy experience and proof that her hormones are doing their thing.'

I wondered if the novelty would wear off if the feeling dragged on for weeks. Given everything she'd been through, probably not. I daresay any reminder that she was pregnant was going be made welcome.

'That's great,' I said.

'And I'll tell you what else is great.'

'What?'

'You stepping in and saving the day for us.'

'I've only done what any friend would,' I insisted, waving his words away.

'No,' Theo seriously said. 'You've really gone above and beyond, Liza. All of our decent Christmas sales would have been lost if it wasn't for you.'

'There's still next week,' I reminded him. 'Plenty more shopping days to capitalise on.'

'Be that as it may,' he said, unwilling to let me shrug his appreciation off, 'but it's this week that was always going to be the one that really counted. I reckon once the schools break up there'll be more browsers than serious buyers. Families will come out to walk around the trees and see Santa, but a lot of people will have finished their shopping by now.'

Given how busy the last couple of days had been, I thought he was probably right.

'Well,' I said, 'I'm happy to have been able to help. I wanted to take some of the pressure off the pair of you.'

'You've made all the difference,' he said, pulling me in for a hug. 'It will be business as usual from tomorrow though, so you can have a lie in.'

'You're coming back?' I asked, as he released me.

I didn't want to let on that Chelsea and Liam had given me the lowdown.

'Yep,' he said. 'I'll be here bright and early.'

'And what about Wren? I hope she's not going to miss the party.'

'She's not,' he told me. 'She's starting back tomorrow too, but she'll come in a bit later if she's feeling icky when she gets up.'

That was a surprise. Clearly, the conversation about Wren's return to work had carried on after Chelsea had put in her two pennies' worth and the plan had been amended.

'As much as I would like to wrap my beloved up in cotton wool for the next few months,' Theo carried on, 'it wouldn't be healthy for any of us. I think more than anything, she needs a bit of normality right now.'

Yes, that was Chelsea's influence right there.

'And so, do you, Theo,' I told him. 'I do understand the temptation to handle her with care, but I'm sure easing back into things now is the right way to go.'

Theo smiled. 'I'll go and start carrying over the few bits of stock I've got in the van,' he said. He hadn't taken many steps before he called over his shoulder, 'you haven't been talking to Chelsea about us by any chance, have you?'

'No,' I laughed, 'but that doesn't mean she hasn't been talking to me, does it?'

He shook his head and carried on towards the van. There was no need to elaborate because we both knew that conversations with Chelsea were often one-sided.

With the stock rearranged, Theo announced he was going to stay on for a bit, which gave me the opportunity to take a break. I'd discovered it was hard work manning the hut all day and standing on my feet for so long, especially in the cold, and I decided to take a walk around the plantation, collecting Bandit who was in the office with David, on the way. There was no sign of either Ned or Maya and I hoped I wouldn't come across the pair canoodling among the trees. Although it was a little chilly for a clandestine outdoor lover's tryst.

When I came to the tree where I'd caught Liam hiding out, I felt a renewed rush of affection for the boy. He had proved himself in so many ways since I'd found him cowering among the branches and ended up offering him a job. Just as it had been for Dad, Wynter's Trees was a very special place for Liam and he had worked tirelessly, quickly picking things up and reaching way beyond everyone's expectations. He'd even gladly volunteered to don an elf outfit for pity's sake and, on that occasion, for no financial gain.

I hoped he wasn't still dwelling on what his two former acquaintances, Bradley and Kyle, had said. It was cruel of them to try and sabotage his fresh start but he needn't have worried that their meanness had made an impact on either me or Ned. We'd talked about it briefly the evening before and Ned was as unfazed by it as I was. We could see Liam for what he was: a hardworking, honest lad, eagerly embracing the break we'd given him and, if I had anything to do with it, he was soon going to be offered an even bigger one.

'Come on!' I called to Bandit, who had slunk off without me realising. 'I need to talk to Ned.'

I didn't know if he'd been thinking about it already, but with Liam poised to head into his last few months at school, I thought it would be the ideal time to offer him a permanent position, one with real prospects, to take up when he left.

It would give him something to work towards and, hopefully, make sitting his final exams more bearable. Surely, it couldn't be that complicated to set up a traineeship or apprenticeship. If Ned was onboard, he could suggest a position that would combine working at the plantation with a formal forestry or arboriculture qualification. There might even be scope to do some volunteer work in the reserve too.

'Bandit!' I called again, laughing as he came tearing out of the trees.

He had as much energy as Liam and I allowed myself the luxury of imagining the look on Liam's face when Ned shared the proposal with him. He would think all his Christmases had come at once!

Bandit was panting when we arrived back at the barn and rather than stop and greet the Wynter's Trees customers who were always pleased to see him, he bypassed them all and headed straight for the office and his water bowl. I followed his lead and found David still at his desk poring over a pile of paperwork.

'Any chance of a word with Ned?' I asked him. 'Is he about?'

David looked up from the papers, took off his reading glasses and rubbed his eyes before leaning back in his chair and grimacing as he stretched out his back and neck. He'd obviously been hunched over in the same position for some time and I wondered what had held his attention so intently, but didn't ask. Now I had declared my disinterest in the business, it was none of my, well, business.

'Afraid not,' he said. 'He went off early this morning and said he'd most likely be away all day.'

I was surprised to learn of his defection from the plantation. With just a few more shopping days before Christmas,

I would have thought he would have wanted to be more firmly melded to the place than ever.

'He didn't say where he was going,' David elaborated, before I asked. 'Is it anything I can help with?'

'No, no,' I said. 'It'll keep, but thanks. I'm going back to help Theo now, so I'll leave Bandit with you if that's all right.'

'Yes,' said David, putting his glasses back on and picking up the papers again. 'He'll be fine in here with me.'

I'd barely made it out the door before I collided with Maya.

'Shit,' she muttered, bending to collect the decorations she'd dropped. 'Sorry, Liza.'

'No, it's my fault,' I said, rubbing my arm which had borne the brunt of our coming together. 'I should have been looking where I was going. Are you all right?' I added, noticing her unusually less than sunny disposition.

She looked distinctly ruffled. It wasn't a state I'd ever seen her in before. What had happened to everyone all of a sudden? Ned was off on an impromptu away day, David was preoccupied with paperwork and now Maya was stressed. It unsettled me a bit. December the seventeenth was not the ideal date on the Wynter's Trees calendar to let things slide.

'No,' said Maya, with a huff. 'To tell you the truth, I'm not. I'm fed up. Ned has buggered off, David's stuck in the office and I'm left selling the trees *and* trying to organise things for the party.'

She sounded in a right grump.

'And then there's . . .' she let out a long breath, but didn't finish her sentence.

'And then there's what?' I asked.

She looked at me for a long moment. 'Oh nothing,' she said, shaking her head and dredging up a smile that didn't quite reach her eyes. 'Ignore me. I've just got my knickers in a knot, that's all.'

'You do sound as though you've got your hands full,' I sympathised. 'And I would offer to help, but I'm supposed to be taking over from Theo again.'

She really had been left in the lurch. I hoped whatever Ned was up to was worth it.

'It's fine,' she said. 'Really. Worst case scenario, I'll leave the party stuff until we're closed. I'd just planned to get it sorted early because I'm going out tonight and wanted a bit of time to get ready at the end of the day.'

'Hot date?'

'Something like that,' she said, her smile fading.

'Well, in that case,' I said, 'as I haven't got a date tonight, hot or otherwise, you can leave anything you don't get finished for me to sort, if you like.'

Her smile brightened and this time looked a lot more genuine.

'Really?'

'Of course,' I insisted. 'Just leave me a list and I'll get it done.'

'You wouldn't mind?'

Given my recent behaviour, it was the very least I could

do. Not only would I be helping Maya out, but my act of kindness might also go some way to assuage the bad feelings about myself that I still harboured. The post-kiss guilt which had gathered was proving to be far longer lived than the tingling sensations Ned's warm, soft lips had aroused.

'After rescuing me from the tree muddle,' I reminded her, 'I still owe you one and this can be a start.'

'You don't have to pay me back for that.'

'I know I don't,' I swallowed, 'but I want to. Only, make sure you leave the ladders out for me. My reach is nowhere near as long as yours.'

'You're a star Liza Wynter,' she said, making me feel even worse. 'No wonder Ned . . .'

'Excuse me,' a woman's voice cut into our conversation. 'Is there anyone available to help me with a tree?'

'I am,' said Maya, thrusting the box of decorations into my arms. 'Just pop those in the barn, would you Liza?'

'Of course,' I said. 'No problem.'

I deposited the box as requested, then went back to help Theo. When I returned to the barn at the end of the day, I discovered that Maya had managed to do everything anyway.

She really was the ultimate multitasker and, taking in the transformed space, a fabulous decorator too. The barn had been beautiful before, but now it was party-ready perfection. It seemed that there was nothing in the Wynter's Trees world that Maya couldn't turn her hand to. It really was no wonder that Ned was so taken with her.

Chapter 24

I hadn't intended to sleep in on the Saturday, but with no hut to open I hadn't set an alarm and discovered that dawn had already breached the horizon by the time I opened my eyes and stretched out in the bed. Even though I had plenty to occupy my mind, my first thought, as my brain caught up with my body, was to wonder how Maya and Ned's date had gone.

Maya hadn't specifically said she was going out with Ned, but it was obvious the pair were a couple now. Even though I'd played a part in successfully pushing them together, the realisation didn't cheer me at all. If anything, it made me feel as bilious as Wren currently did at the beginning of the day. It didn't seem to matter how hard I tried, and whatever tactics I adopted, I still couldn't shake off my feelings for Ned and the thought of him with Maya, although painful to imagine, was also impossible not to dwell on.

'It's for the good of Wynter's,' I quietly muttered to myself as I pushed back the duvet and swung my legs out of bed.

'Ned, Maya and Liam are the ultimate dream team and the ideal candidates to take Dad's vision far into the future.'

Which reminded me, I still needed to talk to Ned about offering Liam a job at some point. I might have felt that I no longer had the same right to comment on what went on in the business as before, but I was determined to help secure the lad's future before I repacked my belongings and left Wynter's Trees for good.

I took a long shower and once dried and dressed, I turned off the light and opened the bedroom curtains. The place was already a hive of activity, with light streaming out of the barn and all of the huts. I cracked the window open a little and along with the sound of a robin in full voice, wisps of conversation and shouted seasonal greetings met my ears. Everyone was abustle, but then with just a week until Christmas day, that was no surprise. Today was the last Saturday to shop before the twenty-fifth and there were sales to be made.

I knew I should go out and offer to help, but I just couldn't face it. My dip in mood and lack of festive cheer had initially been brought on by imaginings of Maya and Ned, but there was something else niggling at me too.

Whereas before I couldn't wait to wave goodbye to Wynter's Trees, the thought now appealed less and less. Of course, I wasn't going to be banished and could visit whenever I wanted to, but I didn't know how I'd cope with seeing the place being solely run by someone else. Especially as that person was going to be Ned.

Resolved not to bring the celebratory outdoor ambience down, I lingered indoors on the pretence of easing myself into the day and catching up on a few chores. The recycling box was fit to burst, so I thought I'd start by emptying that.

'What's this doing in here?' I frowned, as I pulled out the large brown envelope which had arrived, addressed to me, and had now been thrown on top of the flattened cardboard and rinsed out jars.

I might have forgotten all about my unexpected post, but that didn't give Ned the right to recycle it. Abandoning the job in hand, I ripped open the envelope and reached inside.

'Forest schools,' I reminiscently smiled as I pulled out the brochure, then flicked through the pages and read the cover letter.

When I'd started utilising the small area of wild outdoor space at the school I'd been made redundant from, the headteacher had been completely onboard with the idea of incorporating nature into the groups I worked with and had even looked into signing us up to the forest school project with a view to sending me on some specific training.

Unfortunately, there were no formal sites near enough to make visiting an option and then further funding cuts saw the idea shelved completely and my training opportunity lost. However, the idea of being properly trained had never completely taken flight.

If, in my new business, I could incorporate my passion for art as therapy, utilising things collected from nature to create art, and combine it with the benefits of forest school training, then I would be on to a winner. So many students would gain from spending time outdoors and creating something unique and if I added to that the opportunity to take a few risks in a safe environment, then their confidence and self-esteem would skyrocket.

As I read the listed endorsements from the students in the brochure, along with what the leaders and assistants had to say, it dawned on me that this might well have been what Chelsea had been referring to when she mentioned the 'forest thingy' and Liam had cut her off, but why had this information been sent to me? I hadn't requested it.

I stared into space as the cogs slowly whirred and my mind eventually worked it out.

This had to be a venture Ned had, at some point, thought I might consider setting up and running at Wynter's Trees. He knew how much I loved my job and art, and how I had embraced nature to help further nurture those students most in need.

My heart skittered at the thought and I felt giddy as the realisation dawned that Wynter's Trees would be the perfect place to set up a forest school, especially with the reserve right next door. Why hadn't I thought of that before?

'Because all you've been focused on,' I scolded myself out loud, 'is leaving it all behind.'

Reading through the descriptions and looking at the images again, I could see quite clearly that the plantation, the reserve and forest schools were the ideal match. There would be no need for me to look for another site to launch my venture, because I already had access to everything I needed right here.

'Is this Ned's way of showing me that I can have it all?' I whispered, imagining myself working with visiting students, helping with the trees and also maintaining the decorative touches around the place. 'If he's given it this much thought,' my heart danced along, 'then he must really want me to stay.'

Just as my excitement was about to get the better of me, I remembered Ned had thrown away the information in my hand and Liam had told Chelsea that Ned had said the 'forest thingy' wasn't important anymore. This idea must have originally occurred soon after I'd come back, most likely when David had thought there was a chance that I would change my mind about selling my shares.

Dangling the forest school carrot might have been a tactic father and son had previously dreamt up, but thanks to my persistent insistence that I was leaving, they hadn't considered it worth deploying the bait. The fact that I'd found the brochure in the bin confirmed they were both now resigned to my decision. A decision, I realised, I was beginning to regret.

I desperately needed to talk to Ned because the thought of setting up a forest school at Wynter's Trees had taken hold and was growing at breakneck speed. It was a thrilling, challenging and enticing prospect and I didn't dare entertain the thought that I had embraced it too late. He might have tossed his hope out with the brochure, but it was down to me to restore it. I needed to tell him that I'd changed my mind.

'Liza!' called Noah, the second I'd hopped down from the veranda and was pulling on my coat. 'Just the person I need.'

'Can you hang on a sec, Noah? I just need to try and catch Ned.'

'Not really,' he said, looking about him. 'But don't worry, I'll grab someone else.'

I looked about the place, but there was no one else. Everyone was engrossed in their own business.

'It's all right,' I said. 'Don't worry. It'll keep. What do you need?'

And that was how the morning panned out. I went from one hut to the next, then to the barn and back again, helping out wherever I was needed and it felt like I was needed *everywhere*. After lunch, I made it a priority to check on Wren, who was looking a million times better and then, reassured that she and Theo could cope, had donned an elf hat (thankfully the rest of the outfit was too big) and helped out in Santa's grotto while Liam returned to his beloved netting machine.

I had assumed we wouldn't sell any more trees, but I was wrong and there looked to be a steady flow of carts going backwards and forwards to the car park all day. I caught glimpses of Ned, but there was no chance to talk to him and I resigned myself to trying to grab a moment with him at the party instead.

As I moved from one task to another, I couldn't shake off

a floaty, out of body sort of feeling. My physical self was present and just about functioning, but my mind was away, imagining a future I hadn't realised might even exist, until I had opened that envelope. I couldn't recall a time when my head had ever felt so full and there was an endlessly spinning carousel of thoughts running through my mind.

If Ned did come around to the idea of me staying and setting up a forest school, then I was going to have to properly curb my feelings for him and, given the lack of success on that front I'd had so far, I wasn't sure how I would do that. But then, that envelope had been cast aside so there was every possibility that he'd say no anyway and the time spent worrying about it wouldn't have been worth it. As I said . . . my head was full.

'Okay folks,' shouted Ned, a few minutes after six as the last of the customers cars disappeared down the drive. 'We're now officially closed for the day! We'll see you all back here for the party at half seven! Yes?'

'Yes!' everyone cheered.

I hesitated for a moment, wondering whether to try and talk to him then, but Maya was quicker than me. The cheer had barely died down before she had linked her arm through his and steered him back over to the barn.

It didn't take me long to get ready as I hadn't got a wardrobe of party gear to pick from. Had I known a celebration was on the cards when I had been packing to come, I would have added something a little more special, but my priorities then had been leaving again as soon as possible and piling in clothes that would keep me warm.

'Are you ready, Liza?' Ned called up the stairs, just after seven. 'I thought we could go over together?'

Assuming we were alone, I went to rush down and take the opportunity to talk to him, but then I heard Maya's voice in the background.

'Not quite,' I said, my voice cracking as I stepped back into my room. 'Don't wait for me. I'll lock up and follow you over in a minute.'

I didn't think I would be able to bear the sight of them smiling up at me. They would be all dressed up and no doubt looking every inch the perfect couple. For two pins I would have shrugged off my cord jacket, hung my dress back in the wardrobe and buried myself under the duvet, but I didn't. I listened to them leave, then took a deep breath, ran a brush through my hair, which I'd left loose, added a layer of lip gloss and pulled on my boots.

My look was definitely more boho than conventional Christmas, but it didn't matter. I would never be able to compete with Maya's natural sparkle and shine. Not that it was a competition. And besides, given the turmoil coursing through my system, I thought it would be best if I stuck to making small talk and blending into the festive background. I might even slip out and head back to the lodge once I'd done the rounds.

'Wow!' beamed Noah, who happened to arrive just as I was leaving the lodge. 'Look at you!'

'Don't,' I said, sounding sulkier than I intended. 'It's

all I had with me. I wasn't expecting a party when I packed to come.'

Noah dropped the hand of the guy next to him, placed his hands on his hips and tutted.

'I'm being serious,' he said. 'You look gorgeous. I had no idea you had legs and a waist under all those layers. You've been hiding out in baggy jumpers and long coats.'

'I haven't been hiding out,' I told him, a smile tugging at my lips. 'I've been trying to keep warm.'

'And your hair's so long,' he carried on. 'You should wear it down like that more often.'

'Thanks,' I said, feeling better as I smoothed it over one shoulder.

Suitably satisfied with appraising my look, Noah turned back to his companion.

'Now,' he beamed, 'let me introduce you to Michael.'

'Michael,' I said, 'it's lovely to finally meet you.'

He was unbelievably good looking and perfectly groomed. Tall, tanned, fit and with not so much as a hair out of place.

'Hello,' he smiled, revealing teeth which were as impeccable as the rest of him. 'I've heard so much about you, Liza.'

'Have you now?' I said, narrowing my eyes at Noah, who was looking adoringly at his partner.

'All good,' he flustered, when he noticed I was frowning at him.

He quickly linked one arm with Michael and the other with me.

'Now, come on,' he insisted, 'we need to make an entrance.'

That was the last thing I wanted to do, but Noah refused to let me go. However, as we crossed the barn threshold, I became too distracted by the transformation to notice whether anyone was looking at me.

I had assumed the barn was party-ready before, but in the ninety minutes since Wynter's Trees had closed, the space had morphed again and into something even more beautiful. There were yet more lights, another tree, tables laden with platters of covered food, a small bar and much more mistletoe. It was cosy and warm too, thanks to some strategically positioned space heaters.

'Wow,' I gasped.

'Right?' Noah sighed, sounding every bit as taken aback as me. 'How stunning is this?'

'Do you like it?' asked Maya, rushing over when she spotted us. 'Is it okay?'

'It's stunning,' I told her, 'and, so are you.'

She gave us all her trademark smile and an elaborate twirl.

'Isn't it cute?' she laughed, looking down at her dress.

Her outfit wasn't at all what I had been expecting. A red sleeveless skater dress with a silver ribbon around the waist and reindeer prancing at the bottom. The bodice was covered in tiny diamante crystals which sparkled as they caught the light. With her blonde hair in a fancy up-do she looked exquisite. Where I had been expecting slim-fitting and sophisticated she'd embraced quirky and fun. She was endlessly surprising.

'Totally,' I told her, 'but I wish you hadn't worn heels, Maya,' I scolded.

She giggled and rushed off to welcome yet more guests.

'She makes me feel short,' tutted Noah, 'so goodness knows how you feel, Liza . . .'

'Noah,' Michael frowned.

'What? I'm only saying . . .'

Michael dragged him off before he could further dig himself into a hole and I followed my nose to the mulled wine that Sophie, Hope's mum, was doling out.

Before long, the barn was full of people, music was playing and practically everyone was dancing. I'd never known a party like it. It certainly knocked my Christmas nights out with Caitlin and our other exhausted school colleagues into touch.

Ned was looking gorgeous in a navy long-sleeved shirt, which complimented his hair colour and freckles wonderfully, and smart jeans. I tried not to stare as he talked and laughed with everyone because the sight of him filled my stomach with butterflies and made my heart flutter. I was going to need another glass of wine before I plucked up the courage to talk to him even though I had been building up to it all day.

'Are you having a good time?' David asked, coming to sit next to me. 'I haven't seen you dancing much.'

'I have been dancing,' I reassured him, smiling as Noah took Abbie for a spin on the dancefloor in her wheelchair. She certainly wasn't letting the confines of her chair stop her from having a good time. 'I'm just taking a breather. It's a wonderful party, David. It reminds me of the shindig Fezziwig threw for his employees in *A Christmas Carol*.'

David looked delighted.

'Ned would be thrilled to hear you say that,' he beamed, nodding over to where his son and Maya were now cutting quite a dash on the dance floor. 'He told me earlier that was exactly the atmosphere he was hoping to evoke.'

My heart beat all the faster as I watched him and Maya dancing. They looked so right together. I must have been mad to imagine after our kisses that Ned had ever felt anything for me when he had a woman like Maya by his side.

'Mission accomplished then,' I said, emptying the last dregs from my glass before turning my attention back to David.

'You should tell him,' he said, as the track came to an end. 'Ned!' he shouted, beckoning him over.

'No,' I began to protest, plucking at his sleeve, but it was too late.

I might have been wanting to talk to Ned all day, but on my terms not when his dad saw fit.

'Liza,' said Ned, walking over alone as Maya set about helping Hope and Sophie uncover the food. 'I've hardly seen you all evening. You look lovely by the way.'

'Thanks,' I blushed.

'I hope you're having a good time?'

Was it my imagination, or was he not quite as smiley talking to me as he had been with everyone else?

'Yes,' I said, 'it's a great party.'

'Tell him what you just told me,' David encouraged.

I explained what I had already said and Ned's broad smile finally reappeared.

'How about that then?' laughed David.

'Fantastic,' grinned Ned. 'That's exactly what I was aiming for.'

'So, your dad told me,' I nodded.

As there seemed to be a lull in the revelries while everyone lined up to pile their plates with festive food, I screwed my courage to the sticking place and grasped the opportunity to ask Ned if we could meet for a moment in the office. I wasn't sure the timing was right but the request was made before I could talk myself out it.

'It won't take a minute,' I told him, as he looked around. 'You won't be abandoning the party for long.'

'All right,' he said. 'Come on.'

'I'll save you both some food,' David called after us.

I wasn't sure I would have the stomach to eat it.

'It's about Liam,' I blurted out, as soon as the door was closed and Ned had turned on the desk lights.

It wasn't really, but I thought starting with him might be easier.

'What about him?' Ned frowned. 'Those lads haven't been back causing trouble, have they?'

He rolled up his shirt sleeves, revealing wonderfully toned forearms, then leant back against the desk and crossed his arms.

'No,' I swallowed. 'Not as far as I know. This is something different.'

'Go on.'

'Well,' I said, 'I know you weren't impressed when I first took him on, but you have to admit, he's been invaluable in the few weeks he's been here.'

'He certainly has,' Ned readily agreed. 'The kids love him as much as the parents and he's picked things up very quickly.'

'And we know he's honest,' I pressed on, emboldened by his enthusiasm. 'In spite of what this Bradley and Kyle have implied.'

'Yes,' Ned nodded. 'I haven't forgotten that he looked after that purse until Catherine Connelly claimed it.'

'Exactly.'

'So, why are you bringing him up now?' Ned asked. 'Do you think we should give him a Christmas bonus or something?'

'Not quite,' I said. 'It's a rather bigger request than a few extra pounds in his pay packet.'

'Oh?'

'The thing is, he finishes school next year and I was wondering if there would be any possibility that you might be able to take him on full-time. Offer him a traineeship or something. I think he could be a great asset to the business.'

Ned looked at me and smiled.

'What?'

'I didn't know you had telepathic skills,' he smiled.

I rather wished I had. It would certainly have saved me some recent heartache.

'You've thought of it already?' I frowned.

'It had crossed my mind.'

'Really?'

'Yes,' he said. 'With Dad going and you, of course.'

My gaze dipped to the floor. I would get to the part about me going once we'd finished talking about Liam.

'It's going to be important to have someone else working here and learning the ropes.' Ned carried on. 'Maya's great of course.'

'Of course,' I agreed.

'But can only be here when she isn't needed on her family farm.'

'So, you'll talk to Liam.'

'Yes,' he said. 'I'll ask him and Chelsea to come and see me next week.'

'That's fantastic,' I smiled.

I knew Liam would be over the moon and Chelsea would be too. The pair might not have had the ideal start to their mother-son relationship, but I could see their lives coming together now and I was thrilled for them.

'And it will give Liam an incentive to keep studying,' I said, my teacher brain kicking in and forcing to the front of my mind what I was going to say next.

'It will,' said Ned, uncrossing his arms. 'Thanks to Wynter's Trees, and your insistence that we took him on in the first place, his young life has had a total turnaround.'

My breath caught as I geared up to confess that mine might be poised to, too.

'Right then,' said Ned, standing straight. 'We'd better get back to the party.'

He'd reached the door before I found my voice again.

'There's just one more thing,' I hurriedly said, my voice barely audible.

'What's that?' he asked, turning to look at me.

My heart beat a rapid tattoo against my ribcage.

'I . . .' I faltered. 'I sorted the recycling earlier.'

'Oh,' he said, looking confused. 'Great. Thanks.'

'And I found the envelope in there addressed to me,' I pushed on.

The change in his expression told me the penny was about to drop, in spite of the roundabout way I'd approached the subject.

'And I opened it,' I further said. 'It was the brochure about forest schools.'

He looked at the floor.

'You sent for it, didn't you?' I whispered, my voice thick in my throat. 'You sent for it because you thought it might be a way for me to carry on doing the job I love and stay here at Wynter's Trees.'

'Yes,' he simply said, his eyes still on the floor.

'Well, it's brilliant,' I blurted out. 'Inspired!'

'What?' he said, his gaze snapping back to me.

'It's the perfect solution,' I said, as a wave of emotion shot through me. 'I love it.'

He opened his mouth to say something, but I rushed on.

'So inspired in fact,' I beamed, 'that it's made me change my mind.'

'It's made you change your mind?' he repeated.

'Yes,' I choked. My voice trembled as a tear rolled down my cheek. 'I want to stay. I want to live here in the lodge at Wynter's Trees and set up a forest school in the plantation.'

The volume of the music in the barn was suddenly cranked up and I had to raise my voice.

'I think we could make the place available to Norfolk and Suffolk schools, maybe even have a summer camp for kids who . . .'

Ned shook his head. 'It's too late,' he quietly said.

He didn't need to shout for me to grasp what he'd said.

'No, it's not,' I protested, shaking my head. 'It's not. I really mean this, Ned.'

'It's doesn't matter whether you mean it or not,' he said, louder now, as the light in his gorgeous eyes dulled. 'I spent all day yesterday finalising everything. I've had the loan I need to buy you out approved. It's done.'

I sunk into the chair behind me.

'It's all arranged,' he shrugged, 'just like you wanted.'

'But you sent for that brochure . . .'

'Weeks ago,' he cut in, 'and then I binned it because you called that second meeting to make sure that I knew, and Dad knew, that you hadn't changed your mind.'

I didn't know what to say. Literally, just as I had been

having my lightbulb moment, Ned had been flicking the switch of his off.

'You said this was what you wanted and I've gone through hell and high water to make it happen!' The words came out as a shout and I flinched.

'I'm sorry,' I whispered. 'I'm so sorry.'

'Not as sorry as I am.' He glowered, running his hands through his hair. 'Liza . . .'

'Oh my god!' shouted Maya, flying in through the door. 'Ned, you have to come!'

She grabbed his hand and started to tug him away.

'What is it?' he frowned, resisting. 'What's wrong?'

'Nothing,' she breathlessly laughed, pulling him harder. 'Nothing's wrong. Come on, Liza!' she said, spotting me. 'You too.'

'What is it?' Ned asked again, his feet finally moving.

'It's Noah,' she grinned. 'I think he's about to propose to Michael.'

Chapter 25

Maya's hunch was right. By the time we rejoined the party, there were a circle of guests standing where we'd all been dancing and Noah and Michael were in the centre of it. Noah was saying something, but I couldn't work out what because of the buzzing in my ears which had started when Ned had told me he'd raised the money to buy me out. However, reading the expressions on the faces of those closest to the two men, I guessed it was something romantic and when Noah dropped down on one knee, I knew exactly which four words he was going to utter next.

Tears sprang to Michael's eyes and his hands flew to his face in surprise, but I knew he had said yes. He pulled Noah to his feet and the pair hugged as the circle around them erupted into cheers and Abbie, wheeled herself forward to let off a confetti cannon, showering the happy couple in a cloud of rainbow coloured paper. Clearly, she'd known what Noah had in mind for the evening and had come prepared.

As everyone began to sing a rousing rendition of 'For

They Are Jolly Good Fellows', my gaze flicked to where Ned was standing. He was with Maya who was singing and clapping along, but he looked as absent as I felt and I wished I knew what he was thinking. It was utter torture, but I couldn't seem to stop my head from imagining the same scene playing out next year, only with him and Maya at the centre of the circle and a very beautiful solitaire diamond sparkling in a turquoise box.

I tried to push my way out of the crowd, but couldn't and then Noah and Michael were doing the rounds, hugging and kissing everyone with the happiest smiles lighting up both their faces and I knew I was going to have to endure it a little longer. If I left now, my absence would be noted and that was the last thing I wanted.

'Congratulations!' I beamed. 'I'm so happy for you both.'

'I can't believe it,' said Michael, who hugged me as if he had known me forever. 'I had no idea.'

'I blame my brother,' said Noah, trying and failing to sound as if this was an everyday occurrence. 'What with all his talk of romance and marriage. It must have been catching!'

'Well,' I said, 'I'm truly thrilled for you. This is certainly one Christmas party that no one's going to forget in a hurry.'

I knew certain details were going to be imprinted on my memory forever.

'Are you suggesting the party I had planned needed something extra, Liza?' Maya pretended to pout, as she appeared at my side with a tray of champagne.

'No,' I told her, unable to meet her eye. 'Of course not. It was already amazing Maya.'

'I know,' she giggled, 'I'm only teasing. I wonder who'll be next,' she then beamed, with a blatant look in Ned's direction.

I couldn't bring myself to answer and looked away as her gaze swung back to me.

'Where did you find fizz at such short notice?' Michael asked, thankfully deflecting her train of thought.

'Yes,' said Noah, handing me a glass, before passing another to Michael and picking up one for himself. 'I didn't arrange this.'

'I did,' said Abbie, who came to join us. 'I just knew Michael was going to say yes, so I couldn't resist making sure we had something other than mulled cider to toast you both with. Not that the cider isn't delicious,' she added, winking at Maya who was pouting again.

'You,' said Noah, stooping to kiss Abbie's flushed face, 'are a total sweetheart.'

'I know,' she said, looking a little misty eyed. 'It's why you love me. Although, apparently, you love Michael more.'

'Afraid I do,' said Noah, reaching for Michael's hand and kissing the back of it. 'I would have asked you instead Abbie, but with you wanting all those babies, I thought I'd better stick to my man here. He doesn't want offspring either. Do you?'

'No,' laughed Michael. 'Don't panic, Noah. I'm not going to change my mind about that.'

'In that case,' said Abbie, raising her glass, 'cheers to you both.'

'Cheers!' Maya and I joined in, but I didn't drain my flute as the others did. I needed a clear head and no more alcohol flowing through my system for what I had in mind to do next.

It didn't take long for everyone to start dancing again and as they were all so absorbed in having a good time, I was finally able to slip out unnoticed. My path across the yard back to the lodge caused the floodlights to come on, but I didn't look back until I reached the veranda. Thankfully, no one had followed me out.

'Come on then,' I said, letting Bandit out of his sanctuary in the utility room. Ned would have heard his barking between songs, and the dog wouldn't stop now he knew someone was in the house. 'You can come upstairs with me, but you have to be quiet and promise not to tell anyone.'

The daft dog cocked his head to one side and I bent to give him a hug, instantly dissolving into tears the moment my fingers buried into his thick warm coat.

'I'm going to miss you pooch,' I told him, once I was all cried out and having wasted precious minutes. Not that I expected the party to end anytime soon, but I had things to do.

It was well past midnight by the time I heard Ned come in and, assuming my ears weren't playing tricks on me, he had Maya with him. I strained to listen and knew there were definitely two voices talking in the room below and one of them was female. I rolled over in the bed and pulled the duvet right over my head as Bandit scrambled to get out.

'Traitor,' I muttered.

A couple of minutes later, I heard light footfall on the stairs.

'Liza,' I then heard Ned whisper, 'are you awake?'

I ignored him and he quietly closed the door. I gave it a few seconds, then rolled on to my back and looked at the clock. How long should I give them, I wondered, before I made my move? I didn't have to wait long. The noise of the shower was the perfect cover and I snuck out of bed, arranging the pillows to look like I was still in it, and then went downstairs.

I'd had the foresight to stash everything I'd packed out of sight behind the sofa. Obviously, I couldn't take everything I wanted with me, but hoped David would send the rest on to my flat after Christmas. I lingered for a moment to look at the tree, remembering the day Ned and I decorated it, along with all the other things we had done together, mostly because he'd gone to the trouble of arranging them and then, with a heart filled with longing and regret, not only for the man I was leaving behind, but also for what might have been at Wynter's Trees, I picked up my bags and walked out of the lodge for the very last time.

The boot catch on my car had a habit of sticking so, rather than risk setting off Bandit, who was upstairs with Maya and Ned, I shoved everything on to the back seat. I knew getting out of the gate was going to be tricky so rushed to open it before I started the car. That way I could shoot off and leave it open. I would apologise for the security breach when I messaged and asked David to send the rest of my things on.

Everything went like clockwork until I put the key in the ignition and turned it. The car made a sort of grinding noise, but didn't start. I turned the key back, counted to five and tried again. Although temperamental, it generally got there in the end. I just had to be patient and hold my nerve.

'Third time's a charm,' I whispered, crossing the fingers on my left hand and squeezing my eyes shut.

I turned the key with conviction and this time the engine spluttered into life. I opened my eyes, ready to put it in first and release the handbrake, but then caught sight of the one person in the world I simply couldn't face.

Ned charged out of the lodge door, soaking wet and wrapped in yet another inadequate towel. It was my arrival, all over again, only this time, I was leaving. I tore my eyes away and went to move forward, but he had let Bandit out with him and the mad dog leapt about the wheels, barking his head off. I didn't dare move forward or back for fear of running him over.

'Wait!' Ned shouted, rushing over to the car. With Bandit on the case, he'd halted just long enough to pull on his boots which sat, like Dad's always had, by the lodge door. 'Liza, wait!'

'I can't!' I shouted back, giving a blast on the horn. 'Get hold of Bandit, will you? I need to go.'

'No,' said Ned, placing his hands on the bonnet. 'You're not going anywhere.'

I feared for the security of his towel, but no more than I feared for my heart. This was exactly the sort of scene I had been hoping to avoid, not that I had really been expecting him to go to such lengths to stop me from leaving.

Given the look he had given me back in the office when I told him I'd changed my mind about everything I wouldn't have been all that surprised if he'd come out to wave me off and locked the gate behind me. Good riddance and all that.

But then, did I *really* think he'd react like that? If that had formed part of my thought process, then why had I engaged in such an elaborate cloak and dagger moonlight flit?

'Please Ned,' I said, opening the window a little so I didn't have to shout. 'Just let me go. Go back inside to Maya and forget I ever came back.'

He frowned at me through the windscreen.

'Maya's not here,' he said, shaking his head.

'I heard her,' I told him. 'I heard the pair of you come back earlier.'

'She did walk back over with me,' he said, starting to shiver, 'because we needed to properly finish a conversation, we'd started days ago.'

Could that mean that there had been two proposals rather than one? I really hoped not. The thought made me feel sick.

'But she went ages ago,' Ned carried on.

'Even so,' I said, feeling marginally mollified, but still a

369

bit bilious, 'I still have to go. Just go back inside Ned. You're freezing and I don't know how long my car will keep going if I don't move it.'

He didn't budge and I wondered if his hands were actually frozen to the bonnet. It was certainly cold enough for that to happen.

'I'll move if you promise you'll come back in.'

I shook my head.

'Please, Liza,' he pleaded, his teeth chattering.

'What's the point?' I shouted over the noise of the engine as I revved it a little and my voice cracked. 'What's the point in me staying now?'

'The point is,' he shot back, his voice louder as he stared intently at me.

'What?' I demanded, revving the car again.

Perhaps the heat from the engine might warm him a little. If he persisted in standing there much longer, he was going to catch a chill and then I'd be held responsible for ruining his health on top of everything else.

'The point is,' he said, his eyes never leaving my face, 'I need you.'

'Why?' I shrugged.

Why would he need me? Our relationship, professional or otherwise, was over, wasn't it? His reaction to hearing that I'd changed my mind and wanted to build a life at Wynter's Trees had certainly made me think it was.

'Because I love you.'

My foot slipped off the accelerator and the engine

spluttered and died. Thankfully I hadn't put the car in gear or released the handbrake.

'I'm in love with you, Liza Wynter,' he confidently declared, smiling in spite of the bone-chilling cold, 'and I have been from the very first moment I set eyes on you.'

Wasn't that the line I'd had stuck in my head for the last few weeks?

'Did you hear what I said?' he shivered.

I felt rooted to the spot, but not because of the cold. The heat coursing through me and blazing a trail to my face was searing enough to thaw even the deepest frost. I was rigid with shock. I did manage to open and close my mouth a couple of times, but no sound came out.

'Are you going to say anything?' Ned asked, finally letting go of the bonnet and tucking the towel tighter around his waist.

I shook my head, not knowing what to say. But then the image of him dancing with Maya popped into my head.

'But what about Maya?' I spluttered. 'You're in love with her, aren't you?'

Ned walked round to the driver's side door and pulled it open.

'No,' he said, looking down at me. 'I'm not in love with Maya. I never have been and she's fine. A little bemused perhaps, but totally fine.'

'I don't understand.'

How could she be fine? She was head over heels for him, wasn't she?

'She knows everything,' Ned softly said.

'What do you mean?'

'I'd been working my way up to telling her that I'd fallen in love with you for days,' he chuckled, 'but in the end, she beat me to the punch.'

'She did what?'

Ned's smile widened and my heart kicked in response.

'She sat me down and told me that she'd worked out how I felt about you, and having talked to you the day you swapped the trees and watched you since, she was pretty sure you felt the same way about me, too.'

I wasn't quite ready to admit the depth of my feelings for him just yet, but could feel my cheeks were still brightly blazing, which no doubt gave me away anyway.

'Was she upset?' I asked. 'Was she angry?'

I knew how much Maya liked Ned and hoped she didn't blame me for what had happened. It had never been my intention to steal her man. The kisses Ned and I had shared had never been planned. They were completely spontaneous and although arousing and unforgettable, guilt inducing too.

'Not at all,' Ned said, sounding as bewildered by the turn of events as I felt. 'She told me that the heart wants what the heart wants and you can't force it to want something different.'

I didn't think I could have been so magnanimous about it. She really was an incredible woman. She'd gone to a lot of effort with all that mistletoe during the last few weeks and apparently, with no success.

'She's amazing,' I whispered.

Ned grinned. 'She also said she knew something was amiss, because I was impervious to her charms,' he further added. 'Contrary to popular belief, our kisses under the mistletoe have been few and far between and definitely one-sided.'

I felt my face grow even warmer.

'But you looked like the perfect couple,' I pointed out. 'If you really weren't interested in having a relationship with her, then why did you go along with it?'

Ned ran a hand through his wet hair.

'Because I couldn't let myself believe that I'd fallen in love with you, Liza.' He seriously said and I knew there was no deception behind his words. 'I did everything I could to convince myself that you weren't the one for me. You were all set to leave and with no intention of ever coming back. But tonight . . .'

'Tonight,' I interrupted. 'I told you I'd changed my mind and you were furious.'

'I was frustrated,' he amended. 'Not furious. After the party, I told Maya what you'd said and she told me I had to confess all tomorrow. I'd already made up my mind to do that and I'd got it all straight in my head. I was going to apologise and declare my feelings, but then,' he added, with a nod to the car, 'you pulled this stunt and I knew I couldn't wait until tomorrow because you'd be gone.'

He shivered again. So focused on listening to him, I'd forgotten we were outside and that he was still soaked from the shower.

'So, the kisses we've shared have really meant something to you?' I asked, wanting to be absolutely sure before I gave my heart free rein to fall completely in love.

'Of course, they have,' he said. 'You're beautiful, Liza, all the more stunning because you don't know it. Why do you think I haven't been able to resist kissing you?'

'Because you were drunk.' I teasingly reminded him.

'That was only the first time,' he blushed. 'The beer made me brave. I'd wanted to press my lips to yours from the very moment you turned up here and set the alarm off. You set an alarm off in my head and my heart that night too, and I've been trying to keep a lid on it ever since, because I knew letting it ring out wouldn't end well.'

'Well,' I said, still feeling cautious, 'you were right about that, weren't you? Things haven't turned out well. You've just told me you love me, but I'm still about to leave and you're up to your ears in debt.'

'You're not going anywhere,' he huskily said, holding out his hand. 'And I have every intention of cancelling that loan first thing Monday morning.'

I looked at his outstretched hand, swallowed away the lump in my throat and, a few seconds later, reached out. Our fingers, beautifully entwined, felt like the perfect fit.

'If it is still what you want,' he said, gently drawing me out of the car, 'you can stay here forever and we can run Wynter's Trees between us, both as partners in business and in life.'

My eyes searched his face.

'No one else, besides Dad, knows you were planning to leave,' he reminded me. 'I know you haven't told anyone, and I haven't, so there's no muddle to unravel or explain.'

I felt relieved about that because it would make properly settling in so much easier. I was going run my business at Wynter's Trees and I was still going to see the northern lights, but with Ned by my side. We could go together. From then on, we could do everything together. It would be an adventure.

'What do you say?' he asked, gently pulling me to him. 'Is that what you want, Liza?'

'Yes,' I nodded, finally voicing my heart's desire. 'That's exactly what I want.'

With that he swept me up into his arms and carried me back to the lodge and I spent the rest of the night coming up with inventive ways to warm him up again.

Chapter 26

When I woke the next morning, Ned was sitting on the edge of the bed pulling on his boxers. I reached out and lightly ran a finger down his spine, tracing the length of the tree tattoo which I now knew in intimate detail. The action made him shiver, but not with cold.

'Good morning, Miss Wynter,' he lazily smiled, twisting round to face me.

His eyes were aflame and the sight of them caused my insides to dance with desire.

'Good morning,' I whispered back.

'How are you feeling this morning?' he asked.

'Wonderful,' I said, stretching out and feeling more relaxed than I had in, well, forever. 'Rested, refreshed and raring to go.'

Given that I'd had such little sleep, that wasn't at all how I'd expected to feel, but apparently love really did conquer all. Even postcoital exhaustion.

'Good,' Ned laughed, pinning my arms above my head

and straddling me in one swift movement, 'I was hoping you were going to say that.'

I would have quite happily spent the whole day in bed, but as it was Sunday, the last Sunday before Christmas in fact, Wynter's Trees was going to be open for business and there was work to do. Although, not by me, apparently.

'Are you sure you can manage without me?' I asked Ned a while later, once he had eventually forced himself back into the shower and then into some clothes. 'What about clearing up from the party? Surely you'll need some help with that.'

Ned shook his head.

'Maya and I sorted most of that last night. It gave us more opportunity to carry on talking about my feelings for you.'

I still felt guilty about that and as much as I wanted to talk to Maya, and clear the air, I didn't think I could find the words just yet. Neither did I feel ready to face David and the Wynter's Trees beach hut brigade either, but that was for a different reason. Ned and I had agreed not to tell everyone our news too soon and I knew my expression, and the not so secretive smile lighting up my face, would give the game away.

'Right,' I swallowed, feeling jittery about Maya again.

'She really doesn't mind, you know,' Ned insisted, before swooping down and planting a sensuous and lingering kiss on my willing lips.

'Well, that's good,' I sighed, feeling all floaty again as the kiss ended. 'I'd hate to hurt her. She's such a good friend. Sorry,' I then added, as I tried but failed to stifle a yawn.

The previous night's exertions were catching up with me after all and Ned looked well pleased to be the cause of my exhaustion.

'You stay inside and finish wrapping the puddings,' he grinned. 'If it gets too manic later, I'll call you over.'

'All right,' I relented, eager to stay out of sight. 'If you insist.'

Once Ned had gone, leaving Bandit snoozing next to the log burner, I spent a wonderful couple of hours sorting through a large wicker hamper which had belonged to Mum and was full of fabrics.

She had always hoarded scraps of material and ends of rolls, including those featuring Christmas designs and they were going to be just the thing for wrapping up the pudding bowls. I found a bundle of raffia too, which would be ideal for tying the material in place. But most poignant of all was the box of old Christmas cards which Mum painstakingly cut up to make labels. I could remember her doing it every year when the decorations came down.

Ordinarily the rush of memories would have either been pushed away or resulted in a flood of tears, but aside from slightly damp eyes, there was no dramatic reaction. In fact, I was happy to let the remembrance come and took comfort in it. I could think of Mum now feeling light of heart and with no gnawing bitterness about Dad's decision to move us south to Wynmouth.

What an emotional journey I'd been on since accepting David's invitation to return. Within the last twenty-four hours alone, I'd gone from planning to leave for good, to allowing myself to fall headlong in love and declaring I would be staying at Wynter's Trees forever. It was a miraculous turnaround and almost entirely the result of and reaction to Ned's kind endeavours. What a wonder he was. I closed my eyes and saw myself standing where I had previously imagined Maya to be, right by his side, far into the future.

I hoped Ned had correctly interpreted our friend's reaction to everything. The last thing I wanted was to upset Maya and I knew I mustn't delay talking to her for long. In fact, the sooner I saw her, the better.

'Knock, knock.'

And as if by magic, there she was.

'Maya,' I croaked, stunned to have summoned her. 'Hey.'

My hands started to sweat and my internal thermostat soared as my brain scrabbled for something to say.

'Have you got a sec?' she asked.

'Of course,' I said. 'Come in. I was just thinking about coming to find you actually.'

'I had a feeling you might be,' she said, stepping properly in and closing the door behind her. 'Ned said I should come over.'

'Did he?' I squeaked, shifting from one foot to the other.

I would have to thank him later.

'Oh Liza,' Maya then kindly said. 'Please don't look so worried. I haven't come over here to bawl you out, because there's really no need.'

'Isn't there?' I gulped.

I was still finding it hard to believe that she could be so generous and forgiving, even though nothing she had said or done suggested otherwise.

'No,' she said, as she pulled off her muddy boots. 'Absolutely not. The heart wants what the heart wants and there's nothing anyone can do to change that.'

'Ned told me that's what you'd said,' I whispered, my bottom lip trembling a little.

I reached for the kettle before I succumbed to the tears of relief I could feel waiting in the wings.

'And I meant it,' she firmly said. 'In fact, I should have backed off that first morning I tried to kiss Ned under the mistletoe and you walked in,' she further added.

'You should?' I frowned, taken aback.

'Yes,' she laughed, elegantly sitting on one of the stools I had to scramble to get a foothold on. 'I should. Now I've thought it all through, I've realised it was as plain as the nose on my face right from that very moment.'

'What was?'

'That Ned was smitten with you, of course.'

'Really?'

From what I could remember I thought he'd looked knocked sideways by Maya's flirty antics. It never entered my head that he'd noticed me.

'And you looked pretty keen on him too,' she carried on, dreamily staring off into the distance.

'Are you sure?' I flushed.

'I am now,' she nodded. 'And you know, I would have given him up straightaway, only you said you were certain that he liked me.'

I knew now that that was the result of them looking like the perfect match, coupled with my desire to see Wynter's Trees left in the hands of the best possible team to run it. Had I factored my feelings into the equation and confessed them far sooner, things would have been different weeks ago, but there was no point dwelling on that now.

'Anyway,' Maya shrugged, as if her derailed romance was all part of life's great plan, 'all's well that ends well and I'm delighted for you both. I really am.'

'That's so kind of you, Maya,' I said.

Her smile was both generous and genuine and she didn't look at all fazed.

'Would you like a coffee?' I offered, as the kettle boiled.

'Not really,' she said, wrinkling her nose. 'But I wouldn't say no to a mug of your hot chocolate.'

'With extra marshmallows?'

'Of course!' she laughed.

I added a flake to her mug and a swirl of squirty cream and sprinkles as well as marshmallows.

'So,' I said, sliding the packed mug towards her as she eyed it greedily, 'how's it looking out there so far today?'

'It was a slow start,' she told me, 'but it's picking up, though there aren't many trees going out now.'

I supposed it was getting a bit late in the month to sell many more.

'Mind you, the lack of early customers gave Noah the chance to tell us all about his and Michael's plans for the wedding.' Maya carried on, pulling out the flake and dipping it in the cream before taking a bite.

'Oh really?' I sighed. 'I'm sorry I missed that.'

'Don't worry,' she said, scooping up another dollop of cream. 'He's currently running on repeat, so you won't miss out. In fact, you'll most likely get to hear it all twice.'

I had to laugh at that.

'It's going to be the wedding to end all weddings, isn't it?' I said, imagining the elaborate scene.

'Definitely,' she giggled. 'Beach themed of course.'

'Don't tell me,' I said, feeling disappointed that I wouldn't get to witness the nuptials first-hand, but excited for the ecstatic couple nonetheless. 'My guess is the Caribbean or the Maldives.'

'Wynmouth,' Maya said, deadpan.

'You're kidding?'

'Nope,' she grinned. 'They want to keep it local, although Sophie will be doing the catering which will mean a very Caribbean twist.'

'Well, I never,' I said.

'You look as shocked as we all did.'

'I am.'

'Apparently, Noah has ancient grandparents who refuse to fly and, as they've always been so supportive, especially when he was a teenager and fell out with his dad, he and Michael want to wed somewhere they'll be able to get to.'

'That's so sweet,' I choked.

'Don't,' she said, waving her hands in front of her eyes. 'You'll set me off again. Oh,' she added, 'and I almost forgot, they've asked Wren to design and make the rings.'

'Oh my god,' I squeaked, feeling more tears gathering.

'I know, right?' she sniffed, blinking hard.

I felt thoroughly content once Maya and I had talked, drunk more hot chocolate and made serious inroads into the Christmas tub of Roses which Ned had thought was out of sight because it was on a shelf too high for me to reach. Maya's height came in handy once we'd decided to liberate it.

She told me she was already looking forward to working the next season at Wynter's Trees and that she knew the business was going to go from strength to strength now Ned and I had got our acts together. I was sorely tempted to tell her about the forest school plan, but didn't. Ned and I really needed to sit and talk it all out and prepare a proper schedule before we went public.

By the time Maya left, promising to keep mine and Ned's relationship secret, I felt like I was floating again, and it wasn't all down to the extra sugar I'd ingested. As I set to, cutting out large circles of fabric to wrap the puddings in, using the pinking shears to crimp the edges, I made sure I had my new journal to hand to jot down the sudden influx of new ideas which were crowding in.

Top of my personal to-do list was packing up my flat. I wouldn't need to renew the lease, which was fortunately due to run out in the new year, now I was moving back to the lodge. I also made a note to talk to Ned about my travel plans, not that I was likely to forget, but who doesn't love a list?

I wouldn't be giving up my trip to see the northern lights and would persuade Ned to take the time off to come with me. I knew the stunningly illuminated Icelandic skies would be a spectacle he would enjoy. And a romantic one too. And I was very much looking forward to playing out that reindeer rug fantasy . . .

I had just finished wrapping up the last pudding bowl when I had another visitor.

'David,' I said, opening the door, 'come in.'

'I'm not going to keep you,' he said, almost before I'd got the door shut, 'and I know he wasn't supposed to say anything, but I just wanted to tell you how absolutely thrilled I am about you and Ned.'

'Oh David,' I said, the sight of him so happy, causing my eyes to fill with tears.

I reached out and pulled him into a hug.

'I can't begin to tell you how happy I am,' he said, sounding choked himself. 'I just knew you two would make the perfect pairing.'

'You never really did give up hoping that I'd change my mind about selling my shares in the business, did you?' I smiled, releasing him.

'No,' he admitted. 'I didn't, although when I caught sight of Ned's face after your chat and during Noah's proposal last night, I did begin to wonder.'

Was it really less than a day since Ned and I had talked at the party? It felt like eons ago already.

'I'd had no idea Ned had gone to the bank and to see the solicitor,' David carried on, 'and when he told me after the party that you'd changed your mind about leaving and he'd told you it was too late, I couldn't believe it.'

'Oh David.'

'I soon told him he had to fight for you and tell you how he felt.'

Apparently, Maya wasn't the only one who had borne witness to mine and Ned's true feelings for one another during the last few weeks.

'I hope you don't think I was interfering,' David then said, sounding less sure.

'Not at all,' I reassured him.

'Not that I think he really had any intention of letting you go,' he added.

Had my car started first time, he might not have had any choice. Thank goodness for that dodgy starter motor.

'And when he walked into the office this morning,' David continued, his smile back in place, 'I just knew everything had come good.'

'More than good,' I told him, matching his with a very happy smile of my own. 'I truly can't remember a time when I've ever felt so happy, David.'

'It's nothing less than you deserve and I know you and Ned are going to more than successfully carry on your dad's legacy.'

'I hope so.' I swallowed.

'I know so,' he declared. 'Now, when are you planning on telling everyone the wonderful news?'

'Not just yet,' I said, 'Ned and I need to get used to the shift in our relationship first and of course, we wouldn't want to steal Noah and Michael's thunder.'

'Well, in that case,' David laughed, 'you'd both better amend your expressions, because if you go around grinning like Cheshire cats, then everyone's going to know, whether you want them to or not!'

With David's words ringing in my ears, and Ned's face as worn out from smiling as mine was, I was extremely grateful that Wynter's Trees was closed the next day. No one was due to replenish the huts and the uninterrupted twenty-four hours of peace and quiet gave us ample opportunity to get to know each other better.

We walked alone through the reserve, with Bandit around the plantation, and spent hours talking through our plans for the future, making love and gazing into the warming flames of the log burner.

'Come on,' I laughed, as I started and gave up trying to wrap the presents I'd got from the huts, as Ned began kissing my neck. 'You need to get outside. Let's go for another walk.'

'You make me sound like Bandit,' he smiled.

'You've certainly got as much as energy as him!' I giggled.

'I have,' he agreed, crossing the room and throwing me a coat from the rack, 'and I have to warn you,' he added, waggling his eyebrows, 'fresh air gives me an appetite.'

'Why does that not surprise me?'

The cold initially took my breath away, but by the time we'd walked to the family tree, I was feeling warmer.

'It's looking all right, isn't it?' I said, staring up into the branches.

'It's a bit too soon to say to be honest,' said Ned, also scrutinising it. 'But I'm pretty sure it's going to be fine. It's bound to take a little while to realise its roots aren't bound to the confines of the pot, but then it will hopefully romp away.'

'A bit like a Victorian miss released from her corsets,' I grinned.

Ned looked at me, a wicked smile playing about his lips.

'I'd like to release you from your corsets,' he said, reaching towards me but I jumped out of the way.

'Oh, no you don't,' I said, 'not out here anyway. It's freezing!'

I skipped further away as he lunged for me again and our silly antics set Bandit off.

'Don't you go running off,' Ned called as I hid behind a tree. 'I know what happened last time and I can't believe you think this is cold. You should try standing out here naked, soaking wet and with nothing more than a tiny towel between you and the elements.'

I stepped out from my hiding place, laughing.

'Yes,' I said, taking the hand he offered, 'I've been meaning to ask you about that. Why are all your towels so small?'

'They're not,' he said, squeezing my fingers, 'but the first time I grabbed the one that was closest to hand.'

'And the second?'

'Well,' he said, 'the second time, I knew you were about to head for the hills and selected what I thought would show me off in the best light.'

I let out an inelegant, but uncontainable, snort.

'You mean you thought that if I got another look at your toned torso, then I simply wouldn't be able to resist following you back inside?'

'Exactly,' he said, marching ahead and pulling me along with him.

'That's terrible,' I tutted.

'My body?'

'Oh no,' I said, 'that's stunning.'

He let out a bark of laughter and pulled me into his arms for another lingering kiss. The resulting goosebumps and tingles were nothing to do with the temperature.

'I didn't really grab that tiny towel to seduce you,' he said, when we finally came up for air. 'It was sheer panic. The thought of losing you had me down those stairs and out the door before I'd given it a second thought. There was no way I was going to let you go, Liza.'

I felt even warmer after he'd said that.

Back inside the lodge, and after our appetites for each other had been sated again, I finally wrapped the presents and our talk turned to business.

'Have you made arrangements to talk to Liam about his apprenticeship yet?' I asked.

'No,' Ned frowned. 'I wanted to discuss it with you again

before I went ahead. Are we sure we can afford to take him on now our plans for the future have changed?'

I thought about what David had told us about Wynter's Trees having had its most lucrative season so far. The books were looking better year on year and with the huts now in place, and additional new events planned, the bumper seasons looked set to continue.

'Absolutely,' I firmly said. 'I'm not going to draw more from the profits than I do already and the extra share of mine, that I usually keep in the business, can be invested in setting up the forest school next year. As long as we don't overstretch ourselves and we make sensible choices, we'll be fine. Does that sound okay to you?'

I'd already set enough money aside for my trip and didn't think it would be too much of a stretch to make it an adventure for two.

'Yes,' Ned nodded. 'That's fine by me. Exactly what I thought you had in mind. I'm not expecting the extra events throughout the year to make much to begin with but they will eventually and that will help.'

I was feeling excited about both our personal and professional futures.

'I'm going to be kept busy setting up my new business and with all these extras we keep coming up with, we're going to need an extra pair of hands.'

'And Liam's will be ideal,' Ned agreed. 'We'll see him at the solstice celebration tomorrow so I'll ask him and Chelsea then to come out and see us on Wednesday.'

'He's going to be so happy,' I beamed, imagining the look on Liam's face when we told him what we had in mind.

'He is,' Ned agreed.

'Did you say solstice celebration?'

I knew there always was one in the village, but I'd never taken part.

'I did,' said Ned, adding another log to the burner. 'And you'll need to wrap up. It's happening on the beach and as we're keeping our relationship a secret, I'm not going to be able to give you a hug to keep you warm, am I?'

'No,' I said, 'I don't suppose you are. I'll see if I can find some thermals.'

'Sexy,' he laughed, eyeing me up again, with a mischievous twinkle in his eyes.

Chapter 27

December the twenty-first was a bright, crisp and cloud free day which started out with a sharp frost and ice underfoot. Everyone in the huts was in agreement about closing up a little early so we could all attend the solstice celebration, which was organised by Lilith and some of her friends, together.

Ned had hung a sign on the gate to explain the change in opening hours and he'd added a note to the Wynter's Trees website and social media accounts too, so hopefully no one would be caught out. I had to smile when I read how he had worded it – *we're opening for a shorter time on the twenty-first to celebrate the shortest day* – very clever.

'Are you ready?' he asked, when he came back from locking the barn, when it was time to leave. 'Everyone else has gone.'

'Yes,' I said, adding a coat to my many layers and picking up my hat, scarf and gloves. 'All set.'

Ned eyed me speculatively.

'What?' I frowned, looking down to see what had caught his attention.

Nothing looked amiss to me, although my appearance was a bit padded out.

'I was just wondering if you found those thermals,' he mused.

'Well,' I said, 'you'll find out later, won't you?'

'No time for a quick peek now, I suppose,' he suggestively said.

'Nope,' I responded, brushing by him, with a smile. 'No time at all.'

He looked disappointed but there really was no time to further speculate over my all-encompassing undergarments, and having promised Bandit we wouldn't be too late back, he locked the door and we headed over to the truck.

'So,' I said, when we arrived in the village, which was busier than I had expected, 'what's going to happen at this solstice celebration?'

'No idea,' Ned grinned, expertly reversing into a tiny space at the side of the green which a much smaller vehicle had just vacated. 'I've never actually managed to get to one before. The only thing I know about is the burning, which is a new addition this year. Have you got your paper, by the way?'

'Yes,' I said, thrusting my hand into the coat pocket to check.

Lilith had explained that all the attendees were welcome to write down anything they wished to leave behind from the year on a piece of paper which they could then burn in the ceremonial bonfire.

I wasn't sure how I felt about the idea, from a spiritual point of view, but had nonetheless decided to give it a go and had spent a long time composing a whole list of things. By the time I'd finished, I realised I'd tracked back much further than just the last twelve months. I hoped that was all right.

'Have you?' I asked Ned.

'Yes,' he said seriously.

I wondered what was written on his piece of paper, but knowing I would have felt awkward sharing the details of mine, didn't ask.

'Come on then,' I said. 'We'd better go. Everyone's meeting outside the pub, aren't they?'

'Apart from Abbie and Noah,' Ned told me. 'He's driven them near to the site because they can't get on to the sand with the wheelchair. They're going to set up and watch as close as they can from the clifftop.'

I felt a little nervous as we approached the large group milling about outside the pub. It was only half two in the afternoon, but I could see lots of people had torches and lanterns with them.

'Oh,' I said to Ned. 'I didn't think to bring anything to light the way. I suppose it will be almost dark on the walk back, won't it?'

We were to walk along the seafront and over to the beach huts where a large fire had been built near the shore and then back into the village after the formalities to celebrate in the pub. As it would be dark by four, we'd most likely need something to light the path back.

'Don't worry,' said Ned, 'I've got a torch.'

He pulled the red Maglite I recognised from the office out of his pocket.

'Good,' I said, 'but it doesn't look very in keeping.'

Some of the group, who were wearing hooded cloaks which reached the floor, had traditional lanterns and jars adorned with lengths of ivy.

'I don't suppose it matters,' said Ned. 'As long as there's light coming out of the end of it, I'm sure it will suffice.'

The level of chatter began to rise as everyone found and paired up with family and friends. Ned and I stuck together, with Wren and Theo in front of us and Sue and her partner behind. Then a hush fell over the group as the two cloak-clad people at the front turned and led the way down to the beach. I imagined we looked like the elves leaving Rivendell in the *Lord of the Rings* trilogy, only perhaps slightly less elegant.

As we progressed, the walk began to feel properly ethereal and, in the distance, I could see the bonfire had been lit. With every step we took, the light seemed to be fading and it felt quite eerie as we approached. Without a word we all formed a circle around the crackling fire and those with lanterns set them down or drove their handles into the sand.

We held hands with the people next to us and I felt grateful to have Ned on my left and Sue on my right. Bathed in the orange glow from the fire it was harder to pick familiar faces out and in spite of the warmth I felt a shiver run through me. Not of fear, more of the unknown. I'd never experienced anything like it before.

Another hooded figure, which I hadn't spotted in the shadows, stepped seemingly out of the fire, and I gasped. Ned squeezed my hand and the ceremony began. Once a circle of protection had been drawn, there was much talk of the lengthening of days and then two men, wearing masks and carrying sticks, battled. One was the holly king, the other the oak and it was the oak king who rose victorious, regaining the crown and once again reigning supreme.

The light had faded completely as a quiet chant began to echo around the group. I stared into the flames feeling, I wasn't sure what, but definitely something. Tears gathered in my eyes which had nothing to do with the woodsmoke and when I felt a light tap on my shoulder, I let go of Sue and Ned's hands, stepped forward and dropped my note into the flames. I watched as the edges of the paper curled and then suddenly, it burst into flames and along with it went my guilt and all of my regrets from the past and I stepped back, ready to embrace my future.

Once everyone had taken their turn, the circle was opened, the lamps retrieved and the slow walk back to the village began. I would have liked to have thanked the woman who had officiated but she seemed to have disappeared as quickly as she'd emerged.

'That was quite something, wasn't it?' said Ned, as everyone around us streamed away while we lingered behind.

'Yes,' I huskily said, still staring into the flames. 'I don't know what I had been expecting, but it wasn't that.'

'When those men jumped out to battle with those masks on,' said Ned, shaking his head, 'I almost jumped out of my skin.'

'I felt you,' I smiled, tearing my eyes away and breaking whatever spell it was that had drawn me to the glowing blaze.

It was completely dark now and when my eyes readjusted, I could make out the pinprick of stars in the inky sky and I could hear the sea too. I hadn't noticed the lapping waves at any point during the ceremony but they sounded loud now.

'I think the tide's coming in,' I said, looking across the sand. 'We should move, Ned.'

'You're right,' he said, cocking his head to listen.

'But before we do,' I said, catching his hand, 'I want to ask you something. Do you think it would be all right if we told everyone straightaway that we're together?'

He pulled me into his arms and held me close.

'I thought you wanted to wait,' he said, smiling down at me.

'I did,' I said. 'But I've changed my mind. Is that all right?'

It was fast becoming a habit since my return to Wynter's Trees.

'More than all right,' he said. 'We'll have a kiss under the mistletoe in the pub. That'll give everyone the right idea.'

'What about a kiss now?' I suggested.

He was more than willing to oblige.

'Hey!' shouted voices from the cliff above. 'We can see you down there, you know!'

It was Abbie and Noah.

'I knew it!' Noah bawled, sounding ecstatic and when Ned shone his torch, I could see he was jumping up and down and clapping his hands.

'So, did I!' added Abbie, who was by his side.

'Not such a secret after all then,' Ned said to me.

'What gave us away?' I called up to the two of them.

'Ned was like a cat with two tails the morning after the party,' Noah laughed. 'So, we knew something had gone on and as it didn't seem to have anything to do with Maya *and* he kept slipping back to the lodge . . .'

'All right,' cut in Ned. 'We get the idea.'

'And you'd better get off the beach,' called Abbie. 'Unless you're planning to swim back to the pub!'

The cheer that erupted when Ned and I finally walked into the pub, having stopped for another kiss once we'd safely reached dry land, left us in no doubt that Noah and Abbie had made it back first. Ned swept me up into his arms and spun me around, just to confirm the news that our two mischievous friends had already announced.

'Congratulations!' said Sue, rushing over and pulling me into a hug the second Ned set me down. 'I'm so happy for you both.'

Her warm embrace was swiftly followed by another from Wren, a third from Maya and a final one from Noah. There was much back slapping and handshaking for Ned and from what I could make out, the whole gang had been secretly thinking we were made for each other right from the moment I'd arrived.

'You guys,' I said, feeling my face flush scarlet.

'I hope you didn't want to keep your new-found love under wraps,' said Abbie. 'Because I couldn't stop Noah.'

'Oh, you fibber,' he cut in with a gasp. 'You were the one who burst in—'

'No,' Ned then interrupted him, 'we didn't want to keep anything under wraps.'

'That's all right then,' the pair chorused. 'No harm done.'

Everyone wanted to buy us a celebratory drink. As Ned was driving, he stuck to Coke, but I was happy to have a beer. With a drink apiece we found a table and sat down, both grinning like loons. Ned took my hand and squeezed it and I felt drunk before I'd even had so much as a sip of my pint. Yes, I was giddy with love but there was something else that had shifted deep within me during the ceremony on the beach and I felt like a whole new person. It was a strange, but wonderful feeling.

'Hey!' said Liam, rushing over, 'I've just heard the news. I'm so pleased for you both.'

Chelsea was right behind him.

'What did I say, weeks ago?' she said, giving him a nudge. 'Didn't I say they'd be together before Christmas?'

Liam rolled his eyes. 'You and everyone else,' he laughed.

'But I said it first,' she insisted.

'Well, thank you,' I said. 'We're really happy.'

Ned leant over and kissed my cheek.

'And we're really pleased to see you both, too,' he then said to the pair. 'Because we'd like to officially invite you to the plantation tomorrow for a chat. If you can spare the time. If not, we can see you in the evening instead.'

Liam looked worried.

'It's nothing to stress about,' I quickly said.

'The opposite in fact,' added Ned. 'You should be excited, Liam, and you'll be happy too, Chelsea.'

'In that case,' said Chelsea, 'we'll come over when I finish my shift at the care home.'

'I haven't done anything wrong, have I?' Liam frowned, still not convinced that he wasn't in trouble.

'No Liam,' I insisted. 'In fact, you've done everything right.'

He looked happier after that and followed his mum over to the bar. I watched them go, content that not only had I settled my differences with my old adversary, but that I was also now able to help her son with the next stage of his life.

It was quite a turnaround, but then everything that had happened since I'd arrived back at Wynter's Trees had been a total change.

Ned and I were both touched the next day when Liam and Chelsea arrived and Liam took off his coat to reveal a shirt and tie. I offered everyone coffee and then we sat facing each other on the chairs Ned had rearranged in the office. It was Chelsea who spoke first.

'Can I just ask that you hurry up and say whatever it is that's on your minds,' she pleaded, 'because he's been like a cat on a hot tin roof since we saw you in the pub. Put him out of his misery for pity's sake.'

'Don't,' Liam hissed, looking mortified.

'He's thinking it's something to do with that Bradley and Kyle,' Chelsea added in spite of Liam's warning. 'Is it?'

'Oh Liam,' I said, upset that he'd been so worried. 'It's absolutely nothing to do with them, is it, Ned?'

'Nothing at all,' he confirmed, turning to me. 'And in view of your concerns, Liam, I think we'd better get straight to the point. Would you like to do the honours, Liza?'

I looked at Liam. In spite of our reassurance, he was wringing his hands and his gaze had dropped to the floor.

'We'd like to offer you a job, Liam,' I quickly said and his head snapped up. 'If you're interested, we'd like to take you on, when you leave school, and make arrangements for you to study land and wildlife management, or something similar, at the local college.'

Chelsea burst into tears.

'You'd need to keep working hard at school to get the results you need to get into college, but the job's yours if you want it,' added Ned.

Liam looked from one of us to the other. He'd gone from pale to poleaxed. I hoped excitement would take over once our offer had sunk in.

'You obviously love Wynter's Trees,' I carried on when he didn't say anything. 'And Ned and I would love you to work alongside us. We want you to be a permanent member of the team, Liam. What do you think?'

'I don't know what to say,' he eventually stammered, as Chelsea continued to sniff next to him. 'Do you really think I can do it?'

His self-doubt made my heart twist.

'Which bit?' Ned seriously asked.

'All of it.' Liam croaked.

'Well, you've no worries where the practical side's concerned,' Ned told him. 'And your experience here, and the knowledge you've already gained, will definitely help on the course and we'll be here to help if you get stuck with anything.'

'These are the details of the courses we've been looking at,' I said, handing him the sheets I'd printed out, 'and we can easily arrange your working hours around the days you need to be at college.'

Chelsea reached for Liam's hand and Ned and I exchanged a glance.

'We'll leave you to look through it all and come back in a few minutes,' said Ned, 'but there's no rush. You don't have to decide today. Take your time.'

'I don't need to,' said Liam, jumping up and holding out his hand. 'I'll do it.' He beamed. 'I want to do it.'

'In that case,' I said, shaking his hand and feeling my own excitement leap to meet his, 'welcome to the full-time team.'

He pummelled my hand and then Ned's and spun Chelsea

around in a wonderful show of affection. The sight made me feel quite choked and Chelsea was still teary when they left. She'd barely uttered a word. I don't think I'd ever known her to be speechless before.

'Give us a ring later if you want to talk anything through,' Ned said to Liam as we waved them off, 'and to let us know she's all right,' he added with a wink at Chelsea.

'She'll be fine,' Liam grinned, looking a million times happier than he had when he'd arrived. His tie was skew-whiff and his previously flattened hair was stuck up on end. 'That said, I'm hoping she'll be like this until at least Boxing Day.'

Seeing him so happy further confirmed that as soon as the new year arrived, I would be putting proper plans in place to start my training and launch my business. Wynter's Trees had already transformed Liam's life and I knew there were plenty more students just like him, who would benefit from the place too.

'I know exactly what you're thinking,' said Ned, as we walked back to the office and he pulled me into his side. 'And I couldn't agree with you more.'

I was thrilled to hear it.

Chapter 28

Wednesday was an exciting blur as last-minute shoppers descended in droves, the butcher delivered the goose, pies and other meat Ned had ordered, and then in the afternoon a huge grocery shop destined for the lodge arrived too.

I knew that Ned and David had planned to have Christmas lunch together, but the fridge and cupboards were fit to burst with enough supplies to see us through the whole of January and when Ned arrived back from the meeting to cancel his loan with the bank, I pointed that out and he explained that was the idea.

'I'm going into hibernation,' he told me, looking proudly at the vastly stocked kitchen. 'After the rented trees are back in the plantation and checked, Wynter's will be closed and I'm planning to do absolutely nothing from then until February the first.'

'I see,' I smiled.

'You will be joining me, won't you?' he temptingly asked.

'You know,' I purred, 'I think I will. I can sort out

arrangements for my flat and book my training while you're checking the trees and then we can hunker down. It will be the perfect time to get our plans for next season in place, won't it?'

Ned rolled his eyes.

'Crikey!' he laughed. 'You've changed your tune! You've gone from not wanting to think about the place at all, to not being able to stop going on about it.'

'Well,' I said, pretending to pout, 'that's your fault, isn't it? And I thought it was what you wanted.'

'Oh, it is,' he said, pulling me close and lightly brushing his lips against mine. 'It very definitely is.'

'Stop complaining then,' I told him, kissing him back. 'And maybe during our hibernation we can start properly planning our holiday too.'

I'd broached the idea that Ned and I could travel to see the northern lights together and he was looking forward to it as much as I was. David had said that as long as we went before he left to meet his sister, he'd keep an eye on the place, and further told me that he knew it was a trip Dad had always wanted to make too. Knowing that made the prospective adventure feel even more special.

When Christmas Eve dawned, I was thrilled to discover it brought with it a formerly familiar feeling which coursed through my veins and made my heart thump. The old child-like excitement had landed in full force and I was delighted to embrace it. It was an emotion I recognised, but hadn't experienced since Mum had died, and when I opened the curtains it was cranked up even further.

'My goodness!' I gasped, as my eyes took in the surprising scene.

'What is it?' Ned asked sleepily, turning over in the bed.

'When you disappeared after your trip to the bank,' I laughed.

'Yes?' he said, suddenly wide awake.

'It wasn't to order a snow machine, by any chance, was it?'

'Funnily enough, no,' he yawned, 'but I have been wondering if it might be fun to have one next year for the late-night events. I'm going to try and find out if an eco-friendly model exists.'

I rolled my eyes. Trust festive loving Ned to take my question seriously.

'In that case,' I said, pushing the curtains further back along the pole, 'I'm guessing this must be the real stuff!'

Ned, suddenly wide awake, jumped out of bed and joined me at the window.

'No way,' he breathed. 'I don't believe it. We hardly ever get snow here and certainly not this amount.'

'I know,' I laughed. 'I used to live here, remember!'

Plump flakes were steadily falling and there was already enough of a covering to have transformed Wynter's Trees into a winter wonderland. Ned threw open the window, which swept the snow from the sill. It landed with a soft thud on the veranda roof below. There wasn't a breath of wind and everything was silent. Even the birds seemed to be in shock.

'Come on,' said Ned, pulling the window shut again. 'Let's get dressed and get outside before it's all gone.'

He began haphazardly pulling on his clothes. His T-shirt, I noticed, was inside out.

'It's not going anywhere anytime soon,' I told him, also dressing, but at a steadier pace. 'There's too much of it. There's no need to panic.'

But he wasn't listening. He rushed along the landing to his own room for the rest of his clothes and Bandit began to bark, catching his master's excitement.

Seconds later, and suitably attired, we ventured out. Bandit hesitated for a moment and then was off. The pristine blanket wasn't untouched for long. He leapt and rolled, buried his nose in it and came up snorting. He had an almost wild look in his eye and Ned wasn't much better. I'd never seen him in such a playful mood and I couldn't have wished for a more romantic lead into Christmas.

'Do you wanna build a snowman?' he sang out, making me laugh.

I did and so did he, but the snow was too soft to compact, so we settled for a walk through the plantation as it began to get light and a snowball fight instead.

'Dad never saw it like this,' I said, when we eventually reached the family tree. 'He would have been in his element.'

Ned took my hand and gave it a squeeze and I refused to give in to sentimentality. At least there was one Wynter who could appreciate the snowy spectacle.

'Come on,' I said, 'let's go back. I wonder if everyone will be able to get here to open their huts today?'

'I hope so,' said Ned. 'Sophie's prepared a festive feast and I'd hate to see it go to waste.'

The plan was to close the huts and the plantation at lunchtime, and then we were all going to eat together in the barn. It was both a festive celebration and a farewell to David, but with minimal fuss. Just like he'd insisted he wanted.

When we arrived back at the lodge, hungry, with flushed cheeks and damp coats, Ned opened the gate and I refilled the feeders and replenished the water bowls at the bird feeding station. Our feathered friends must have been surprised to wake and find their world so transformed and would need some extra support to make it safely through the chilly snap.

'Now you've fed the birds,' said Ned, 'how about I make you some breakfast?'

'Those supplies of yours are coming into their own already!' I laughed.

Thankfully, everyone made it to the huts, although Sue hadn't felt comfortable about driving in and with her partner at work, Theo had kindly made a detour to pick her up. There weren't many customers who ventured out, but it was still worth opening for the final few hours of the season and with the excitement of the unexpected snowfall, there was quite a party atmosphere even before we all descended on the barn.

Sophie and Hope arrived with a huge glazed ham, along with a vegan Wellington and a variety of pickles, chutneys and cheeses and Ned and I supplied multiple baked potatoes and warm baguettes, which we had cooked in the lodge oven. We'd also brewed a festive non-alcoholic punch and there were Christmas cookies, courtesy of Hope, for afters. My mouth was watering a good hour before we were ready to eat.

It was a very jolly party that gathered around the make-shift table in the barn. Michael had driven in with Noah at the start of the day and between them they'd been able to guide Abbie safely into her hut. Her wheelchair wasn't great in the snow and she was grateful for the no fuss help they offered. Joe had come along with this brother, Charlie, and Liam had convinced Chelsea to drive out too. The roads had been worse than she expected and Michael offered to drive her car back, if she didn't feel up to it.

'Thanks, Michael,' said Liam, immediately accepting on his mum's behalf, 'otherwise we would have been heading straight off again.'

Once I knew Chelsea wasn't going to be driving home, I poured her a tot of brandy. She swallowed it down in one swift gulp.

'Thanks,' she said, a little colour returning to her cheeks. 'I needed that. The roads beyond the village haven't been gritted at all. I've never been a nervous driver, but I didn't enjoy that trip one little bit.'

I willingly poured her another measure, to speed her recovery along.

Maya was last to arrive and she came with a very hand-some plus one.

'This is Harry,' she said. 'We met at the young farmers' years ago, and bumped into each other again in the pub after the solstice celebration.'

She looked adoringly at the golden-haired guy next to her and he looked equally smitten with her, but then who wouldn't? I still found it hard to believe that Maya had been single for so long.

'Hey Harry,' everyone chorused.

'Hi,' he grinned back.

He wasn't at all fazed by the sea of faces, and I guessed he recognised a lot of them. Having acknowledged the group, he strode over to Ned and handed him a bag clinking with bottles.

'He's back visiting family for Christmas,' Maya whispered to me, as Harry and Ned chatted. 'But I'm doing my utmost to persuade him to stay.'

'In that case,' I grinned up at her, 'I can't imagine he'll be going anywhere anytime soon.'

After we had eaten and drunk our fill, it was time for some toasts, announcements and speeches. Had my life not been so utterly changed by the father and son sitting either side of me, I would have been dreading that part, but as it was, it felt like a most appropriate way to end what had turned out to be a most exciting and transformative season at Wynter's Trees.

Ned tapped a spoon against his glass and everyone fell silent.

'I would just like to say,' he began, reaching for my hand,

'a huge thank you to you all for making these last few weeks at Wynter's Trees so wonderful and for making the beach hut project such a huge success.'

We raised our glasses and toasted everyone around the table.

'And in turn,' Sue quickly chimed in, 'we'd like to thank you for giving us the opportunity to move here, Ned. We all thought the plan was going to be shelved before you stepped in.'

'Hear, hear!' the rest agreed.

'It's worked well,' Ned smiled, 'so well in fact, that Liza and I are going to discuss the possibility of opening the huts on further occasions throughout the year, so if you'd be interested in selling here again, please let us know before you leave today. We haven't thrashed out the details yet, but we will soon.'

An excited whisper wove its way around the table after that announcement.

'I'd also like to take this moment to welcome a new member to the Wynter's Trees team,' Ned continued and everyone stopped talking.

Chelsea gave Liam a nudge and he turned bright red.

'He's part of the team already,' Ned explained, 'but from next year, when he leaves school, he'll be joining us here on a permanent basis.'

Everyone's gaze turned from Ned to Liam.

'Welcome Liam,' said Ned, raising his glass.

This time the reaction wasn't confined to a whisper and

Liam found himself the centre of attention and the recipient of kind words, well wishes and congratulations from everyone present.

'Thank you,' was all he could say, but the look on his face told us all how proud he was, and that went for Chelsea too.

Ned looked at me and smiled and I shifted a little in my seat, panicked that I was next on his list, but thankfully he let me off the hook.

'And last,' he said, 'but by no means least, I'd like you all to raise a glass to my dad, David.'

David shook his head.

'I know you don't want a fuss, Dad,' Ned carried on, sounding choked, 'and I have no intention of making one, but I couldn't possibly let this opportunity go by without saying thank you. Thank you for encouraging me to come here and join you in this incredible and much-loved business that Liza's dad established. Thank you for giving me the chance to put my plans into action and of course, the biggest thank you of all, for somehow managing to get this wonderful woman sitting next to me to come back.'

I let out a long breath, aware that everyone's eyes were on me. So much for getting off the hook.

'Liza,' he said, and I felt tears prick my eyes as I looked up at him. 'I know we've had a few differences of opinion these last few weeks, but Dad was determined I shouldn't give up trying to convince you that you belong here.'

I was aware of some muttering around the table. It was hardly surprising, given that no one beyond myself, Ned and David had known I'd felt otherwise. David had already told me he'd never stopped hoping I would change my mind about selling and now I realised that the many things that Ned had had me do – replanting the tree, decorating the lodge and so on – had been his way of trying to ignite the Wynter's Trees flame in my heart too.

'But of course,' he carried on, 'I was never going to stop trying to do that, because you captured my heart the moment you arrived and I would have done everything in my power to prove to you that your future was destined to be here.'

'Even risk hypothermia,' I laughed.

'Even that,' Ned joined in.

He leant down to kiss me on the lips and a cheer went up as I willingly reciprocated.

'So,' Ned then said, getting his toast back on track. 'To Dad, with love and thanks. We hope you enjoy your travels and your retirement, but not so much that we can't tempt you out of it again next Christmas, when we need a hand!'

We all stood and raised our glasses.

'To David,' we chorused. 'Happy retirement.'

We were all a little teary eyed after that, so Ned set some music playing and refilled everyone's glasses and the emotional atmosphere was soon replaced with something far more festive. I was able to briskly gloss over the questions which came my way about what Ned had meant and no one was still any the wiser that I had originally been planning to leave and never come back.

By three o'clock, the light was fading and everyone began pulling on their coats and saying their goodbyes. I positioned myself next to the door so I could hand out the puddings I'd made, along with the few other gifts I'd picked up, and was very touched to receive presents back. I hadn't expected that at all. It was astounding to think that I could have been in my flat, ignoring the season and not feeling anything other than lonely and sad. Not that I would have admitted to that.

Liam, bringing with him a large cardboard box, had shyly come to stand next to me and he was handing out gifts too.

'There's a care label in with each one,' he explained, as he gave everyone small bowls planted with bulbs which would flower soon after Christmas. 'This was what my nan used to do,' he quietly told me with a wobbly smile, 'and I thought it would be nice to carry on.'

'Family traditions are important,' I agreed, kissing his cheek as he gave me a bowl filled with hyacinths, the scent of which I knew would fill the lodge in a week or two.

'They really are,' he said, turning slightly pink.

Standing in the barn, surrounded by my new friends and with the love of my life at my elbow, I could accept that now and embrace and enjoy my own family's traditions. I felt incredibly grateful that David had never given up on me. His determination to make me come back to Wynter's Trees had been a very definite blessing. A life changing one.

'Right then,' said David, who was last to leave, 'I'll leave you two lovebirds to it.'

413

The barn had been cleared and tidied and all that was left to do was lock up.

'Are you sure you wouldn't rather stay?' I suggested again. 'I'm worried that if there's more snow tonight, you won't be able to get here tomorrow.'

'Thank you for the offer,' he said, 'but I prefer my own bed and there's no more of the white stuff forecast, so don't worry.'

'Lunch at two.' Ned reminded him.

'I'll be here,' he firmly said. 'I take it you won't be coming to church tonight?' he then asked.

'No,' said Ned, 'I'm not going to risk it. It's bound to be icy again later. Unless you'd like to go, Liza?'

'No,' I said. 'I don't mind staying here. There'll be plenty more years to attend the midnight service after this one.'

'That there will,' said Ned, reaching for my hand.

Hearing him confirm that caused my heart to flutter. I really was home for good.

'I don't blame you,' said David. 'Right, I'd better head off.'

'Just let me know when you're back, Dad,' said Ned.

David looked at me and rolled his eyes.

'Three rings please,' I said, siding with Ned, as I kissed David on the cheek.

We had planned to take a walk around the reserve, but it was already too dark so after locking up the barn and the gate we headed back to the lodge instead. It was an even more magical sight in the snow.

The lights on the veranda made the snow glisten and

through the windows, I could see the fire glowing and the lights from the tree twinkling. It was picture perfect and as Ned and I walked hand in hand towards it I felt a deep rush of affection for the place.

I had felt it long ago, during that time before Chelsea's teasing had made me loathe rather than love it, but now it was back in full force. I welcomed it, knowing I would never turn my back on it again.

'Come on,' I said squeezing Ned's hand, 'let's get inside. We can catch *Carols from King's* on catch-up in lieu of going to church later.'

'That,' said Ned, dropping a kiss on my head, 'is a wonderful idea.'

I was fast beginning to learn that when one opportunity didn't work out, there was always another waiting in the wings.

David was right about the snow. No more fell overnight, but there was a dramatic drop in temperature so the scene beyond the lodge windows on Christmas morning was frozen solid and sparkling. If anything, it was even more beautiful than the day before.

I woke early. Far earlier than I had expected to and crept down the stairs, remembering to step over the one from the bottom which had always been prone to creak. Bandit had followed me down, his claws skittering on the wooden floor.

'Merry Christmas,' I whispered to him.

Thankfully, he didn't bark back.

Underneath the Christmas tree looked rather different to when Ned and I had gone to bed and I wondered how long he'd waited for me to fall asleep before he came down and arranged everything. Clearly, he knew about the trick step too. Unless of course, Santa himself had managed to squeeze in a trip to Wynter's Lodge on his whistle-stop trip around the world.

'Look Bandit,' I whispered. 'Who do you suppose did that?'

The carrot we had left for the reindeer was missing and where there had been a mince pie there were just a few crumbs. The tot of whisky had gone too. I hoped it had warmed Santa's cockles on such a cold night.

I flicked on the tree lights, all the better to show off the gifts which had been set out beneath it.

'Couldn't you wait just a little longer?' said a sleepy voice, making me jump.

Ned, at the bottom of the stairs, looked seductively tousled and I rushed into his arms. He was still warm from the bed.

'Merry Christmas, Liza,' he said, kissing me.

'Happy Christmas, Ned.' I smiled back.

'You bypassed your stocking completely,' he pointed out, as our second Christmas kiss came to a reluctant end.

'I was coming back up,' I told him. 'I just wanted to let Bandit out and make us a drink and then I was coming back to bed.'

'You wanted to sneak a look at the presents more like,' Ned grinned, looking down at me.

'Perhaps,' I admitted, sweeping my hair over my shoulder in a gesture that I knew would give me away.

'And has he been?' asked Ned, playing the game.

I led him over to the tree.

'He has,' I said. 'Look.'

'Wow,' he gasped. 'That's quite a selection. How on earth are you going to resist?'

I took a purposeful step back.

'Presents underneath the tree were always left until after lunch when I was growing up,' I told him, 'so if I could do it when I was little, I can manage it now.'

Ned shook his head. Clearly, he didn't have much faith in my resolve.

'Are you sure?' he teased.

'Of course,' I forthrightly said, but my gaze flicked back to the pile. 'Well,' I caved. 'Perhaps a peek at just one wouldn't hurt, would it?'

'I don't see why not,' he said, kneeling down for a closer look. 'But it has to be the right one.'

He reached towards the back of the pile and pulled out a small flat present. My guess was that it was a wrapped envelope. I was intrigued as to why he'd picked that one out of the stack surrounding it.

'How about this one?' he suggested, holding it out. 'If you're going to have an early one from under the tree, then I think it should be this one.'

My heart began to hammer as he took my hand, pulled me down next to him and handed the envelope over. It weighed practically nothing, but the smile on Ned's face told me it contained something very special indeed and I was right.

'We're going on an adventure!' he burst out as I tore through the paper to find very exclusive travel documents and a luxury itinerary to see the northern lights.

'Oh Ned!' I gasped, as I admired the image of a glass igloo, complete with a large bed covered in reindeer rugs. 'This is perfect. Thank you!'

'It will be,' he said, pulling me onto his lap. 'Everything will be perfect now we're together.'

He kissed me deeply and for the longest time, and there, underneath the Christmas tree, I embraced my fate and my future and a lifetime dedicated to celebrating the most wonderful time of the year.

Acknowledgements

Can you believe that *Underneath the Christmas Tree* is my sixth Christmas book? No, me neither! I've had to count on my fingers just to make sure and I'm right, it's definitely six! This one is unique in that it's the first winter adventure in Wynmouth and I hope there will be more trips there to come. There are a couple of characters from the seaside who really don't want to be left behind.

As always, there are a huge number of people to thank for helping me breathe life into this book.

My wonderful editor, Clare Hey, and agent, Amanda Preston, who were as excited as I was to spend Christmas on the Norfolk coast. Pip Watkins who has created my first properly pink cover, which I absolutely adore – and given the response on reveal day, I know you all do too! Special thanks also to Judith Long, Harriett Collins, Sara-Jade Virtue and Amy Fulwood for the fabulous work you do.

Huge and heartfelt thanks to my author and real life (even though we've barely seen each other in real life this year) friends, Jenni Keer, Clare Marchant, Rosie Hendry and Ian Wilfred.

Thanks also to my dear friend and hugely talented jewellery designer, Claire Howard. She's an inspiration and would be most welcome to set up in any one of the Wynter's Trees beach huts! Thanks also to Jeremy Preston for the fabulous Christmas label idea and Trish Fearnley for her love of animal-print PJs.

Massive, massive thanks to my mum and dad. I hope you both know why.

Thanks also to each and every one of my fellow authors, supportive bloggers, librarians, booksellers, book club organisers, virtual event hosts and Swainettes. I have read and appreciated every kind word, rave review, cheerleading tweet and stunning Insta pic.

Love and thanks to Fiona Jenkins and Sue Baker who run the Heidi Swain and Friends Facebook Book Club. The club has gone from strength to strength again this year as a result of your continued wonderful work. This book is especially for you two.

And as always, last but by no means least, thank you dear reader for picking up this book and celebrating the run-up to Christmas with me on the Norfolk coast. I hope you have enjoyed the adventure and I look forward to sharing many more with you.

Merry Christmas my loves, may your bookshelves – be they virtual or real – always be filled with fabulous fiction.

H x

A Taste of Home

Fliss Brown has grown up living with her mother on the Rossi family's Italian fruit farm. But when her mother dies, Fliss finds out she has a family of her own, and heads back to England with Nonna Rossi's recipe for cherry and almond tart and a piece of advice: connect with your family before it is too late ...

Fliss discovers that her estranged grandfather owns a fruit farm himself, on the outskirts of Wynbridge, and she arrives to find a farm that has fallen into disrepair. Using her knowledge gleaned from working on the Rossi farm and her desire to find out more about her past, Fliss rolls her sleeves up and gets stuck in. But what will she discover, and can she resurrect the farm's glory days and find a taste of home?

AVAILABLE IN PAPERBACK AND EBOOK NOW

The Winter Garden

Freya Fuller is living her dream, working as a live-in gardener on a beautiful Suffolk estate. But when the owner dies, Freya finds herself forced out of her job and her home with nowhere to go. However, with luck on her side, she's soon moving to Nightingale Square and helping to create a beautiful winter garden that will be open to the public in time for Christmas.

There's a warm welcome from all in Nightingale Square, except from local artist Finn. No matter how hard the pair try, they just can't get along, and working together to bring the winter garden to life quickly becomes a struggle for them both.

Will Freya and Finn be able to put their differences aside in time for Christmas? Or will the arrival of a face from Freya's past send them all spiralling?

AVAILABLE IN PAPERBACK AND EBOOK NOW

The Secret Seaside Escape

Tess Tyler needs a break. Weighed down by her high-pressure job and her demanding father, she's left little time to take care of herself. But after a shocking discovery sends her spiralling, she flees to Wynmouth, the seaside town she fell in love with as a child, to escape it all.

With its sandy beaches, stunning rock pools and welcoming community, Tess feels like she can finally breathe again. And as she grows ever closer to local barman Sam, she dares to dream that she might never return to her real life. But when a familiar face returns to town, Tess realises that there are secrets in Wynmouth too, and that her own past may be about to catch up with her . . .

AVAILABLE IN PAPERBACK AND EBOOK NOW

The
Christmas
Wish List

After being let go from her job, Hattie is feeling lost. Even
more so when her boyfriend announces he's landed his
dream job in Abu Dhabi and asks her to move with him.
Luckily, Hattie's long-time friend Dolly is on hand to help
and invites Hattie to spend one last holiday in Wynbridge,
determined to give her a Christmas to remember . . .

The residents of Wynbridge are preparing for their most
spectacular Christmas yet. But for Hattie, it'll take more
than mince pies and mistletoe to open her heart to the
season once more. Relishing the task of reigniting Hattie's
Christmas spirit, Dolly suggests they create a wish list of
all the things the season can offer. And with the help of
Wynbridge's resident handyman, Beamish, Hattie finds her
frosty exterior is starting to thaw . . .

AVAILABLE IN PAPERBACK AND EBOOK NOW

Poppy's Recipe for Life

*Treat yourself to a glorious novel full of food,
sunshine, friendship and love!*

Things haven't always been straightforward in Poppy's
life but her dreams are finally within her reach.

She's moving into a cottage in beautiful Nightingale
Square, close to the local community garden, where she
can indulge her passion for making preserves and pickles.
She may not have the best relationship with her family,
but she is surrounded by loving friends, and feels sure that
even her grumpy new neighbour, Jacob, has more to him
than his steely exterior suggests.

But the unexpected arrival of Poppy's troubled younger
brother soon threatens her new-found happiness, and as
the garden team works together to win community space
of the year, Poppy must decide where her priorities lie
and what she is prepared to fight for . . .

AVAILABLE IN PAPERBACK AND EBOOK NOW